THRONES, DOMINATIONS

THRONES, DOMINATIONS

DOROTHY L. SAYERS
&
JILL PATON WALSH

G.K. Hall & Co. • Chivers Press
Thorndike, Maine USA Bath, England

This Large Print edition is published by G.K. Hall & Co., USA and by Chivers Press, England.

Published in 1998 in the U.S. by arrangement with St. Martin's Press, Inc.

Published in 1998 in the U.K. by arrangement with Hodder and Stoughton.

U.S. Hardcover 0-7838-8438-9 (Mystery Series Edition)
U.K. Hardcover 0-7540-1143-7 (Windsor Large Print)
U.K. Softcover 0-7540-2100-9 (Paragon Large Print)

The text of this Large Print edition is unabridged.
Other aspects of the book may vary from the original edition.

Set in 16 pt. Plantin by Juanita Macdonald.

Printed in the United States on permanent paper.

British Library Cataloguing in Publication Data available

Library of Congress Cataloging in Publication Data

Sayers, Dorothy L. (Dorothy Leigh), 1893–1957.
 Thrones, dominations / Dorothy L. Sayers and Jill Paton Walsh.
  p.   cm.
  ISBN 0-7838-8438-9 (lg. print : hc : alk. paper)
  1. Large type books. I. Paton Walsh, Jill, 1937– . II. Title.
 [PR6037.A95T48   1998b]
 823′.912—dc21   98-4979

I was delighted and deeply honoured when Lord Peter Wimsey's associates asked me to write up a case which he worked on early in his marriage, a period of adjustment in his life and that of his wife, and of upheaval on the public stage. I have loved and admired Lord Peter since first I met him in my schooldays. As one might expect of a person born in 1890 he has some old-fashioned mannerisms; but his undying charm arises from a characteristic which he shares with Ralph Touchett (in *Portrait of a Lady*); Benedick (in *Much Ado About Nothing*) and even somewhat with Mr Rochester in *Jane Eyre*, but with none too many others in literature or in life: that is, that he requires as his consort a spirited woman who is his intellectual equal.

Such an unusual alliance as Lord Peter's with Harriet Vane has naturally aroused widespread curiosity; a curiosity which, within the limits dictated by the literary form of a detective story, and respect for his earlier chronicler, I have tried to satisfy.

Jill Paton Walsh

ACKNOWLEDGEMENTS

I would like to thank Mr Bruce Hunter and the trustees of Anthony Fleming for entrusting to me the completion of *Thrones, Dominations*.

I gratefully acknowledge the indispensable help of Dr Barbara Reynolds; the friendly assistance of Mr Christopher Dean, chairman, and Bunty Parkinson, archivist, of the Dorothy L. Sayers Society; help given by Marjorie Lampe Meade, and the staff of the Marion E. Wade Centre, Wheaton College, Illinois; Cambridge University Library; Mr Richard Walduck for the loan of *The Lost Rivers of London*; Ms Carolyn Caughey and Ms Hope Dellon for their capable editorial advice, and help received as always and in everything from John Rowe Townsend.

Thrones, and imperial powers, off-spring of heaven,
Ethereal virtues; or these Titles now
Must we renounce, and changing stile be call'd
Princes of hell?

Thrones, Dominations, Princedoms, Virtues, Pow-
ers . . .

John Milton

1

They order, said I, this matter better in France.
LAURENCE STERNE

'I do not,' said Monsieur Théophile Daumier, 'understand the English.'

'Nor does anybody,' replied Mr Paul Delagardie, 'themselves least of all.'

'I see them pass to and fro, I observe them, I talk to them — for I find it is not true that they are silent and unfriendly — but I remain ignorant of their interior life. They are occupied without ceasing, but I do not know the motives for the things they so energetically do. It is not their reserve which defeats me, for often they are surprisingly communicative; it is that I do not know where their communicativeness ends and their reserve begins. They are said to be rigidly conventional, yet they can behave with an insouciance without parallel; and when you question them, they appear to possess no definable theory of life.'

'You are quite right,' said Mr Delagardie. 'The English are averse to theories. Yet we are, for that reason, comparatively easy to live with. Our conventions are external, and easily acquired; but our philosophies are all individual, and we do not concern ourselves to correct those of others. That is why we permit in our public parks the open expression of every variety of seditious opinion — with the sole proviso that nobody shall so far forget himself as to tear up the railings or trample on the flowers.'

'I beg your pardon; I had for the moment forgotten that you also were English. You have so much the outlook, as well as the accent of a Frenchman.'

'Thank you,' replied Mr Delagardie. 'I am actually only one-eighth French by blood. The other seven-eighths is English, and the proof is that I take what you have said as a compliment. Unlike the Jews, the Irish and the Germans, the English are pleased to be thought even more mongrel and exotic than they are. It appeals to the streak of romantic sensibility in the English temperament. Tell an Englishman that he is pure-bred Anglo-Saxon or a hundred per cent Aryan, and he will laugh in your face; tell him that his remote ancestry contains a blend of French, Russian, Chinese or even Arab or Hindu, and he will listen with polite gratification. The remoter, of course, the better; it is more picturesque, and less socially ambiguous.'

'Socially ambiguous? Ah! you admit, then, that the Englishman in fact despises all other races but his own.'

'Until he has had time to assimilate them. What he despises is not other races but other civilizations. He does not wish to be called a dago; but if he is born with dark eyes and an olive complexion, he is pleased to trace those features back to a Spanish hidalgo, cast away upon the English coast in the wreck of the Great Armada. Everything with us is a matter of sentiment and association.'

'A strange people!' said Monsieur Daumier. 'And yet, the national type is unmistakable. You see a man — you know at once that he is English, and that is all you ever know about him. Take, for example, the couple at the table opposite. He is, undoubtedly, an Englishman of the leisured and wealthy class. He has a slightly military air and is very much bronzed — but that may be due only to the habit of *le sport*. One would say, looking at him, that he had no interest in life beyond fox-hunting — except indeed that he is clearly very much enamoured of his extremely beautiful companion. Yet for all I know, he may be a member of parliament, a financier, or a writer of very successful novels. His face tells nothing.'

Mr Delagardie darted a glance at the diners in question.

'Ah, yes!' he said. 'Tell me what you make of him and the woman with him. You are right; she is an exquisite creature. I have always had a *faiblesse* for the true red-blonde. They have the capacity for passion.'

'It is, I think, passion that is in question at the

11

moment,' replied Monsieur Daumier. 'She is, I imagine, mistress and not wife — or rather, for she is married, not *his* wife. If any generalization is possible about Englishmen, it is that they take their wives for granted. They do not carefully cultivate the flower of passion with the pruning-scissors. They permit it to seed away into a settled affection, fruitful and natural, but not decorative. Observe them in conversation. Either they do not listen to what their wives say at all, or they attend with the intelligent courtesy one accords to a talkative stranger. *Ce monsieur là-bas* is inattentive, but for another reason: he is absorbed in the lady's personal charms and his mind is concentrated on favours to come. He is, as you say, over head and ears — and I have noticed that in an Englishman that condition betrays itself. He does not, like ourselves, display assiduity to every woman in right of her sex. If he exhibits himself in attitudes of devotion, it is for good reason. I hazard the guess that this is an elopement, or at any rate an adventure; one, perhaps, which he cannot well carry on openly in London. Here, in our wicked Paris, he may let himself go without embarrassment.'

'I agree with you,' said Mr Delagardie, 'that that is certainly not the typical English married couple. And it is true that the Englishman on the Continent tends to cast off the English convention of reserve — in fact it is part of his convention to do so. You say nothing of the lady.'

'She also is in love, but she is aware at the same

time of the sacrifice she has made. She asks nothing better than to surrender; nevertheless she knows how to make herself courted; after all, it is the one who risks most who confers the obligation. But when she gives herself, it will be with abandonment. The bronzed gentleman is on the whole to be envied.'

'Your observations are of the greatest interest,' said Mr Delagardie. 'The more so that they are to a large extent erroneous, as I happen to know. The English, as you say, are baffling. What, for example, do you think of the very different pair in the opposite corner?'

'The fair-haired diplomat with the eye-glass and the decided-looking brunette in orange taffeta?'

'He is not precisely a diplomat, but that is the man I mean.'

'There,' said Monsieur Daumier, in a more assured tone, 'I perceive exactly the English married couple *par excellence*. They are very well bred, the man especially, and they offer a lesson in table manners to the whole room. He consults her about the menu, is particular that she has what she requires, and orders his own dinner to suit himself. If she drops her napkin, he picks it up. When she speaks, he attends and replies politely, but with imperturbable phlegm and almost without looking at her. He is perfectly courteous, and perfectly indifferent, and to this heart-breaking self-possession she opposes a coldness equal to his own. They are no doubt good friends and even agreeable companions by force of custom, since they converse smoothly and with no pauses. The English, when they dislike one another, seldom shout; they withdraw into taciturnity. These two do not, I feel sure, quarrel either in public or in private. They have been married so long that any passionate feeling they ever had for one another has long since died; but perhaps it was never very much, for she is not exceptionally good-looking and he has the air of a man to whom beauty is of some importance. Possibly she was rich and he married her for her money. At any rate he probably conducts his private affairs as he chooses and she accepts the situation, so long as there is no parade of infidelity, for the sake of the children.'

Mr Delagardie poured a little more Burgundy into both glasses before replying.

'You called the man a diplomat,' he said at length. 'And you have succeeded in proving that at least he does not carry all his private history written in his features. As it happens, I know both couples fairly well, and can set you right on the material facts.

'Take the first pair. The man is Laurence Harwell, and he is the son of a very distinguished and very rich KC who died a few years ago leaving him exceedingly well off. Though brought up in the usual country-house and public-school surroundings, he is not particularly addicted to sport in the English sense of the word. He spends most of his time in town, and dabbles a little in the financing of theatrical ventures. He is bronzed at present because he has just returned from Chamonix; but I think he went there rather to please the lady than himself. She, so far from being his mistress, is actually his own wife, and they have been married just over two years. You are correct in thinking that they are deeply in love with one another, for the match was a highly romantic one. The sacrifices were, however, on his side and not hers; in so far, that is, as there can be any sacrifice in acquiring a supremely beautiful woman. Her father was involved in certain fraudulent transactions which reduced him from considerable wealth to poverty and a short term of imprisonment. Rosamund, his daughter, had been forced to take a post as mannequin in a fashionable dressmaker's establishment when Harwell arrived to rescue her. They are frequently cited as the most idyllic — some go as far as to say, the only — married lovers in London. It is true that they have as yet no children; and this perhaps accounts for the fact that the passion-flower has not yet lost its bloom. They are never happy out of each other's sight — and that is just as well, since both, I fancy, are of a jealous temperament. Needless to say, she has many admirers, but they do not get very much satisfaction, since hers is the kind of amorous temperament that is cold to all but one.'

'I repeat,' said Monsieur Daumier, 'that Mr Harwell is to be envied. The story is certainly romantic, and different from what I had supposed.'

'Yet in essentials,' said Mr Delagardie, 'you were not very far wrong. The relation between the two is, to all intents and purposes, that of lover and mistress and not of husband and wife. The other pair are more enigmatical, and perhaps even more romantic.

'The man is certainly well bred, for he is the second son of the late Duke of Denver and, incidentally, my own nephew. He has dabbled a little in diplomacy as in most things, but that is not his profession; if he has any profession at all, it is criminology. He is a lover of beauty in old wine and old books, and has from time to time shown himself a considerable connoisseur of beautiful women. His wife, who is with him now, is a novelist who had hitherto earned her own living; rather over six years ago, she was acquitted, largely by his intervention, of the charge of murdering her lover. My nephew fell in love with her at sight; his pursuit of her was conducted with patience and determination for over five years; they were married last October, and have only just returned from a prolonged honeymoon. I do not precisely know what their present relations are, for it is some weeks since I heard from them; and the honeymoon was complicated by some unfortunate occurrences. A murder was committed in their house and the emotional currents set up while bringing the assassin to justice introduced, I believe, a disturbing factor. My nephew is nervous, fastidious and inhibited; my niece by marriage, obstinate, energetic and independent.

16

They are both possessed of a truly diabolical pride. Mayfair is awaiting with interest the result of this curious matrimonial experiment.'

'Do all Englishmen,' enquired Monsieur Daumier, 'present themselves to their brides in the role of Perseus?'

'All of them would like to do so; but all, perhaps fortunately, have not the opportunity. It is a role difficult to sustain without egotism.'

At this moment the man with the monocle got up in response to a summons by the waiter and came down the long hotel dining-room, as though making for the telephone. He signalled a greeting to Mr Delagardie and passed on, walking very upright, with the swift, light step of a good dancer. As he went, his wife's dark and rather handsome eyes followed him with a peculiarly concentrated expression — not quite puzzled or anxious or apprehensive, though all three adjectives passed through Monsieur Daumier's mind, only to be dismissed.

He said, 'I was wrong about your nephew's wife. She is not indifferent. But I think she is not altogether sure of him.'

'That,' replied Mr Delagardie, 'is quite likely. Nobody is ever sure of my nephew Peter. But I imagine that he is not altogether indifferent, either. If he speaks to her without looking at her, it is probably that he has something to conceal — either love or hatred; I have known both the one and the other to be developed at the end of a honeymoon.'

'*Evidemment*,' acquiesced Monsieur Daumier. 'It appears to me, from what you say, that the relations between those two must be of a most delicate nature; the more so as neither of them is in the first youth.'

'My nephew is rising forty-six, and his wife is in her early thirties. Ah! The Harwells have seen us; I think they are coming over. I know them just a little. The old Harwell was a friend of Sir Impey Biggs, who is a family connection of the Wimseys, and I have met the son and his wife from time to time at social functions.'

Monsieur Théophile Daumier was pleased to have the opportunity of viewing Rosamund Harwell more closely. She was a type of which he thoroughly approved. It was not merely the smooth red-gold of the hair, or the liquid amber of the eyes, set a little slanting under the widely springing and delicately pencilled brows; nor was it solely the full red curve of the mouth, or the whiteness of the skin; though all these had a good deal to do with it. The face was heart-shaped; the body, which let itself be rather more than divined beneath the close-fitting gown, suggested to him the unveiled charms of a Botticelli Venus. Such features Monsieur Daumier could appraise at their worth with the controlled appreciation of the connoisseur. What stirred him was the pervasive exhalation of femininity, which went to his head like the ethers of a vintage wine. He was sensitive to such emanations, and was astonished to find them in an Englishwoman; since in the

English he was accustomed to encounter either an aggressive sexlessness or a suffocating maternal amiability, almost equally devoid of allurement. The voice, too, in which Mrs Harwell uttered the commonplace greeting: 'How do you do?' — it was warm, vibrant, musical, like a chime of golden bells, a voice with promise in it.

Mr Delagardie enquired whether the Harwells were making a long stay in Paris.

'We are here for a fortnight,' said Rosamund Harwell, 'to do some shopping. And, of course, to amuse ourselves.'

'Did you enjoy the sports at Chamonix?'

'Very much; but the place was horribly crowded.'

Her glance at her husband seemed to pick him out of the crowd and get him alone with her in some kind of isle of enchantment. Monsieur Daumier got the impression that Laurence Harwell was impatient even of this casual exchange of remarks with two gentlemen of mature age in a dining-room. He judged the husband to be about thirty, and the wife at least five years younger. Mr Delagardie prolonged the conversation with a few more unimportant enquiries — it might have been for the deliberate purpose of allowing his friend to study the romantic English at close quarters. A diversion was caused by the arrival of Mr Delagardie's nephew, who had meanwhile returned from telephoning and collected his wife.

'*Vous voilà, mes enfants,*' said Mr Delagardie, indulgently. 'I hope you have dined well. Peter,

I think you know Mr and Mrs Harwell?'

'By name only; we seem always to have just missed one another.'

'Then let me introduce you. My nephew, Lord Peter Wimsey, and my niece Harriet. This is my friend, Monsieur Daumier. It is curious that we should all be staying in the same hotel, without connivance, like the characters in a polite comedy.'

'Not so very curious,' said Wimsey, 'when you consider that the cooking is, for the moment, the best in Paris. The comedy will, I fear, not extend to three acts; we are leaving for London tomorrow. We only ran over for a day or two — to get a change of scene.'

'Yes,' said his uncle. 'I read in the papers that the execution had taken place. It must have been very trying for you both.' His shrewd old eyes shot from one face to the other.

Wimsey said in a colourless tone, 'It was most unfortunate.'

He was, thought Monsieur Daumier, colourless altogether: hair, complexion, and light unemphatic voice with its clipped public-school accent.

Wimsey turned to Mrs Harwell, and said politely, 'We shall no doubt have the pleasure of meeting before long in town.'

Mrs Harwell said, 'I hope so.'

Mr Delagardie addressed his niece: 'Then I shall find you, I suppose, in Audley Square when I return.'

Monsieur Daumier awaited the reply with some

curiosity. The woman's face was, he considered, interesting in the light of her history: dark, resolute, too decided in feature and expression to attract his fancy; intelligent, with a suggestion of temper about the mouth and the strong square brows. She had been standing a little aloof, quite silent and, he noticed with approval, without fidgeting. He was anxious to hear her speak, though he disliked in general the strident tones of the educated Englishwoman.

The voice, when it came, surprised him; it was deep and full, with a richness of timbre which made Rosamund Harwell's golden bells sound like a musical box.

'Yes; we are hoping to settle in now. I have hardly seen the house since they finished decorating. The Duchess has organised it beautifully; we shall enjoy showing you round it.'

'My mother has been in her element,' said Wimsey. 'If she had been born a generation later, she would undoubtedly have been a full-fledged professional decorator with an independent career. In which case, I suppose, one would never have existed. These chronological accidents are a check upon one's natural vanity.'

'We are excited too,' said Mrs Harwell. 'We have just taken a new flat in Hyde House. When we get home we are going to give a party, aren't we, darling?'

Her smile enveloped her husband, and then passed with a charming friendliness to Mr Delagardie, who promptly replied, 'I hope that is an invitation. Hyde House? That is the big new block in Park Lane, is it not? I am told that its appointments constitute a positive miracle of convenience.'

'It is all absolutely marvellous,' said Mrs Harwell. 'We are thrilled. We have spacious rooms, and no kitchen at all — we can eat in the restaurant on the first floor, or get our meals sent up. We have no difficulty with servants, because the service is all run for us. All the heating is electric. It is just like being in a hotel, except that we can have our own furniture. We have a lot of chrome and glass things, and lovely modern curtains designed by Ben Nicholson, and some Susie Cooper vases. The management even keep the cocktail cabinet fully stocked for us; we don't have a large one, of course, just a very neat design in walnut with a built-in wireless set and a little shelf for books.'

For the first time Monsieur Daumier saw Wimsey look at his wife; his eyes, when fully opened, turned out to be a clear grey. Though not a muscle in his face moved, the observer was somehow conscious of a jest silently shared.

'And with all the marvels of science at his command,' commented Mr Delagardie, 'my benighted nephew takes his unfortunate wife to live in an out-of-date and, I strongly suspect, rat-haunted Georgian mansion, five storeys high, without so much as a lift. It is pure selfishness, and an uneasy challenge to advancing middle age. My dear Harriet, unless you are acquainted with a great many Alpine climbers nobody will call upon you but exceedingly young and energetic people.'

'Then *you* will be our most constant visitor, Uncle Paul.'

'Thank you, my dear; but my youth, alas! is only of the heart.'

Laurence Harwell, whose impatience had been visibly increasing, now broke in: 'Darling, unless we tear ourselves away we're going to be late.'

'Yes, of course. I'm so sorry. We're going to see the new programme at the Grand Guignol. There's a hair-raising one-act play about a woman who murders her lover.'

Monsieur Daumier felt this announcement to be ill-timed.

Wimsey said smoothly, 'We, on the other hand, are improving our minds at the Comédie.'

'And we,' said Mr Delagardie, rising from the table, 'are refreshing our spirits at the Folies-Bergère. You will say that at my age I should know better.'

'Far from it, Uncle Pandarus; you know too much already.'

The Harwells commandeered the first taxi that presented itself, and departed in the direction of the Boulevard de Clichy. As the other four stood waiting a few moments upon the steps of the hotel, Monsieur Daumier heard Lady Peter say to her husband, 'I don't think I've ever seen anybody quite so lovely as Mrs Harwell.'

To which he replied, judicially, 'Well, I think I have. But not more than twice.'

An answer, in Monsieur Daumier's opinion, calculated to excite surmise.

'Of course,' said Peter, with a touch of peevishness, 'we *would* run into Uncle Pandarus.'

'I like him,' said Harriet.

'So do I; but not when I happen to be feeling like a caddis-worm pulled out of its case. His eyes are like needles; I could feel them boring into us all through dinner.'

'They can't have got far into you; you were looking magnificently petrified.'

'I dare say. But why should a man whose blood is warm within sit his grandsire out in alabaster merely on account of an inquisitive uncle? No matter. With you I breathe freely and can apply the remnants of my mind to rebuilding the caddis-case.'

'No, Peter.'

'No? Harriet, you have no idea how naked it feels to be unshelled . . . What are you laughing at?'

'The recollection of a strange non-conformist hymn, which says, "A timid, weak and trembling worm into Thy breast I fall." '

'I don't believe it. But give me your hand . . . To cherish vipers in the bosom is foolish; to cherish worms, divine. Later on, Cytherea — *Zut!* I keep on forgetting that I am a married man, taking my wife to the theatre. Well, my dear, and what do you think of Paris?'

'Notre-Dame is magnificent; and the shops very expensive and luxurious, but the taxi drivers go much too fast.'

'I am inclined to agree with you,' said his lordship, as they drew up with unexpected suddenness before the doors of the Comédie-Française.

'Did you enjoy it, darling?'

'I adored it. Didn't you?'

'I don't know,' said Harwell uneasily. 'Pretty brutal, don't you think? Of course, gruesomeness is the idea of the thing, but there ought to be limits. That strangling scene . . .'

'It was terribly exciting.'

'Yes; they know how to get you all worked up. But it's a cruel kind of excitement.' His mind wandered momentarily to the London manager who was looking to him for backing, if a suitable play could be found. 'One would have to modify it a bit for the West End. It's witty, but it's cruel.'

'Passion *is* cruel, Laurence.'

'My God, I ought to know.'

She stirred in the dimness, and his nostrils were filled with the scent of crushed flowers. By the turn of her head, silhouetted against the passing lights of the boulevard, by the movement of her body against him, he was made aware that the damned play had somehow done the trick for him. That was the maddening, the intoxicating, the eternally elusive thing: you never knew what was going to do it. 'Rosamund! What did you say, my darling?'

'I said, isn't it worth it?'

'*Worth* it . . . ?'

Mr Paul Delagardie, carefully depositing his
dentures in a glass of disinfectant, hummed a little
air to himself. Really, there was no ground whatever for saying — like that old fool Maudricourt
whom he had met in the foyer — that legs were
not what they had been. Legs — and breasts, for
that matter — had improved very much since his
young days; for one thing you saw a great deal
more of them. Maudricourt was getting senile;
the natural result of settling down and giving up
women in your sixties. That sort of thing led to
atrophy of the glands and hardening of the arter-
ies. Mr Delagardie knotted the cord of his dressing-gown more tightly about his waist, and resolved that he would quite certainly go and look
up Joséphine tomorrow. She was a good girl, and,
he believed, genuinely attached to him.

He drew back the curtain and gazed out into
the garden court of the great hotel. In many windows the lights still shone; others were already
extinguished; even as he looked one, two, three,
of the glowing rectangles turned black, as in
abrupt secrecy the sojourners sought their comforted or uncomforted pillows. Overhead, the
January sky flamed with unquenchable cold fires.
Mr Delagardie felt himself so young and sprightly
that he opened the window and ventured out
upon the balcony, the better to observe Cassio-

peia's Chair, which had for him a sentimental association of a pleasurable sort. Phyllis, was it? Or Suzanne? He was not clear as to the name but he recollected the occasion perfectly. And the constellation — like the legs which old Maudricourt had libelled — had in no way diminished its splendour with the passing years.

From one of the darkened windows just across the corner of the court came a woman's low laugh. It rippled softly down the scale, and ended in a quick, eager sigh. Mr Delagardie retreated from the balcony and shut the window in gentlemanly haste. Besides, he had no wish to hear more.

It was a long time since they had laughed in his arms like that. Phyllis, Suzanne: what had become of them? Joséphine, to be sure, was a good girl, and in a dutiful way devoted to him. But a sharp twinge of rheumatism in the joints reminded him that it was unwise for elderly gentlemen to stand admiring the winter sky on balconies. Fortunately, his excellent man was always very particular about his hot-water bottle.

Extract from the diary of Honoria Lucasta, Dowager Duchess of Denver:

6th January
Went round to Audley Square to take another look at household while Peter and Harriet are in Paris. Poor dears have hardly had time to look at it themselves, although Harriet did thank me

27

very nicely, and said she liked it. Also said, 'all very new to me,' which is probably the truth. Realise have very little idea how a doctor's daughter or those Bohemian people she used to live among would arrange their houses. Foolishly wondered aloud to Helen when she called to take me to cinema to see new film with Greta Garbo. Helen said she should think squalid was the right description, but can't believe her. Greta Garbo very stylish young woman, and Harriet can change things as she goes along if she wants to. Have promised to visit Delagardie cousins in Dorset for a week on Friday, and so shall miss Helen's dinner-party to launch Harriet on London. Hope she doesn't need reinforcements — Harriet that is, Helen needs rather the opposite. Unenforcements? Disenforcements? Must try to improve vocabulary.

2

Strange to see how a good dinner and feasting reconciles everybody.

SAMUEL PEPYS

Don't you know
I promised, if you'd watch a dinner out,
We'd see truth dawn together?

ROBERT BROWNING

Helen, Duchess of Denver, was a woman conscientious in the performance of social duties. However deeply she might disapprove of her brother-in-law and his bride, it was her duty to give a party in their honour as soon as possible after the honeymoon. It had been a difficult thing to arrange. The Wimseys had (characteristically) become involved in a vulgar murder investigation the very day after their hurried, secret, and ill-managed wedding. They had then gone abroad. Instead of returning to London, they had buried themselves in the country, emerging only to give evidence against the murderer at the Assizes. They had then chosen to remain where they were until after the execution, during which time Peter had been reported to be suffering from nervous depression. This was a favourite trick of his at the conclusion of a 'case'; why anybody should upset himself about the fate of a common criminal the Duchess could not understand. If one did not like hangings, one should not mix oneself up with police work; the whole thing was a piece of exhibitionism which ought to be treated with the wholesome severity it deserved. The Duchess ascertained the date of the execution, issued invitations for Friday of the week following, and wrote to Lady Peter Wimsey a letter, whose gist beneath the formal phrasing was: 'Herein fail not at your peril.'

This firmness had been rewarded. The invitation had been accepted. What means Harriet Wimsey had used to persuade her husband, the Duchess neither knew nor cared to know. She merely observed to the Duke: 'I thought that would do the trick. That woman isn't going to let slip her first chance of social reinstatement. She's a climber if ever there was one.'

The Duke merely grunted. He liked his brother, and was disposed to like his sister-in-law, if only people would let him. He thought they were a trifle mad; but since their madness seemed to suit one another, let them get on with it. During the past twenty years he had gradually given up hope of ever seeing Peter married, and was now thankful to see him settled down. After all, he could not disguise from himself that the heir-apparent was an only son, much given to reckless driving; and that, failing him, there was only Peter's possible line to stand between the title and an elderly and mentally deficient third cousin on the Riviera. In the Duke's harmless and rather stupid existence, only one passion held permanent sway: to keep the estate together, in spite of the monstrous imposition of land-tax, super-tax, and death duties. He was bitterly conscious that his own son did not share this passion. Sometimes, sitting at his desk and struggling with his agent's books and reports, he was haunted by horrible visions of the future: himself dead, the entail broken, the estate dismembered, the Hall sold to a film magnate. If only St George could be got to realise — he *must* be made to realise . . . And then would follow the thought, disconcerting and oddly disloyal: Peter's a queer devil, but I could have trusted him better. Then he would dismiss the thought with a grunt, and write an angry letter to his son at Oxford, complaining of his debts, the company he kept, and the rarity of his visits to the Hall during vacations.

So the Duchess made preparations for a dinner-party in Carlton House Terrace, and the Duke wrote to Lord St George, who was staying with friends in Shropshire, that he must, in decency, turn up to receive his uncle and aunt, and not make the beginning of term an excuse for absenting himself. He could perfectly well travel to Oxford the following morning.

'Can you face the family?' asked Lord Peter Wimsey of his wife. He was looking at her down the length of the breakfast table, holding the gold-edged invitation in his hand.

'I can face anything,' said Harriet cheerfully. 'Besides, it has to happen some time, doesn't it?'

'There is an argument for getting on with it,' said his lordship. 'While we can still sit together.'

'I thought husbands and wives were always placed apart,' said Harriet.

'No; for the first six months after marriage we are allowed to sit together.'

'Are we allowed to hold hands under the table?'

'Best not, I should think,' said Peter. 'Unless about to go down with the ship. But we are allowed to talk to each other for the duration of one course of the dinner.'

'Is it stated which course?' asked Harriet.

'I don't know that it is. Will you have me as hors d'oeuvres, soup, fish, entrée, pudding, cheese, or dessert?'

'As just desert, my lord,' said Harriet, solemnly.

If the Duchess's guests were all either of the highest social position or the most fashionable style of beauty, or both, that must not be put down to any desire on her part to put the bride at a disadvantage. Such a gathering was due to Peter's position. The Duchess sincerely hoped that 'the woman' would behave well. It was a most unfortunate match, but one must put a good face on these things. And if the arrangement of the table seemed likely to leave one or two of the guests but dismally situated, that could not be helped. There was the question of precedence, of the required seating of bride and groom, and of separating husbands and wives. People must learn to accommodate themselves. The Duke made a wry face, all the same.

'Couldn't you have found someone a bit livelier opposite Harriet than old Croppingford? He can't talk about anythin' but horses and huntin'. Give her young Drummond-Taber; he can chatter about books and stuff and help me out with her.'

'Certainly not,' said the Duchess. 'It's Harriet's party, and she ought to have Croppingford. I can't give her Charlie Grummidge, because he's got to take me in.'

'Jerry is sure to be rude to Marjorie Grummidge.'

'Jerry is the son of the house, and surely can be polite to his mother's friends for once.'

'Hum!' said the Duke, who detested the Marchioness of Grummidge with a cordiality that was heartily reciprocated.

'Jerry has got Mrs Drummond-Taber on his other side, and she's very beautiful and charming.'

'She's an awful wet blanket.'

'He can talk for both of them. And I've given Belinda Croppingford to Peter. She's lively enough.'

'He hates women with green fingernails,' objected the Duke. The Earl of Croppingford's second marriage had disconcerted his friends and relatives. But he was the Duchess's cousin on the mother's side and, true to her standards, she made the best of him.

'She's the best-looking woman in London. Peter *used* to appreciate good looks.'

It crossed the Duke's mind that there was a conspiracy to make Peter feel what he had missed. But he only said mildly, 'Was it really necessary to invite Amaranth Sylvester-Quicke? She made herself a bit conspicuous about Peter two seasons ago.'

'Not at all,' said the Duchess sharply, adding rather inconsistently, 'That was a long time ago. I must say I think it's a pity he couldn't have had the sense to marry her, if he had to marry somebody. It would have been much more suitable. But to say she made herself conspicuous is absurd. Besides, she's Lady Stoate's niece, and lives with her; we can't ask Lady Stoate without her. And we had to have Lady Stoate, to bring this man Chapparelle.'

'I don't see why we want Chapparelle, if it comes to that. He's a painter or something, isn't he? What's he doing in a family party?'

'I really cannot understand you,' said the Duchess. 'First you complain that we have nobody to keep Harriet in countenance with books and art and that sort of thing, and then you object to Gaston Chapparelle. I don't care for that type of person myself, as you know; but he's painting everybody just now, and they say his work's going to be valuable.'

'Oh, I see,' said the Duke. Clearly, the Duchess had set her mind on securing the right artist for a few additions to the family portrait-gallery. There was St George, of course, and next season, he supposed, his daughter Winifred. The Duchess had no taste, but an excellent business head. Buy early, was her motto, before the price ran up; and one could expect a proper discount for dinner and patronage.

'He will take in Mrs Drummond-Taber,' pursued the Duchess. 'If he says anything peculiar, she won't mind; no doubt Henry, being a publisher, has accustomed her to these odd, Bohemian people. And Belinda Croppingford will rather like it. He'll have a good-looking woman on each side of him and Amaranth Sylvester-Quicke opposite. I can't see what you're making all the fuss about.'

The Duke saw plainly that his wife had already 'placed' a couple of portraits as a step towards pinning the painter down to her service. He resigned himself, as he usually did. And Lord St George, who — when he really put his mind to it — could wheedle his mother into almost anything, found himself unexpectedly in no position to argue. On the very morning of the dinner-party a piece of information reached his father's ears which led to a row so long, loud and infuriated as to be memorable, even in the Wimsey annals.

'How I'm to look your uncle in the face I don't

35

know,' said the Duke, breathing stormily. 'Every ha'penny will be paid back and docked off your allowance. And if I ever hear of anything of this sort again . . .'

So that when the young man voiced his reluctance to partner Lady Grummidge at table, the Duke, slamming over to his wife's side with the noisy suddenness of a boom in a squall, thundered, 'You will do as you are told!' and settled the matter.

'I hope,' murmured the Duchess, 'Peter is not going to be late. It would be just like him.'

Actually, she knew it would not be at all like him; he was punctual both by inclination and courtesy. But it would be like him to arrive last and so time his entrance for the most theatrically effective moment; and the other guests had played into his hands by putting in an exceptionally prompt appearance, as though unanimously resolved to miss nothing of whatever social sensation was likely to present itself. The Wimseys had returned from Paris only the previous afternoon; nobody had yet seen them; the scandal of the trial had whetted curiosity. They had also whipped up the sales of the bride's novels, so that the notorious name of Harriet Vane on vivid green and orange jackets assaulted the eyes of her relations-in-law from every bookstall and bookseller's window. The Hon. Henry Drummond-Taber, who, though an earl's son and socially unimpeachable, had become a partner in the publishing firm of Bonne and Newte, appeared to consider this circumstance a matter for congratulation. The Duchess, suddenly sensing a commercial preoccupation behind his agreeable chatter, wondered whether she had not made a mistake in inviting him to Carlton House Terrace. Patronising fashionable foreign artists was one thing; helping to sell detective stories was another.

She said, graciously smiling, 'Of course, Harriet won't really need to do any writing now that she is married. And her time will be very much occupied.'

Mr Drummond-Taber sighed. 'Our women authors ought to sign a penalty contract debarring them from matrimony,' he said, with feeling. 'Still, we mustn't be pessimistic.'

In the meantime the dowager Lady Stoate, who looked like a faded photograph of Queen Victoria, and was one of the most inquisitive and irrepressible old women in London, had flung Gaston Chapparelle into the unwelcoming arms of Lady Grummidge, and was bombarding her host with every kind of unnecessary question about 'the murder'. The Duke, stolidly disclaiming all inner knowledge, uneasily watched his son, who, neglectful of his duty to the distinguished and elderly, had attached himself to Amaranth Sylvester-Quicke. By the look on his face, he was being both malicious and indiscreet. Lord Grummidge and Lord Croppingford had got together to talk about drainage on rural estates.

Lady Grummidge, disentangling herself from Gaston Chapparelle, and casting a vicious glance at Lady Croppingford's viridian green frock, addressed herself in ringing tones to the Duchess: 'I am afraid, Helen dear, I am not very gaily attired for this *festive* occasion; but really, with this distressing news from Sandringham, gaiety seems scarcely appropriate.'

The footman at this moment announced, 'Lord and Lady Peter Wimsey,' and so launched the pair, like consort ships, on the interminable voyage up the long drawing-room, under a crossfire of scrutiny from the harbour by the fireplace.

Gaston Chapparelle, whose business it was to read the mind in the face, and was, moreover, well primed by the gossip of Lady Stoate, took one glance and said to himself: 'Oh, oh! It's defiance, I see. Amazing! Madame la duchesse wrongfooted at a stroke. Exquisite dress in perfect taste; three incomparable rubies. What can one say? Is she pretty? Not at all; but, cristi! What a figure! And strong character. She'll acquit herself well, that one. But the clue to the enigma is the husband. *Il est formidable, mon dieu,* the little white sparrowhawk . . .'

And as the greetings went round he added inwardly, 'This is going to be vastly amusing.'

The Duke approached the new Lady Peter Wimsey with some apprehension. He had met her before, of course, during the period of the engagement, but there had always been somebody

— his wife, Peter, the Dowager Duchess of Denver — to bear the brunt of the conversation. Now, for the next five minutes or so anyway, he would have to do what he could with her, unassisted. He was exceedingly conscious that Oxford-trained female novelists were not in his line of country. He opened tentatively: 'Well, how have you been getting on?'

'Very well, thank you. We had a lovely time in Paris. And the house is simply perfect. Oh, and now I've seen your tapestries in place, I must thank you all over again. They're absolutely right, and so beautiful.'

'Glad you like them,' said the Duke. He could not in the least remember what the tapestries were like, though he dimly remembered that his energetic mother had pitched upon them as a suitable and valuable wedding present with interesting family associations. There was something he felt he ought to say, though he did not quite know how to approach it.

'Afraid you had a stiffish sort of time over that murder and so on. Sorry about that.'

'Well, it was rather an unfortunate thing to happen. But it couldn't be helped. One must just try and forget about the bad bits.'

'That's right,' said the Duke. He glanced uneasily at the assembled company, and added impulsively, 'They'll keep on asking questions. Bunch of tabbies. Pay no attention.' His sister-in-law smiled gratefully at him. In a low voice he asked, 'How's Peter taking it?'

'He was badly worried, but I think he's got over it now.'

'Good. Looking after you properly?'

'Splendidly.'

Something reassuring in the tone of that. The Duke examined his sister-in-law with more attention. It dawned upon him that, brains or no brains, the general shape or appearance of what sat beside him did not differ markedly from those of other women. He said earnestly, 'I'm glad of that. Very glad.'

Harriet read the genuine anxiety in his face. 'It's going to be all right, Gerald. Really and truly.'

The Duke was surprised, and could think of nothing to say except: 'That's splendid.' He felt that in some way a confidential relation had been set up between them. He lost his head and plunged recklessly: 'I told 'em they'd better leave Peter alone. He's old enough to know what he wants.'

Having thus delivered his family into the enemy's hands, he became embarrassed, and fell silent.

'Thank you. I'll try to see he gets it.'

The announcement that dinner was served saved him from committing himself further, and threw him into the ready conversational clutch of Lady Grummidge.

It was ridiculous, thought the Duchess, lending half an ear to Grummidge on sanitation, to imagine that Peter did not like Lady Croppingford; he was provoking her to little spurts of laughter — quite an achievement, surely, at the soup stage of the proceedings. Lady Croppingford was, in fact, delivering a merciless assault on her neighbour's sensibilities, and he was clowning his way through, exhibiting distress only by a fixed vacuity of countenance, and a tendency to drop all his 'g's. St George, with a mutinous expression, was listening to Lady Grummidge; she was probably rebuking him for having spent his vacation in Shropshire. On the other side of the table, Lord Croppingford and Lady Stoate, Henry Drummond-Taber and Amaranth Sylvester-Quicke were conversing smoothly in pairs. Only the beautiful Mrs Drummond-Taber sat silent and aloof; Gaston Chapparelle, having finished his soup with unnecessary haste, was not attempting to entertain her, but was gazing in an abstracted way at Harriet. A Frenchman should have better manners, even if he was an artist. To do Harriet justice, she was doing nothing to attract notice; she was talking quietly to her brother-in-law, and her oyster satin, though obviously expensive, was discreetly cut. Fortunately, Mrs Drummond-Taber did not seem to notice that she was being neglected. Somebody had once told her that she achieved an exquisite repose, and she was rather given to displaying this achievement.

Nevertheless, the Duchess felt it her duty to draw Miss Sylvester-Quicke into conversation with Lord Grummidge and remove Peter's attention from Lady Croppingford, when, in a momentary lull, she heard Harriet say cheerfully to Drummond-Taber: 'You'd better go on calling me Miss Vane; it'll be far less confusing.'

It was Lady Grummidge's face that informed Harriet of the shock she had (quite unthinkingly) administered to the company.

The Duke said with unwonted quickness, 'I suppose that's the usual thing, what? I never thought about it.'

'Well,' said the publisher, 'some authors like it one way, and some the other. And they're often very particular about it. It's simpler for us, of course, to use the name that appears on the title page.'

'I suppose it wouldn't do to change that,' observed Lady Grummidge.

'Oh, no,' said Harriet, 'readers would never remember.'

'Are the husbands consulted beforehand?' enquired Lady Grummidge.

'I cannot,' said Peter, 'speak for husbands as a class. I was consulted and agreed with alacrity.'

'With what?' asked Lady Stoate.

'Alacrity,' said Peter. 'It gives one the illusion that one has a mistress as well as a wife, which is obviously gratifying.'

The Duchess said coldly, 'How absurd you are, Peter!'

'Well,' said Lady Grummidge, 'we shall all look forward to the new book. Unless, of course, my dear, you find a husband and family a full-time job, as some of us do.'

'Job?' said the Duke, exploding, as he occasionally did, in a quite unexpected direction. 'My dear Marjorie, what do you know about jobs? You should see some of my cottagers' wives. Bring up six children with all the cooking and washing to do and a hard day's work on the land as well. Pull down jolly good wages, too, some of them. Damned if I know how they manage it.'

The Duke had certainly succeeded in changing the subject of conversation, but having reproved Lady Grummidge with unusual emphasis, he hastened to make amends with a prolonged exchange of society gossip.

This left Harriet at the mercy of Lord Croppingford, and the Duke wondered how they were getting on. What in the world would Croppingford make of a woman who didn't know one end of a horse from the other? He heard the loud, cheerful voice begin on the weather, and the hunting season, and was seized by an inexplicable impulse to dart to the rescue.

Lady Grummidge said reprovingly, 'Gerald, you're not attending . . .'

'Never ridden in your life?' said Croppingford, shocked, but trying not to show it.

'Only on a donkey at Margate, when I was six. But I've always madly wanted to try.'

'Well, well,' said Croppingford. 'We must get you out.'

'Yes — but tell me, is thirty-three too old to learn to ride without looking silly and making a nuisance of oneself? Honestly? I don't want to behave like the comic female in *Punch*, always getting in the way and being shouted at.'

'I'm sure you're not that sort,' said Lord Croppingford, warming to his subject. 'Now, look here, if I were in your place, this is what I'd do . . .'

'Are you hoping,' enquired Miss Sylvester-Quicke, 'to include the next Harriet Vane in your autumn list?'

'We all hope,' said Drummond-Taber. 'But to take active steps in the matter would be, as the Americans put it, unethical.' One had to watch one's step, he reflected, with this girl; she was suspected of supplying gossip paragraphs to the Sunday papers.

'Can she really write? I suppose she can. Those foreheady people do as a rule. Peter's looking washed-out, don't you think? A honeymoon and a murder both at once seem to have been too much for him.'

Henry Drummond-Taber said carefully that murders in real life must have their trying side.

'It doesn't seem to have affected her much. But, of course, she's used to it. I mean, I suppose she looks on it all as good copy. Anyway, it's refreshing to see a bride and bridegroom so healthily detached. None of that their-eyes-sought-one-another-across-the-table touch which is so embarrassing. The Harwells do it still — quite indecent, after two years. They're coming back to

44

town next week, aren't they? Is it true that Chapparelle is going to paint her?'

The publisher admitted that he had heard as much.

'I think he's a most alarming man. Did you see those terribly revealing portraits he did of Lady Camshaft and Mrs Hartley-Skeffington? Of course *they* can't see what everybody else sees. It's too comic. But it's the done thing to be turned inside out by Chapparelle. I suppose it's a kind of vicarious exhibitionism.'

'Is it?'

'You're looking rather shocked. Don't say he's promised to paint your wife, or anything! But I'm sure her psyche is robust enough to stand exposure. I don't believe she could possibly have an inhibition or a repression or anything with that face; like the Venus of Milo, isn't she?'

'She is, rather,' agreed Drummond-Taber, who admired his wife's looks very much.

'I think she's quite the most beautiful person I know. She could let any painter do his most Freudian. But I should be terrified.'

Mr Drummond-Taber deduced, quite correctly, that Miss Sylvester-Quicke would give both her ears to be painted by Gaston Chapparelle.

With the arrival on the table of dessert Peter turned to his wife. 'Have you anything to say to me, upon the present occasion, Harriet?' he said in a low voice.

45

'Nothing, my lord,' said Harriet, aware that all eyes were upon them, and pauses were occurring in the flow of talk.

'Well, conversation can perhaps be overvalued,' said Peter. 'Suppose a wife to be of a studious or argumentative turn, it would be very troublesome, for instance, if a woman should continually dwell upon the subject of the Aryan heresy.'

'I think I can undertake not to do that. But as to studious conversation . . .'

'Later, Josephine?'

'Later she planted a rose garden,' said Harriet.

'So she did,' said Peter. 'And so, should you wish to, Harriet, you shall.'

The Duke circulated the port. He would permit no interference with this ancient ritual. Men might drink less than their fathers, but they must drink after the same prescribed fashion. Lord Grummidge put forward a few words on politics. Lord Croppingford returned to the subject of sport. Drummond-Taber, who disliked port, but remembered that Peter had a palate for it, put a tactful question about vintage years. Lord St George sat in uneasy silence, wondering whether he would be able to get a word in with his uncle before his father got hold of him. Gaston Chapparelle sat listening, his full lips amused in the shadow of his beard. Suddenly Lord Croppingford addressed him, with a bland and wholly unconscious insolence, as though he were ordering a mutton chop.

'Oh, by the way, Monsieur Chapparelle. I should like you to do a portrait of my wife.'

'Ah!' said Chapparelle, slowly, in his heavily accented English. 'The lady on my right? Quite so. Well, Lord Croppingford, I will think of it.'

Croppingford, taken aback, said in stiff and incredulous tones, 'Not, of course, if you don't like the idea. I am sorry I mentioned it.'

'Monsieur Chapparelle,' said Peter, 'reserves to himself the artist's privilege of caprice. The wind of inspiration carries him whither it will. If he is in a mood to be idle, nothing will make him work, not even the most beautiful subject, *n'est-ce pas?*'

'Beauty?' said the painter. 'I snap my fingers at beauty. That is for commercial artists. The true beauty, maybe; but that is not what you mean when you use the word in this country. Beauty-parlours, beauty-spots, bathing-beauties — it stands for everything that is commonplace.'

'Can't stick all these grinning girls in bathing-dresses,' said Lord Grummidge, helpfully. 'Nothing else in the papers nowadays.'

'Don't tell me,' said Peter, 'that you paint everybody with green complexions and triangular busts. Or has that fashion gone out?'

'Come, Wimsey,' said Drummond-Taber, 'are you going to confess that you don't know Chapparelle's work?'

'I am. Openly. Shamelessly. I haven't been in town since last March. Give me full marks for candour, monsieur, and tell me what you do paint.'

'With pleasure. I paint women. Sometimes men, but usually women. I should like to paint *your* wife.'

'Would you, begad!'

'She is not beautiful,' pursued Chapparelle, with startling frankness. 'There are at least two other ladies here tonight who would look better on the picture page of the daily paper. But she is paintable. That is not the same thing. She has character. She has bones.'

'God bless my soul!' said the Marquis of Grummidge.

'She interests me. Will you let her sit to me?'

'Look out, Uncle,' said St George, with sudden, unexpected malice. 'His motto is "Where I paint, I sleep." '

'St George!' said the Duke, awfully.

'Sleep,' said Peter, 'is a singularly harmless occupation, though an inactive one.'

'Young devil!' said the painter. 'But your nephew has got hold of the wrong end of the stick. I do not care whom my sitter loves, provided she loves somebody. Her husband, another woman's husband, myself at a pinch. But I prefer that it should not be myself. It saves complication and is less fatiguing.'

'I am obliged to you,' returned Peter, 'for that very frank and manly statement, which clears the ground for negotiations. Your proposal is that my wife should provide the bones, you provide the paint, while I do my best — I hope I understand this part of it correctly — to provide the human interest.'

'I also,' said Chapparelle, 'provide the genius, which you seem to have forgotten.'

'That is an important item, of course. Can you paint?'

'I am a very good painter,' said Chapparelle, simply. 'If you will visit my studio any day, I will show you.'

'It will give me very great pleasure.'

'Oh, yes,' said Chapparelle, 'you will be pleased. I speak with confidence. I may then say to your wife that you permit me to paint her?'

'I don't know that I should recommend that form of words. It's her permission that you want. But I am ready to hover sympathetically in the background and lend you my moral support.'

Chapparelle met the mocking eyes with an exaggerated humility. 'Favoured by your alliance, I shall hope for success.'

Lord Croppingford, feeling obscurely that everybody had behaved rudely except himself, refilled his glass.

'Peter,' said the Duke, as the men rose to rejoin the ladies, 'now you're here, I'd like to have a word with you. Do you mind going on up without us, Grummidge? We won't be long. Gerald, ask your mother to excuse us.'

He waited till the door was shut, and then said, 'Look here. How much money have you lent Gerald?'

'Not a penny,' replied Peter, coolly. 'This is the Tuke Holdsworth, isn't it?'

The Duke reddened between the eyebrows.

'It's no good your trying to shield the boy. I made him admit that you'd been paying his debts and helping him out of a scrape with some woman or other.'

'Whatever I let him have was a gift. I don't believe in hanging millstones round a boy's neck. The other business cost nothing but a letter from my solicitor. I wish you hadn't tackled him about it. Unless, of course, he told you of his own accord.'

'He tells me nothing. He'll go to anybody rather than to his parents. But I'm damned if I'll have him sponging on you. I've made out a cheque, and you'll have the decency to take it. I made him tell me the amount — though I dare say he was lying.'

'No,' said Peter, accepting the cheque. 'That's quite correct. But look here, old man, why don't you make him a really adequate allowance? He's bound to play the fool when he's kept so short.'

'He's not fit to handle money.'

'If he doesn't learn now, he never will be. After all, he knows he's got to come into the money some day. And if you can't trust him now, what's going to happen to the land when you go?'

'God knows,' said the Duke, gloomily. 'He doesn't give a damn for anything. Nothing but girls and fast cars. Now he says he wants to take up flying. I won't have it, and I've told him so.

He's got to have some sense of responsibility. If anything happens to him —' He broke off and fiddled with the stem of his glass; then said, almost angrily, 'I suppose you realise that you're next.'

'I realise it perfectly,' said Peter. 'I assure you *I* have no wish to see Jerry break his neck. Country estates aren't in my line and never were.'

'You run your London property pretty well, though.'

'Yes, but it *is* London. I rather like handling houses, and people. But pig and plough — no.'

'Well,' said the Duke, 'I'm glad you're married, anyway.'

Peter's eyes narrowed. 'I didn't marry with the idea of founding a dynasty.'

'I did,' said the Duke. He got up and walked heavily across to the fireplace. 'Don't blame Helen. I made several kinds of fool of myself, and she got fed up with me. But I wish Winifred had been another boy.'

'Looking at the matter logically,' said his brother, 'either one is the parish bull, or one is not. But our generation is neither one thing nor the other. You want me to secure the collateral line for you in case of accident. All right. A Victorian would simply have ordered his wife to do her duty. The young man and woman of today would refuse to recognise any duty in the matter.'

'It's you I'm asking, Flim.'

'I know,' said Peter, moved in spite of himself

by the school nickname. 'And I see your point. But the decision isn't in my hands and I don't intend that it shall be. If my wife has children, she shall have them for fun and not as a legal instrument for securing the orderly devolution of property.'

'Have you mentioned the matter to Harriet?'

'She once mentioned it to me.'

The Duke's face expressed a lively apprehension: 'Do you mean that she definitely objected to the idea?'

'No. Nothing of the kind. But see here, Denver, I will not have you saying anything to her about it. It would be damnably unfair to both of us.'

'I'm not goin' to interfere,' said the Duke, hastily.

'Then why the devil *do* you interfere?'

'I'm not. I only asked you. You needn't be so dashed touchy.' He was sorry Peter had been so quick to frustrate his idea of speaking to Harriet and putting the thing to her in a straightforward manner. A sensible modern woman surely would not mind, and her attitude at dinner had given him encouragement to hope for the best. But his brother had always been full of queer, baffling reluctance. Still, if the thing had been for any reason impossible, Peter would have said so. He ventured: 'Harriet's made quite a conquest of Croppingford. He told me she was a damn fine woman.'

'With no bigad nonsense about her! I'm obliged to Croppingford.'

'Well, I say you did dead right,' said the Duke. 'Good luck to it.'

'Thanks, old man.'

The Duke hoped something would be forthcoming, but Peter's usually busy tongue was well bridled tonight. A queer business, thought the Duke. Independence. Silence. Reservations. Modern marriage. Was there any sort of mutual confidence? A slippery affair, and he could get no grip on it. He led the way upstairs. At the turn of the landing he paused, and said with an air of defiance, 'I've been planting oaks in Boulter's Hollow.'

Oaks! Peter met his eyes firmly and said without emphasis, 'They should do very well there.'

At the door of the house the Daimler was waiting for them. Peter said, 'Would you mind very much if I walked home? I'd like the breath of air.'

'I wouldn't mind; but may I come with you?'

'You won't be cold?'

'In the bride's mink coat? I don't think so.'

Peter dismissed the car with a wave of the hand, and drew Harriet's arm through his. They passed the top of the Duke of York's Steps, and saw in the pallid lamplight a number of people passing up the Mall. Without a word they descended the steps, and joined the tide of people flowing towards the Palace. Harriet was glad of her coat, for there was a brisk wind under a clear sky, dry and threatening frost. There were cars parked all along the Mall. The monument to Queen Victoria was covered with people standing; people were clustered in front of the Palace railings; some of them had climbed up and were holding on to the bars. The crowd stirred, moving round the bulletin board which was hanging at the gates.

Peter said, 'Stand just here, Harriet, under this lamp-post, and I'll see if I can get through and read it.'

Harriet leaned against the lamp-post. The crowd around her were of every possible kind of person: men and women, some in evening dress, some poorly clad enough to be shivering in the wind. They spoke to each other in a curious muted and reverent excitement. A group of men speaking German pushed past. Then a policeman passed Harriet in the throng.

'What is the latest bulletin?' she asked him.

'It has not been issued,' he said, and moved on.

There was a stirring in the crowd next to the Palace. Peter returned to her. 'It says: "His Majesty's life is drawing to a peaceful close",' he said.

'Do you want to keep watch here?' she asked.

'No need,' he said, and taking her arm again he led her away. They walked silently up St James's, stepping from pool to pool of lamplight, crossed Piccadilly, and into Mayfair. As they turned into Audley Square he said, 'It's an odd thing how people come out on the streets, how they gather at the scene.'

'Like a chorus in a Greek tragedy,' she said. 'Perhaps that's why the chorus seems perfectly natural to us — people have always gathered . . .'

'When times change,' he said, turning his key in the lock.

Extract from the diary of Honoria Lucasta, Dowager Duchess of Denver:

21st January
Up late listening to the wireless for news of the poor dear King. No change in the bulletins, but Franklin came in from her night off saying that the street was full of people, just milling around. Woken later by shouting in the street. The little carriage-clock beside my bed showed three in the morning. A newsboy was hallooing, 'King dies! Read all about it — King dead!' Opened window to call out to him for a paper, but only to see Franklin in her dressing-gown running after him to get one. We had cocoa together reading the front-page report — all in black borders. Remember him very well as a little boy in a sailor suit at Windsor, when I was taken there to play with him. Remember how difficult it was to let him win at Battledore. Seems only yesterday. Cried a little on going back to bed, not for the dignified old King but for the little boy. So silly. Often can't help being silly . . .

3

Oh, Mrs Corney, what a prospect this opens! What a opportunity for a jining of hearts and housekeepings!

CHARLES DICKENS

Matrimony . . . is no more than a form of friendship recognised by the police

ROBERT LOUIS STEVENSON

Although, with the academic person's deceptive tendency to understatement, Harriet tended to dismiss her own share in the household management as negligible, she was discovering that domesticity had its problems. There was, for instance, the delicate affair of Emmanuel Griffin, the footman. It had been decided (partly in his own interests) that he should be known as 'William'; but a number of politically minded friends had persuaded him to see in this arrangement a manifestation of upper-class tyranny. He had taken umbrage and been impertinent to Meredith. The matter having been adjusted by an apology on his part to the butler and his restoration (by consent) to his baptismal name, there ensued trouble between him and the chauffeur, Alfred Farley. Farley, Emmanuel complained, would bring the car to the front door and 'sit singing Christmas hymns to it, quiet-like', while Emmanuel, immobilised in attendance with his arms full of rugs, was in no position to make his resentment felt. The quarrel came to a head at a moment when Peter had been called away to Denver by family business. Harriet, left in authority, suggested that the affair should be honourably settled in the boiler-house. The result was satisfactory: one black eye, one cut lip, and Emmanuel's spontaneous decision to adopt the name of Thomas for everyday wear.

Then there was Harriet's personal maid, an experimental novelty embarked on with gingerly reluctance. To a naturally untidy person with an ingrained habit of impatient independence the very idea of a trained lady's-maid was intimidating. Even the resourceful dowager had been at a loss. It was Peter, who, from an unexpected quarter of his illimitable acquaintance, had produced Juliet Mango. She was the daughter of a cinema attendant, and had attracted the unenviable notice of authority by pinching illustrated magazines from bookstalls. Her record and character were otherwise good, and her thefts limited to magazines; and it appeared on enquiry that her sole motive for misdoing was to imagine herself into that strange world of the titled and wealthy whose clothes and houses and activities decorated the

57

pages of *Vogue* and *Country Life*. Of the cinema (a more usual sublimation of such appetites) she complained that 'mostly the people were dressed all wrong and the real top-liners didn't behave like that.'

Peter, feeling that anyone of such natural discrimination should be encouraged, had consulted with the probation officer and got her work with a dressmaker, where she had done very well. In the September of his engagement, finding his mother at her wit's end, and his bride in a state of suppressed panic, he had sought out Miss Mango, and brought her home on approval. The interview being satisfactory, he had obtained her release from the dressmaking establishment and packed her off to learn the art of hairdressing, and now here she was in Audley Square, accompanied by a whole library of manuals on etiquette and the complete works of Mr P.G. Wodehouse whom, not without justice, she took seriously as an infallible guide to high life above and below stairs. Like d'Artagnan, she had no practice but a profound theory of her profession; like a university scholar, she absorbed information readily from the printed text; she had, in short, the kind of mind that Harriet knew how to cope with.

For Miss Mango herself, there was the excitement of living her own dream. She was a stickler for propriety. To be addressed by her surname gave her a thrill of exquisite satisfaction; the severity of her garments and the primness of her manner made Mrs Trapp appear over-dressed and Bunter expansive. In her time off, she attended theatres and talkies, noting errors of social procedure and writing condemnatory letters to producers. She seemed to look upon Peter as a cinematograph entertainment that had been, by some miracle, correctly produced in every detail, and accorded him a prostrate admiration accordingly. Her reverence for Mr Bunter as his producer, though profound, was tinged with rivalry. She was so eager that her own show should compete with his, that Harriet felt bound in decency to co-operate by taking a hitherto unwonted interest in dress.

There were mysteries as well as problems in the running of the house. Meredith, it seemed, was called upon by his station in life to clean the silver, whereas Mrs Trapp in person washed the Sèvres dinner service. Only the lowly dishes came within the competence of the kitchen maid. Harriet applied herself to learning this domestic lore with an anthropological curiosity — for surely she was of a different tribe — and then was nonplussed one day to find Bunter cleaning an austerely beautiful pair of silver candlesticks that adorned the library side table.

'Why doesn't Meredith see to those, Bunter?' she asked.

'His lordship is particularly attached to these, my lady,' said Bunter, pausing in his task. 'He has had them, I believe, since his father gave them to him to brighten his rooms at Balliol. They are by Paul de Lamerie, my lady, a London silver-

59

smith, circa 1750. I have always cleaned them myself.'

Apart from a lien to a pair of candlesticks, the master of the house himself offered fresh fields for discovery. His wife had already realised that he had other interests in life besides cricket, crime and old printed books; she now saw these interests take the practical form of conferences with the estate agent, occupying an average of two mornings a week. The estate agent was on the outer border of north London, in a rapidly growing district. Peter, it seemed, was not merely the ground landlord but the actual landlord of the greater number of the properties, and had architects and builders at his command. Mr Simcox the agent bustled about continually, bringing estimates and correspondence and blueprints. Peter took infinite care of even the smallest details, as though, Harriet noticed, fascinated, he were particularly determined to refute allegations that his wealth and title put him out of touch with the everyday world and the ordinary concerns of plainer people. On the other hand he was aesthetically ruthless, so that features of the Wimsey Estate were the roomy comfort of its public houses, the exceptional splendour of its scullery sinks, and the landlord's ferocious veto upon bungalows, galvanised iron, and bastard Tudor half-timbering.

Peter had also personal peculiarities to be reckoned with. His physical fitness had sometimes puzzled Harriet. Though he could, when called upon, ride, swim and play cricket, he bore none of the obvious stigmata of the sports addict; yet he was obviously in first-class training, and, except for an occasional nervous headache, never seemed to be ill. A solution of this problem was offered by Monsieur d'Amboise and Mr Matsu. Harriet preferred the attitude of Monsieur d'Amboise, in spite of his tedious and scarcely credible anecdotes directed to prove his descent from the great Bussy. He treated Peter with a proper respect, and complimented him on his mastery of fence. But Mr Matsu, a wiry Japanese who scarcely reached his pupil's shoulder, was laconic and sparing of praise. One had imagined Peter would be an accomplished ju-jitsu performer, until one saw Mr Matsu throw him effortlessly about like a brisk housemaid handling a clumsy eiderdown. Mr Matsu had seen nothing of Peter for some months, and affected to find him gravely deteriorated. 'Can't be helped, Matsu,' said Peter, writhing under the vigorous attentions of the masseur. 'I don't get any younger, you know.'

'Not too old,' replied Mr Matsu, brutally. 'Too much restaurant, too much automobile, too much lady wife.'

'You be damned,' said Peter; and in the next bout put Mr Matsu on his back for nearly six seconds.

'Better,' said Mr Matsu, extricating himself, 'but please not to lose temper; very disadvantageous to lose temper in sustained encounter.'

Then there was a whole series of fads and ab-

surdities: the interminable dawdling in the bathroom; the agonised fuss over a pimple or a care-
lessly rolled umbrella; the haunting and irrational
terror of being some day obliged to wear false
teeth which sent my lord post-haste to the dentist
at the first sign of trouble, breaking every engagement to be encountered in his headlong flight.
There were the incunabula and piano, whose
health involved the daily taking of temperatures
in library and music-room; there was the passion
for ritual that set ten feet of mahogany between
husband and wife at a solitary meal and that
prefaced any request for Harriet's presence in
another part of the house by the dispatch of a
footman with compliments. And there was the
preposterous contrast between Peter's diffidence
as a husband and his confidence as a lover, so
that his bedside manner displayed no inhibitions
but only an infinite series of courtesies; while his
hatred of any exhibition of feeling in public was
only equalled by his shattering frankness in the
disregarded presence of his own servants.

Lady Peter Wimsey, thoughtfully chewing her
cigarette-holder, paused in her writing and stared
out of the window. She had begun to realise why
marriage is sometimes a handicap to a novelist's
career. The emotion of love — fulfilled and satisfactory love at any rate — does not stimulate
the creative imagination, but puts it to sleep.
Hence, she supposed, the dearth of really cheerful
poems about love in any language. She had

wasted a great deal of her working time that morning owing to sheer inability to concentrate. This afternoon she had sat down determined to get the chapter finished. It was raining remorselessly, so that there was no temptation to go out; and Peter had gone to keep a business appointment, so that, being out of sight, he might be presumed to be out of mind. In the little room adjoining Harriet's study Miss Bracy the secretary sat before the silent typewriter, reproachfully knitting a jumper. Miss Bracy always looked reproachful when there was no manuscript for her to get on with. She was a quick and efficient worker, and it was very difficult to keep her supplied.

Cormorant! thought Harriet. She lit a fresh cigarette and squared her elbows, preparing to tackle afresh her detailed and scientific description of a ten-day-old corpse as it appeared when removed by the police from the city reservoir. It was a subject well calculated to dispel daydreams.

But like Dr Donne at his prayers she was in a mood to neglect her occupation 'for the noise of a Flie, for the ratling of a Coach, for the whining of a door . . .' A jingling of harness and a clatter of hooves under the window were sounds unusual enough to merit investigation. She looked out. A brougham with a rotund coachman and two fat, shining horses, passed and drew up before the door. It was evident that something of a portentous sort was coming to call — something that would never have called on Miss Harriet Vane, but was liable at any moment to descend without warning upon Lady Peter Wimsey. Her ladyship, repressing Miss Vane's natural inclination to crane her head out of the window, laid down the author's pen and wondered whether she was suitably dressed to receive whatever fairy godmother should descend from this pumpkin equipage.

The card came in on a salver.

'The Countess of Severn and Thames, my lady. Is your ladyship at home?'

Obviously one must be at home to Lady Severn, who was of fabulous age and terrifying reputation. Harriet said faintly that she was at home, and had sufficient presence of mind not to bolt out into the hall, but to wait until the formidable antediluvian had had time to ascend into the drawing-room and recover breath.

When, after this suitable interval, she followed, she found Lady Severn seated bolt upright on the sofa, her hands crossed upon a crutch-handled stick and her eyes fixed implacably upon the door. The room was large, and Harriet, crossing it, felt unusually conscious of her own arms and legs; yet the novelist in her registered the visitor at once as a frowsy little old vulture in a black velvet toque.

'How do you do?' said Harriet. 'Please don't get up. It is very kind of you to call.'

'Not in the least,' retorted Lady Severn. 'Sheer curiosity. It's the only pleasant vice I have left. I was ninety last week, so I can do as I like. Thank you, yes; I am wearing quite well. I came to see what Peter had married, that's all.'

'But it *is* very kind of you,' said Harriet. 'You might so easily have sent for me.'

'So I might,' said Lady Severn, 'only Peter would have come trailing along to protect his property. As it is, I happen to know he's out of the way.'

'He will be very sorry to have missed you.'

'Very likely. H'm. Well, you seem to have a sensible sort of face with eyebrows in it. Eyebrows have gone out; I'm sick of looking at human eggs. You've got plenty of bone. Your skin looks healthy, if it's natural.'

'It is, except for a little powder.'

'H'm. You'll do. Helen Denver is a fool. Well, how do you like it?'

'Like what, Lady Severn?'

'Being part of the Wimsey Estate.'

'Peter doesn't treat me as part of the estate.'

'I suppose not. He always had good manners. An excellent bedside manner too, or so they tell me.'

Harriet said gravely, 'I don't think they ought to have told.'

In spite of herself, the corners of her mouth twitched and the vulture chuckled again.

'You're quite right, my dear, they oughtn't. You won't tell, I can see. Never tell *me* anything; I always repeat it. Are you in love with him?'

'Yes. I don't mind having that repeated.'

'Then why didn't you marry him sooner?'

'Obstinacy,' said Harriet, and this time she grinned openly.

'Humph! You're probably the first woman that ever kept him waiting. What do you do with him, now you've got him, hey? Lick his toes, or make him sit up and beg?'

'What do you advise?'

'Honest dealing,' said the old lady, sharply. 'A man's none the better for being fretted to fiddle-strings. You're going to amuse me. Most of these young women are very dull. They either take offence or think I'm a scream. What do you think?'

'I think,' said Harriet, feeling she might as well be hanged for a sheep as a lamb, 'you are behaving like a character in a book. And I think you are doing it on purpose.'

'That's rather shrewd of you,' said the vulture.

'When I put you in a book,' pursued Harriet, 'I shall make that aspect of your psychology quite clear.'

'All right,' said Lady Severn. 'I'll take six copies. And I'll promise to live till it's published. Are you going to have any children, or only books?'

'Well,' said Harriet, reasonably, 'it's easier to be definite about books. I mean, I know I can produce books.'

'Oh, I see,' said Lady Severn, and proved that she did see by adding, 'Good girl. You must come and see my Siamese cats. I breed 'em. I have six children, ten grandchildren, and only three great-grandchildren Cats are more reliable.'

'I expect it's simpler for them,' suggested Harriet. 'No economic problems, and no prolonged connubial life.'

'You're wrong there,' said Lady Severn, triumphantly. 'The Siamese kind are very monogamous. So's Peter, but everybody doesn't know that. Did you know it?'

'I suspected it. I hope you will stay to tea.'

'Politeness? Or good, what d'ye call it, copy?'

'That's the first really rude thing you've said to me, Lady Severn.'

'So it is, my dear, and I apologise, but so many people don't know the difference these days. It's quite a long time since anyone put me in my place. Very refreshing. I like you,' she added abruptly. 'There's good blood in you somewhere. I don't care where Peter picked you up, or what you did. I wish I were younger. I'd enjoy taking you about, and seeing people's faces. I suppose you know you're the worst-hated woman in London?'

'I hadn't thought of it quite like that,' said Harriet. 'Do you think it will be good for sales?'

The vulture laughed — a baritone chuckle. 'I shouldn't wonder,' she said. 'And yes, I should like some tea. Proper tea. Not this Chinese stuff that tastes of damp hay. While it's coming you can show me the house. Stairs? Rubbish. I've still got the use of my limbs.'

Lady Severn's criticisms had their own pungency. 'What do you call this? The drawing-room? Oh, the music-room. Peter's music, I imagine. That's the piano he had in the flat. Ever let you touch it? Oh, you don't play; well, I shouldn't begin, if I were you . . . Oh, yes, the library. Very handsome. Peter's books, no doubt. Where do you keep yours? I suppose you have a little dog-kennel to yourself somewhere?'

'We both use this,' said Harriet mildly. 'I have a separate study on the ground floor, and Peter has a little room for interviewing architects and agents and policemen and people. The Dowager Duchess arranged it all beautifully.'

'Peter's mother? I hope she consulted you occasionally. I like Honoria, but she always was a perfect fool about Peter . . . Housekeeper's room? Nonsense, of course I'm going in. Dear me, it's Trapp. How are you, Trapp? Keeping his lordship in order, I hope. Thanks; if my asthma wasn't better, I shouldn't be here . . . Yes; I thought that pretentious staircase would stop at the first floor — these Georgian houses are all alike . . . Whose bedroom? Yours? That bed's a good specimen. Those curtains are unhealthy.'

'But they're beautiful, don't you think?'

'Yes, they are, but it seems unnatural for your generation not to be faddy about fresh air. Or is there a new fad for stuffiness coming in?'

'I've never lived among really beautiful things,' said Harriet by way of apology for the curtains.

'No, I suppose not. What was your father? Country doctor or something? No, there wouldn't be much in the way of William and Mary bedsteads. And the lodgings in Bloomsbury? When you lived with that poet person, which of you paid the rent?'

She shot the question out so suddenly that Harriet was quite taken aback. After a moment's hesitation she said quietly, 'The expenses were shared.'

'Humph! I shouldn't mind betting I know which of you took the heavy end of the load. Never mind, child, I'm not asking you to give the man away. Were you in love with him?'

'I realise now that I wasn't. But he's dead now, and please may we leave him alone?'

'Oh, don't mind me. My lover died fifty years ago. Nobody knew about him, which was good luck. But I was in love with him, and that was bad luck. Does Peter manage to let the poor dead poet creature alone?'

'He has never mentioned him.'

'Then don't *you* go digging him up. Let him be. And let Peter's women be . . . wallowing in remorse is pure self-indulgence. Don't do it. Who sleeps in here? Why on earth do you put the head housemaid next to that man of Peter's? Nobody could possibly be as respectable as that man looks,' and, giving the door a peremptory knock, she marched straight in.

'I don't know whether Bunter is . . .' Harriet protested, but Bunter, knowing her ladyship, had clearly taken care not to be there. Lady Severn made a rapid inspection. In spite of her sense of decorum, Harriet, who had never before been in the room, looked round too.

'I've always wondered whether that man had any private life,' said Lady Severn. 'Who are all the photographs? His wives and families?'

'I expect they are his brothers and sisters. He has six, including Meredith.'

'Your butler? Is *he* married? Oh, yes, here he is, with three children. What's become of them?'

'They're in service, I believe.'

'Who took all these photographs of Peter?'

'Bunter; photography is his hobby.'

'You'd think he saw enough of Peter without eight photographs. I suppose it's a kind of craze. It's a pity Peter isn't better looking, it'll come so hard on the girls. What's on this floor? The footman? That good-looking young man? You keep your eye on him. Human nature's human nature. And the two other maids together? Well, keep your eye on *them* all the same. Your linen-closet might be worse . . . I hope your cook doesn't take advantage of that electric fire. In my day, cooks didn't expect luxuries and expensive electricity . . . What are you going to do with those two rooms, hey?'

'I don't know,' said Harriet thoughtfully. 'We might keep rabbits here, don't you think?'

'Rabbits?' cried Lady Severn in some alarm. 'Good heavens, child, don't take it into your head to have quads or quins or anything vulgar. Making a man look a fool. That kind of thing should be kept for the zoological gardens. Don't you even *dream* of rabbits. With all this subconsciousness going about, it's not safe. And don't have any-thing you don't fancy. I don't care what Denver says, or Peter either. Men are a lot of Pharisees — always binding heavy burdens for women to carry. A bunch of silly peacocks. I ought to know. I've had a husband and three sons and two grand-sons and more lovers than most people know about, and there's not a halfpenny to choose be-tween 'em.' She broke off abruptly. 'I want my tea.'

In the drawing-room they found not only tea, but Peter, who started like a guilty thing, and said, '*Dear* Lady Severn,' in a voice faint with apprehension.

'Humph!' said Lady Severn. 'I came to inspect, and I've remained to tea. I like your wife. *She's* not afraid of me. Are you treating her properly? You look disgustingly smug, and you're fatter in the face than you used to be. I hope you're not battening on her. I hate husbands who batten. Sit down, man.'

'Yes, Godmamma . . .'

(So it was a fairy godmother, after all, in the pumpkin coach . . .)

Harriet poured tea, while Peter began a long series of enquiries about Lady Severn's extensive family and acquaintance, unto the third and the fourth generations, and including the generations of her cats. He seemed determined to keep the conversation on the enemy's home ground through cucumber sandwiches, and fruit cake, and a fresh pot of tea.

But eventually he made a strategic error: 'It is very good to see you here, Godmamma. Do you approve of the house?'

'You'll be able to manage for a few years,' said Lady Severn, graciously. 'What are you going to call the children?'

'Matthew, Mark, Luke and John,' said Peter, rather deliberately not catching Harriet's eye. 'Keviah, Jemoma, and Keren-happuh. After that we shall begin on the nine muses and the kings of Israel and Judah. And then there are still the major and minor prophets and the eleven thousand virgins of Cologne. Your carriage is waiting, Godmamma, and the horses are catching cold.'

'Verywell,' said the vulture. 'And you needn't try smiling sideways and waving your eyelashes at me; it won't work. Ever since some idiot told you you had charm you go about practicing it. Well, don't. It's silly and it's wasted on me. You're not *my* white-headed boy.'

'Isn't he?' said Harriet. 'Do you know, you quite gave me the impression that he was.'

'I'm sorry about that,' said Peter. 'I knew we'd have to go through the hoop one day soon, but I never thought she'd come in person. She never puts herself out for people. She must have been suffering agonies of inquisitiveness for the last three months. She was mercifully laid up for the wedding — safe in bed in Devon. Was she very awful to you?'

'No. I don't mind her.'

'I do. I had the most frightful grilling, with my head stuck in at the carriage window and the rain coming down on my behind. Vain, selfish, neurotic, never had to do a hand's turn, married to a girl with twice my guts and expecting her to sit around and hold my hand. Born with a silver spoon in my mouth, and all I could do was to wave it around and strike attitudes. And that damned fool of a footman stood there waiting to hand in the rug and never had the sense to hang it on my cruppers. Is it lumbago or sciatica you get from being lectured in the rain?'

'Floating kidney, I expect, my beautiful.'

'Don't laugh at me, Harriet, my self-respect won't stand it. There was more. It wasn't as if I was good-looking. A vapid Apollo had at least a set of features to be conceited about, but why should I give myself airs? Or she may have meant heirs with an H — I didn't dare ask. I've seldom seen the godparent in such form; she must have taken an extraordinary fancy to you. In fact she told me she had.'

'She thinks my eyebrows are amusing.'

'Oh, that accounts for it. Mine have been a sad disappointment to her. In fact, I have never asked you how you came to find acceptable eyebrows as pallid and faint as mine.'

'Not faint Canaries, but ambrosial,' said Harriet, regarding him gravely.

'Didn't we trade that quotation before? And wasn't it about something rather more profound?' he asked, smiling.

'Perhaps. Your eyebrows had better be remote Bermudas, then.'

There were, of course, one's own friends, too; a few staunch-hearted women who had stuck to the ship ever since the bad old days, and a number of literary acquaintances who came professing admiration for one's work and displaying unconcealed curiosity as to one's adaptation to new conditions. These caused little difficulty, and Peter was pleasant to them all — except to one repulsive young novelist who sneered subtly at Harriet's sales and put down a hot cigarette end on a Sheraton table. He departed hastily, surrounded by an atmosphere that might be felt. The Drummond-Tabers called, bringing with them Sir Jude Shearman, who owned three theatres and asked Harriet with kindly interest whether she had ever thought of writing for the stage. 'No; I'm afraid not. I'm afraid trying so hard not to be melodramatic has turned my thoughts from being dramatic, *tout court*.'

'Well, a novel can be a very good novel and still make an excellent basis for a play,' he said. 'One is reading something and it strikes one as, well, stagey; eminently adaptable.'

'Oh, I know what you mean,' said Harriet. 'Or at least, I do in reverse. One sometimes sees plays which appear to have emerged uneasily from novels. Did you see *Distinguished Gathering* at the Cambridge Theatre last month?'

'Alas, no,' said Sir Jude. 'Poetry is an even more

interesting case. What did you think of *Murder in the Cathedral*?'

'It is magnificent on the page,' said Harriet. 'We haven't seen it on the stage.'

'Let me urge you to do so,' said Shearman. 'It makes wonderful drama.'

'It isn't an obstacle to success that the work is in poetry?' asked Wimsey.

'Not if it's good enough,' said Sir Jude. 'A certain section of the public likes to preen itself on appreciating fine language.'

Shortly afterwards Harriet invited her own publisher to dinner. Mr Drummond-Taber behaved exceedingly well on this occasion, talking perceptively to Peter about Mussolini and the situation in Abyssinia, and only mentioning twice his concern for Harriet's literary future.

But the sight of his anxious and appealing eyes forced Harriet to face the central problem of the married author; am I really a writer or only a writer *faute de mieux*? If one was really a writer, then one must write, and write now, while the hand still kept its cunning, while the technique was still in one's head, while one was still in touch with one's public. A little slumber, a little rest, a little folding of the hands to sleep, and one would drowse into an endless lethargy, waiting for a dawn that might never break.

No; that was not the real difficulty. Peter was the problem. He had allowed it to be taken for granted that one would go on writing. He had made it a matter of principle that one's work came before one's private entanglements. But did he mean what he said? Not everybody cares to see his principles put into practice to his own inconvenience. And if it ever came to a choice between being Harriet Vane or Harriet Wimsey, then it didn't matter much which one chose; the mere necessity of choice would mean that something had suffered defeat. Talk settled nothing; the only way to find out the facts was to start writing and see what happened.

The first thing that happened was the realization that the new story was going to be a tragedy. Previous books, written while their author was struggling through a black slough of misery and frustration, had all been intellectual comedies. The immediate effect of physical and emotional satisfaction seemed to be to lift the lid off hell. Harriet, peering inquisitively over the edge of her own imagination, saw a drama of agonised souls arrange itself with odd and alluring completeness. She had only to lift a finger to make the puppets move and live. She was a little startled, and (rather apologetically) brought this interesting psychological paradox to Peter for treatment. His only comment was: 'You relieve my mind unspeakably.'

With this encouragement, if it could be called so, she proceeded to the brewing of her hell-broth. At the end of a week's work, she found herself in need of a little technical information, and, going into the library in search of it, discovered Peter, laboriously collating a black-letter folio.

He looked up enquiringly.

'I've got the corpse out of the reservoir at last,' said Harriet.

'I'm glad of that. As a conscientious landlord, I was beginning to worry about the town water supply.'

'That was just what I came to look up. But perhaps you can tell me. All about water pollution, and sewage, and filters, and that sort of thing. And what the borough council — would it be the borough council? — would do about it, or does there have to be a water board? I've got a humorous sanitary inspector I'd like to work in.'

'I'll try,' said Peter, making a careful note on a slip of paper before closing the black-letter volume. 'Is it London or a big town, or a country town or merely an urban district? Where does it get its water from? What is the capacity of the reservoir? How long has the bloke been inside it, and how far is he supposed to have gone on the way to eventual liquidation?'

'That's the problem,' said Harriet. 'Can the forensic people tell accurately how long a body has been immersed? Could there be any doubt about such a thing?'

'Do you want there to be a doubt?'

'Oh, yes. Ideally I would like an appearance that the body had been submerged for a much shorter time than is actually the case. If plausible, that is.'

'Well, why not contrive to have it washed up somewhere high and dry for a bit, and then re-immersed. That should confuse the time scale nicely.'

'But a washed-up body would be found.'

'Not necessarily. Suppose you got it into the water not in a municipal reservoir, but somewhere like Highgate Ponds. They are one of the sources of the Fleet River, long since gone underground and out of mind. I've got some interesting old maps which would let you trace the course.'

'But wouldn't it just wash down the river into the Thames, and pop up quite quickly?'

'No, it wouldn't, as a matter of fact, because these lost old watercourses are dry some of the time. There's a system of intercepting sewers. Look at the map: you see the old rivers ran into the Thames roughly at right angles, and they were grossly polluted and seething with cholera and dysentery. So after the Great Stink of 1858 —'

'Whatever was the Great Stink?' asked Harriet, charmed.

'A stench so awful from the tidal mudbanks in the Thames that curtains soaked in chloride of lime had to be hung at the windows of the Palace of Westminster to allow MPs to get through necessary parliamentary business.'

'So they had to do something about it?'

'Yes. An engineer called Joseph Bazalgette, whose name would be immortal and known to every schoolboy if there were any justice in the world, built intercepting sewers, running parallel with the Thames at three levels, that carried away the muck to outfalls below London. Look, you see, here they are, running east to west on the map.'

'Does this still work?' asked Harriet.

'Yes, it does. There are treatment works at the outfalls now, of course. And the poor ensewered rivers still run forgotten beneath our feet. Where are the streams of yesteryear? The Walbrook, the Fleet, the Westbourne?'

'So Westbourne Grove was once a stand of trees beside a western brook? Funny how one doesn't stop to think what place names really mean — they might as well be in Chinese.'

'Far in a western brookland that bore me long ago . . . What I had in mind, you see, Harriet, was that if your body was sucked into the underground system of watercourses at Highgate Ponds, it might get washed down the Fleet in stages, first to the upper-level sewer where it sticks on a weir; then a downpour flushes it over the weir, and down it goes as far as the middle level, and then the lower, and finally out into the Thames to frighten a lighterman. Would that meet the bill? Of course there might be grilles and sluices and things. I could find out if you wish me to.'

'For the purposes of fiction we could ignore the grilles,' said Harriet.

'How I envy you your capacity to take facts or leave them,' said Peter.

'I shall have to consider removing the scene of the crime from country to town. But, thank you, Peter, that's a great help.'

'Glad to be of use,' said his lordship. 'Now as to the effects on a corpse of intermittent submersion in dirty water . . .'

'Thirdly,' murmured Harriet, with a rich thrill of emotion, 'marriage was ordained for the mutual society, help, and comfort, that the one ought to have of the other.' She sat down on the opposite side of the table, and they plunged eagerly together into the statistics of putrefaction.

4

It is amazing how complete is the delusion that beauty is goodness.

COUNT LEO TOLSTOY

Some women are not beautiful — they only look as though they are.

KARL KRAUS

It was Mr Paul Delagardie who coined the epigram: 'One should have women like shirts, one for day and one for night.' And when it was pointed out to him that this solution was repugnant both to law and morals, he added, shrugging his shoulders, '*Pour être bonne femme il faut être bonne à tout faire* — a good wife must be a maid of all work.' The law (which, like Minerva's owl, sees better by night than by day) in its wisdom takes more account of bed than of board, considering that satisfaction in the one activity should imply satisfaction in the other. It has its private justification for this attitude, having its eye riveted upon the inheritance of property; but it is a common error, very rife among persons unskilled in applying constructive imagination to the art of living, that what is lost on the daily roundabouts can be made up on the nightly swings. Mr Delagardie did not share this delusion, and therefore remained a bachelor. He was too lazy and selfish to apply his insights to his personal concerns. It gave him more amusement to sit back and watch the mistakes made by others than to provide a shining example for their imitation.

Yet in his wiry make-up there remained a vulnerable spot. To know that his nephew Peter was unhappily married would, he realised uneasily, upset his digestion. Contrary to his usual practice, he had offered his counsels of worldly wisdom before the event, anxious in this special case to avert, and not merely to relish, disaster. That there were obscure corners in his nephew's temperament to which the dry light of his own shrewdness could not penetrate he was uncomfortably aware. For nearly thirty years now he had assisted Peter to keep night and day in separate compartments, conscious all the time that for Peter this disjunction was wholly artificial. Seeing his nephew now committed to the perilous synthesis, as to chemical experiment, he held himself warily aloof, since, when one can do nothing to help, one can at least refrain from jogging the experimenter's elbow. To look on had always been his *métier;* to look on with anxiety was something new. During their brief meeting in Paris, his nephew's face had been an enigma to him; it was the face of a man who takes nothing for granted.

Laurence Harwell, on the other hand, had been accustomed from childhood to take everything for granted. He took it for granted that he should have been born well-off, should be popular at his public school and should, without over-exertion, take a respectable degree at his university. His inherited interest in his father's investments was in reliable hands; and he took his continued prosperity just as much for granted as was reasonable in a sensible man. He knew, from what he had read, that wealth in these days should be usefully employed; he understood that the pursuit of mere unproductive pleasure was ill-thought of, and that a touch of art and letters did no harm to anybody's reputation, and he had concluded from this that the theatre was as pleasant an area as any other in which to keep superfluous money moving about. Like most people, he took it for granted that he knew a good play when he read it, and on this assumption had backed a number of flops. He was, however, far better justified in supposing that he knew a successful play when he saw it; so that he had, on the whole, done well with the productions he had brought in from the provinces. He had never clearly understood why some of his ventures had failed and others succeeded, because he had not an analytical mind. Theatre managers, whose philosophic method is purely empirical, observed the rule of his success without troubling their heads about the reasons; they strained every nerve to induce him to attend try-outs, and received with the utmost caution any manuscript he brought to their notice. Actually, the reason behind the rule was simplicity itself. He could not visualise a play from the text, because he lacked constructive imagination; but show him a performance, and no imagination was necessary — he took it for granted that what he liked the British public would like, and rightly, for in taste and training he was himself the British public.

Thus he took for granted a number of other things that are publicly so taken, and in particular that congruence of night and day on which all matrimonial law is founded. He knew his own marriage to be a success, because the night sky blazed with so many and such splendid constellations, with such tropical heats and fervours as wait upon Sirius ascending. If the noons that followed brought sometimes an atmosphere of Scirocco, that was only to be expected in the dog-days. If the one thing was right, everything else must surely be right; the thing was axiomatic. It was true that happiness had often to be wooed, pleaded for, struggled for; but he took it for granted that a woman was made like that — she did not come halfway to meet desire, or if she did, there was something wrong with her. She shrank instinctively from passion, but her shrinking inflamed it in spite of herself; then, when she reluctantly yielded, her compassion prompted her response. No passion without compassion, no compassion without love, so that her passion was proof positive of her love. Since every act of love was an act of compliance, it was right to be grateful for it — her surrender was so beautiful — an intoxicating compliment that filled one with a perpetual consciousness of achievement. For the territory was never won; Alexander, had he been a lover, need never have lacked for new worlds to conquer — it would have given him sufficient exercise to reconquer the same world over and over again.

There were moments when Harwell found the endless ever-renewed warfare exhausting. To come so near, to achieve a conquest so absolute, and then, never to sit and enjoy his heritage in peace, but to find himself hammering at the defences again — there was something baffling about it. He believed there were indeed men who came to a placid understanding with their wives in this matter. They were the men that people wrote plays about: cheerful, stupid, complacent men who were always cuckolded in the third act, amid the acquiescent laughter even of the upper circle, that stronghold of propriety. The author always made it clear that these men roused no passionate response in their wives; the corollary followed that so long as you could rouse passion all was well with you. As for those plays in which women went about offering spontaneous passion to all and sundry, they were clearly perverse and very seldom box-office; and if a play was not box-office, it was because the public did not recognise it for truth. A play in which a husband and wife tormented each other through three acts and came together just before the curtain was sure-fire, for it bore by common consent the stamp of true love, clearly characteristic and conformable to all experience.

It was comfortable to Laurence Harwell to know that for Rosamund's womanly dower of love and beauty, he could exchange the gifts proper to a man. He had protection to offer her as well as love, and all the luxuries of wealth and position to which beautiful womanhood entitled her. Theirs had been true romance of that old-fashioned sort which never (no matter what high-brows say) grows old. Of all the fairy tales, one could count most confidently upon the evergreen appeal of Cinderella. It had been mere kind-hearted curiosity that had led Harwell to enquire after the welfare of old Warren's daughter. His own father had died, rather suddenly, at the con-clusion of the trial which had sent the defaulting director to a short but disastrous term of impris-onment, and he had been left with a sympathetic compassion for all orphans. After all, none of it was the poor girl's fault. He had hunted her out and come up with her at Madame Fanfreluche's off Bond Street, shining, Cinderella-like, in glo-ries not her own. Madame Fanfreluche, an odd, commercial fairy godmother, had been amiable enough to Prince Charming when he arrived to fit her handsomest mannequin with a glass slipper and a gold ring. If she hoped that the Princess might in future deal at her establishment, she was disappointed; any Fanfreluche creation would always have a touch of the witch-broom and the pumpkin about it for Rosamund, who asked nothing better than to put the whole humiliating episode out of her life. No wonder she had greeted her rescuer with adoring gratitude — but there was happily more to it than that. The raptures had been real and reciprocal. The Prince had stooped his head eagerly to pass beneath the lintel of the humble door, and Cinderella had shed her rags and asked to enter joyfully into his kingdom.

'And as for the two Ugly Sisters, they were put into a barrel full of spikes and rolled down a steep hill into the sea.' That was how the fairy tale had ended in the robust old days. Some versions had even added, callously enough, 'So that was the end of them, and a good riddance it was.' Modern susceptibilities shrink from this kind of conclusion to a romance. The Ugly Sisters — or, in the present case the Ugly Father — must be graciously forgiven and made to some extent free of the kingdom. Certainly ten months in the second division had by no means been the end of Mr Warren. On his emergence, he had been comfortably settled in a south-coast watering place, in receipt of a modest pension. From time to time he came to visit his daughter and was indulgently received by the magnanimous Prince. He had not indeed been altogether to blame for his disgrace; he had meant no harm, and had merely allowed his name to be used by persons clearer-headed than himself. He was, in short, a muddler — had always been a muddler; even now, it seemed, he muddled away his little income, which had to be supplemented rather more often than the indulgent Prince had expected. He was less unhappy in his exile than he thought he was, contriving to extract a flavour of romance from his own misfortune and wrapping himself in the dim aura of importance which always surrounds the man who has handled — however incapably — large sums of money.

Laurence Harwell looked at his wife. He was glad that a woman could once again keep her hair long and remain in the fashion; the two thick plaits of red gold drew him as with a cart rope. The bedroom, with its lucent surfaces of green and blue, had about it an illusion of water. Through its chilly depths one sank, entranced, to find the embraces of the Siren, whose voice, mocking and caressing, was like a carillon of drowned bells. This thought presented itself to Harwell in a less fanciful form.

He said, 'I rather wish we'd chosen warmer colours for this room. It'll be lovely in summer, of course, but then we shall probably be spending most of our time at the cottage. I'd have liked to see you in something like that Carpaccio interior we used for *The Winter's Tale*.'

Rosamund made no direct answer. She said, looking up from the newspaper, 'I suppose one will have to go into black.'

'By Jove, yes, of course,' said Harwell, shocked

at his own forgetfulness. He put back the tie he was fingering.

'It's a nuisance. Such a farce. And as though one couldn't be sorry without. Father has phoned to say he's coming up to town this afternoon.'

Harwell noted, as a vexatious coincidence, that something invariably happened to disturb the rosy harmony that should normally follow a night of stars and love. He had come upstairs a little after midnight, emotional from his vigil beside the loudspeaker. Rosamund had not expected him quite so soon. The monotonous announcements had gone on so long unchanged, it seemed as though time had sunk into a stupor that nothing could break. He had said, 'Go to bed now, darling; probably it won't happen till about two in the morning.' His sudden arrival startled her. She said, 'Not already?' and he answered, 'Yes; he's gone,' and she could only cry, 'Oh, Laurence!' and cling to him. A rich melancholy enfolded them. They felt the grief of a nation lap them in luxurious sheets of sympathetic bereavement. A whole epoch was collapsing about them, while at the core of darkness they lit their small blaze of life and were comforted. It is a pity that reality can never be content to keep the curtain down on a climax.

'Oh, well, that'll be all right,' said Harwell, absently. A disquieting thought had just come into his own mind: 'This'll knock business flat.' *Gee-up, Edward!* was due to open the following Thursday, and it suddenly struck him, that, under the circumstances, the playwright could scarcely have selected a more unfortunate title.

'I wish he wouldn't. Town doesn't suit Father. You know it doesn't.'

'Oh, well,' said Harwell, a little uneasily, 'he enjoys it very much, and what's the odds? It must be pretty slow for the old boy down at Beachington. He can' — he cast about for a harmless and dignified occupation — 'He can help choose your frocks for you. He'll like that.'

This was true. There was nothing Mr Warren enjoyed more than the illusion of spending the money he no longer possessed.

'I hate wearing black,' said Rosamund.

'Do you? But you look wonderful in it. I've often wondered why you've given it up. The first time I ever saw you, you were in black.'

'Yes. I always showed the black models.' An expression of distaste crossed her face, which Harwell, hunting for a tie, did not see.

'I've always wanted to see you in black again. You looked like a Venetian portrait.'

'It's obliging of the poor King to die and allow you to gratify a long-felt wish. But it's rather horrible somehow.'

'Yes, I know.' Harwell was dimly conscious that he had not said quite adequate things, but his brain felt lethargic, and he could not rouse it to cope with this domestic problem in the middle of a national catastrophe and what he knew only too well was going to prove a frightful business emergency. 'One's got to do the same as other people.'

The telephone rang, and he snatched up the receiver. This, of course, was Leinster, sounding the tocsin in a frenzy.

'Yes . . . yes, old man . . . yes, I know; I'd thought of that too . . . Yes — well, it's no good getting the wind up . . .'

While he telephoned, sitting on the edge of the bed, she lay watching him, wondering for the hundredth time what it was about him that so fascinated and excited her, so that she was always in a sick agony of impatience if his attention was given to anybody or anything but herself. He was big, and rather stiffly, though not clumsily, built. She could see the movement of the wide shoulder muscles under his shirt as he reached forward with a grunt to stub out his cigarette in the ashtray that lay on the telephone table beside her. His thick, dark hair, rigorously clipped and disciplined, had an obstinate tendency to wave above the parting; his anxious severity with it amused her daily. His hands, like his voice, were masterful; that they should be passively defied by this outlying and unimportant suburb of himself filled her with a secret zest — it was the impudent self-assertion of the weak confounding the strong. He was being decisive and heartening now to the manager, who, if one side of the conversation was anything to go by, had fallen into a panic. An aroma of authority diffused itself about him, mingling with the male odour of bay rum and shaving-soap. It was perhaps his sheer, unmistakable maleness that she at once adored and resented;

he dominated her senses and at the same time infuriated her by his large masculine arrogance. He was so certain of everything, including herself, that she felt she must keep pinching him to remind him that she was there to be noticed. She could always, of course, bring him to heel by withholding herself but the triumph was not lasting. She always gave way too soon, the victim of her own excitement. Yesterday, he had been alert to her. This morning, it was only the voice of the outside, masculine world of affairs that could call the note of awareness into his voice.

'All right, all right,' he soothed that barking telephone. 'I'll come round straight away.' He turned to his wife. 'I shall have to push along to the theatre. Leinster has lost his head. They always do.' He swept the entire theatrical profession into a limbo of fluttering indecision. 'No good getting the jitters. One must take a line and stick to it.'

'Then we'll meet at lunch?'

He shook his head. 'They want me to run down to the City at one o'clock and see Brownlow. He came in with me fifty-fifty, and he's all up in the air, thinking he sees his hard-earned dollars vanishing down the drain. Shouldn't be surprised if he's right, but one's got to take risks in this business. I'll have to try and graft a backbone into him . . . Oh, Hades! We were lunching together, weren't we? Sorry, sweetheart. We'll have to make it another day. Somebody's got to stiffen up this bunch.'

He blazed serenely, out of her stars, handling money and men with careless assurance.

'It doesn't matter. I'll ring up Claude Amery.'

Claude was the obvious, because the certain card to play. She had only to beckon, and Claude would cancel an appointment with a rich actor-manager. But it was extremely difficult to work up a scene about Claude.

'Yes, that's a good idea. Why not? He always seems to be at a loose end.'

'Claude's always ready to break his engagements for me.'

'I dare say,' said Harwell, getting up and resuming his search for the black tie. 'Not that I suppose he's got many to break. He thinks you'll wheedle me into backing that lousy play of his. Nothing doing. But there's no harm in it, if he amuses you.'

How touchingly, how maddeningly blind men could be! The siren smiled a small secret and provocative smile. Unfortunately it was wasted on Ulysses, who had found his tie, and was knotting it with his chin in the air.

'It's quite a good play, Laurence. Have you read it?'

'My dear child, Amery couldn't write a commercial play to save his neck. He hasn't the guts. He can talk fast enough, but he knows I won't listen to him. Let him blow it all off on you, bless his little heart. I don't know how you have the patience with these limp youngsters. What is it? Maternal instinct gone wrong?'

She said, 'Nothing of the sort!' with more energy than the occasion warranted, and had the pleasure of seeing him flush.

'I didn't mean that,' he said, shortly.

'If you want to go into all that again, I'd rather you did it openly. I hate being hinted at.'

'I'd no intention of going into anything of the sort. You know quite well what I'd like, Rosamund, but if you don't feel that way, it's no use arguing.'

'You always sound as though you thought I was being hard and selfish, Laurence. It isn't that. Of course I'd sacrifice myself in any way. But don't you see?'

'I know, darling, I know. Great heavens, I'd be the last person to want to force you into anything.'

'It worries me so, Laurence. It makes me feel as though our love was slipping away somehow. I want you to love me for myself — not for — not for . . .'

'But of course I love you for yourself, dearest,' he said desperately, coming over to her. 'How can you possibly think anything else? Oh, damn that telephone! Rosamund, listen . . .'

'Sure?' She smiled over his head as he knelt, in agitated surrender at the bedside, while the bell shrilled on unheeded.

'Certain. Don't you know it? Can't you believe it? What more can I do? Surely, I've proved it by this time.'

Her face hardened. She said coldly, 'Hadn't

94

you better answer the telephone?'

London had an odd feeling about it that morning. There was a stir of mournful excitement: people walked purposefully, yet abstractedly, as though something of secret importance awaited them at the end of their journey. Harriet Wimsey, strolling slowly along Oxford Street, turned her novelist's mind to wondering what it was that made the crowd seem so unlike its ordinary daily self. Nearly everybody was still wearing colours, yet the atmosphere was that of a funeral — of a village funeral. That was it. London had turned into a great village overnight, where every inhabitant knew the other's business and could read the other's mind. All these shoppers in Oxford Street, for instance; they were buying black, thinking about buying black, wondering how much black they could afford, or with how little black they could satisfy the instinct for decent self-expression. Behind the glittering barriers of plate-glass were shop assistants, window-dressers, buyers, managers, displaying black, checking the stock of black, issuing orders to the manufacturers for fresh supplies of black, anxiously calculating how far the demand for black would compensate for inevitable loss on coloured spring goods already ordered. Harriet found herself performing a private calculation about her own wardrobe and checked her thoughts hastily in the middle of a secret lament over a flame-coloured evening gown. She had been rather looking forward to that gown; but still, if you mourn, you mourn, and from that point of view, the more unbecoming the more mournful. One must, however, draw the line at unrelieved black; that, on a simple commoner with a sallow skin and dark colouring, would be mere ostentation of grief. Besides, Peter was taking the thing gravely enough already; there was no need to harrow his feelings further by offending his eye. The black costume she was wearing would do very well — though the addition of the white shirt and tie made her feel as though she were back in Oxford, and bound for the examination schools — but something simple and suitable must be found for the afternoon and evening.

Habit, and the fellow-feeling that prompts one to mingle with the crowd, had taken her to Oxford Street. Now, however, she turned south, and sought counsel of Alcibiade. This gentleman, to whose establishment she had been introduced by Peter's mother, had furnished her with a number of frocks for her trousseau. He was, name, appearance, and a plum-coloured velvet jacket notwithstanding, a completely normal Englishman with an artistic eye, a sense of humour and a wife and three children in Battersea; and he had the unusual recommendation that he adapted his creations to the figure he saw before him, and not to an ideal form existing only in the morbid imagination of dress designers. He welcomed Harriet with an air of sincere relief and, deserting several other clients, invited her into his private office.

'Have a cigarette,' said Alcibiade. He looked into three glass boxes one after another, and pressed a buzzer. 'Here, Miss Doubleday, take these stinking horrors away and get me a packet of Players.'

The secretary removed the perfumed cigarettes and Harriet offered the young man her own case.

'Thank you. That's better. One of these days I shall break out and bawl for a job' with Colonel Blimp, or join the North-West Mounted Police. It's nice to be natural with somebody for a change. Well, now — black, I suppose?'

'Yes, please. I'm afraid I'm not a very good subject.'

Alcibiade cocked his sleek head sideways.

'Not very,' he said frankly. 'But it'll be all right if we keep it away from the face. I've got a model you can wear. With a sort of Elizabethan collar — rather entertaining. Not feminine, I give you my word of honour, but on the other hand quite definitely female. Ah, thank you, Doris. There, you see, that is undoubtedly your frock, and what is more, I will lay any money you can walk straight into it. I thought of you when I composed it; and that's a lie, though you'd be surprised to know how many of one's vainer customers believe it. I was really thinking of a Breton cook we had last summer holidays. The collar is pleated the Breton way, over straws.'

'I like it very much,' said Harriet, 'only . . .'

'Only what? It's not fussy. I wouldn't dream of

giving you anything fussy.'

'No; but won't these pleats . . . ?'

She was on the point of saying, '. . . take a lot of laundering and keeping in order?' Years of hard work on a restricted income had ingrained in her a distrust of the 'little white collar' and the 'starched frill'. She readjusted herself sharply. 'Will my maid understand them?' As the words were uttered she realised that Mango would find the things a heaven-sent challenge to perfection.

'Send her to us,' said Mr Hicks (for that was, in fact, his name), 'or let us have the collars and we'll keep them in order for you. You'll want them clean every day this weather. A dozen? I'll see how quickly we can get them made. And there's a design just gone into the studio that is rather your style, which we could carry out at once if you liked it. Well, yes, we are a little rushed, but we'll let the Pretty-pretties and the Ugly-wugglies wait. I don't know,' he added dubiously, 'which of the two kinds I dislike most. You'd like to slip into this, I expect?'

Harriet said she would, and asked whether Mr Hicks had borne her in mind while designing any black evening dresses.

'You were constantly in my thoughts,' said he, unblushingly. An album of sketches lay beside him, and he slid out the contents upon the desk.

The material side of life was becoming too easy, thought Harriet. One was in danger of forgetting the bad old times altogether, and if one did, what sort of books would one write?

Lord Peter sat on the edge of his brother-in-law's desk at Scotland Yard.

'It gives me,' he said, 'the curious sensation of having suddenly grown very old.'

'Old?' retorted Chief Inspector Parker. 'We shall all be grey-headed here in about two ticks.' He sat surrounded by reports on the whereabouts and recent behaviour of alien undesirables, all of whom had to be checked up, located, put under supervision, admonished, or, in extreme cases, evacuated in preparation for a royal funeral, with its inevitable complement of foreign bomb-fodder. The Jubilee had meant plenty of hard work and extra policemen; but that had been a domestic affair. Nobody but an out-and-out loony would want to throw things at an English constitutional monarch. But the moment you opened the door to the uneasy continent of Europe, the shadow of a 'regrettable incident' came looming up on the threshold. And an incident at a funeral was unheard of. Quite apart from international complications, such a thing would be revolting to the British mind, which feels respectably about funerals.

'I liked the old man,' said Peter, unheeding. 'He stood for something.'

'You're right there,' agreed Mr Parker.

'Hell!' said Peter suddenly. 'Well, there it is.'

'It had to come some time.'

'Yes, well. I'll clear out of your way. Give my love to Mary. When are you both coming to see us?'

The Chief Inspector scowled at his littered desk. 'If I ever have a moment to call my own — but Mary would love to. Are you all settled in?'

'Quite, thanks.'

'All well?'

'Yes.' The affirmative was decided, and Mr Parker nodded. 'I think,' pursued Peter rather hastily, as though he had in some way betrayed an unbecoming emotion, 'marriage is going to have a bad effect on me. I feel mental arthritis setting in. I shall probably renounce the merry murder-chase, and abandon myself to the care of landed property and the supervision of a household.'

'Uxorious beast,' said his brother-in-law severely, contradicting himself a moment later by observing: 'Then you *must* be getting old. You don't feel drawn to a nice little nest of agitators in Bloomsbury? Unlicensed firearms, seditious pamphlets and incitement to violence?'

'Not in the least. Political offenders don't count. They have only a courtesy title to crime.'

'I always knew you were an intellectual snob. Well, we must do our bourgeois best. But I'm glad you looked in.'

He watched Peter drift through the doorway, and a feeling of depression came over him as he turned to his lists again.

Mr Paul Delagardie, warming his elderly bones on the French Riviera, found himself called upon to receive the dignified and exceedingly well-expressed condolences of Monsieur Théophile Daumier.

'To you, my dear friend, therefore,' concluded Monsieur Daumier, who had arrayed himself formally for the occasion, 'as to a representative of the great nation with which France is so closely linked in bonds of alliance and mutual amity, permit me to offer the expression of that cordial sympathy by which the heart of every member of our republic must feel itself today profoundly moved.'

'*Merci, mon cher, merci,*' replied Mr Delagardie. 'Believe me that I am sincerely touched by your friendly visit, and by the condolences which you so amiably offer to my nation and to myself on your own behalf and that of your compatriots.'

Here the two gentlemen bowed, shook hands, and (the hour of *déjeuner* approaching) sat down to partake of an *apéritif.*

'Strictly speaking, however,' observed Mr Delagardie, 'I am in no way representative of my nation. Indeed, I congratulate myself that I am not at this moment in London, where the feelings of the average Englishman are doubtless expressing themselves in that singular mixture of sentiment and snobbery which characterises the public utterances of our remarkable race.'

Monsieur Daumier raised deprecating eyebrows.

'Some, no doubt,' pursued Mr Delagardie, 'will be genuinely distressed. My sister, with whom I have a great deal in common, will experience that natural melancholy which attends the closing of a chapter in history. And my nephew Peter, who has occasionally displayed an awareness of the importance of public affairs . . .' He paused, and then went on uncertainly, 'King George was a safe man and the country had grown used to him. The English do not care for change, and any new idea is repugnant to them. I say again, to be absent from England now is a matter for congratulation.'

After his friend's departure, Mr Delagardie sat for a long time gazing from his window across the palms to the blue Mediterranean waters. Once his hand went out to the newspaper lying at his elbow; but he checked the movement and returned to his meditation. Presently, with a small impatient sigh, he took up a paper-covered novel and read for some fifteen minutes with determined concentration. At the end of this period, he put the volume down, carefully inserting a marker to keep the place, and rang the bell.

'Victor,' he said to the servant who answered, 'telephone for sleepers and pack my bag. We are leaving tonight for London.'

'I say,' repeated Harwell for the twentieth time at least, 'it would be madness to open on Thursday. If you'll take my advice, you'll put out an announcement, simply saying that in view of the national calamity, and so forth, the production of Mr Clandon's new play is postponed. Then find a new title, rewrite that scene in act two, and call a rehearsal to keep the company from going broody. If you do that, I'll stand by the show, and I think we shall make good.'

He looked round the room with the challenging confidence of the man who, with money to lose, is prepared to figure as the strength and stay of upholding a chicken-hearted creation.

'Do you really expect me,' demanded Claude Amery, 'to mark with black the day on which you asked me to lunch?'

He delivered this admirable line sincerely enough, but a little theatrically, as though, having written a play, he had become touched by a sort of anticipatory stage-infection.

'That,' replied Mrs Harwell, extricating her latchkey, 'is pretty but foolish. Now we're here, you'd better come in and have a cup of tea.'

As Mr Amery, protesting delighted acceptance, stumbled vaguely after her into the sitting-room, they were greeted by a small elderly man, who rose up from an armchair by the fire, rather hastily setting down a tumbler as he did so.

'Rosamund! My dear child . . .'

'Oh, here you are, Father,' said Rosamund, receiving his embrace with graceful detachment. 'I'm sorry I'm late. I hope they looked after you. I think you know Mr Amery.'

'Yes, of course,' replied Mr Warren. 'How do you do? My dear, this is all terribly sad. I hope I shall not be in your way, but I felt that we must be together. At times like this one feels the call of London. My place, after all, is here. I couldn't stay at Beachington; a very nice little town, of course, but out of touch with the pulse of the country. Whatever misfortunes one may have experienced —'

'Of course, Father,' said Rosamund, ringing the bell rather hastily, 'I'm delighted to see you, and so is Laurence. Claude, come and sit down.'

'No doubt,' pursued Mr Warren, with a kind of shaky dignity, 'you are aware, Mr Amery, that I was, not so long ago, the — shall we say — the guest of His Majesty's government, under somewhat distressing circumstances. I committed the fatal error of placing too much trust in my fellow-men. I have paid for that error, Mr Amery, and though I no longer move in my accustomed circles, my friends have been very kind to me. My daughter and my generous son-in-law are always ready to welcome a — let us call it a prodigal father, and now that a great bereavement has overwhelmed us all —'

'I don't know when Laurence will be in, Father. He's very busy down at the theatre. Would you ring down and ask them to send up tea for three, please. No, Claude, how absurd! Of course you're not in the way.'

Peter Wimsey found his wife having tea in company with a book and a large tabby cat. He sat down with a brief apology, and a soft grunt of satisfaction.

'Tired?'

'Low-spirited. Why has that excellent phrase gone out of fashion? Thinking of the old'un. I haven't done much. Lunched with Gerald, who was in an exceedingly damping frame of mind. Went up north and wrestled in prayer for nearly an hour with the local authorities about the collection of dustbins.'

'Can't the tenants deal with that for themselves?'

'They seemed to think my personal influence might have some weight with the borough council. I had to go up, anyway, to see about getting rid of a frightful row of speculative villas in Lilac Gardens, a beastly relic of the post-war period when I was neglecting my duties as a landlord. Be sure your sins will find you out. And the Peculiar People want to build a quite blasphemously ugly chapel just opposite my beautiful new pub in Billington Road. And one thing and another. One set of tenants making a devil of a fuss about noisy neighbours, and another couple wanting to be moved because the block they are in is eerily quiet.'

'Couldn't you just swap them around?'

'As it happens, yes, this time. If only they always presented themselves in opposing pairs; you'd be surprised how bothersome people are about noise. At four o'clock I felt exactly like a lost dog. I was just preparing to approach the nearest bobby and whine to be taken to Battersea, when I suddenly remembered that I had a home to go to.'

He let his glance wander for a moment over the serene Georgian proportions of the room, before bringing it to rest on his wife.

'It all sounds very trying.'

'It is, Domina, it is. An endemic low-level crisis, not important enough to screw one's courage to the sticking point, but requiring fortitude, none the less.'

'Couldn't you keep them sorted out? Noise-haters, I mean?'

'Build a special block of flats for them? With soundproof walls and floors, situated between a convent and a retired solicitor's residence.'

'And special rules to enforce quiet.'

'The keeping of children, dogs and tomcats is strictly forbidden; the hours of music and entertainment are rigidly regulated, and any complaint about noise, if made by three tenants in writing, renders the disturber of the peace liable to instant ejection,' Peter intoned. 'Perhaps I should. On the other hand, people who like noise suffer as much by being deprived of it as nervous people do from noise.'

'You'll need another block of complementary flats for them,' suggested Harriet. 'Something sturdily built with moderate rentals . . .'

'Where children, animals and musical instruments are heartily encouraged, the inner court is laid out as a playground, and complaints about noise receive only the stern reply, "Agree with your neighbours or go." Harriet, I do believe we are on to something.'

'Of course, there might be neighbours across the road from your noise-lovers' block, or on either side of it.'

'I shall have it built on a site with a school on the one side, and a brickmaker's yard on the other, to ensure a proper distance from nervous residents. I had been wondering what would best occupy that space.'

'Are we joking, Peter?'

'Certainly not. I lay my troubles at your feet, and you proffer solutions. Balm to my weary heart. I shall make the experiment. What shall we call these mansions of diverse contentment? Scylla and Charybdis Court?'

'I do rather wonder what it would be like to be ill in the noise-lovers' block. With a splitting headache, for instance.'

'The charitable landlord will add a small soundproof sanatorium for the isolation of the sick,' said Peter. 'All will be provided for, and people will fight savagely to get on to the waiting lists.'

'You may or may not be joking, Peter, but you do look rather jaded. Will tea cope with it? Or is it a fever of the spirit that calls for homeopathic treatment?'

'Tea and sympathy will meet the case.' He came over to take the cup from the tray, pausing by Harriet's chair for information and action.

'It's a very handsome pie-frill. Discouraging, perhaps, to the well-meant expression of a husband's feelings. But becoming. The head of the

107

family sent you his blessing, by the way. I believe Gerald is almost persuaded that you are capable of taking the family madman in hand . . . Hi! That's my chair, you miserable striped ruffian. Up you come! Is a man never to be master in his own house?'

5

For God s sake, let us sit upon the ground
And tell sad stories of the death of kings
                WILLIAM SHAKESPEARE

As the tiny procession came down Whitehall a curious illusion moved with it. At its passing, hats were lifted from bald heads, faces were tilted upwards to peer over obstructing shoulders. Long before you could distinguish the outline of the gun-carriage in the distance, you knew where it was, seeing the dark crowd turn pink, as though a pale sun were following it westwards. It was a small procession — not as many as fifty — some mounted, some walking. The new King walked behind the coffin, deathly pale, seeming bowed by the weight of his long dark overcoat. There were no parading soldiers, and no music. The intense quiet of the crowded streets allowed the footfalls of the passing men and horses to be clearly heard. And in the whole scene, muted in the misty January light, the only splash of colour was the royal ensign draped across the coffin, and the crown borne along on top of it, looking strangely like a theatrical prop.

Harriet's throat felt tight. The woman on her left was bringing out a pocket-handkerchief; on her right, she was insistently aware of a frozen rigidity that was Peter. She lowered her eyes to the parapet; his hand lay there quietly, but she could see white semicircles where pressure had forced back the blood from the nail-tips. Cautiously, as though even so small a movement might break the tension, she slid her own hand along till their little fingers touched.

It passed; and the crowd, closing in its wake like blown leaves, began to drift away. It was unlike all other crowds in this, that it was voiceless. It only moved, with a sound like waves breaking on a shingly beach.

'You are a very remarkable nation,' said a deep voice behind them. 'You permit a casual crowd to arrange itself with the assistance of a few unarmed policemen. Then you take your new King and all the male heirs to the throne, throw in the crown of England for good measure, collect them into a bunch that you could cover with a handkerchief, and walk them slowly for two miles through the open streets of the capital. Who was to say that I had not a bolshevist fury in my heart, and a Mills bomb in my pocket?'

'This is just a village funeral,' said Peter. 'Nobody would dream of making a disturbance. It is not done. When it comes to a public ceremony, precautions will be taken. But not when we are private.'

'It is fantastic,' said Gaston Chapparelle. 'You think of yourselves as a practical people, yet your empire is held together by nothing but a name and a dream. You laugh at your own traditions, and are confident that the whole world will respect them. And it does. That is the astonishing thing about it.'

'It may not last,' said Peter Wimsey.

'It will last so long as you do not take it into your heads to become theoretical. You are like the centipede, which walked perfectly until it tried to explain which leg went after which. Let us ask what questions we like, but take care you never try to answer them. Once you have secured to yourself the sort of government that nobody dares to criticise, the way is open for the bullet-proof car, the bodyguard armed to the teeth, and the iron hell of a discipline tightened to hysteria. I am impressed. With every disposition to be cynical, I am nevertheless impressed.'

They descended slowly through the building, pausing on their way to thank the government official who had welcomed them to a place on the roof. On the lower landing they exchanged surprised recognition with the Harwells, who had old Mr Warren in tow. A few commonplaces led to the suggestion that they should all proceed to Audley Square for drinks. Rosamund's momentary hesitation gave Chapparelle his chance.

'Admirable!' said he, with such firmness as to make refusal seem impossible. 'It amuses me to see two of my sitters together. For me they create new aspects of one another.'

'I am afraid,' said Rosamund, 'it will tire my father.'

'Not at all, my dear, not at all,' said Mr Warren, 'why should it? So Monsieur Chapparelle is painting you too, Lady Peter?'

Harriet began to explain that Peter and she had just been paying a visit to the studio, when Chapparelle broke in: 'This man is cautious. He comes to find out whether I can paint before he will commission a portrait. I show him my work. I do not need to ask the result. I shall paint his wife. *Hein?* You will not pretend, I hope, that I am a bad painter.'

'You are a hellishly good painter,' said Wimsey, with an emphasis on the adverb.

'You have nothing to fear,' replied Chapparelle, with a scarcely perceptible emphasis on the pronoun.

Harriet caught a flicker in Harwell's glance, as though, despite their context, the words had reminded him that Chapparelle enjoyed a certain reputation, not only as a painter, but as a man.

Peter said quietly, 'I am quite aware of that, Chapparelle.'

It was Rosamund's turn to notice a faint embarrassment in Harriet's face. The ambiguous phrases evidently held a clear enough meaning for her.

'Then,' retorted the painter triumphantly, 'we will begin our sitting tomorrow.'

'You must arrange that with my wife. When it

comes to two industrious artists fighting over a timetable!' Wimsey's gesture disclaimed responsibility. 'Between the devil and the deep sea!' He opened the door of the car.

Rosamund Harwell, her fingers perilously clenched about the thin stem of a Waterford wine-glass, was suffering the torture of the damned. Through a cheerful barrage of conversation put up by the three men beside her, she could hear fragments of what her father was saying to Harriet. With a childlike absence of self-consciousness, he was talking about his prison experience. Harriet, her dark head sympathetically inclined, was listening with an appearance of grave interest. It was bound to happen, of course. It happened every time. If only Father would stay quietly at the seaside! No doubt he talked there, too, but so long as one did not hear it. So long as one need not sit pretending to hear nothing! It would be a relief if Laurence would lose patience, and forbid him the house. One could scarcely ask him to do so, of course, and one was very grateful.

'Don't you think so, Mrs Harwell?'

'Oh, yes, I agree absolutely.' Chapparelle's eye was like a sharp pin skewering one like a moth to the setting-board. Mr Warren had glanced across at her, shaken his head, and begun to fumble for his handkerchief. He had reached the intolerable point where he lamented his folly and praised his daughter's courage in finding herself a job.

'I assure you, Lady Peter, she has never uttered a single word of reproach . . .'

'Perfectly damnable,' said Peter, gently taking the glass from her hand and refilling it. 'Of course, every management is hit to some extent.'

'That's the worst of it,' agreed Harwell. 'It means bad business all round. And once people get out of the theatre habit, it takes a long time to get them going again. I shan't put money into anything this year, you bet, unless it's a sure-fire certainty — in which case one isn't likely to need outside backing.'

Mr Warren was now blowing his nose.

'Are there any sure-fire certainties?' demanded Chapparelle.

'There are two or three authors,' said Harwell, 'whose plays get a following more or less automatically.'

'And two or three actors, I suppose?' suggested Peter.

Harwell paused consideringly. Mr Warren's voice filtered through. 'I say to myself, I must not become bitter or resentful. I must not brood and bottle things up. One must open the windows of the spirit and let in fresh air, fresh air . . .'

'Not so many as there used to be. Authors are more important at the moment. A sound play on an established author's established lines means a pretty safe return for one's money. Though it's all a speculation, of course. Still . . .'

'I always think,' said Mr Warren, 'it is a mistake to pretend that a thing has not happened. Nowadays, when I meet anybody . . .'

'But, Laurence,' objected Mrs Harwell, 'backing plays isn't your bread and butter. It's only a hobby. And it's the new writers who need the backing. Otherwise, how is one ever to discover new talent?'

'My wife,' said Harwell indulgently, 'is always finding swans among the Bloomsbury goslings. It's no good, darling, trying to argue me into putting on that thing of young Amery's. It hasn't a chance in Hades. Not even in an ordinary season, much less now.'

'Amery?' said Peter. 'I seem to know the name.'

'Claude Amery. One of those stringy lads with a forelock.'

'He's published some poems,' added Rosamund.

'Harriet may know.' Peter detached Harriet's attention from Mr Warren with an apology. 'Harriet — excuse me, sir — have you ever heard of a Bloomsbury poet — slight build and floppy hair — by the name of Claude Amery?'

'Yes. He wrote a thing called *This Forked Plague*, all rather outspoken and disillusioned, about fat bald men making love in brothels. In a very complicated verse form with inner rhymes and overriding couplets. I had it to review. And he is rather stringy, now you come to mention it. Why?'

'I thought I'd seen his name about the place. Have I met him?'

'I don't think so. I ran into him once at a

publisher's party. But you might have seen the book on my table in Mecklenburgh Square about three months ago when you came back from Italy; but I didn't know you'd looked at it.'

'I didn't. I had something better to look at. But no doubt it registered itself on my subconscious. The young man has written a play.'

'Yes; I saw a mention of it somewhere.'

'It's very good, I think,' persisted Rosamund. 'But Laurence won't even read it.'

'I looked at it,' said Harwell. 'It may be good. But it certainly isn't commercial.'

'I expect you're right,' agreed Harriet. 'All the same, it might pay to keep your eye on that lad. I shouldn't wonder if he did something interesting one of these days.'

'Think so?' Harwell looked dubious. Out of the corner of her eye Rosamund saw Peter leading Mr Warren away upstairs to examine a set of tapestries on the landing. 'Well, you may be right. Perhaps if I sent you the script you'd like to give me your opinion.'

'I don't think my opinion would be much use,' said Harriet quickly. 'I'm a novelist. I know nothing about what would get across on the stage.'

'*A chacun son métier,*' observed Chapparelle approvingly. 'To know one's own limitations is the hallmark of competence.' He put away his empty glass and made a tentative motion to rise. 'Your husband promised to show me a Gainsborough.'

'Yes, of course. It's in the library. Would you like to go up?' Harriet turned to the Harwells. 'I

116

don't know whether you would care to look at the house. It's old, of course, and Peter — there are some rather beautiful family things.'

The move was made. Harwell, his attention caught by the suitability of the eighteenth-century tapestries for stage sets, added himself to the male section of the party, and Harriet found herself escorting Rosamund to the upper storeys.

'Are you domesticated?' enquired Rosamund, rather abruptly.

'Not at all,' said Harriet. They were standing in her bedroom, which looked down into a small garden containing a brick path and a small dried-up fountain surmounted by a small cupid struggling with a very large dolphin. 'It does seem an absurdly big house for two people, doesn't it? But Peter said he was tired of being cramped up in a flat. He was brought up spacious, you see.'

'So was I. But I wanted to get out of it all. Servants and all that bother.'

'I was rather terrified of that. I'd never had to manage a staff or anything. But we've got a domestic dragon who does the whole thing. She's called Mrs Trapp, and she was Peter's old nurse. She gave notice to the Duchess twenty-three years ago, when Peter got engaged — not to me, of course, to somebody else. He didn't get married, so she stayed on to oblige the family. Then when he did get married, she walked out. Helen didn't like it, but Mrs Trapp said she'd given twenty-three years' warning, and nobody could be expected to do more. That's the sort she is.'

'I shouldn't know how to get on with that sort. Don't these old servants rather interfere?'

'Well,' admitted Harriet, 'she does rather tend to tell Peter to eat up his nice bread and milk and not be fussy. But she doesn't interfere with me, because Peter's impressed it on her that I'm a writer and mustn't be disturbed. I expect she thinks it all rather odd, but she sees the published volumes, you know, and people always find that impressive.'

'Oh, yes. But I shouldn't like to have an old nurse coming in between Laurence and me.'

'It's dreadful, isn't it?' said Harriet lightly. 'Peter's overrun with old servants, like mice. His man, Bunter, has been with him for twenty years. And the butler is Bunter's brother. Only, of course, we can't have two Bunters in one house, so we call him by his Christian name, which happens, most conveniently, to be Meredith. Goodness knows what they think of me. Mrs Trapp and Meredith run everything between them, and I look at the books and try to look as though I'd always thought in pounds instead of in pence.'

'Do you have to go into all the accounts? It's frightfully tedious. Thank goodness, we live in a service flat, and just have things up from the restaurant.'

'To tell you the truth, I don't. At least I've only just started, of course, but I shan't, not unless things go over the housekeeping allowance. After all, Mrs Trapp must be trustworthy — she's housekept at Gerald's place at Duke's Denver for donkeys' years. I'll wait till there's a revolution and we have to live on twopence a week — that's the only sort of housekeeping I know about, and I don't enjoy it anyway. Still, Peter could help. He once had a job in an advertising agency and told people how to make grand family stews for fourpence.'

Rosamund began to think she was being made fun of. Harriet saw her unbelieving expression and hastened to explain: 'He was investigating a murder and had to go about disguised as a copy-writer. He earned four pounds a week, and was terribly proud of himself.'

'Really, how absurd!' Rosamund Harwell was seized with a sense of impatience. Something — something she had had obscurely in mind when she began the conversation had gone wrong; it was as though there was a guard up somewhere. Baffled, she returned to the commonplace of politeness. 'It's a beautiful house.'

'Isn't it? It's a little frightening. One feels gravely responsible, as though it would be shocked if one lost one's temper, or shouted things. I suppose it's because we've rather lost the habit of being ceremonious, though I've no doubt its original eighteenth-century owner drank himself under the table every night and roared at his wife and kicked the flunkeys downstairs without a qualm.'

(So, she thought to herself, would Peter, no

doubt, if he felt like it. So far he had shown no disposition to roar. But Gerald would roar like twenty tigers. No, it was a matter of what you were used to.)

Rosamund had gone over to the mirror and was dealing swiftly and competently with her face.

'It's a nuisance, having to go into black, isn't it? Don't you find it needs an entirely different make-up?'

'Make-up doesn't suit me much,' said Harriet. 'In fact, a stern tyrant forbids me to use it.'

'Do husbands still forbid things?'

'Oh, not Peter. My dressmaker. He has an artistic conscience. Says I should ruin his artistic effects. One artist must respect the other's conscience, naturally. It's Alcibiade — do you know him? Or are there dreadful clan feuds between him and Fanfreluche, like the Campbells and MacDonalds?'

'I haven't the least idea,' said Rosamund, coldly furious.

(Help! thought Harriet, now I've gone and put my foot in it. And that's why Peter — how stupid of me not to see!)

The situation was relieved by the appearance of a maid at the door.

'His lordship's compliments, my lady, and Mr Harwell is afraid he must be going as he has an appointment. The car can come back, if madam is not quite ready.'

'Oh, no,' said Rosamund, 'I'll come at once. It was so kind of you to ask us in, Lady Peter. You must come and see us some day.'

Harriet replied that she should be delighted.

'Very decent people,' said Laurence Harwell. 'I'm glad we ran across them. They're important among the stalls public, and that woman is in touch with writers and so on. We'll have to ask them to something. Can't throw big parties just at the moment, of course, but we could have a little dinner . . .'

'No,' said Rosamund, almost violently. 'I'm sorry for her, but I can't stand that man.'

'My dear!' ejaculated Mr Warren. 'I thought he was very civil indeed. Went out of his way. As Laurence says, he's important. Nobody more so. The Denvers —'

'Yes, and he knows it. That's what I loathe so. Look at the way he treats his wife.'

'Treats his wife?' exclaimed Harwell in amazement. Rosamund's tone suggested at the very least public discourtesy, if not personal abuse, corporal chastisement and open infidelity, and he had noticed nothing of the kind. 'I thought his manners to her were excellent.'

'I thought they were condescending and horrible. All that business about the portrait, referring Monsieur Chapparelle to her as though it were no business of his. "I won't interfere between one artist and another" — sneering beast! — just to remind us all that she used to have to work for her living.'

'Well,' said Harwell, 'she needn't go on writing

now unless she wants to.'

'I expect it's the only bit of independence left her, poor thing. I don't suppose he likes it, and that's why he sneers. And look at that absurd great house — absolutely unnecessary except to impress her with his own grandeur. She daren't even say *we've* got this or that. It's Peter's heirlooms, Peter's money, Peter's titled relations, Peter's attached family retainers. She told me about it. She isn't even allowed to run the place herself — Peter's old nurse takes charge. I know it is so. She poured it all out to me the minute we were alone.'

'I believe,' said Mr Warren, 'he was always rather a spoilt young man; very much his mother's favourite.'

'I must say,' Harwell put in, having had his own perplexities to contend with, 'I can't see why he wanted to marry her. He might have made a far better match. She's nobody, and she's not even particularly good-looking; and wasn't there something fishy about her?'

'Oh, yes, there was a dreadful story. He saved her from prison or something worse. I forget exactly. That gives him a lovely opportunity to be patronising. He's probably one of those people who always have to be king of their company.'

'I can't say I found him patronizing,' objected Mr Warren. 'He was very pleasant. Of course, I explained to him, to both of them, I always do, about my own circumstances. I never like to leave people in the dark.'

'Father, dear, *why* should you humiliate your-self? It's absolutely unnecessary.'

'I can't help feeling these things,' insisted Mr Warren. 'He said he thought I'd had very bad luck. Well, so I did, you know. Very bad. I wasn't fairly treated.'

'Well, well, Dad,' said Harwell, 'we all make mistakes, and that's how rogues manage to live. One's got to keep one's eyes open, that's all. We needn't have anything to do with these people if you don't like them, darling. Leave it to me. We'll ask them round some time when we know they can't come and that'll be an end of it. I don't want you to do anything you don't like.'

'Of course, if you need this man to do any-thing . . .'

'I don't need anybody. If you dislike him, that's quite enough. We can do without him.'

'Oh, Peter, I was so grateful to you for taking Mr Warren away. Tact is your second name, isn't it?'

'Tiresome old ass. I don't suppose he meant any harm, but there's no reason why you should have to put up with it. He probably didn't re-member anything about it.'

'Oh, that!' (So Peter had not seen, after all. He had only been thinking of her. That was like him.) 'I don't mind that a bit. He did know, as a matter of fact, but he didn't think much of my experi-ence. Not a *real* convict, only a prisoner on re-mand; he was the real thing, and rather proud of it in an upside-down way. At least, I expect his pride is a sort of defence mechanism. Probably he's rather made to feel his position at home. I gather he's usually kept isolated at Beachington.'

'Poor old sinner! Nothing to do with himself all day. I expect he needs an outlet. And so long as you didn't mind; but anyhow I thought it was all getting rather trying.'

'Yes. Peter, do you really want this portrait painted?'

'I should like to have it, if you can spare the time and don't mind. Not that storied urn and animated bust are exactly necessary to make me think of my blessings. But I have sometimes suspected you of an unwarrantable modesty. I should rather like Chapparelle to show you to yourself.'

'Oh! Dearest, couldn't you sometimes pay compliments a little more — frivolously? Does everything mean so much to you?'

'No, not everything. Only everything to do with you.'

'You'll have to grow out of that, Peter.'

'Too late. I've stopped growing. Henceforth I shall only become slowly ankylosed in an attitude of devotion. Time shall make me marble. The soul is its own monument. As certain also of your own poets have said. Chapparelle will have got home by now. Ring him up and make the appointment.'

6

Look here, upon this picture, and on this . . .
WILLIAM SHAKESPEARE

I would rather see the portrait of a dog that I know, than all the allegorical paintings they can shew me in the world.
SAMUEL JOHNSON

Dear Mrs Harwell,

Sir Jude Shearman was here yesterday and happened to say he was looking for 'unusual' plays to put on at the Swan Theatre. As you know, he tries out interesting shows there for short runs, and there is always the chance of transfer for anything that looks like having commercial possibilities. I mentioned Mr Claude Amery's name, and Sir Jude said he knew his books and should be interested to see anything he had written for the stage. Perhaps Mr Amery might think it worth while to send him a script.

I was so sorry you and your husband were unable to lunch with us last week. We must hope for better luck another time.

Yours sincerely,
Harriet Wimsey

Exasperating! thought Rosamund. It was not as though she hadn't herself thought of the Swan as a possibility; she had several times asked Laurence to put her in touch with Shearman, but had encountered a blank wall of unwillingness. It seemed as though, for some reason, Laurence did not like the man.

Actually, the head and front of Sir Jude's offending was that he had made a smash hit three years previously with a highbrow poetical play that Harwell had contemptuously refused to back. Being a North Countryman, who liked to say what he thought, Sir Jude rather made a point of rubbing in his triumph every time he happened to encounter Harwell in the bar at a first night. Harwell was wont to retort that one could get away with almost anything, given a lavish production and a snob audience. That did not alter the fact that the foolish play (completely pseudo in every respect) had run eighteen months in the West End, before embarking on a successful provincial tour and a fresh career of triumph in the United States. The thing was an affront to one's judgement. But since all this had taken place before Harwell's marriage, Rosamund knew nothing about it. Her husband was accustomed to say that Shearman was a vulgarian and unscrupulous man of business with a stranglehold on half the theatres in London; he was quite correct in saying so, and was probably sincere in supposing that these were the reasons for his distaste.

It was really unfortunate that Rosamund should

find herself under an obligation to the Wimseys, just as she had made up her mind to dislike them. And it would be a disappointment, in a way, for Claude. She would have loved to say to him, 'Claude, my dear, I've got Sir Jude Shearman to promise to read your play.' He would have loved it too; he was really so devoted — foolishly so — and so ready to be grateful for her kindness. But now the little scene of delight and gratitude would be spoiled, because she would have to add: 'You'd better remind him that Lady Peter Wimsey spoke about it.' Managers were all like that; nothing ever got read unless it came with some sort of memoria technica of a personal nature attached to it. Poor Claude would have to divide his gratitude between her and a stranger, which would be tiresome for him. And meanwhile, she would have to return an appreciative answer to Lady Peter, and it would be difficult not to get involved in exchanges of hospitality, always under the distinguished patronage of Peter Wimsey, whose personality affected her so disagreeably.

'Laurence, what's Sir Jude Shearman like?'

'Shearman ? Oh, he's one of these domineering North Countrymen with no manners. Been divorced twice. First time it might have been the woman's fault, but the second time there was a whiff of scandal. Not the sort of fellow you'd care for. Why do you ask?'

She passed the letter over to him.

'Good Lord!' Harwell was conscious of a moment's sickening disquiet. If Shearman thought there was anything in Claude Amery . . . No! This time the blighter couldn't possibly hope to crow over him. There was a better explanation, more probable and infinitely more comforting: 'Oh, I can see through Shearman all right. He wants to stand in with Harriet Wimsey because Harriet Vane's got a name and might write a play some day. Anyhow she's good snob value. He probably thinks she's personally interested in Amery.' He read the letter through again. 'Obviously, that's it. Says he knows his books, good God! Do you suppose Shearman spends his time reading little volumes by Bloomsbury poets? Tell Amery to send the thing along, by all means, but he'd better not build any hopes on Shearman.'

'Couldn't you mention it to Shearman yourself some time, Laurence? I'd so much rather it came through you. I mean, Claude's bound to think it funny that I should get an introduction through outsiders when I've got a husband who's connected with the theatre.'

'Oh, but that's quite an ordinary thing. Everyone gets introductions in the most casual and unexpected ways. If I praised the thing it would only put Shearman off. He and I never think the same way about plays.'

'Well, tell him you dislike it. Then he might take a fancy to it.' Her smile was pleading as well as mischievous.

Harwell hesitated. To be asked and to give, even to the half of one's kingdom, should be accounted one of the seven joys of marriage. And it could do no harm. Rosamund would be pleased, the play would be returned with thanks in due course and he would have done his best. Shearman wouldn't be ass enough to put the play on, and if he did it would be damned. It must be. It couldn't possibly turn out to be the case of *The Brazen Serpent* all over again. That had been the purest fluke. All the same, perhaps it would be wiser to have another look at the script. Confound the Peter Wimseys; why did they want to interfere?

'Look here, darling, I'll tell you what I'll do. I'll read it again myself, and if I think it's got a dog's chance . . .'

'Will you put it on yourself?'

'I couldn't promise that,' said Harwell, a little taken aback. 'It means getting a management and a theatre.' To women, everything always seemed so simple. When one tried to explain the enormous diplomatic complexity of the theatrical world, they simply couldn't grasp what one was saying.

'Oh, Laurence, don't be absurd. Of course any management would put a play on if you backed it.'

He was flattered by her certainty of his omnipotence. And it was true that he could probably get *a* management — not any management, not Shearman, for instance — to put on even an uncommercial play, provided (he thought a little contemptuously) he was ready to shoulder all the risk and pay all the losses. And in a dazzling moment he saw himself making the magnificent gesture, pouring thousands down the drain, so that Rosamund might go on looking as she was looking now. What had he married her for, if it was not to fulfil her every whim, however unreasonable?

'Are you really so keen on it?'

'Oh, Laurence!'

'You're a witch,' he said. 'I don't believe there's any tomfool thing you couldn't persuade me to do.'

'Isn't there?'

Her smile mocked and invited him.

'I haven't promised.'

'Oh, but you will.' She put out her hands to ward him off. 'Not till you promise.'

'All right. I promise.'

'Darling . . . Claude will be so thrilled, poor boy.'

'Damn Claude. I'm not doing it for him. I'm doing it for you.'

This time her laugh was at once triumph and enchantment. It was like an exultant arpeggio upon the harp. He was committed now, he supposed, to making a fool of himself, but it was worth it, to justify her confidence and her pride in his power.

'You do spoil me, darling, don't you?'

'Well, what am I here for?'

Yes, by God! If there was anything in the world his wife wanted, he would give it to her. She could tell the world, show 'em she didn't need favours from the Wimseys or Jude Shearman either. Shearman! A tight-lipped, tight-fisted Yorkshire tradesman, who turned over every bit of his brass before he spent it. No wonder two wives had found him impossible. Women liked men to be generous; it was their delight to return surrender for surrender.

'Happy now?'

'Terribly happy. Yes, but — no, sweetheart, no, not now. Let me go. I must write and tell Claude.'

'He can wait till tomorrow. Dash it, you can ring the fellow up. You stay exactly where you are. He doesn't want you as much as I do. Or perhaps he does, but he's not going to get you.'

'Poor Claude!' said Rosamund, dismissing her poet with another little arpeggio of laughter. She let Harwell pull her back upon his knee, and then sprang up again with an exclamation.

'Oh, Laurence, we must behave ourselves. There's the waiter coming to clear the coffee things.'

'Damn!' said Harwell. He released her and took up a newspaper rather hurriedly. Rosamund stood before the fireplace, arranging her hair in the mirror. The waiter attached to the service of the flat entered and collected the china in a detached manner.

'Will there be anything further tonight, sir?'

'No, thank you. Tell the valet I shall be wearing the brown suit tomorrow.'

'Very good, sir.'

The man withdrew.

'Well, thank God for a service flat,' said Harwell. 'When the staff goes, it goes. You can come back.'

Rosamund shook her head. The interruption had destroyed her mood. 'I'm going to ring up Claude straight away. He's waited such a long time.'

'Another few hours won't hurt him.'

'No, it's a shame to keep him waiting. Don't be so selfish, darling.'

She picked up the scarlet-enamelled telephone and dialled, while Harwell had time to think that it would have been more satisfactory, in a way, if she had been a little more selfish. To spend money on her was his prerogative; to spend money on her tame poet might look to some people like a weakness. Everybody might not understand, as he did, her naïve and uncalculating pleasure in making others happy. Then he grinned; Bootle, the Sealyham pup, had sat up suddenly in his basket, and was beginning to trundle his fat body across the hearthrug. Ludicrous little dog. He made for Rosamund and began to play foolishly with her silver slippers; she stooped to pat him with her free hand, playing with him, laughing at his lavish red tongue and his frantic mumblings of adoration. Claude's incoherent ecstasies on the phone would be just another rapturous and absurd puppy-gambol. All in a moment Harwell saw happiness tossed like a ball from him to Rosamund, from Rosamund to

Claude, from Claude to the whole preposterous litter of theatre folk to whom a new play meant work and money and self-importance, from them to their children: a ball that gathered as it went like a snowball. He put his hand beneath the sofa cushions and found Bootle's rubber ball tucked away there. He bounced it across the floor. It hit Bootle on his round hindquarters, startling him, so that he looked round with an idiot face. Harwell laughed.

'Hi on, Bootle! Fetch him. Good dog.'

Rosamund slowly put down the receiver. 'He doesn't seem to be in.'

Her voice sounded a little chilled, as though she had surprised Claude in an act of ingratitude. She called to Bootle, who had chased his ball under the edge of the rug and was whuffling at it in what he considered to be a menacing and grown-up manner.

'Bootle! Stop it, precious. Come to Muzzer. You're destroying that rug.'

'He won't hurt it,' said Harwell, easily.

'He mustn't get into a habit of worrying the furniture. Bootle, give it to Muzzer. There! Now, then, where is it? Where's your good ball? Who's got it? No, Muzzer hasn't got it. Look! Hand empty. Ozzer hand empty. *Now* where's ball? Wow, wow!'

She crouched by the puppy, passing the toy from one hand to the other behind her back, thrusting it into his eager face and spiriting it out of sight again, teasing and exciting him.

'He'll ruin your frock.'

'No, you wouldn't. No, you wouldn't ruin Muzzer's lovely frock, would you? No-o-o! Clever dog, zen.'

The ball rolled away as she caught the puppy up in her arms. He scrabbled and licked her face.

'Oh, darling! Muzzer's beautiful make-up! Isn't it lucky it's kissproof?'

'You shouldn't let him lick your mouth. It's dangerous.'

'Oh, did you hear zat, Bootle? As if you wasn't a nice little clean dog! Kiss Muzzer again. Master's cross because he's jealous of poor Bootle!'

Harwell recaptured the ball and bounced it invitingly across the parquet.

'Oh, Bootle, don't be so rough! Whatever did you do that for, Laurence? He's laddered my stocking all to bits and scratched me right across the arm.'

'I'm sorry, darling. Show me.'

'That'll *do*, Laurence.'

'Damn it, you let the blasted dog kiss you. What's the matter with you tonight? You'd better go and wash your face.'

'You needn't be rude.'

'And put some iodine on your arm.'

'It's all right, thank you; it hasn't broken the skin. He didn't mean to hurt. It was only you calling him off like that. It's silly to be jealous of a puppy.'

'I'm not jealous. That's ridiculous.'

'You are, or you wouldn't sound so cross.'

'I tell you I am *not* jealous.'

'You're jealous of Claude, or you'd have done something for his play months ago.'

'My dear girl, don't be absurd. How on earth could anyone be jealous of Claude?'

'Why not? He's a very attractive boy.'

'Is he? I suppose he appeals to women.'

'Yes, darling. That's what I was trying to convey to you.'

'Well, dash it! If you prefer that sort of limp rag —'

'I didn't say I did. I didn't marry a limp rag, did I?'

'By God, you didn't. And why you should accuse me of being jealous —'

'But you are. You're always being jealous. You're jealous of Gaston Chapparelle.'

'I'm not jealous of him. But he doesn't have a good reputation.'

'I suppose that's why you come and wander round the studio while he's painting. It's rather insulting, I think, and must be frightfully irritating for him.'

Bootle, finding his grown-ups self-absorbed and unhelpful, withdrew to worry his ball in the corner behind the walnut cocktail cabinet.

'My dear girl, do get this straight. I don't care about Chapparelle and I don't like his manner with women, but it has never for one single moment occurred to me to be jealous of him or anybody else. I won't come with you again if you'd rather I didn't. I thought you might prefer it, that's all. But if you can put up with his insolence, I'm sure I don't mind. You don't imagine I'm afraid of competition from a hairy painter with a thick French accent?'

'I do love your self-satisfied way of dismissing people. It would be more flattering to me if you were, wouldn't it?'

'Good God! But I thought that was what you were attacking me for. Well, I'm not jealous, and I absolutely refuse to pretend I am.'

'I'm glad, because I might find people to be jealous about, too. All those actresses you take out to lunch and kiss at the stage door.'

'One has to kiss actresses. They expect it. It doesn't mean a thing.'

'I know it doesn't, darling. That's why I don't mind it. But you object if I even kiss Bootle.'

'Kiss him as much as you like, so long as you don't catch anything from him. Anyway it's not good for that sort of dog to make a baby of him. If only you would —'

'I know what you're going to say. If only we had a child of our own —'

'Well, I will say it. If we had a child, you'd have something to occupy your time —'

'And keep me happy and quiet while you're taking actresses out to lunch. That would make you feel freer, and be very nice for you.'

'Well,' said Harwell, steadily, 'say if you like, while I'm taking actresses out to lunch and soothing their vanities, and calming down managements, and working out costs, and attending to my business. I'm afraid you do often have a dull time when I'm out. There isn't much to do in a place where everything's run for you.'

'I'm glad you aren't suggesting I should take up housework to keep me out of mischief. No, Laurence; we've been over all this so many times. Please don't bring it up again. It isn't that I don't love children, and I wouldn't be a bit afraid of having one — in that way. But it wouldn't do. It would just be Bootle all over again, only worse. You think it wouldn't, but I know it would. You'd be terribly, terribly jealous, and I couldn't bear it.'

'Jealous of my own child? Really, Rosamund, that's a dreadful thing to say.'

'Heaps of men are, all the same. Or else you'd love him better than me, and I should be miserable. Darling, can't you see? It's so wonderful, just you and me, and if anything, anything at all came to divide our happiness —'

'Oh, but Rosamund, darling . . .'

'Yes, and suppose I were to die. Well, I shouldn't mind that so much, but suppose it made me get all out of shape and ugly, and I lost all my teeth or something horrible so that I couldn't be your Rose of the World any more. It's an awful toss-up, having babies, and I've got nothing *but* my looks to give you, no money and only a thief's name.'

'You mustn't say that.'

'But it's true. I'm so thankful Father's gone home. It's terrible for you to have him always

137

talking to people about prisons and making things so uncomfortable.'

'Poor old boy. I don't mind him.'

'I mind for you. And Laurence, suppose that sort of thing's in my blood. If I had a baby and he turned out like — like Father, you know, weak and dishonest . . .'

'Rosamund, sweetheart, don't. You're tormenting yourself. You're being hysterical. My darling, I'd no idea it was worrying you like that. Hush, now. We won't talk about it any more.'

'You do see, don't you?'

'I don't think there's the least risk of anything like that happening, but of course if you feel like that it's no good arguing about it.'

'Honestly, I'm not being selfish, but I should be worrying and worrying all the time. Of course, if you say I *must* . . .'

'Should I be likely to say anything so disgusting? Darling, I'm sorry. Forgive me. I didn't understand. We won't think about it any more. Look! There's old Bootle, wondering what on earth has happened to his missus. He has got a silly face, hasn't he? Just like a white cloth boot.'

'Poor Bootle. Oh, Laurence, I'm so glad we've had all this out. It's such a relief. So long as I've just got you I don't want anything more.'

'Nor do I, darling. Only you. I *have* got you, haven't I? All mine? Every bit?'

'Every bit. You see, you *are* jealous.'

'Of course I am. Jealous as hell . . . Sweetheart . . .'

Dear Lady Peter,

Many thanks for your letter. It was very kind of you to think of mentioning Mr Amery to Sir Jude, and I am sure he will be most grateful when I tell him. However, in the meantime, my husband has decided to sponsor the play himself, so I expect it will be better to leave it to him to approach a London management. But thank you very much all the same. Yes, indeed, we must meet again some time. Just at the present, of course, in view of the poor King's death, we are not doing any entertaining, but we must make an opportunity later on.

With again many thanks,
    Yours sincerely,
    Rosamund Harwell

Bless me, thought Harriet, what it is to be able to twist one's husband round one's little finger! 'Peter, would you put money into a play you didn't believe in, if I asked you to?'

'Harriet, you alarm me. You're not writing a play?'

'No, my good lord, I am not. I meant somebody else's play.'

'Nothing would induce me to back a play. Whose play?'

'Claude Amery's. Mrs Harwell has wheedled her husband into backing it.'

'And beauty draws us with a single hair. No, Harriet, I have already informed you that as a husband I am the world's worst wash-out. I am very proud, revengeful, ambitious, with more offences at my beck than I have thoughts to put them in. You might bump your head in the dust to me and I would still refuse to back any play, more particularly, of course, a bad one.'

'I was afraid not.'

'Nor,' pursued Peter, warming to his subject, 'should you entangle me by any less honourable means. I may be an effete aristocrat, but I am not the King of France. I will not hold a Bed of Justice — still less, a Bed of Dramatic Criticism. In a moment of weakness one concedes everything. Kindly understand, here and now, that I make no official pronouncements except clothed and in my right mind, between breakfast and bedtime.'

'Does that go for me, too?'

'Certainly. By the way, last night, somewhere about midnight, you voluntarily informed me that you would pull yourself together and return Lady Severn and Thames's call. You are at liberty to rescind that decision.'

'Thank you. I will reconsider the matter and let you have a memorandum through the Secretary of the Home Office.'

'It shall be read to me, as Disraeli once observed, "by a Privy Counsellor". Are you going out this morning?'

'I have a date with Gaston Chapparelle.'

'Oh, yes, the gentleman who is in love with your bones. I hope he is making a good job of your flesh. I hold certain mandatory concessions in that department.'

'I think it'll be a good bit of painting,' said Harriet, doubtfully. 'I don't know whether you'll like it.'

'I shall wait till it's finished and then issue a speech from the throne. At present I am urgently called for in a little matter of local sewage. Can I drop you at the studio in passing? I am going St John's Wood way.'

'Thank you,' said Chapparelle, putting down his palette. 'That is very good. You may sit down now, and withdraw your mind from the agreeable thoughts upon which I requested you to fix it. You obey instructions *à merveille.* If the wife is as obedient as the sitter, everything in your household should march as if on wheels. I would just make one little reservation — a cigarette? — that the behaviour of married women with other men affords no criterion of their behaviour with their husbands. I am not drawing any conclusions, I simply state a little fact.'

'That is a perfectly true observation, though perhaps not strikingly original.'

'Truth seldom has the chance to be original. There is so little truth in the world that very little of it can have escaped comment in the three hundred thousand years of mankind. Happily, there are more pleasant subjects of contemplation than there are truths. It is a hundred to one that the thoughts which produced an expression so suitable to my *Portrait of a New Bride* were simple illusion. Nevertheless, they serve the purpose.'

'I was thinking,' said Harriet, 'about a little matter of local sewage.'

'Sewage? *Ah! j'y suis — les égouts,* that is what is sewers, *n'est-ce pas?* That is certainly not an illusion, at least, we will hope not, if we are not to be swept away by the cholera. *Evidemment,* it is only the English who can think rapturously on the subject of sewage. It's all a matter of taste! Love, sewage, a new dress, a diamond necklace — it is all the same to me, provided it evokes the rapture.'

Harriet had no intention of enlightening Monsieur Chapparelle's inquisitive mind on the fascination of sewage. She roamed the big studio, examining the finished and unfinished canvasses.

'Isn't this Mrs Laurence Harwell?'

'Ah! She is difficult, that one. I mean, in your English sense of the word. She is not difficult to please. The husband, he is another matter. He thinks I am the big, bad wolf that will gobble up his beautiful red-haired Riding-Hood. So he is here all the time to watch what I do. Since I paint without stopping and he does not know the first thing about painting, he dies of boredom. *Je m'en f—* forgive my language! — if he wants to sit there in the corner, kicking his heels. I give him the paper. I say, sit down, amuse yourself. In five minutes he is up again, looking over my shoulder to see how the trick is worked. He looks at my picture, and he looks at his wife, and that puzzles him. He looks at her again a long time, and he does not know that what he sees is not there at all. But look! I will paint him what he sees, *quand même*. *You* notice, the sitter is holding something in her hands. No, it is not there yet. What I give her at present, it is the lid of a saucepan. Not inspiring, is it? The lid of a saucepan. *Bon!* Tomorrow she shall have what she will like better.'

'A mirror?'

'That is not a bad guess. It will please her like a mirror, and with the same kind of pleasure, because, you know, when she looks in the mirror, she too does not see at all what is there. But no, it could not be a mirror. And why? You that write books to detect the fact from the appearance, you will look again and tell me why it is not a mirror.'

Harriet examined the portrait, which was nearly completed, except for the background and accessories.

'A mirror would throw up a reflected light on the lower part of the face, and there is no reflected light.'

'*Bien, très bien!* I will buy one of your books and read it. Now I will show you. This has been made by a young man I know, who makes a little use of my studio, because he is poor and talented. I do not think he will always be poor, because he paints what other people like to see, and there is a good market for that. So, you see, Mrs Harwell will like this, better, perhaps, than my portrait.'

'A mask!'

'Be careful, it is papier-mâché. Yes, it is clever, *hein?*'

'Very clever, and very beautiful.'

'That is how she sees herself: "the beautiful woman with red-gold hair", *tout simplement.* But in my painting she is "The Bewitched", because, you see, the bad witch has shut her up close, close in a black tower without windows, and there is only one gate, and that is of ivory, and all her dreams come through that ivory gate. That is between her and the reality of things; which is just as well, because if she ever saw one glimpse, one smallest little glimpse of what is real, she would run away screaming and hide in the deepest dungeon beneath the castle moat. *Avec ça,* that in the *Moyen-Age* the dungeons were never beneath the moat but beneath the keep, but since that's how the saying goes, let it pass.'

'You see much too much, Monsieur Chapparelle.'

'You do not believe me? *Je suis psychologue:* I have to be. But you need not be afraid. A lady who can be enraptured by sewage is not sheltered from the realities. *Allons! Au travail.* Return quickly to your subterranean meditations, and I will return to my paints. *Des goûts, et des égouts;* about matters of taste as about sewers, no discussion is possible.'

7

O, what can ail thee, knight-at-arms,
Alone and palely loitering?
The sedge has wither'd from the lake
And no birds sing.

JOHN KEATS

'Mr Amery, isn't it? Lady Peter Wimsey — Harriet Vane.'

Harriet had walked past the despondent-looking young man, sitting with his head in his hands on the park bench, before she recognised him, and now he was looking at her blankly as though he did not recognise her.

'Oh, oh, yes of course,' he said, belatedly getting to his feet and taking the hand she held out to him. 'I'm sorry; I . . .'

'Are you all right?' she asked him. He was wearing a somewhat threadbare overcoat, not buttoned up, the hand he had offered her was stiff and blue with cold, and he was looking distraught. Perhaps he was even trembling slightly.

'I don't think I shall ever be all right again!' he said.

'Oh, come,' said Harriet. 'You have just let yourself get extremely cold. How long have you been sitting on this bench?'

'Ages,' he said. 'I don't remember.'

'Come with me,' said Harriet firmly. 'Let's get you some hot soup, or coffee and a brandy.'

'I can't afford anything,' he said. 'I'm flat broke.'

'I can . . .' Harriet began, and then seeing at once that it would be better if the question of payment were not to arise, said, 'I can get you something at home. It isn't at all far. And, look, don't argue. You really had better have something warm. You don't want to fall fainting in the street.'

He shambled along beside her. She permitted herself a moment or two of rueful regret for the loss of the afternoon's work. It was a habit of hers when a chapter was stuck to take a brisk walk round the park, and she often found that on her return to her study a mysterious change had occurred and she could see exactly how to proceed. This time the walk had put paid to the chapter till tomorrow; but then she could hardly have left a fellow-author freezing to death on a bitterly cold January afternoon, even if he was behaving like a byword for stupidity — what was it? — having not enough sense to come in from the cold.

A bright fire was burning in the empty drawing-room at Audley Square, and Harriet settled her guest in an armchair, and rang for Meredith.

'Would there be soup, Meredith, do you think?

Something warm, as quickly as possible, anyway.'

Meredith regarded the shivering guest impassively. 'May I recommend, your ladyship, that the gentleman does not sit too near the fire, for fear of chilblains, your ladyship, and that I should bring a tot of brandy immediately?'

'Thank you, Meredith. Quite right,' said Harriet.

She watched Claude while warmth, food and brandy stilled the quaking of his limbs, and turned his hands and face gradually from bluish pallor to rosy pink. He was still looking remarkably dejected.

'Are you feeling better?' she asked him, when Meredith had removed the tray.

'You shouldn't bother yourself about me,' said Amery ungraciously. 'Nobody else does.'

'Isn't Laurence Harwell getting your play put on?' she asked.

'Yes, he is,' said Amery, shortly, and colouring slightly. 'I should be grateful to the enemy. I am, of course, I am. But . . .'

'Mr Amery —'

'Do call me Claude. You're not an enemy. You gave me a very favourable review, and I haven't thanked you for it.'

'You shouldn't say thank you for a good review,' said Harriet. 'That would imply that one had done a favour to the author, whereas one has simply done justice to the book. And, Claude, do have a care. I don't know what you can mean by calling Laurence Harwell your enemy, but I am very sure you should not be calling him one to me.'

'Why not? If I can't tell you, who can I tell? At least you have lived a bit, not like all these monsters with boiled shirts and whalebone corsets and pursed lips, pretending to be totally respectable. Laurence Harwell is my enemy because I am horribly in love with his wife. What do you say to that?'

Harriet was silent. Then she said, 'I am sorry for you.'

'But why?' he said, suddenly getting up and pacing up and down the room. 'Why should you be sorry for me? Do you assume that I cannot succeed?'

Help! thought Harriet. She had, she realised, stepped straight into that lethal gap that separates people's view of themselves and their situation from the view taken by other people. And the poor young man was clearly in deep water.

'It must be a misfortune to fall in love with a married woman,' she said quietly. 'And the Harwells are famous all over London for being incandescently in love with each other. So yes, Claude, I am sorry for you, and I do assume you cannot succeed.'

'I don't know where I am with her,' he said, returning to his chair and sitting down again facing Harriet. 'She's so wonderful with me sometimes, so kind, and so determined to help me get my work put on. And then another time she just brushes me aside. I look forward for days to seeing her, and then she puts me off to go shopping or to have her hair done, or she has a headache and can't come out. She was supposed to be meeting me in the park this morning to take a walk,' he added woefully.

'Good heavens,' said Harriet. 'Had you been waiting in the cold since morning? But it was almost dark . . .'

'Since ten o'clock,' he said. 'But I couldn't go until I was sure she wasn't coming. I don't know what to do, Lady . . .'

'Do call me Harriet,' said Harriet quickly. She was still having a certain amount of difficulty in taking absolutely seriously a conversation in which she figured as Lady Peter Wimsey.

'Harriet. I can't work, I can't sleep, I don't go out in case she telephones . . . I think I am going mad. If this goes on I can't be responsible for my actions. I might do anything.'

'You mustn't let it go on. You should be working hard on your next play. If the present one does as well as we all hope it will, there will be an immediate demand for another one, and it would be as well to have something ready.'

'Would it?' he said, looking slightly less miserable.

'I'm sure it would. You owe it to yourself to work hard, Claude. Indeed you owe it to everyone; you have it in you to write something really magnificent. And, I found myself, you know, that in times of trouble there is nothing like work to get you through the days. I think you should keep warm, and keep working, and stop seeing Mrs Harwell.'

'Oh, but I couldn't do that!' he cried, leaping out of his chair again, and standing over her, actually, she noticed with interest, wringing his hands. So that was the gesture referred to in that famous phrase . . .

'Ask me anything but don't ask me to give up hope!'

'But what can you hope for?' she asked him. Her patience with him was wearing rather thin. 'You can hardly hope to entice Mrs Harwell into leaving her husband, and living with you. It would ruin her.'

'You ought to know,' he said, bitterly.

'Mr Amery, I shall pretend that I did not hear that,' said Harriet coldly.

'I'm sorry!' he said. 'I'm dreadfully sorry. How awful of me, when you are being so kind to me! But you see what I mean when I say she is driving me crazy! Can you ever forgive me?'

'I will forgive you if you go home and take my advice.'

'Just the same, you do know what I am hoping for.'

'And I do think you have no hope of it. She is in love with her husband, and, I think, enjoying her standing as Laurence Harwell's wife.'

'But it must be very boring having to be grateful all the time,' he said. 'She might like a turn at being the one who gives favours.'

Flinching, and enraged, Harriet was wondering

desperately how to get rid of him before he perpetrated any more terrible indiscretions, when Meredith appeared to announce the Dowager Duchess. This welcome visitor bustled into the room, embraced her daughter-in-law, and on being introduced to Claude Amery deluged him with effusive praise for his poems, and looked forward eagerly to his play.

Thus cheered up he pulled himself together, and took his leave.

As the door closed behind him, Honoria said, 'I do believe that young man is devoted to you, Harriet.'

'Sorry, Mother-in-law, but those tearful romantic eyes and all that quivering angst are not for me. I am merely a suitable wailing wall to resound to his distress. And I am very glad to see you; you appear like the relief of Mafeking. I seem to have been listening to him for hours.'

'May one know who is the lucky object of all that adoration?'

'Mrs Harwell. I don't see why I shouldn't tell you since the burden of the song is that he has got nowhere with her.'

'She is very lovely, isn't she?' said the Duchess. 'I suppose men see the world differently. Not all men, of course.'

'You mean, not Peter, no doubt,' said Harriet, smiling. 'But what difference of view do you mean?'

'In the rating they give to beauty. As though it had an entertainment value in itself. But beautiful people are often rather boring, don't you think?'

'Less beautiful people might rather like to think so,' said Harriet.

'But you know what I mean, my dear. All those wealthy men choosing a wife like a piece of furniture or a fine picture, to furnish the house, and then having to listen to her at breakfast twenty years later.'

'Well, at least,' said Harriet, 'you needn't fear that Peter chose me as house furnishing. He'll be back very soon; will you have a drink and wait for him?'

As well as black dresses, of course, one needed black hats. Every woman in London needed black hats, and the hat shops were crowded, even the little very exclusive milliner in Mayfair, to which Alcibiade had directed Harriet. She had to wait for a chair at the wall of looking-glass to be free, and as she sat down the woman sitting next to her pulled off a thick, folded velvet cloche, and tossed her head, releasing a heavy braid of copper-coloured hair.

Harriet recognised Rosamund Harwell.

'Good morning, Mrs Harwell.'

'Good morning,' Rosamund said. 'See if this suits you — it looks dreadful on me.'

Harriet put on the cloche, and they both considered it, and said 'no!' in the same breath.

The milliner bustled about, and brought Rosamund a little close-fitting cap, and Harriet a rather trilby-shaped item with a black feather in the hatband.

'That's better,' said Rosamund, considering the cap. 'But how I hate wearing black!'

'It doesn't suit me, either,' said Harriet.

'Oh, it's not that it doesn't suit me,' said Rosamund quickly. 'Laurence says I look ravishing in black, but I promised myself I would never wear it again; and now I can't help it.'

'I rather agree that you look good in it,' said Harriet. 'But it doesn't suit a dark complexion.'

'Oh, but that clever little collar thing makes all the difference,' said Rosamund, studying Harriet with an expert eye.

'The pleated collar would suit you too, Mrs Harwell,' offered the milliner, 'especially with that little skull cap and the dress you are wearing now.'

Rosamund's dress was patterned in silk and velvet lozenges, lightening the effect of the black.

'Would you like to try?' said Harriet helpfully. 'I'm sure we could get some made for you if you like them.' She unhooked the little confection, and passed it to Rosamund.

The effect of it on the diamond-patterned dress and the little cap was electrifying. Rosamund looked like some exquisite Columbine.

'Ah!' cried the milliner with deep satisfaction.

'It's lovely,' said Rosamund, fretfully. 'But it would take too long to have some made. Haven't you anything I could wear tonight?'

Harriet was struggling with herself. The sight of a beautiful and rich woman staring at herself discontentedly in some of the most expensive looking-glass in London, and declaring that she hated wearing what her husband liked to see her in, was bound to irritate her. Rosamund was behaving so exactly as Harriet thought women ought not to behave. But something about her, some atmosphere of pathos, brought on no doubt mostly by the Columbine effect, pulled her the other way.

'I could lend you a couple of the collars, if you would like,' she said. 'My dressmaker had a dozen made, and I don't need nearly so many.'

She expected the offer to be brushed aside, but Rosamund eagerly accepted. 'I will take the little cap, in that case,' she said. 'And now we must find something for you, Lady Peter. Something very plain and understated,' she added, turning to the milliner, 'and elegant rather than mannish. Something like the one on the model in the window.'

Rosamund turned out to be right; the hat on the model in the window looked rather good on Harriet, and was duly bought.

'Will you come and have some coffee with me, Lady Peter? I know a very amusing little place just off Sloane Square. Do say yes; Laurence is out all day today and I have nobody to talk to.'

'Just for an hour, then,' said Harriet. It was borne in on her that the 'Old Tabbies', whom Gerald had told her to ignore, and who had audibly doubted if Peter's wife could have time to write, had been thinking in part of social duties such as this. Harriet Vane would not have dreamed of spending time with Rosamund Harwell, with whom she had nothing in common; but the awful truth was that as Lady Peter she did have something in common with Mrs Laurence Harwell; rather too much for comfort, in fact. Certainly it would be better not to mention a need to work, since having needed to work had been found to be a sore point with her companion.

Once settled on chromium chairs amid enormous potted palms, and having ordered black coffee and declined petit fours, the two women fell silent for a moment.

'Are you enjoying being married, Lady Peter?' Rosamund asked.

'Yes, I am,' said Harriet simply. 'Very greatly,' and then saw, disconcertingly, a passing expression of surprise in Rosamund's eyes. 'Aren't you?' she hazarded.

'Well, of course, it's wonderful when Laurence is at home,' said Rosamund. 'But he's out such a lot, working with all those theatre people. I had no idea how much time it took. I find myself at a loose end, rather, just sitting around longing for him to come back. Don't you find the same thing?'

'Not really,' said Harriet. 'I seem to be doing — trying to do — everything I used to do, and a lot of other things as well.'

'I thought all those servants were rather cutting you out of running things,' said Rosamund.

'Well, for example,' said Harriet, 'I shouldn't have needed all these black dresses and hats if I had not been Lady Peter, living in London. I would have got by with very little. In fact perhaps the answer to our problems, Mrs Harwell, would be to flee to the countryside, and lie low.'

She thought longingly for a moment of Talboys, standing quietly among the fenland farms, where life tickered along gently without all these metropolitan exigencies. She hadn't yet seen the chimney pots she and Peter had found, and had had put back in place.

'We do have a bungalow in Hampton, beside the river,' said Rosamund. 'We were going to spend some time there in the summer, and have boating parties, but we hardly got there at all last year. It needs doing up to be really comfortable. But I couldn't get Laurence to come down with me now. He's very fussed at the moment about some play they have had to postpone.'

'Not Mr Amery's play?'

'Oh, no, that's still in the future. Something called "*Gee-up, Edward!*" '

Both women burst into laughter. 'Well, no, I do see! That really wouldn't do,' said Harriet at last. 'Can't they call it something else?'

'Oh, I expect so,' said Rosamund. 'I just don't see how it can take Laurence all day.'

'Well, he has to work . . .'

'But that's just it, Lady Peter, he doesn't have to work. He could give it all up tomorrow, and be no worse off. In fact he'd be better off, because plays don't always make money. Some of them lose money — quite a lot sometimes. In fact, being a theatre angel is more a hobby than anything for Laurence, and I don't know what he would say if *I* had a hobby that meant leaving *him* alone for hours!'

'Well, why don't you try it? Not leaving him alone for hours, but having a hobby? There's such a lot to do in London, isn't there? You could make a point of seeing all the exhibitions, for example, or find a worthwhile charity to support.'

'I don't know . . .' said Rosamund dubiously. 'I don't see how it would help.'

'You wouldn't have so much time on your hands,' said Harriet. 'And you would be demonstrating a bit of independence. Showing your Laurence that you are not completely dependent on him. He might like that; he might find it intriguing.'

'Do you think so? But I can't think of anything I'd like to do.'

'Well, what about going down to your bungalow for a few days, and getting a redecoration in hand? You could choose nice new furniture for it — wouldn't that amuse you?'

'You poor thing,' said Rosamund suddenly, 'they didn't let you have any fun doing up that great new house of yours, and I expect Lord Peter neglects you even more than Laurence does me, going out detecting all the time.'

Harriet bit her tongue in vexation, stopping herself from saying, 'I have better things to do with my time.' She was just no good at this sort of woman-to-woman conversation. In a minute Rosamund would start talking about having children. 'Well, no,' she said, 'Peter hasn't had a case since we got back from honeymoon.'

Pat, like the resolution in the old comedy, Rosamund said, 'And I suppose you'll have to have children in a family like that with titles floating around. I've told Laurence definitely that I won't.'

'I'll have to wait and see,' said Harriet. 'And I really do have to go now. I'll send my maid round with a couple of those collars, and I do hope you enjoy the outing tonight.'

'Oh,' said Rosamund, shrugging, 'it's only some affair of Laurence's.'

'Gosh, Harriet,' said Sylvia Marriot, 'what a perfectly stunning hat!'

'It's all part of the great change,' said Eiluned Price. 'You never used to have an eye for that kind of thing. And now here you are wearing about a year's income. It's amazing you can bring yourself to come slumming with us.'

'Do shut up, Eiluned,' said Sylvia. 'It's no way to thank Harriet for inviting us to lunch.'

'And I wasn't thinking of slumming,' said Harriet, mildly. 'I thought you might like lunch at the Ritz.'

'I'd love it,' said Sylvia. 'Let's be Sybarites, just for once. And I don't care how much that dress cost, it's worth it.'

'Well, everything's relative,' said Harriet. 'It isn't Balenciaga or Schiaparelli. Just something bought in London. And Eiluned, you are right about the hat; someone helped me choose it last week — quite one of the silliest women I have ever met. You've no idea how good it is to see you both.'

'Heavy relief, you mean?' said Eiluned, gruffly.

'Come on, let's jump into a taxi, and on the way you can tell me how you are, and how everyone else is.'

'What I want to hear about,' said Sylvia, once they were settled at a table, and had ordered oysters, to be followed by mutton chops, 'is the exotic family tree. Harriet, how are you finding your relations?'

'A rather mixed bag, to tell you the truth,' said Harriet, launching into a description of Helen, Duchess of Denver's dinner-party.

'But you can't mean that you like the Duke?' said Eiluned, by and by. 'What could there be to like about him?'

'He's very stupid,' said Harriet thoughtfully. 'It's amazing really, when he has such a clever brother. And he's like some great bear, somehow; sort of baffled. I suppose it's that he is so unlikely to succeed in his life's only project that gives him a sort of pathos.'

'What's his life's only project?' asked Sylvia.

'Transmitting the estate intact to his only son, and getting that son to do his duty,' said Harriet. 'But I suppose I like him really because he admires Peter, although he doesn't understand him a bit, and so he is on my side. You can imagine: "I can't think why Peter has married this weird woman, but if he has married her she must be all right." '

'It does sound rather zoological,' said Sylvia, 'having a bear to protect you in a nest of vipers.'

'Well, I won't have mother-in-law problems, anyway,' said Harriet. 'The Dowager Duchess is wonderful.'

'What about work problems?' said Eiluned. 'How's the next book?'

'I'm having difficulty,' said Harriet. 'But then you know, I always do.'

'I'm not sure I would go on painting, if I didn't need the money,' said Sylvia.

'Yes, you would,' said Eiluned. 'And I would go on composing. We don't do it for the money. I'm very glad you are working, Harriet. I was afraid you might stop.'

'Well, I haven't,' said Harriet. 'Look, Sylvia, do you know anything about a painter called Gaston Chapparelle?'

'Not a lot,' said Sylvia. 'Very successful. Much hated. Not much admired by other artists.'

'Why is he hated?'

'Jealousy, mostly. You know, those society portrait painters make buckets of money painting in a very old-fashioned way. The up and coming want to paint like Picasso or Modigliani, or like Cubo-futurists or something, and they think it's not fair that old fogies get all the money.'

'And he's French,' said Eiluned. 'Don't forget our attitude to foreigners.'

'I think he would make rather a good spy,' said Harriet, 'if France weren't a friendly country.'

'You can't tell these days, with Fascists springing up everywhere,' said Eiluned.

'I want to know who the silly woman is who helped you choose your hat,' said Sylvia.

'Rosamund Harwell. And oddly, that's her husband over there, lunching with a very pretty young woman. I've just noticed him.'

Eiluned swivelled round in her chair to look. 'Oh, don't worry about her. I know her. She's just a young terp. Phoebe Sugden: a friend of mine was at drama school with her. I expect he's giving her a part. Though now I come to think about it, I heard she had a part in a forthcoming production of Sir Jude Shearman's.'

'Well, one certainly wouldn't have a secret assignation in the Ritz,' said Sylvia. 'And don't theatre people have to plan a long way ahead? Perhaps he's giving her a part in something coming up after the thing she's playing next. Can we have crêpes suzettes for pudding?'

Walking along Piccadilly towards Hatchards, Harriet was amazed to see Lord St George emerging through the shop doors.

'Jerry, whatever are you doing here?'

'Buying a book,' he said, grinning.

'But it's full term; shouldn't you be in Oxford?'

'Couldn't get the book there,' he said.

'Thought I'd just nip down to jolly old Hatters and nobody would be any the wiser.'

'Whatever is it in the universe of print that defeats Blackwells?' she said in mock astonishment.

He pulled the book from the bag, and showed it to her. '*Modern Aircraft: A Manual for Trainee Pilots.*'

'But I thought your father . . .'

'Bished again!' he said. 'Look, you won't tell, Aunt Harriet, will you?'

'No, I won't tell,' she said. 'But don't you think . . . ?'

'It's dashed unfair, having a literary aunt,' he said. 'I'm not used to it. It used to be that Uncle Peter was the only family member one could possibly run into in a bookshop.'

'And Uncle Peter would not be likely to shop you for learning to fly against your father's wishes?'

'He might scold, but he wouldn't shop,' the young man told her. 'Look, Aunt Harriet, could I walk you wherever you're going?'

'You don't have time, do you, if you are going to nip back to Oxford in time not to be missed? In my day junior members were not allowed more than five miles from Carfax.'

'I can nip back faster than you think,' he said.

'You can drive like your uncle, you mean?' she said, shuddering.

'Well, not exactly,' he said. 'I don't have his spiffing motor, for one thing. But a chum of mine

162

has a Cub, parked at Northolt. Do let me walk with you; I am capable of good manners sometimes.'

'You'll be frightfully bored, Jerry. I'm only going into Swan and Edgar's.'

They crossed Piccadilly at the Belisha beacon, and came face to face with a window full of prams, cots and cradles. Jerry stopped. 'Just look at that,' he said to Harriet.

'At what?' said Harriet, flabbergasted.

'Well, that maroon and gold carriage job,' he said. 'That's got some pizzaz, don't you think?'

'Jerry, whatever has got into you?' she said. 'I very sincerely hope you are not thinking of procreating? Not yet, at least.'

'Oh, not me, Aunt Harriet. I rather hoped you were. I mean, I would be infinitely grateful. It would take some of the heat off me, don't you know.'

'And what do you imagine your sainted Uncle Peter would say if he heard you proposing it to me?'

'He wouldn't like it,' said Lord St George, gravely. 'Of course, I suppose he might be past it, but if he isn't . . .'

'I've never known anybody like you for perpetrating an outrage in every sentence,' said Harriet. 'Fall silent at once.'

'I'm not putting it well, I can see,' he said. 'It isn't funny. The thing is, dearest Aunt, it does put a great weight on a fellow's back, all this inheritance stuff. If the pater — well, all the family

163

— had someone else to fall back on, it would be a great relief. I'd be inexpressibly grateful. I'd even buy the little fellow that pram myself.'

'Jerry, if you are really being serious, you must see that I would hardly be likely to discuss it with you.'

'Oh, no, very private and all that. Until it starts to show, of course. But you do see what I mean?'

'Uneasy lies the head that wears a crown?'

'Something like that. So you will think about it?'

'Be off with you to Oxford,' Harriet said, 'before you drive me to shop you, if not to the university proctors, at least to your avenging uncle.'

'Peter, what kind of a car is a Cub?' asked Harriet.

It was the day following her encounter with Lord St George. They were sitting companionably beside the fire in the library, drinking sherry before lunch.

'It isn't a car,' he said, 'it's an aeroplane. A Piper Cub. An American job. Rather a jolly little thing, bit like a Tiger Moth. Why do you ask?'

Harriet's reputation as the aunt who would not shop an errant nephew was saved by the appearance of Bunter.

'Chief Inspector Parker on the telephone, my lord, would be grateful for a word with you.'

'Aha!' said Peter, 'I thought the faithful bloodhound would not forsake me for ever. Excuse me for a moment, Harriet.'

Harriet watched him leave the library with a light and rapid step. Affection for him made her smile. Unlike her sister-in-law — the Duchess of Denver, that is, for Harriet had nothing against Mary — she did not find Peter's occupation ghoulish. It was the use he had found to make of his unusual talents, and she approved of using one's talents. The boyish eagerness with which he had gone to the telephone charmed her; she herself might, when a book was going well, have raced off to the notebook in just such a way to write something down.

But Peter returned to the library quietly, shut the door behind him, and offered Harriet a white and sombre face.

'Peter, whatever is it?'

'Rosamund Harwell has been found dead,' he said.

8

The hunt is up, the hunt is up!

OLD BALLAD

All other men are specialists, but his specialism is omniscience.

CONAN DOYLE

'But she can't — I saw her only the other day,' said Harriet. 'Surely — whatever happened to her?'

'She has been murdered, I am afraid. Strangled.'

'Oh, God, Peter, how horrible!'

He came to her, and put a hand on her shoulder.

'I can't believe it,' she said, 'and whoever would want to murder her, poor silly harmless thing?'

'It looks like a break-in. Not in London; she was in the country. Harriet, Charles wants my help. It might be useful that I — we — knew the Harwells slightly.' He spoke in a quiet, dead tone of voice.

She heard, rather than saw, the danger. 'Of

course you must help,' she said. 'Of course. I thought we had that settled.'

'I thought last time you . . .'

'I hardly knew you then.'

'After all those years of plaguing you!' he exclaimed.

'We had only been married for a day. I know you better now, dearest. I have it worked out, I think.'

'Do you? I — Harriet, if I am to take this on, I must go at once. And it's a horrible shock; can I telephone to Sylvia or someone to come over?'

'Just go, Peter. I'll be all right.'

Peter stooped to kiss her, and rang for Bunter. 'Bunter, let Chief Inspector Parker know that I'm on my way. Bring the Daimler round to the front door, and put your photographic gear and tackle and trim in the boot.'

'I am to accompany you, my lord?'

'Of course you are, man. Stop waffling and get your skates on, will you?'

And the change in Peter's voice, the confident, businesslike note, was not more noticeable than the joy on Bunter's face.

As the door closed behind them she felt herself shaking with shock and revulsion. Poor Rosamund! Poor Laurence Harwell too — how horrible and destroying for him, out of all the husbands in London . . .

When Meredith announced lunch, she sat down distractedly, and began to eat, but within minutes she stopped, feeling sick, and then very sick, and hastily abandoned the table to run for her bathroom. When Mango appeared — Meredith must have witnessed Harriet's retreat and sent her — she found her mistress pitiably vomiting, and when the paroxysm ceased she comforted her efficiently, and helped her to bed.

The Harwells' country retreat was on the riverbank. It was the last but one of a line of dwellings strung out along a little lane, and stood on a sloping lawn, surrounded by trees. The drive was full of police cars, and Peter parked the Daimler on the verge in the lane. He and Bunter stood for a moment in the gate, surveying the scene. Rose Cottage was a large modern bungalow, built in a fashionably rustic style, with a veranda running the length of the house on the side facing the river. It was smartly painted, and the lawns and flower borders were well kept. The view of the river, and across it, was pleasantly unspoiled and green. There were indeed some climbing roses round the door, neatly pruned and trained.

Chief Inspector Parker appeared, framed in the rose arch, and came towards them.

'Thank you for coming, Peter. I'm sorry to let you in for this, it isn't pleasant.'

'When was murder ever pleasant?' said Peter.

'Some are worse than others,' Parker replied. 'Come in. My people are just about finished here.'

'Give us a guided tour, Charles. Starting here. Was the door locked?'

'Not when we got here.'

'Fingerprints on the doorknob?'

'Multiple. All yet to be identified. And a broken pane in the French windows on the other side of the house. Intruder probably got in that way, and cut himself doing it. Blood all over the place. I'll show you that in a minute.'

They stepped inside. A corridor led past the kitchen to the back of the house, where a large, L-shaped room with windows to the balcony was arranged as a sitting-room one end, and dining-room the other. At the dining-room end of the room the table was laid with a white cloth, and set for dinner: napkins, silver flatware, glasses, flowers and candles in crystal candlesticks — new candles, unlit.

'She was expecting someone,' said Peter.

'Who didn't come,' said Charles. 'It looks like it, doesn't it?'

'What were they going to eat?' asked Peter. 'I'd be surprised if she could boil an egg, in person.'

'Hamper in the kitchen.'

'Can I look?'

'Of course.'

They stepped into the kitchen. The usual kitchen range, dresser and deal table was supplemented by a new Easywork cabinet. Little gingham curtains hung at the windows. On the table a large wicker basket with Fortnum and Mason's labels on it stood open and partly unpacked.

'What were they having?' asked Peter.

'No expense spared: caviar, venison pie, salads,

apricots in brandy, coffee, fine chocolates, champagne sent down in ice, melted now, of course.'

'Any of it touched?'

'No. But there's a bottle of sherry in the drinks
cupboard in the sitting-room that's had about two
glasses poured from it.'

'And the glasses?'

'None left out. Of course, the sherry might have
been opened last time the bungalow was used.'

'Of course.'

Peter moved to inspect the broken pane in the
French window.

'Classic outside-in breakage pattern,' he said.

'Yes. Only one or two fragments of the glass
have fallen outside,' said Charles.

Peter took the silk handkerchief from his breast
pocket, shook it out, and draped it over the door
handle of the French doors. Gingerly, he tried
the door.

'This is locked, Charles — had you noticed?
Breaking the pane would not have allowed the
door to open. Where's the blood you mentioned?'

'Over there,' Charles indicated the corner of
the room containing a bookcase.

The two men stared at the thick pool of co-
agulating blood on the carpet. The bookcase had
been joggled: three books and the vases that had
stood on top of it had fallen into the pool of
blood.

'This is the intruder's blood, you reckon?'
asked Peter.

'It must be. There are no surface wounds on

the body,' said Charles. 'We'll be getting it typed.'

'So he cut himself over there — and he bled profusely here?' Peter mused. 'Are there some blood spots between the window and here?'

'We haven't found any.'

'Odd. And what was he doing here? I mean, if I had happened to cut myself badly I would make for the kitchen taps, not for the bookcase.'

'Dark room; unknown premises?' said Charles.

'Curtains all open, and nearly full moon,' countered Wimsey. 'And if he didn't get in by the French window, how did he get in?'

A police officer approached Charles and said, 'We're ready to move the body, sir.'

'Hold it just a minute,' said Charles. 'Do you want to see this, Wimsey?'

He indicated a corridor that led from the sitting end of the room to the bedrooms.

'Hello,' said Peter. 'Door lock broken here.'

'Yes; she had locked herself in when she went to bed, it seems.' Charles pushed the door wide, and was surprised by Peter's intake of breath.

Rosamund Harwell lay on her back, her knees slightly flexed, her right hand dangling to the floor, among piles of silk pillows and sheets. Her spectacular red-gold hair was spread in a tousled halo round her darkened and swollen face. Her tongue was protruding slightly between blackened lips. She was wearing a white dress and a white pleated collar.

'My God, Charles!' said Peter faintly.

'Sorry, old man, am I being inconsiderate? I thought you'd be used to a body or two, by now.'

'Harriet wears a collar exactly like that,' said Peter.

'Damn silly fashions, women all wearing them like sheep,' said Charles. 'Thank God Mary's got more sense. But you see the problem, Peter?'

'Oh, yes,' said Peter, 'I see it all right. More than one, in fact. Let them take her, Charles, I've seen enough.'

A police constable with huge, beefy hands stepped forward, and drew a sheet delicately over Rosamund's disfigured face. The stretcher party were waiting in the corridor as Peter and Charles beat a retreat.

'I asked Bunter to take some photographs, Charles. Would you mind? Before you seal up the place. Of course, I know your people will have done it, but . . .'

'By all means. I've been impressed by Bunter's photographs, and he knows better than to disturb the scene of the crime. Are you feeling better for a spot of lunch?'

'Top hole, thank you. Sorry to have made a blinking ass of myself.'

'Not at all. I should have realised that murder is very different when one knew the victim.'

They were sitting ensconced in the snug of the local pub, over beer and sandwiches beside a bright fire. Through the windows they could see a pleasant prospect of the river, stooped over by drooping willow branches in festoons, and enlivened by the occasional rowing boat or skiff passing by.

'So, problem one, who was she expecting, and did he show up, or not show up, and if not why not? Doesn't her husband know, poor fellow?'

'He's in no state to ask, at the moment. He discovered the body himself, early this morning. We can question him when he's had time to collect himself. I wanted your reaction.'

'Why, particularly?'

'Because I wanted to know if it looked like a lovers' assignation to someone in your elevated circle, or if that thought was just my policeman's dirty mind.'

'The table was set for two. So unless she was expecting her husband . . . How far have you got, Charles?'

'Not very far at all. My men are doing a house-to-house, to see if anyone saw or heard anything. Harwell says Mrs Harwell was spending a few days in the country to rest her nerves, or something, and he got worried about her being alone, and drove down here first thing this morning. He found his wife dead in bed. He seems to have been in a traumatised state, and there's no telephone in the bungalow, but by and by he pulled himself together and drove off to the police station to raise the alarm.'

'Locking the doors behind him, I take it? Did he say why he was worried enough to come down?

Presumably he knew when she set out that she would be alone.'

'He saw a report in *The Times* this morning of an outrage quite nearby, in Sunbury.'

'Did he now?' said Peter. 'I suppose you've checked that?'

'It's there all right. Nasty case: man broke into a house and assaulted an elderly woman living alone. Took some money and some jewellery.'

'But until Mr Harwell recovers himself you can't ask if any jewellery was missing here.'

'No. I shouldn't think there's any connection. But all the same it might be why Mr Harwell came down here.'

'Of course it might. But what do you make of the other problems?'

'What other problems in particular?' said Charles cautiously.

'To start with, a pane broken in the French window that could not have allowed entry to the place. Whoever broke it would have been able to reach the door handle, admittedly, but would not have been able to open the door.'

'Well, whoever it was wouldn't have known that the door had a lock and key, and not just a handle, until the pane was smashed and he could reach in and try it. Not every criminal manoeuvre is successful.'

'No indeed. But how, in that case, did the intruder gain entry?'

'Mrs Harwell might have let him in.'

'After he broke the window, or before? Then

there's the bedroom door. Why was that locked?'

'Well, a woman alone in a house surely might lock the bedroom door when she goes to bed.'

'She might. But she hadn't gone to bed — or only just. She was fully dressed, even her shoes still on, and that ridiculous collar.'

'So the murderer got in by means unknown at the moment, when she had only just locked the door, I suppose.'

'Which would give us quite a tight time scheme if we could establish when she went to bed.'

'The pathologist will give us a time of death more precisely as soon as he can. His rough guess is shortly after midnight.'

'And the cause of death?'

'Asphyxia. Smothering, I should think, with all those pillows around.'

'Don't think so, Charles. Something more violent, I'm afraid. That amount of occlusion and facial darkening; smothering leaves less trace, I think. And there was a marked depression in the pillow beside the head.'

'Downward pressure from the smothering?'

'Beside the head. Not under it. I wondered about that. And anyway —'

'If it was smothering, where is the pillow used as the upper one?'

'Exactly. Well, Bunter will take pictures for us. And there will be marks when they strip the body.'

'Yes. Well . . .'

'Charles, old fruit, why don't you come right

out with whatever it is you have on your mind, instead of eyeing me like a frightened horse?'

'I wondered if you would sit in on the interview with Harwell,' said Charles.

'Now why would you want me to do that?' said Wimsey. 'Frightfully irregular, isn't it? Do you think the sight of my vacant features will lull the suspect into a full confession?'

'He isn't a suspect at the moment.'

'The husband is always a suspect in the case of a murdered wife,' said Wimsey lightly, 'although from what I know of the fellow he is a rather unlikely one in this case.'

'He was absolutely distraught this morning,' said Charles. 'The presence of a friend might help.'

'Amazing discovery!' said Peter. 'Sensitive policeman found in Hampton pub . . . What is it, Bunter?'

Bunter had appeared and was standing at the end of the pew.

'Beg pardon, my lord, but I am unable to develop the plates immediately, as you requested, because the sink in the scullery at Rose Cottage is blocked. I have obtained permission to avail myself of the sink in the pantry in the next-door bungalow, my lord, where the owners are absent, and not expected today, and the housekeeper is a sensible woman by the name of Mrs Chanter. Should you require me during the next hour, my lord, I will be at Mon Repos.'

'Splendid. Very fly of you, Bunter. And while

you are availing yourself of the freely flowing sink at Mon Repos, you can also avail yourself of anything that the excellent Mrs Chanter saw or heard, or knows about her neighbours.'

'That thought had occurred to me, my lord.'

'Bunter, have you had some lunch?'

'Thank you, my lord. Mrs Chanter mentioned a freshly baked cottage pie, and an apple charlotte.'

'Excellent. Run away then. The Chief Inspector and I are off to interview Mr Harwell.'

'Indeed, my lord,' said Bunter gravely.

'The Chief Inspector has intimated,' said Wimsey, 'that the presence of an acquaintance might induce calm and coherence in the man; but I can't help wondering if what he has in mind is that Harwell has friends in high places, and it might be wise to have a witness to the fact that velvet gloves and the entire rule book were used in dealing with him. Good God, Charles, don't blush like that; Bunter will think I have caught you out in some peccadillo.'

Harwell was in a room in a local hotel: a room with a policeman outside the door. When the Chief Inspector entered, with Wimsey close behind him, Harwell was sitting on the end of the bed, hands clasped between his knees, staring out of the window at the view. It was of bleak, leafless trees, and a brown flood, overspilled from the river across the fields, and empty of action except for the silent gliding across it of a pair of swans.

Harwell jumped up, and turned towards the door an expression of eager desperation, as though, perhaps, hope against hope, there could be some good news. This expression was succeeded at once by one of misery.

'Sit down, Mr Harwell,' said Charles. 'I am going to have to ask you some questions. I am afraid they may be distressing to you, but . . .'

'I will tell you anything you need,' said Harwell, bleakly.

'I have brought Lord Peter Wimsey with me,' said Charles. 'In case he is able to assist. If you have any objection . . .'

'No, why should I have?'

'This is a terrible thing, Harwell,' said Wimsey, quietly. 'You have all my sympathy.'

Tears sprang to Harwell's eyes. He turned to Wimsey, and said, 'I loved her.'

'The immediate need, sir,' said Charles, 'is to find and apprehend her assailant. He is clearly a very dangerous man. We need him under lock and key.'

'What? Of course, of course. What do you need to know?'

'Well, firstly, sir, could you give us an account of your wife's movements on the day of her death?'

'No,' said Harwell, thoughtfully. 'Not really. She went down to the bungalow on the previous day.'

'That would be Wednesday, would it? The 26th?'

'Yes. And I stayed in London. I don't know how she spent the next day. She telephoned the flat some time that afternoon, and left a message that she was feeling better and would return to town on Friday. That is the last I heard of her before . . .'

'There is no telephone at the bungalow?'

'No. We thought of having one put in, but the purpose of the place was as a quiet retreat, out of reach of constant demands. In London the phone rings all day and half the night. Theatre people get very obsessive. There is a perfectly convenient telephone box on the odd occasions when we need to make a call, a little way down the lane, opposite the farm cottages. She phoned from there while she was walking the dog.'

'But you did not take the call yourself?'

'No; I was at my club. The service porter took the message.'

'Good. We can check the time with him. The message said she was feeling better; had she been unwell?'

'Not exactly. She was a little tense. She was very moody, Inspector. Very highly strung. Well, you know, Lord Peter, she had not had an easy life.'

'Did she often go down to Hampton by herself?' asked Charles.

'No. It was the first time. The first days we had spent apart since our marriage. I was very uneasy about it, but I could hardly have forbidden her to go, could I?'

'Harwell, we had better ask you bluntly if there was any special reason why she went?' said Wimsey. 'Had you, for example, quarrelled about anything?'

'No,' said Harwell. 'We had not quarrelled. We never quarrelled, why should we? I always give her — oh, God! — gave her anything she asked for.'

'But nevertheless, she was spending three days apart from you, for the first time?' pursued Charles.

'Yes. She thought a little fresh air, a change of scene would lift her spirits. I think she found the Park Lane flat dull when I was out at work. And I have been unusually busy recently.'

'And was she going to meet anyone while she was down there, do you know?'

'There was some talk of getting a decorator to look at the place. Oh, and she thought Mr Amery might visit her there.'

'The poet,' Wimsey told Charles.

'A friend of the family,' said Harwell.

'But you don't know whether or not he did go?'

'No, I don't,' said Harwell. 'He could more easily see her when she was in town.'

'And would there be anyone else you know of who might have wished to see your wife, perhaps specially when she was out of town?'

'Did she have a lover, you mean? That's what you are suggesting, isn't it?' Rage and distress made his voice rise.

'Try to keep calm, old man,' said Wimsey, gently. 'The Chief Inspector has to ask these things.'

'She could have had dozens of lovers,' said Harwell, sullenly. 'People are drawn to anyone as beautiful as that.'

'But can you think of anyone in particular?'

'There's that odious painter fellow Chapparelle,' said Harwell at length. 'He has a pretty awful reputation, and he certainly ogled her. He was painting her portrait. But she wouldn't have had anything to do with him apart from the sittings, I'm certain.'

'Yes, I see,' said Charles. 'Now, sir, your own movements, please. In the afternoon, when the call from Mrs Harwell came through you were at your club . . .'

'Yes. I spent the afternoon discussing a project with some business associates there. I dined there, and then played several rounds of bridge with Colonel Marcher. The flat was not very tempting to return to, with my wife absent.'

'We can confirm all that,' said Charles. 'When did you leave?'

'I can't remember exactly,' said Harwell. 'Fairly late.'

'Did you go straight home?'

'No. I had things on my mind; professional concerns. I wandered about a bit.'

Charles caught Peter's eye. Wimsey's face was frozen.

'About how long did you wander for, sir?' asked Charles.

'I don't know!' cried Harwell, exasperated. 'What does it matter?'

'So you don't know when you got in that night?' said Wimsey. His tone was neutral. He did not catch Charles's eye.

'No!' said Harwell. 'No, I don't. But the night porter does. I found I had left my doorkey on the hall table in the flat, and I had to knock him up to let me in. I had to make a hell of a racket before I could attract his attention; he was sleeping on the job, I think, so I gave him a bit of a dressing-down for it. He's certainly going to remember that.'

'That's very helpful, sir. Now, the next morning — this morning, that is . . .'

'I got up and had breakfast as usual. I was uneasy. Then I saw the story in *The Times. I* cancelled my morning's appointments, and drove down to Hampton, to make sure she was all right . . .' His voice began to shake.

'Just a few more questions, sir, and then we'll leave you in peace,' said Charles. 'When did you arrive at the bungalow?'

'A little before nine. It takes about three-quarters of an hour to drive down there.'

'And how did you get in?'

'How? I don't understand you.'

'Did you enter the premises by the front door?'

'Yes, of course.'

'And was it locked? Did you let yourself in with a key?'

'Yes. And yes. I have my own key to the bungalow.'

'And what did you think when you saw the

table?' asked Wimsey, quietly interjecting.

'The table? I didn't see the table. I called out for her, and when she didn't answer I went straight to the bedroom.'

'And the bedroom door, Harwell, was it locked?' asked Wimsey.

'It was shut, but unlatched — I think it was swinging loose. I pushed it. And she was . . . she was . . .' He fell silent.

'Did you disturb or move anything in the room, Mr Harwell?' asked Charles.

Harwell didn't answer at once. He was staring into space.

'Mr Harwell, is there anything in the room, anything in the entire house, anything at all, which was not as you found it when we found it? Did you move anything?'

'I took her up in my arms,' he said, sadly. 'I held her for a long while. Then I laid her back, and went for help.'

'Just one more thing, sir. Did you by any chance lock the French door to the living-room some time that morning? Before leaving the house to fetch the police, perhaps?'

'No, I —' Harwell broke off, and coloured up. 'There was a broken pane in it,' he said. 'I supposed that's how — that's how someone got in.'

'The door was locked, sir, and the key not there,' said Charles. 'The broken pane indicates an attempt at forced entry, but it must have been unsuccessful.'

'Oh, but I remember now!' said Harwell. 'Of

course; I did lock the door. Just as you say, I locked it as I left for help, and put the key in my pocket.'

As he spoke he produced the key, and handed it to Charles.

'Thank you, sir, that is a great help,' said Charles.

'Is that all?' asked Harwell. 'Can I go now?'

'Would you have any objection to letting us take your fingerprints, first, sir?'

'My fingerprints? Why on earth?'

'The police need to have the fingerprints of anyone who had a legitimate reason to be in the house,' said Wimsey, 'so as to be able to identify any prints that shouldn't be there. Yours and your wife's will be all over the place; the domestic help will have left prints everywhere. When we have eliminated those, the ones left over may include those of the murderer.'

'I see. Very well, then.'

'By the way, there was some domestic help, I take it?'

'We didn't keep anybody on. We used to find somebody in the village when we needed. I don't know who she got this time.'

'Don't worry, sir, we'll find whoever it was,' said Charles. 'Now, when we've taken those prints, you should return home, or to your club, and make sure we know where to find you if you go anywhere else for more than half a day or so.'

'I don't think I'm fit to drive,' said Harwell,

holding out his hands to them, showing the tremor in them.

'I'll drive you back to town,' said Wimsey. 'I ought to be getting back. Bunter can bring the Daimler home when he's ready. See you tomorrow, Charles?'

'Certainly. Have no fear, Mr Harwell, we will catch the man who murdered your wife.'

'Man?' said Harwell, looking bewildered. 'Some sort of animal. She was so beautiful. Some vile beast.'

Peter came rapidly into the library, where Harriet was reading beside the fire.

'They tell me you have been unwell,' he said.

'I was sick. It's gone off now. I must have eaten something, I suppose. I've been famously looked after, Peter, don't look so stricken! Mango put me to bed, and Mrs Trapp made me a plain rice pudding — she said that would stay down if anything would — and look at me now, as right as rain.'

'This is a terrible shock,' said Peter, sitting down.

'Worse for you.'

'Why do you say that?'

'Didn't you have to see the body?'

'Yes. And that did give me a jolt, I confess. She was wearing one of those Breton collars like yours. I take it London is full of them?'

'No; but I lent her some. They looked so good on her.'

'Ah.'

He fell silent. Harriet waited, sitting perfectly still, to see if he would tell her about the case. Of course he might not want to, and she was certainly not going to ask. But if he did not want to, something would have been lost. Perhaps he would think she could not bear the brutal discussion of someone she had known slightly. And having known Rosamund did, Harriet thought, make a difference — a considerable difference. When she had been involved in murder before — she did not count the murder of poor Philip Boyes, who had been her lover, that was far too complicated a situation; she was thinking of Mr Alexis, lying in a pool of blood on the shore at Wilvercombe — she had felt disgust and bafflement. Now she felt deep anger. What an outrage it was to hasten a fellow-creature into the dark!

'Harriet, what did you mean, this afternoon,' said Peter, breaking into her train of thought, 'when you said you had got me worked out?'

'Not you *in toto*, Peter,' she said. 'That will be the study of a lifetime. Just your detective urges.'

'Would you be so good as to tell me your explanation?' he said.

His caution lay between them like a fog. She was still paying a price for having said, on their honeymoon, that surely it need not be he who investigated a body in the cellar. They had got straightened that time — or so she thought — but this was the next time, and he was treading carefully.

'It's *noblesse oblige*, isn't it?' she said.

186

'Most of the nobility would be astonished to hear it!' he said, laughing.

'When I was a child,' she told him, 'there was a man in the village who was tall and stout, and as strong as an ox. He would appear as if by magic whenever a job was afoot. Whenever a cart had a broken axle, or the vet couldn't get an animal into a truck, or a car had run into a ditch, or there were bricks to unload, or a sick fat woman had to be carried up the cottage stairs to bed . . .'

'I'm not entirely sure I follow your drift,' said Peter.

'His strength was his *noblesse*,' she said. 'It put him under an obligation to help with feats of muscle power.'

'And in my case?'

'In your case brains and privilege put you under an obligation to see justice done. I've got that clear, I think. And, Peter, I don't just agree that you should do it; I admire you for it. I think you are right that your position entails responsibilities, and I'm rather proud of you for taking them up, and not just idling about.'

'You make a very lucid advocate. When I conduct my own defence I make a very muddled job of it.'

'Peter, you are not on trial. Who accuses you of anything?'

'If you do not, none but my secret self.'

'And, dearest, what charge does your secret self lay against you? Can you bring yourself to tell me?'

'You alone in all the world,' he answered. 'I accuse myself of accepting and enjoying the title and rank and privilege — the unthinking automatic respect given me for reasons of birth — and not giving back value for them; not pulling my weight.'

'Of that I acquit you,' she said. 'You may leave the court without a stain on your character. And after all, my lord, these titles, these thrones and dominations, were not of your choosing.'

'No,' he said. 'And, Domina, I would not have chosen them. I would greatly have preferred to start shoulder to shoulder with others, or even handicapped. As it is, I am always in a false position; anything I can ever achieve is done by a form of cheating, is the result of an accident of birth.'

'Not quite *anything*, Peter. In persuading me to marry you, you *were* handicapped.'

'So I was,' he said. 'Several laps behind the butcher, the baker, the candlestick maker, old Uncle Tom Cobleigh and all. But at least, I think you are saying, I can do an honest turn as a surrogate policeman. You don't think the great detective is a frivolous pose — a rich man's game?'

'No; I think it is very serious. A matter of life and death, after all. What I haven't got clear is how this connects with the war. I think it does, in some subterranean fashion.'

'When you have seen people die,' he said, 'when you have seen at what abominable and appalling cost the peace and safety of England was secured, and then you see the peace squalidly broken, you see killing that has been perpetrated for vile and selfish motives . . .'

'Oh, yes, I can see that,' she said. 'Beloved, I do see.'

'Justice is a terrible thing,' he said, 'but injustice is worse.'

He came suddenly towards her, and knelt in front of her chair, putting his arms round her knees, and laying his head in her lap. When he spoke again his voice was muffled in the folds of her dress. 'Dearest, do you want me to discuss this case with you? Or would you rather not?'

'I'd rather you did, if you can bear to.'

'It's what you can bear that I was thinking of. I would spare you distressing topics, if I could.'

'Nothing you could tell me would be as bad as the thought that there was some subject we couldn't talk over together. That would be really hateful.'

'It is to be the marriage of true minds we try for?' he said, looking up at her.

'I thought it was; yes.'

'Then so it shall be. We'll bear it out even to the edge of doom — Yes, Meredith, what is it?'

'Dinner is served, my lord.'

'Later,' said Peter, getting up and extending her his hand. 'I will tell you all later.'

'You rang, my lord?' Bunter entered the drawing-room, where his master was sitting over a

189

goodnight glass of brandy. Harriet, who had eaten a reassuringly hearty supper, had gone promptly to bed, pleading tiredness.

'Pour yourself a brandy, Bunter, and come and sit down,' said Wimsey. 'I want to hear all about Mrs Chanter and Hampton society.'

'Yes, my lord, thank you, my lord,' said Bunter, doing as he was told. 'I learned a good deal that may not be to the point, my lord.'

'Spill all the beans, Bunter, and we'll sort them out later,' said Wimsey.

'Well, sir, it seems as if the Harwells have been a great disappointment to their neighbours. Mrs Chanter's employers, a Mr and Mrs Sugden, were thrilled when the bungalow next door was sold to the Harwells, because the family are more than somewhat stage-struck. They thought that there would be a continuous stream of famous actors and actresses flowing past their front door, on their way to lavish parties in next door's drawing-room and garden. They had even bought a new book with a leatherette binding in the hope of autographs. And then it turned out that the Harwells were very quiet when they were in Hampton, and that that was not often; in fact they were hardly ever there.

' "What they want to go to all that expense for, just for a few weekends in summer, I'll never know!" Mrs Chanter said. "And as for famous guests — well, there hadn't been none spotted, not but what Mrs Harwell, the poor lady, was as lovely as Dorothy Lamour herself." I am repeating her exact words, my lord.'

'Very convincing, Bunter.'

'There was a good deal in a similar vein to listen to, my lord, because Mrs Sugden has a daughter who is in the theatre, an actress with a great future, I was given to understand. However, it is Mrs Chanter's daughter who might interest us, because she has served as a maid and housekeeper from time to time when the Harwells required someone. She is a young woman called Rose, my lord. I understand that she is a good girl, who helps to look after her father while Mrs Chanter is at work, but who takes any casual jobs she can get to earn herself some pin money. The family are respectable folk, Mrs Chanter assures me, but very hard up owing to Mr Chanter's having fallen off a ladder and being unable to work at his trade for some years past.'

'Aha, Bunter mine — at last some inside information. Was Rose asked to do for Mrs Harwell this time?'

'She was asked to air the house, and light the fires the day Mrs Harwell arrived, and then told to make herself scarce, I gather. On the second day she came in first thing to make the bed, and clear the ashes, and then was asked to return in the afternoon to help with the table for supper. She was told she would not be required for more than an hour in the afternoon, because the supper dishes could be washed up the following morning. I gather neither Rose nor Mrs Chanter were surprised at this, because Mrs Harwell did not usually do anything for herself.'

'But perhaps if the Harwells were very seldom there, Mrs Chanter and family had not seen enough of them to know their habits well?'

'Perhaps not, my lord. I did not see Rose herself, but Mrs Chanter felt involved enough to be very upset. She had jumped to the conclusion, my lord, that the crime was perpetrated by a rapist, who had been lurking in the district, and she became very agitated in case Rose too might be in danger; then she consoled herself with the thought that Rose's young man would be likely to protect her, since he is in the habit of walking her home if they are out after dark.'

'Quite right too,' said Wimsey.

'Apart from Rose, my lord, there is a gardener-handyman who comes in once a week, whether the Harwells are in occupation or not, to keep the garden tidy. Mrs Chanter makes him a cup of tea, and takes it over mid-morning when Rose Cottage is empty. She doesn't hold with asking a man to work all morning without so much as tea and a biscuit.'

'Very proper sentiments. She didn't happen to say if she had heard anything unusual during the hours of darkness on the night of the 27th?'

'I enquired about that, my lord. But Mrs Chanter does not live in at Mon Repos, she comes in daily all day. She lives with her husband and daughter in one of those little terraced cottages at the foot of the lane; we passed them on the way up to Rose Cottage. You might have noticed them, my lord, on the left.'

'I can't say that I did, Bunter. I am becoming a careless beast these days.'

'There is no reason why you should have noticed, my lord. Mrs Chanter lives well out of earshot of Rose Cottage. She did, however, hear a car at some time during the night. It seems that the leafiness of the lane, my lord, means that it is favoured by young people in cars looking for a quiet place to park for a little while, well out of the scope of street lights. The residents on the lane all resent the disturbance. It being a cul-de-sac, they feel entitled not to be subjected to noise from the passing trade. Mrs Chanter was annoyed at being woken by a car, but she had not looked at her alarm clock, and could give me no indication of the time. She recommended talking to Rose, but Rose did not return home while I was there. We should bear in mind, my lord, that a car passing the terraced cottages could have been going to any point on the lane; there are more than a dozen houses there all told.'

'Or it could, as you say, have been carrying roaming lovers, looking for a quiet spot to park a car,' said Wimsey. 'All the same, Bunter, we should spin down to Hampton again, and have a word with Rose, don't you think?'

'It might be worth while,' said Bunter.

'How did your prints turn out?' asked Wimsey.

'In respect of fingerprints, my lord, very well. I have a number of very clear prints from various places in the house which can be compared with those obtained by the police. In respect of the impressions in the pillows, my lord, less good, I am afraid. The sheen on the satin has produced white-outs on the prints.'

'You need not attempt to impress me with technicalities, Bunter, I am deeply respectful already. What is a white-out?'

'The effect is, my lord, to make the twin depressions which we observed in the bedding hard to discern clearly on the prints. I am going to a meeting of the Bayswater Photographic Society on Saturday evening, if I am not required here, at which I will seek the advice of other photographers, some of them very good professional photographers, my lord, as to how to make clearer prints.'

'Well, do your best, Bunter. This could be important, and the state of those pillows might be temporary. I mean, mightn't they puff themselves up again after a while?'

'I don't think that feathers rebound perceptibly of their own account,' said Bunter thoughtfully. 'But the slightest agitation . . .'

'That's what I thought. I'm off to bed now, Bunter. Goodnight.'

Extract from the diary of Honoria Lucasta, Dowager Duchess of Denver:

27th February
 Seems to be scandal about the King already; French newspapers full of it, according to Paul.

194

Paul very difficult these days — becoming impossibly eccentric. (Gerald says it comes of living abroad among benighted foreigners.) First Paul rushed home for the King's funeral, and then rushed back to France again, complaining of the cold, and the price of wine. Now he keeps sending me clippings from French newspapers about King and Mrs Simpson. Would have thought his famous broad mind might have managed a mistress or two for the King without fussing. Also Paul very angry with President Roosevelt over Neutrality Law. Wonder if living in France really is giving him peculiar opinions. On reflection suppose not, he has been peculiar for years. Says Americans all over Paris purporting to be interested in civilization, and yet determined to leave Europe to stew in own juice. Went with Hartley-Skeffingtons to see new Chaplin film, Modern Times. *Pathé News showed Herr Hitler opening Winter Olympics; thought Hitler very like Chaplin, and wondered why Germans don't laugh. Suppose it isn't funny, really.*

9

Singularity is almost invariably a clue. The more featureless and commonplace a crime is, the more difficult is it to bring it home.

CONAN DOYLE

'It is perfectly possible, I suppose,' said Lord Peter to his wife, over breakfast, 'for someone to be murdered while doing something she does not usually do, or behaving in a way unaccustomed to her. But it is an affront to the natural feelings of a criminologist, all the same.'

'It has a feeling of lightning striking twice in the same spot, you mean?'

'It does rather. I would greatly prefer it if every tiny break in precedent was in some way connected to the crime. And therefore could be constructed as a clue by a brainy enough person.'

'Well, if this were a work of fiction, one would certainly make sure that was the case,' said Harriet. 'But in real life, Peter, don't people usually do unusual things? Aren't they always going to places for the first time, mildly surprising their friends by little switches in behaviour, suddenly getting bored, or headachy, and dashing out to parties, or going early to bed, or buying a red dress instead of a blue one, or suddenly marrying, at the age of forty-five, a highly unsuitable person?'

'Do you mean that unpredictable behaviour may simply reveal the secret truth of someone's inner man or woman?'

'In a novel, of course, it would. Things have to be connected or the reader would not believe them.'

'It's odd, that, isn't it?' said Peter. 'If unconnected and spur-of-the-moment things keep happening in the real world, why shouldn't they be plausible in novels? Shouldn't the most plausible picture of life be a portrait of reality in all its bizarre and incoherent confusion?'

'I think a novel has to deal in a different kind of truth,' said Harriet. 'For example, if poor Rosamund's death were in a novel, readers would know at once that the Sunbury attacker who so alarmed Laurence Harwell could not have done it. If a wholly unconnected stranger arrived in a story just in time to commit the crime and disappear, there would be no plot.'

'But in real life random things occur, and there may actually be no plot, in that sense of the word,' said Wimsey, thoughtfully. 'Just the same, Harriet, I would be happier if the random attacker had found Rosamund doing what she usually does, in much her usual way.'

'A certain amount of accident, and no more?'

'Exactly. Whereas in this case there were numerous variations from the usual, starting with her having gone off to the bungalow by herself in the first place. She had never done such a thing before, it seems, and Harwell hadn't any very clear idea why she had done it now. Are you all right, Harriet? You are looking rather pale.'

'A horrible thought has just struck me: Peter, I advised her to go! It may be my fault . . .'

'You advised her to go?'

'I was casting around for some helpful suggestion for her. She was complaining about time on her hands, and I thought it was bad for her to sit around waiting for her husband all the time. She mentioned the place in Hampton, and said they hadn't got round to doing it up . . . Oh, Peter, do you think . . . ?'

'No, I do not,' he said. 'I'm taking a novelist's view of this. It isn't a random thing, some stranger taking an opportunist's advantage of her presence in the bungalow. I think she brought her jeopardy with her, it was built into her life somehow, and every little inconsistency in her conduct is a clue.'

'I hope you're not just sparing my feelings,' said Harriet shakily.

'Wouldn't dream of it,' said Peter. 'My dear, aren't you eating anything?'

'I don't feel like it, somehow,' said Harriet, 'but surely two *cafés au lait* will keep body and soul together till lunch.'

'Are you working this morning?'

'I was thinking of it.'

'Only Charles is coming in to talk over the case, and I wondered . . .'

'I don't think policemen, even Charles, have a sufficiently high regard for detective fiction writers,' said Harriet, laughing. 'I would put him off his stride. Tell me about it later.'

'So how's it looking?' Peter asked Charles. They were comfortably ensconced in the library; Charles might be a policeman, and Peter might have an office for interviewing policemen, among others, but Charles was received in Audley Square with the welcome due to a brother-in-law.

'I'm afraid this is one of those cases that are the devil's own job to solve,' said Charles gloomily. 'No motive in particular; well, a sexual motive if you like, but no reason for the victim to be anyone in particular, so I mean, no motive for attacking *her*, rather than somebody else.'

'Never mind why, Charles. Think about how.'

'It's who that's the priority,' said Charles, reasonably enough.

'Well, what have we got?' asked Peter. 'Have we got the pathologist's report?'

'Preliminary. Cause of death, mechanical asphyxia. Cause of mechanical asphyxia, throttling. Pressure points on each side of the throat, consistent with face-to-face attack. Extensive internal crushing with fracture of the hyoid bone, and cricoid cartilage. External bruising slight. Slight hypostasis, more advanced in lower limbs. Rigor partial when corpse first examined, giving an approximate time of death between eleven P.M. and two or so in the morning. Body temperature consistent with that, given that a fire was burning in the bedroom for most of the night. Intimacy had taken place very shortly before death; slight bruising to thighs and upper arms suggests possibility that some resistance was offered.'

'So what is your guess, Charles?'

'It's all rather commonplace, isn't it? The all-too-usual nasty, squalid crime.'

'There are various aspects of it I don't like,' remarked Wimsey. 'What does the night porter at Harwell's apartment block have to say?'

'Harwell came in a little after twelve, and there was an altercation. The porter had been upstairs in one of the flats, helping an elderly tenant who had slipped getting out of the bath. So of course he was out of earshot of the front hallway. By the time he returned to his desk Harwell must have been banging on the door quite some time, because he was already very worked up. He threatened to get the man dismissed, and wouldn't listen to any explanation. They were arguing for perhaps another ten minutes before Harwell went up to bed.'

'And how long would it really take to drive back from Hampton, Charles, supposing he had driven down there?'

'Certainly not less than forty-five minutes. I'll get one of our men to try it in the middle of the night; in the daytime traffic it would take much longer.'

'What about trains?'

'Last train back to London leaves at eleven ten.'

'So Harwell's alibi . . .'

'Looks pretty good, really. Not absolutely watertight; he can't prove that he went wandering about London between leaving his club and getting home, and we haven't a very tight time of death.'

'I take it that the porter at the club confirms his stated time of leaving?'

'Quarter after nine. They noticed because it's a bit of a joke with them that he leaves early now he's married, and nine fifteen was later than usual these days.'

'On the other hand, Charles, I'm rather favourably impressed by an untidy sort of alibi; I'm always suspicious of very watertight ones. It's unnatural to know precisely where one was precisely when, and to have a witness to every step and every breath, don't you think?'

'Let's call Harwell's alibi natural, then,' said Charles. 'And in any case, Peter, he hasn't the ghost of a motive. He adored her, and all the money was his anyway. She didn't have a bean.'

'I wish you wouldn't get so obsessed by motives, Charles. Motives are ten a penny. There's always a motive for anybody doing anything. Just find out who had the opportunity, and you can make up the motive.'

'I don't really agree with you,' said Charles. 'Juries like motives, you know.'

'So what are your lines of pursuit?' asked Wimsey.

'We are urgently seeking the man whose description we have for the Sunbury attack. We were looking for him already, of course. I don't know that we can look any harder. And we are asking round the neighbourhood for any suspicious persons seen, or noticed, following young women in the days leading up to the murder. We will take descriptions from the station-master at Hampton of everybody unknown to him who arrived at the station during that afternoon and evening. The usual sort of routine enquiry. We are interviewing one Mrs Chanter, and also her daughter, who seems to have been the last person to see the victim alive. And we are looking for a Mr Claude Amery, who might have paid a visit to the deceased in Hampton.'

'Well, he shouldn't be hard to find,' said Wimsey. 'I expect Harriet has his address.'

'He isn't at home. Gone away for a few days, we understand from a neighbour. She doesn't know where. Would you like to sit in on the interview when we find him?'

'If he doesn't object,' said Wimsey. 'He'll come to light the moment he sees the story in the papers, I expect. I take it the papers have got it?'

'Front page,' said Charles, taking the *Daily Yell* out of his briefcase, and showing it to Wimsey. 'Angel's Wife Found Dead', ran the headline. 'The wife of Mr Laurence Harwell, well-known theatrical "angel", was found dead at the couple's

202

country home yesterday morning . . . not un-known to scandal . . . daughter of convicted fraudster . . .' Wimsey glanced through the story with distaste.

'Can you think of anything else we should be doing?' Charles asked.

'Oh, yes,' said Wimsey. 'Find out what hap-pened to the dog.'

'A Mr Warren to see you, my lady,' said Meredith.

'Mr Warren? Whatever . . . ?' Harriet looked up from her manuscript. 'Did he ask for me, or for his lordship?'

'For you, my lady. His lordship went out about an hour ago. Are you at home? The gentleman seems very distressed, my lady.'

'Then I had better be at home,' said Harriet. 'Show him into the drawing-room.'

It was natural to dread encountering Mr War-ren, in the circumstances, but Harriet reproached herself with cowardice as she made her way down to the drawing-room. She hadn't given a thought to how the disaster would affect Mr Warren — poor stupid old man. But surely he — anybody in like trauma — should be able to expect a little kindness. Harriet braced herself to be kind.

Mr Warren was in a terrible state. He was unshaven, red-eyed from weeping, and dishev-elled as though he had dressed in haste and not looked in a mirror before coming out. Poor man, it would not after all be difficult to be kind to him. He stood up as she came in, and he seemed very unsteady on his feet, so that she hastened to sit down.

'Lady Peter, I didn't know to whom to turn . . .'

'Can I offer you coffee, Mr Warren? Or a drink? You look all washed up.'

'No; I . . .'

'I am so desperately sorry to hear of your loss,' said Harriet, offering a cigarette. Mr Warren's hands shook as he lit it.

'This is the worst thing that could possibly happen,' he said. 'Worse than prison. When I thought prison was the worst possible thing I was very wrong, very wrong indeed. If I could go back to prison and have her still alive . . .' He began to weep.

What can I say? thought Harriet. To lose a child probably is the worst thing that could happen to any parent; a horrible inversion of the normal course of nature. To lose an innocent child to violence gave it a loathsome and intolerable twist. How can I possibly comfort him? she wondered, and why has he come to me? I hardly know him.

'Lord Peter is so clever about crimes,' Mr Warren was saying, 'and you were so kind to me when we were here the other day, I thought you would be bound to know what to do, how to advise me . . .'

'I will give you any help I can,' said Harriet, gently.

'You see, it is my fault,' he said. He spoke

bleakly, and suddenly calmly, looking at her hollow-eyed.

She was floored for a moment. 'When someone dies the people around them often think themselves in some way to blame,' she said.

'No, but really,' he said. 'It is my fault and I know who did it. But I don't know what to do now.'

'Mr Warren, if you know anything about your daughter's death, you must go at once to the police, and tell them,' said Harriet.

'The police,' he said, shuddering visibly. 'Lady Peter, I cannot face the police alone. Without a friend . . . I am sure you, of all people, must understand me in that.'

'A lawyer would go with you,' said Harriet, 'and see fair play.'

'Lady Peter, I am ashamed to say this, I who was used to the best of everything, and could command the services of anyone I needed, but I can't afford a lawyer. I haven't a penny in the world above my fare back to Beachington, third class.'

Harriet was flinching with embarrassment at the thought that perhaps this old reprobate had come to borrow money. If he had, he would have to be given it, naturally; but . . .

'Surely, Mr Harwell would help you . . .'

'I can't ask him for another penny,' said Mr Warren. 'I have asked him for money in season and out, quite large sums, Lady Peter, and on an almost daily basis, until he is weary of me, until

even his generosity is exhausted, and he has begun to ask why I need it. I have been reduced to
inventing losses on horses and cards, and even
from pickpockets. And now Rosamund is dead,
why should he? While she was alive, I could
square my conscience about it, Lady Peter; because it was for her sake. It was not my fault that
I had lost everything, and could not protect her
myself. And Laurence would never have grudged
the money had he known it was to protect her.'

'Protect her?' said Harriet. 'Against what?'

'Harm,' he said. 'Death. They were threatening
to disfigure or kill her.'

'Are you telling me someone has been blackmailing you?'

'Oh, Lady Peter,' he said, 'I have been so afraid!
And now the worst has happened, and I don't
know where to turn!'

'You absolutely must go to the police,' said
Harriet firmly.

He was silent. He just sat before her, stubbed
out his cigarette and bowed his head. Harriet
rapidly weighed up the situation. Whatever could
have happened to him in a police station to make
him as reluctant as this to do what he ought to
do? A police station, as she remembered all too
well herself, is a deeply hostile and unpleasant
place in which to be if you are accused of something, but it is not yet a crime in this country to
be a victim of blackmail.

'They said they would kill me if I went to the
police. They said I would be seen at a police

station, and they would know . . .'

So that was it.

'Mr Warren, I think what we had better do is ask Chief Inspector Parker to come here,' she said. 'Your tormentors cannot be watching this house.'

'Whatever you say,' he muttered.

Harriet stepped out of the room, going to the telephone, and met Peter on the stairs.

'Peter! Never have I been gladder to see you,' she said.

'What's up?' he asked.

In a rapid undertone, Harriet told him.

'Whew!' he said. 'That's another silent dog. Look, you are quite right, the thing to do is to get Charles here as soon as possible. I hope he hasn't gone straight back to Hampton after seeing me this morning. You go and sit with old Warren for another minute or two, and I'll call Scotland Yard, and come and join you. Can you bear that?'

'It's the least I can do,' she said. 'Don't be long.'

Mr Warren, having been found to be famished and sleepless, had been given lunch and a bedroom to rest in before Charles, who had indeed been in Hampton, arrived. Bunter had been deployed to give the old man a shave, and tidy him up a bit, and he looked steadier and calmer when he joined the Chief Inspector and Peter in Peter's little office.

'I understand you would like to make a statement, sir,' said Charles.

'Yes, I would,' said Mr Warren. 'That is, I would if Lord Peter is to be present. I know to my cost how easy it is for an innocent form of words to be twisted out of all recognition. Indeed, if I had not been traduced by an unscrupulous policeman, my daughter would be alive today.' His voice shook.

'Try not to upset yourself, Mr Warren,' said Peter. 'Chief Inspector Parker is an excellent man, and will certainly not misinterpret what you say. Trust me for it.'

'But you will stay? You won't leave me alone with him?'

'Yes, if you wish me to, I will stay.'

'Begin right at the beginning, if you would,' said Parker.

'That terrible prison,' said Warren. 'There were awful people there. I know I deserved some punishment, but not to be put among people such as that! I was very frightened nearly all the time. They were *violent* people, Lord Peter. Capable of anything.'

'And someone in particular?'

'I blame myself, I do indeed, for having spoken of my daughter in company such as that, but there were long hours to fill in dismal surroundings, and inmates did come to tell others why they were inside, and about their families and former lives. I had a picture of Rosamund that I showed to many people. I was so proud of her. She was so beautiful . . .'

'So quite a few of your fellow-inmates would have known that Rosamund was your daughter?'

'I didn't think anything about it, you see, at the time. Then of course when she got married she was in all the newspapers. Her picture was on the front page of the *Daily Yell*, and in *The Times*, and . . . I thought our troubles were over. And my son-in-law was so good to me. He's a real gentleman. Generous to a fault.'

'So what happened next?' Charles prompted.

'A horrible man turned up. Someone I knew in prison. He followed me home at Beachington, and forced his way into the house. And he said . . . he said . . .' Mr Warren paused to collect himself. 'He asked for money. For five hundred pounds. Otherwise they would get my poor Rosamund.'

'What did you do?' asked Peter.

'I paid him, of course. I knew only too well what people like that might be capable of. I drew out all my little savings. I told him it was all I had.'

'And that didn't stop him, of course,' said Peter in disgust.

'No, it didn't. When he came back I told him I couldn't pay another penny, and he said of course I could find the money, with a rich son-in-law like that. And if I didn't . . . So I asked Laurence for money.'

'How much did you ask for, sir?' said Charles.

'Fifty pounds. Sometimes a hundred. It went on and on. I had to keep making up reasons. I pretended that I lost money on horses, because Laurence seemed to understand that. I sold all my little souvenirs from my past life. I sold my poor dead wife's wedding ring; but it was for Rosamund, she would have forgiven me. It was getting terribly difficult. I kept coming to London, although I'm sure Rosamund wanted to be alone with her husband — well, it's only natural, isn't it? — not that she ever said anything, but I felt safe in London. They couldn't come to the Park Lane flat, with those porters always in the lobby. Of course, Rosamund was safe in the flat too, but she went about such a lot, shopping, and to the theatre and . . .'

'You said "they" just now,' said Wimsey. 'Were there more than one of them?'

'He had a huge big friend,' said Warren, miserably.

'You didn't tell Mr Harwell what was going on?' asked Charles.

'I was afraid he wouldn't help me with money any more if he knew. He would go to the police.'

'And they threatened you with awful consequences if anyone went to the police,' said Charles, sighing. 'Did your daughter know about it?'

'No!' exclaimed Warren. 'How could I tell her a thing like that? She thought she had been rescued and carried off to a life of wealth and ease. She hated having a jailbird for a father, although she stood by me. How could I tell her that my past deeds had led to this?'

'All right, sir. So nobody knew but yourself?'

'Nobody. And the dreadful thing is, the last time they came I didn't give them anything. I hadn't anything to give them. Laurence said, the last time I asked him for money, "Make this last, Dad, because I'll be a bit tight for a while." So when that was gone I was stuck. And they were very angry.'

'So when you heard that Rosamund had been attacked . . .' said Charles.

'I knew it was them. Yes.'

'We will need to know who they are,' said Charles.

'That's just it!' he cried. 'I don't know! You don't suppose they gave me their real names and addresses, do you?'

'All right, sir, keep calm,' said Charles. 'Just tell us quietly what you do know. Anything that will help us to find them. Did they threaten you in writing? And have you kept any of the notes?'

'They just came and spoke to me,' said Warren. 'It was all by word of mouth.'

'But exactly who came?' said Peter.

'Two men. A little one like a ferret, thin and mean-looking. He was called Streaker in prison. Even the warders called him that. I wasn't to know that I would need to know his proper name. And a big man, very big.'

'What was the big one called?' asked Charles.

'The big one was called Basher. Streaker said, "Cough up or Basher will have to do his stuff." That's all I know.'

'And they visited you at Beachington to make threats, and they collected the money at the door? You didn't have to send it anywhere?'

'No. They just came. It got so I was terrified to open the door at all.'

'Was it always cash you gave them?'

'It had to be cash. Old notes. That's what they said.'

'Do you know how much altogether they got from you?'

'Several thousand pounds,' said Mr Warren miserably. His voice had dropped to a whisper.

'You can give us a good description of these two, I take it?' said Wimsey. 'Did anyone but you ever see them?'

'Yes,' said Warren, 'my neighbour. She said once or twice I had funny-looking friends. I thought she had found out I was a jailbird.'

'Well, it doesn't matter what she thought,' said Parker, robustly, 'only what she saw. Look, sir, you must come down to the Yard with me, and make a proper statement, including full descriptions.'

'You really had better,' said Wimsey firmly. 'You can see that Inspector Parker is a gentleman, and he won't take advantage of you. And then afterwards, I don't think you had better go back to Beachington, and perhaps it wouldn't be a good idea to stay in Harwell's flat, when he's in such a distressed state.'

'So am I, Lord Peter, so am I.'

'Of course you are. Very natural. I was going

to suggest that you let me find somewhere safe and comfortable for you to stay until this is all sorted out, and we have got your threatening friends under lock and key. What do you say? Will you leave it to me? The Chief Inspector will send you back here in a taxi when you have made your statement.'

Mr Warren began stumblingly to express gratitude.

'No, don't bother to thank me, old chap, just dredge your memory for any little thing that might help the police.'

'My dearest, I'm so sorry. I can't think what the old fool was thinking of, coming to you like that.'

'Coming to the only other jailbird in his circle of acquaintance? You can hardly blame him.'

'That's what I was afraid of. Are we never going to live that down?'

'It's always going to be there, Peter, isn't it? It's going to jump out at us from time to time, for as long as we live, I'm afraid. We'll just have to accept it. It's like your shell-shock nerves: we can forget it for most of the time, but when it happens we just have to cope with it.'

'I can't tell you how pleased I am to hear you say "we" in such a context.'

'There aren't any singular contexts left, now.'

He smiled at her.

'What will you do for Mr Warren, Peter? Might he really be in danger?'

'Probably not. Blackmailers don't like to kill the milch cow. That's why, for all the sinister nature of his story, I don't think . . . There's a reformed burglar of my acquaintance. A Bible-thumping, hymn-singing, high-minded Salvation Army officer with a sensible wife. Helped me get a safe burgled once when a lot depended on it. A lot of his congregation are reformed villains, and some of them have plenty of brawn. You might remember him, Harriet — Mr Bill Rumm. He came to our wedding.'

'Yes, I remember him perfectly.'

'I shall place Warren with him as a paying guest, and make sure they keep an eye on him.'

'Is it far?'

'The East End. Safe as in the African jungle. People don't stand out there the way they do in the country. He'll be all right.'

'The endlessly resourceful Lord Peter,' she said, smiling. 'You're sure they won't teach him safe-breaking?'

'He might be less of a menace if he had a profession. Talking of professions, Harriet, I expect he cost you the whole morning's work. I've been meaning to ask you how it's going.'

'Not well, I'm afraid.'

'Is there a reason, other than the incursions of policemen and criminals, and the vagaries of the muse? I would hate it, simply hate it, if it proved difficult for you to write as my wife. I don't want you heading for the divorce courts, or the gin bottle.'

Harriet stopped herself, just in time, from uttering an anodyne 'of course not'. Peter deserved the truth. 'I think there is a reason,' she said thoughtfully, 'and it is connected with being married to you.'

She saw him blanch.

'It used to be a simple thing to do,' she said. 'I needed the money. It was my chosen trade. I didn't have to question it, I simply had to write, or starve. And now, of course . . .'

'You don't have to. As my appalling relatives have gone out of their way to point out to you. But, Harriet, I didn't think you wrote for money *simplissime*. I always thought the money made it possible for you to write. And that writing was important to you in itself. I never doubted for a moment that you would go on.'

'You married a writer, and you want a writer to be married to?'

'I want you, whatever you are. I thought you were a writer to your marrow bones; was I wrong?'

'I think you were right; but just the same it isn't simple any more. When I needed the money, it justified itself. It was a job of work, and I did it as well as I could, and that was that. That was enough. But now, you see, it has no necessity except itself. And, of course, it's hard; it's always been hard, and it's getting harder. So when I'm stuck I think, this isn't my livelihood, and it isn't great art, it's only detective stories. You read them and write them for fun.'

'You underestimate yourself, Harriet. I never thought to hear you do that.'

'Normally I have the pride of the devil, you mean?'

'The pride of the craftsman, yes.'

'There can be intricate and admirable craft in entirely frivolous objects, Peter,' she said. 'Like those cufflinks, for instance.'

He was wearing jade cufflinks carved intaglio with the Wimsey mice. 'Frivolity can give a good deal of pleasure,' he said, mildly. 'But I don't like to hear you call detective stories frivolous.'

'But aren't they? Compared to the real thing?'

'What do you call the real thing?'

'Great literature; *Paradise Lost*; novels like *Great Expectations*, or *Crime and Punishment* or *War and Peace*. Or on the other hand real detection, dealing with real crimes.'

'You seem not to appreciate the importance of your special form,' he said. 'Detective stories contain a dream of justice. They project a vision of a world in which wrongs are righted, and villains are betrayed by clues that they did not know they were leaving. A world in which murderers are caught and hanged, and innocent victims are avenged, and future murder is deterred.'

'But it is just a vision, Peter. The world we live in is not like that.'

'It sometimes is,' he said. 'Besides, hasn't it occurred to you that to be beneficent, a vision does not have to be true?'

'What benefits could be conferred by falsehood?' she asked.

'Not falsehood, Harriet; idealism. Detective stories keep alive a view of the world which ought to be true. Of course people read them for fun, for diversion, as they do crossword puzzles. But underneath they feed a hunger for justice, and heaven help us if ordinary people cease to feel that.'

'You mean perhaps they work as fairy tales work, to caution stepmothers against being wicked, and to comfort Cinderellas everywhere?'

'If you like. Or as belief in ghosts used to work. If you thought you might be haunted by Grandfather's ghost unless you carried out his last will and testament; or if you thought the ghosts of murdered men walked the night howling for vengeance.'

'You have rather an exalted view of it, Peter.'

'I suppose very clever people can get their visions of justice from Dostoyevsky,' he said. 'But there aren't enough of them to make a climate of opinion. Ordinary people in large numbers read what you write.'

'But not for enlightenment. They are at their slackest. They only want a good story with a few thrills and reversals along the way.'

'You get under their guard,' he said. 'If they thought they were being preached at they would stop their ears. If they thought you were bent on improving their minds they would probably never pick up the book. But you offer to divert them, and you show them by stealth the orderly world in which we should all try to be living.'

'But are you serious?' she asked.

'Never more so, Domina. Your vocation seems no more frivolous to me than mine does to you. We are each, it seems, more weighty in each other's eyes than in our own. It's probably rather a good formula: self-respect without vanity.'

'Frivolity for ever?'

'For as long as possible,' he said, suddenly sombre. 'I rather wish the Germans were addicted to your kind of light reading.'

10

We owe respect to the living; to the dead we owe only truth.

VOLTAIRE

'It's an odd thing about this case,' said Chief Inspector Parker to his companion. 'Everyone is devastated. Everyone is distraught about the death of the victim.'

'Yes, you're right,' said Peter Wimsey. He was sitting in the worn leather armchair in the Chief Inspector's office.

'Usually a murder victim turns out to have been not much loved,' said Charles. 'There are almost always people who, while not quite uninhibited enough to say so openly, are far from sorry that the deceased will trouble them no more. Just as there are usually people around with a motive for preferring the victim dead. Or else the victim is somebody friendless, vulnerable to attack.'

'And this time we have a rich and beloved young woman whose death leaves everyone who knows her shattered and incoherent with grief? What does that suggest to you, Charles?'

'Well, it might lend colour to the theory that the Sunbury attacker is responsible. That kind of random attack could strike someone with no enemies.'

'Yes, it could. But Harriet tells me that if we put such a crime into a novel nobody would believe it. She has a point, don't you think?'

'I'm afraid I don't read detective fiction,' said Charles stiffly.

'No; well, I expect all those tomes of theology make just as good an ethical training,' said Wimsey. 'What did you make of Mr Warren's blackmailers, by the way?'

'He had certainly believed in them himself. He was genuinely frightened.'

'Yes, he was, poor old duffer.'

'But when a blackmailing case has led to violence it is, in my experience, almost always a case of the victim turning on the tormentor rather than the other way about.'

'I suppose,' said Wimsey thoughtfully, 'it is possible to imagine — suppose that the money dries up, and the blackmailer wants to turn the screws a bit. So he or they decide to frighten Rosamund, perhaps to leave a mark on her, because didn't Warren say they had threatened disfigurement? And then it went wrong.'

'If they meant to disfigure, they would have used a knife, or a cigarette lighter,' said Parker.

'If they just meant to terrify her, and then they held on a moment too long, or seized her throat in the wrong spot . . .'

'It's possible, I suppose. I think they did turn up at Hampton, by the way, because Warren's description corresponds fairly closely with one of the non-regulars spotted by the ticket collector at the station. We have a search out for a pair of that description all over the country. When they turn up we can question them, but I don't think . . .'

'Neither do I,' said Wimsey.

'Meanwhile, something else has come up. We took a formal statement from the night porter at Hyde House, a Mr Jason, and in the course of making it he remembered that somebody had been asking for Mrs Harwell at about five. He was not yet on duty himself; he was having a cup of tea and a gossip with the day porter. The day porter let the visitor into the hallway, and he said he was calling on Mrs Harwell. So he was told that Mrs Harwell was away for a few days, and he got quite agitated. He said he was a friend of the family, and he had an urgent message for her, and asked for the address to which she had gone. Well, the day porter was not sure he should give it, so he and Mr Jason consulted together, and decided that since the gentleman looked quite respectable, it would be all right to give him the address. Mr Jason didn't think anything of it at the time; only when we asked if anything unusual had occurred that evening did he remember it.'

'I take it he could give you a description?'

'Between the two we have a good description. And it matches one of the descriptions given by the ticket collector at Hampton station. A person not being a regular traveller from Hampton station, who arrived on the evening of the 27th of February and was not seen to catch any train back to town that night.'

'Curiouser and curiouser, Charles. The person cannot be Mrs Harwell's mysterious supper guest, surely; for if she had invited him she would have given him the address.'

'Well,' said Charles, 'I suppose he just about could be the guest, having misunderstood and supposed he was bidden to supper in Hyde House . . .'

'No, Charles; he was too early at Hyde House; he was in that uncomfortable gap between tea and gin and tonic, and much too early for dinner. And he couldn't have just mislaid the address, could he? Because if so he would surely have told the porters so. I don't think he was the expected guest. Have you put out a search for him?'

'I'm about to. We've just got the description typed up, and an artist's impression made.' Charles handed the poster across the desk to Wimsey.

'You don't have to mount a search,' said Wimsey. 'I know who this is. It's Claude Amery. Haven't you turned him up yet? By the way, Charles, I have to apply my mind to something else for a few days. Don't do anything silly while my back is turned.'

'Harriet, I'm afraid I have an urgent job to

attend to today. I hope to be back in time to escort you to the Shearman party, but I must complete the errand however long it takes me. Will you go as arranged? I'll join you there if I can.'

Harriet looked up from the morning paper. 'Of course, Peter. I was thinking of working in the London Library today anyway.'

He hesitated in the breakfast-room door. Then he came across and kissed her lightly on the cheek.

I wonder what that was about? thought Harriet. Something important, obviously. No doubt Peter would tell her about it, by and by. She turned her attention to work.

Her life had turned inside out, she considered. Before she married Peter her professional life had been relatively easy, and private life was full of intense, seeming insoluble difficulties. She had been compelled to keep parts of herself firmly locked away, and manage like a motor engine running on only half its cylinders. And now her private life was almost ridiculously easy, she was waited on hand and foot, and the inner tigers were sleek and purring and prosperous, and as if to maintain some secret fundamental balance, as if to modify the 'happily ever after' cliché, and keep it in the realm of the real, work had become impossibly difficult.

Defying Miss Bracy, who was knitting in a meaningful fashion, working an increasingly elongated sweater, Harriet stared out of the window, her fountain pen idle in her hand. Miss Bracy's knitting advanced in inverse proportion to Harriet's manuscript, and if this dawdling went on much longer the unfortunate secretary would be able to clothe a regiment of relatives. Harriet applied herself to analysing the problem. A detective fiction, she told herself, might be born in a moment of inspiration, but it had to be worked out with almost scholarly calm and detachment.

Very well; but the sort of calm and detachment which had done very well in the past was less than adequate now. Her new approach had begun with Wilfred, that self-lacerating character, of whose agonies — for they had entailed agonies of her own — Peter had said, 'What does it matter if it makes a good book?' The blackness and despair in the book she was writing now had surprised her; clearly it was a subject she had not been able to afford to write until she herself was safely anchored 'out of the swell of the sea'. But that very safety had changed the rules of the game; it was now worth writing only if the result was very good. How good did it have to be? There was no limit.

If Peter thought that the job was to project a dream of justice, an ideal that had to be kept alive in a very unjust and dangerous world, then the first thing she had to do was to convey the disruption, the hideousness of murder, 'murder most foul, as in the best it is', the intolerable violence done to rightful expectations. Harriet's readers ought to feel *desperate* to see the thing put right; not as in puzzle-solving, but with real need. And so the first thing she had to do was to make the body in the reservoir more than a conundrum, to make the victim pitiful, and real.

In real life, Harriet told herself, murder was dreadful in this way. Even the death of deplorable people, like her sometime lover Philip Boyes . . . Harriet found, fascinated, that she could hardly remember Philip now; his face and voice and tiresome demands had faded into oblivion, and she recalled him chiefly as the source of her own danger, and of her debt to Peter. Rosamund, then — ah, yes, poor Rosamund! Still probing her trains of thought, Harriet reflected that she could never have felt much liking for Rosamund alive. Rosamund alive was a pattern of all that Harriet disliked in a woman. Rosamund dead, however, was a different thing. Her death evoked a free flow of Aristotle's cathartic emotions, pity and fear. And, after all, there had been something poignant about Rosamund; Harriet found herself wondering if the disapproval she had felt for the silly woman was sharpened by her own rejection of any such life for herself.

Meanwhile — surely Miss Bracy's needles were clicking louder than ever! — to work. A morning's work, and as good as she could make it. Even her work was put to the test of Peter's opinion. Where had he gone? she wondered. She missed knowing where he was, that intangible sense that he was somewhere in the house . . . Oh, come! she told herself, crossly, and bent her mind to the task.

The first person Harriet saw as she entered the crush in the foyer of the Sheridan Theatre was Henry Drummond-Taber, in conversation with Sir Jude Shearman. And over there Miss Gertrude Lawrence was talking to Noël Coward. If ever society was rightly described as glittering, then this party glittered. The red plush walls and spectacular chandeliers of the Sheridan's foyer, the twinkling champagne glasses offered around on silver trays, the photographs of stars of stage and screen mounted on the walls in silver frames, all sparkled back at the guests. Everyone was in black; that was expected of them, although the new King had shortened the period of mourning to six months. But if you must appear in black, then you may be forgiven a scatter of sequins, and some diamond paste. Harriet had donned one of her white collars, ruthlessly suppressing a twinge of reluctance. She had left her rubies at home; Sir Jude's party would have as many old friends as new ones in attendance, and a show of wealth might look unnecessarily triumphalist.

She was glad to see Drummond-Taber, but he was at the far side of the room. Amaranth Sylvester-Quicke was bearing down on her, and pinning her to the spot.

'Lady Peter! How delightful to see you here. Where is Lord Peter?'

'Unavoidably detained,' said Harriet, diplomatically. Nobody gave information willingly to Miss Sylvester-Quicke, but she was in fact telling all she knew.

'How very right of you to come without him. I do think it's rather ghastly when married people go around together all the time. It didn't do the Harwells any good, did it? And how is the dear Duchess, your sister-in-law?' The woman was looking malevolently at Harriet. 'Such a stickler for propriety.'

'She was well when I last saw her,' said Harriet, taking advantage of the arrival of a young man at Amaranth's elbow to extricate herself.

'Well, I don't know,' she heard the theatre critic of the *Daily Yell* confiding loudly to his companion. 'I'm told the dress-rehearsal was a shambles . . .'

'They always are, darling, they always are . . .'

Harriet manoeuvred her way across the room.

'Ah, Lady Peter!' exclaimed Sir Jude Shearman. 'How good to see you. You will be impressed by the play tonight, I'm sure you will. Lord Peter could not come?'

'Alas, no.'

'Is he involved in this dreadful Harwell business? Perhaps one should not ask. Poor Harwell had troubles enough, without this.'

'Did he?' said Harriet.

'I'm only guessing, mind. But the fellow has a cloth ear for a play. And I would have thought he was over-stretched. He had to postpone his new production, you know, on account of the

King's dying. He had a lot of things on the boil already, without backing Amery's play. I would have liked to look at that myself. I'm sorry it didn't come my way.'

'I always thought Laurence Harwell had inherited a good deal of money,' said Drummond-Taber, who had arrived at Harriet's elbow, and had been listening.

'But then, I suppose plays cost a lot to put on,' Harriet said, as though she had only just thought of it.

'Oh, yes, certainly. A rich man's game,' said Sir Jude. 'You can have a fortune tied up in a production, and not a penny coming in until the first night. Now you mustn't think that I know more about Harwell's affairs than I ought to. One of my contacts in the City mentioned that Harwell was trying to raise a little wind, that's all.'

At that minute a theatre usher came up to Sir Jude, and whispered in his ear. 'Excuse me a minute, won't you?' he said, and went off through a baize door.

Harriet turned to Drummond-Taber. 'It's good to see you, Henry.'

'You're looking well,' he said gloomily. 'Positively glowing.'

'You don't sound pleased,' she said, laughing. 'Do you prefer your authors downtrodden?'

'Rather. Just the place for them. Poor, hungry, frantic for the advance. Seriously, Harriet . . .'

'Seriously, Henry, I am hard at work.'

'I am very glad to hear it. Keep your nose firmly

to the grindstone. No coming out to parties like this; eschew the dizzy whirl.'

'Tyrant!' said Harriet amiably, as the foyer bell announced the first act, and the party streamed through into the auditorium to take their seats.

Just before curtain-up, Sir Jude Shearman appeared between the curtains. He was greeted by a little sporadic clapping, but he gestured for silence.

'I deeply regret, ladies and gentlemen,' he said, 'that Miss Gloria Tallant is unable to appear tonight. Her part will be played by Miss Mitzi Darling, the understudy. Miss Darling will be appearing for the first time on the London stage, and I hope you will give her your warmest welcome.'

He stepped back between the curtains, which rose on a scene in a station waiting-room.

The understudy had certainly seemed a little nervous at first, but she had carried it all off perfectly well, and been rewarded with gales of applause. Harriet, riding home in a taxi into which Henry Drummond-Taber had handed her with a show of gallantry, reflected that she had quite enjoyed the evening, in a way. It made her feel as though she were revisiting her old life, going somewhere like that without an escort. Peter had not turned up. She expected to find him at home, but he had not returned. Surprised at the sharpness of her disappointment, she settled down beside the fire with a book to wait up for him.

It was nearly midnight when the telephone rang. She jumped up, to get to it before Meredith roused himself. 'Hold the line, please,' came the operator's voice. 'I have a call for you from France.'

Uncle Paul? wondered Harriet, astonished. Then Peter's voice came through, faint, and sounding hurried.

'Harriet? You're not in bed.'

'No. Where are you, Peter?'

'In a dim little pension outside Paris. No getting back tonight; and I don't know about tomorrow. I haven't succeeded yet. Look, don't worry about me, Domina. Go to bed. You'll be all right without me for another day?'

'Yes, of course. No, of course not.'

He laughed. 'My feelings exactly,' he said. 'I won't be any longer than I have to be.'

'Peter, can I get in touch if I need to?'

'Possibly. The FO would find me. But I'll be back by tomorrow, please God.'

'Dearest . . .' But the line had gone dead. She waited a few minutes in case he had more to say, and rang in again; then she went sorrowfully to bed. How ridiculous, she told herself, to be mooning about like a calf-struck girl, over a lawfully wedded husband! But Peter's absence was sharply painful to her. It must after all be possible to be in love with one's married lord, a question which she remembered once having debated keenly with Eiluned and Sylvia. They had run through their entire catalogue of married acquaintances, and had been unable to reach a conclusion on the matter.

Harriet had two unexpected visitors the following morning. The first was not strictly for her, and she might never have known about her had she not been extra alert, in spite of herself, for the sound of the bell; for steps in the hall, for the thump of the front door closing. If Peter had been in France last night, he could not possibly arrive home before the evening of today; and yet, hearing the doorbell, Harriet went at once to the top of the stairs to see who was calling.

A woman was standing on the black and white marble pavement of the hall, holding a large flat package done up in brown paper and string. She was quietly and smartly dressed, but had not felt the need to go into black: her coat and hat were brown. Why had Meredith not shown her into the drawing-room? She was looking around her with frank curiosity, so in a moment her eye met Harriet's. Harriet advanced down the stairs.

'Can I help you?' she asked. 'I am Lady Peter Wimsey.'

To her astonishment, the woman blushed. 'Oh, lord,' she said, 'Mervyn will never forgive me for disturbing the quality. Should I have come to the back door? Obviously I should.'

'Mervyn? You mean Bunter? I am so sorry, I believe Bunter is with Lord Peter, away from home at the moment. Can I take a message?'

'May I leave these prints for him? They were

wanted urgently, I believe.'

'Certainly,' said Harriet, indicating the ormolu and marble side table that stood against the wall.

The visitor put down her package. There was a pause. Each of them, Harriet realised, was burning with curiosity: the stranger about the house, Harriet about the stranger. The Lady-Peter mask slipped a bit, and Harriet said, 'It's a beautiful house. Would you like to see round it?'

'I'd love to!' the woman replied.

'May I know your name?' asked Harriet.

'Goodness, didn't I say? Hope Fanshaw. Miss Hope Fanshaw.'

'I've heard that name somewhere,' said Harriet, leading the way up the stairs.

'I should hope you had, Lady Peter,' said Miss Fanshaw, producing a card from her little bag and handing it to Harriet. Before she could look at it, Meredith appeared, evidently very agitated.

'Bunter is not at home,' he said, addressing the visitor, and somehow conveying eloquently his dismay that she had escaped from the hall.

'I thought not,' said Harriet. 'Coffee in the drawing-room in fifteen minutes, please, Meredith.'

She saw his eyebrows go up, as he said, 'Yes, my lady,' and the devil got into her. She took Miss Fanshaw on a long and detailed tour of the house before sitting her down in the glories of the drawing-room for coffee.

'You were much more interested in the portraits than most of my guests,' she said, as they settled in facing chairs. 'I always think other people's ancestors take a bit of being interested in; I'm not sure I entirely manage it myself. Though Lord Peter has perhaps enough to overwhelm one rather.'

'It is my trade,' said Miss Fanshaw, simply, whereupon Harriet looked properly at her card.

'*Hope Fanshaw, Portrait Photography,*' it read. '*Weddings, Anniversaries, Investitures. Coming out a speciality.*'

'It's a very different thing though, photography?'

'Yes, it is. But it makes one interested in the question of likeness. I sometimes think it's easier to get a likeness in paint.'

'That's very intriguing. The common opinion would be the other way about.'

'For how many minutes, Lady Peter, would you say you had looked at me this morning? Looked directly, I mean.'

'I don't know,' said Harriet. 'For some third of the time we have been together? Perhaps less.'

'Probably less. There's a taboo of kinds against people staring at each other. Say five minutes; I am certain it has been less, and it cannot have been more.'

'And a portrait painter has a licence to stare, you mean?'

'Indeed, yes. The painter stares for hours together. The camera, on the other hand, is done in a split second. People can appear for a split second in ways that are unrecognisably strange to them, and their friends.'

'So your cunning is to catch the typical moment?'

'One of them. My cunning is required to guess which of the million ways a person looks, considered second by second, is the way they would like to look, and capture that.'

'And there wouldn't always be an answer to the problem, would there?' said Harriet, musing. 'Since a lot of people don't like any of the ways they look. They don't like their own appearance at all.'

'You are precisely right. For one thing, they have never seen it. Everybody poses themselves when they look in a mirror; they don't see what others see. You yourself would be a good example of that.'

'Why me particularly?'

'Because your features are rather plain when at rest; it is animation that gives them beauty. One would need to give prominence to your eyes. You have a certain seriousness in your glance. Will you allow me to photograph you?'

'Certainly, some time. But to revert to what you were saying about a painted portrait?'

'A painting takes time. It therefore contains time. The changing expressions of the subject, the changing light, the trust or mistrust with which the subject regards the painter are all in play.'

'And the result will show somebody not as they actually appeared for any one of the million split seconds that could have been photographed, but as they appeared for an hour, or a week, or a year?'

'As they appeared to the painter, for that time, yes.'

'I have seen a portrait,' said Harriet, musing, 'that showed the sitter in more than one way, all on the same canvas.'

'That sounds very clever and artificial to me. Who was it by?'

'Gaston Chapparelle. I saw it in his studio when he was painting me. I wonder how I shall fare at his hands,' said Harriet thoughtfully. Peter, she remembered, had wanted somebody to show her to herself.

'Oh, he's quite good,' said Miss Fanshaw. 'Better at women than at men.'

'And you, are you the other way about?'

'Not really. I find women interesting. They have more to hide.'

'Really?' said Harriet. 'You should see my husband when he doesn't like the company he is in, or when he thinks it diplomatic to take cover. In fact, that is what I should ask you to do, photograph Peter for me. So far all his pictures are by Bunter.'

'Mervyn is a very good photographer.'

'But perhaps a touch deferential?'

Miss Fanshaw broke into a broad grin. 'I should rather think he might be,' she said. 'Lady Peter, I have taken up too much of your time, I must be going. If you would really like a portrait taken, you can telephone the studio for an appointment any time.'

'It has been very interesting meeting you, Miss Fanshaw. I shall certainly do that.'

As the guest rose to leave Meredith appeared again, palpably panic-struck, to announce, 'Helen, Duchess of Denver, my lady.' And since Helen did not wait to be announced but followed hot on Meredith's heels, the two women passed on the stairs.

'Whoever was that peculiar woman, Harriet?' was the first thing Helen said.

'A friend of Bunter's,' said Harriet incautiously, wondering what it was about Hope Fanshaw's appearance that struck her sister-in-law as peculiar.

'Great Scott!' Helen almost wailed, looking at the coffee tray being borne away by Meredith. 'Harriet, one doesn't *entertain* that class of people!'

'What class of people do you mean, Helen?' said Harriet. 'Miss Fanshaw isn't a servant, she's a professional woman like myself. Do sit down; would you like a drink?'

'No, thank you, Harriet, I can't stay long. I have come to have a word with you, just the two of us, since I understand from the Dowager Duchess that Peter is away.'

So he telephoned to his mother, Harriet thought. I wonder if he told her what this is about?

'Yes. Peter is away,' she said. She waited to see what Helen embarked on. No need to encourage her.

'I had wondered whether to say to you,' Helen began, 'that if you wanted to get rid of Bunter . . . well, it is quite the done thing, you know, for a bride to choose domestic servants for herself. You don't have to keep people on. Many people prefer not to have an old servant around the place, trying to stick to the old regime, and knowing the husband better than they do themselves. And Bunter —'

'Bunter gives perfect satisfaction, thank you,' said Harriet. 'Is that what you came to talk to me about?'

'No,' said Helen. 'That's just by the by. If you don't object to him, of course . . . The thing is, we all quite understand, in your circumstances — your circumstances before your marriage, I mean — that you had to support yourself. No doubt writing detective stories was all you could find to do. But we were naturally hoping that you would let the whole thing drop now. Frankly it came as a great shock to us the other night to hear you discussing keeping your maiden name on your future books now that . . .'

'Would you rather I used my married name?' said Harriet, coldly.

'Peter's wife has no need to work at all,' said Helen. 'No doubt he has not mentioned it to you, being so famously sensitive and tactful, but it's a slap in the face to him to have his wife involved in paid work, even if it were something more dignified.'

'It is idleness that I would myself find undignified,' said Harriet.

'A married woman must consider the reputation of her husband,' said Helen. 'Surely you must see that. You cannot marry Peter for all the advantages of his position, and then flout convention and cast a slur on his name every time you have a wretched book published.'

'Has it occurred to you, Helen, that I might not have married Peter for the advantages of his position? That his position strikes me as a complex of disadvantages, and was responsible in large measure for my declining his offer of marriage for some time?'

Helen coloured up. 'You aren't going to claim to have married him for love?' she said.

'No,' said Harriet. Her voice was deadly quiet and even. 'I am going to claim only that my motives are no business of yours.'

'The standing of the family is very much my business,' said Helen. 'As Gerald's wife I have a duty to concern myself in it.'

'I cannot see that being Gerald's wife puts you in a position to overcome your natural disadvantages as a literary critic,' said Harriet.

There was a silence. Then Helen said, 'Please, Harriet, don't let's bicker. We all need you to let the writing drop and give Peter some children. I was trying to appeal to your better feelings, that's all. If you knew how Gerald worries . . .'

'I take it we are now discussing the reckless conduct of Lord St George, are we?' said Harriet. 'Isn't it rather more your responsibility than mine to provide a back-up heir?'

Helen's face froze, and she looked so bleakly miserable that Harriet was appalled at herself for unleashing her tongue remorselessly, though it had been in self-defence. The Duchess was not an equal opponent in contests such as this.

'You have a better chance both of achieving it and of surviving it than I do,' Helen said.

'I see,' said Harriet.

'So you will do something about it?'

'I am afraid not. As you know, Helen, Peter married out of his class. And among my sort of people a decision to have a child in cold blood to relieve the feelings of its uncle and aunt about the irresponsibilities of its cousin would seem very wrong indeed. No such consideration will influence me. I shall consider Peter's happiness and my own happiness and nothing else.'

'The family will take this very hard,' said Helen. 'They will think the worse of you for it.'

'The family? Are you speaking for the Duke, and for my mother-in-law? In that case I should perhaps report your request, and the answer I have given you to both of them.'

'No, I mean I hoped this conversation might be just between ourselves. Surely it need go no further?'

'Very well, I will keep it to myself. But I shall draw my own conclusions about how far, in that case, you are speaking for anyone in the family other than yourself.'

'You are a very hard-hearted woman,' said

Helen. 'I suppose I should have expected that.'

'Look here, Helen,' said Harriet, 'there doesn't seem to be much prospect of us understanding each other, leave alone liking each other. But we're stuck with each other, wouldn't you say? So how are we going to manage? Wouldn't the easiest thing by far be if we simply agreed to let each other alone?'

'I shouldn't have come, you mean?'

'You are always welcome to call,' said Harriet. 'We can talk about the weather. Look — these American copies of *Death 'Twixt Wind and Water* arrived this morning; would you like one?'

She allowed herself a grin at the Duchess's back, departing hastily with a new Harriet Vane in her hand.

Peter's voice was faint, and crossed with another line, so that little gusts of French cut into his sentences.

'I'm still roaming, Harriet. And I still don't know for how long. Are you all right?'

'Peter, whatever you're worrying about, there's no need to worry about me too. Why shouldn't I be all right? I'm just sitting in the centre, like the fixed foot of the compasses, and doing a little sublunary leaning and hearkening.'

'I'm certainly running obliquely now,' he said. It was a thing she loved dearly in him, the way he caught and returned allusions. 'Has anything come up?'

'Charles hasn't told me anything,' she said, 'if

that's what you mean. But I heard an odd little rumour that Laurence Harwell might be short of funds. It probably doesn't mean anything.'

'No; probably not,' he said. 'But, look, Harriet, get hold of Freddy Arbuthnot, will you, and ask him in strictest confidence what he can come up with?'

'Yes, of course.'

'It's been a lying sort of winter,' he added. 'Look, I must go. I'll telephone to you again when I can.'

In that intensified silence and loneliness that follows on the end of a telephone call, Harriet went to the library to find the *Songs and Sonnets* of John Donne. The 'Valediction Forbidding Mourning' was easy to find; the book fell open at that page. Harriet took the book to bed with her, and fell asleep before she had found what Peter had meant by a lying winter.

11

Hadst thou the wicked skill
By pictures made and mard to kill
How many ways mightst thou performe thy
  will?

JOHN DONNE

The Honourable Freddy Arbuthnot, hearing that
Peter was abroad, and that his help was required,
became insistently eager to take Harriet out to
lunch. Harriet accepted, and found herself being
swept instantly, escorted by a flunkey, from the
portals of the Bellona Club across the road, round
a corner, and down a side street, into a little
glazed pavilion that might once have been a
greenhouse, and that certainly had a different
address from the club. A discreet brass plate announced this to be the Ladies' Annexe. The flunkey pushed open the door; and she was delivered
to a room full of ferns and little round tables and
the welcoming smile of her host.

'I'm sorry about all that,' he said. 'Ladies are
allowed in here, but nowhere nearer the sacred
halls.'

'Don't worry, Freddy,' said Harriet. 'If I was going to take offence, I shouldn't have come.'

'Ladies do sometimes take offence, though,' he said, following the head waiter, who was leading them to a table in the darkest corner of the room. 'Had one here the other day who kicked up a fearful fuss.'

'Good for her,' said Harriet, cheerfully.

'What? Oh, I see what you mean. Well, I suppose the rules will change one day. Now, tell me what you will have, and I'll order some wine.'

'Peter seemed to think you would know,' said Harriet, when they had eventually ordered the meal, and she had repeated the rumour about Laurence Harwell.

' 'Fraid I don't,' said Freddy. 'Might sniff something out, though. Leave it with me for a day or two.'

'Thank you,' said Harriet. 'But can you satisfy my curiosity by telling me how such things as that are sniffed out?'

'Well,' said Freddy, expansively, 'there's always someone who knows something. And, you see, chaps were at school with one, or they had a handy tip-off some time and they owe a bit of something in return — you get the picture. The thing about Harwell is, he's private. His father made a huge pile in the law courts, and with a bit of canny investment, you know. So the son can do what he likes. He doesn't have a board of directors to square, or trustees or anything. He can make money or lose money, and nobody be any the wiser.'

'It must be fairly well known whether one of his plays is doing well, or flopping.'

'Oh, yes. But you see theatre is a wild sort of field. Not like railway stock, or coal, or shipping, where people have a very good idea of what sort of a return you would be getting. Plays are more like horses, don't you know — odds very slippery.'

'But if he were borrowing money?'

'Mightn't mean a thing. Doesn't mean he's lost his fortune, if that's what you're thinking. In fact if he's lost his shirt, he wouldn't be able to borrow money. To him that hath shall be given, that's the banker's motto.'

'And from him that hath not . . .' said Harriet. 'My parents lost every penny they had in an unwise investment.'

'Sorry to hear it,' said Freddy. 'But you know, not everybody went down, even in 1929. You can make money on a falling market as well as on a rising one, if you're fly enough. Now, the most likely thing is that your man was short of cover — till the next settlement day, or something. And he put out his hand for a bit of short-term help. If he did borrow a bit, I should be able to find out. In general terms, that is. Not why exactly, or how much, just that something was borrowed, and maybe from whom. Tell old Peter that I'll keep an ear to the ground.'

'He'll be very grateful,' said Harriet.

'He's got a lot to be thankful for, if you ask me,

even if it didn't come easily,' said Freddy.

'Thank you,' said Harriet.

'I — I'm jolly glad he took the plunge, you know,' said Freddy, colouring slightly, but plunging on recklessly. 'Best thing I ever did, myself.'

'Tell me about Rachel and the children,' said Harriet, and the conversation turned joyfully personal.

Harriet emerged into the street on a beautiful afternoon, softly warm for the time of year. The season had the spring up its sleeve like a badly kept secret. In the park the willow trees had begun to change colour from dead brown to tarnished bronze. The bustle of the streets amused her, and she decided to walk.

'*News, Star* and *STANdard*! *News, Star* and *STANdard*!' yelled the newsboy. 'Missing actress! Read all abaht it!'

Harriet stopped and bought a paper.

A search has begun for Miss Gloria Tallant, who is missing from her London flat. Miss Tallant did not appear for the opening night of Dance until Dawn *in which she was to play the female lead. The alarm was raised when the actress failed to attend the dress-rehearsal on the afternoon of Thursday last, and messengers from the theatre management sent to her address found her not at home. When she had not returned to her flat by the following morning the police were alerted, and a nationwide search set in motion.*

Miss Tallant was last seen at ten in the morning of 1st March. She was wearing a navy overcoat with a fox-fur stole, and a brown hat. The police have appealed to the public for information, and would be glad to hear from anybody who saw Miss Tallant after ten A.M. on the 1st, or who knows her movements in the few days previously. In the absence of Miss Tallant the part of Cynthia in Dance until Dawn *was played by Miss Mitzi Darling. (See our theatre critic, page 6.)*

The piece was accompanied by a photograph of the missing woman: blonde, sulky and beautiful, wearing an off-the-shoulder gown. She had the fashionable looks of the day. An aura of familiarity hangs about famous faces of stage and screen, thought Harriet, dimly reminded of someone: was it Greta Garbo?

Rosamund had not kept the headline for long, she thought wryly. She put the paper in her bag to be scanned in more detail later: she was on her way to her last sitting with Gaston Chapparelle.

'Well, madame, I see there has been *quelque chose d'éclatant*,' he said, when she had settled into the pose for him. It was not a difficult pose: simply standing, with an open book in her hands, and looking towards him. The canvas on which he was working was at an angle to her; she could not see it. 'What has happened? Not a revolution in sewage, I hope?'

'No; this week's topic is decomposition,' said

Harriet mischievously.

'And to that you do not bring the serenity of contemplation that was aroused in you by sewage,' the painter said. 'I repeat, madame, something has occurred.'

'Peter is away,' said Harriet. 'Is that what your gimlet eyes have discovered?'

'But you trust him, *non?* You expect him back, like the faithful Aucassin?'

'Well, yes,' said Harriet, 'I do.'

'Then you will please to contemplate his return. *Ça doit donner un beau regard.*'

Harriet fell silent. It would be easier to contemplate Peter's return if she knew where he was, and when it would be. Somehow she had expected lawful marriage to lay to rest the switchback feelings of a lover's state. And yet she ought really to have known that she would be vulnerable to this degree; hadn't she once told Miss de Vine that if she once gave way to Peter she would go up like straw? Well, here she was, burning away merrily under the ruthless gaze of Chapparelle, whom she was not even sure she very much liked. Certainly being seen through by him made her feel humiliatingly transparent. But what was he seeing?

She turned her attention to the chaos around her. Chapparelle's studio was a sort of material analogue to her life before Peter; in the centre was a clear space, stripped for working. All around, piled against the walls, were heaps and heaps of stuff, shoved aside, discarded, tumbled any old how, so long as it did not intrude on the area needed for easel, canvas, backdrop, and table with rows of paint tubes. Canvasses old and new, props of various kinds, chairs and stools and boxes were piled up with no visible system at all. In one way she felt very comfortable with it. Living in a clear space in the midst of chaos had been a habit of hers. The trouble was that sooner or later one needed to clear it up. She smiled, thinking how now outside her magic working circle, instead of chaos and pain, there was order and light.

'Better,' said Chapparelle. 'But please to smile with the mind only.'

Aminute later he said, 'This secret: I do not believe it is just the *congé du mari*. Something else has changed.'

'There is no secret, Monsieur Chapparelle.'

'Secrets are like that,' he said. 'That there is a secret itself is a secret.'

'If you say so.'

'But certain is I cannot finish today. You must kindly permit me another sitting. Then I can see if anything changes permanently.'

'You are welcome to another sitting without making such a mystery about it,' said Harriet. 'When can I see the result?'

'Not today, I think. When it is finished will be soon enough.'

'But I would very much like to see the picture of poor Mrs Harwell. You must have finished that.'

'*Mais oui;* but I am desolated that you cannot see it. Mr Harwell has taken it already.'

'Oh, poor man!' said Harriet. 'Yes; I can well imagine . . .'

'It is not so *sympathique,* all the same,' said Chapparelle. 'I am surprised by him. He did not like the picture, you see. It troubled him. But all the same he is round here to pay me for it and carry it away, only two days after his wife is dead.'

'Don't you think the loss of his wife in such dreadful circumstances might have made him urgently need the picture?'

'Ah, you do not believe me. You who once tell me I see too much. But a person who does not look at the picture again before he takes it . . . he is in such a hurry he does not even wish me to have it wrapped for him, he just takes it in the car. I told him the varnish was not quite dry, only — *mouillé* — tacky, I think you say. He replies that very well he will carefully not touch it. So it is gone. If it had stayed I would perhaps have touched up some things more a little — but *c'est ça.*'

'I'm sorry to have missed seeing it finished, or very nearly finished. I thought you had caught something about her which I had not then seen, but have seen since.'

'It is my trade, madame.'

'Perhaps I shall see the picture in Mr Harwell's flat some time, when he recovers enough to see people.'

'It must be hoped. He will recover in not too long.'

'He loved her desperately.'

'Oh, yes. We have a rhyme in French, Lady Peter, for playing with plum stones: *"Il m'aime un peu, beaucoup, passionnément, à la folie, pas du tout."* For my painting it was *pas du tout*. He has paid me what I asked him, which was twice the price because he has hurt my pride.'

Walking back through the park, Harriet met Lady Mary, with the two little Parkers. They stood watching the children playing chase round the beds of spring bulbs. Harriet had barely met her sister-in-law, Peter's younger sister. She was aware of the unspoken family tension around the Parkers' marriage. Peter was fond of Mary, though Harriet had heard him refer to her as a little goose, and perhaps even fonder of Charles Parker, his colleague in many hard cases. The Duchess, on the other hand, could not bring herself to mention either Parker or Lady Mary, who had rather conspicuously not been present at the family dinner-party for Harriet that Helen had organised.

In spite of the pleasant spring weather they were having it was rather cold to stand around in the park. Harriet obligingly chased her nephew- and niece-in-law round a crocus patch, and then Lady Mary said, 'Come back to Bayswater for a cup of tea, won't you? Charles is always late, and it does get lonely.'

'Yes, I'd love to,' said Harriet. 'Peter is away, and I find that great house rather overpowering for one. Not that I'm alone, of course!' she added, her sense of the ridiculous intervening.

'No, one isn't,' said Lady Mary. 'It isn't normal life at all. I can't tell you what a relief it is to be done with live-in servants.'

'I've done without them long enough to be ready to enjoy them,' said Harriet.

'Oh, I'm not criticising old Peter,' said Lady Mary. They were walking towards the park gate, in quest of a taxi. 'And I am glad to have run into you. We black sheep of the family must stick together.'

'Are we black sheep?' said Harriet, and finding her hand tugged by the little boy, said 'Baa!' at him, and made him laugh.

'Very unpopular,' said Lady Mary serenely. 'Me for marrying out, and you for marrying in.'

'What about Peter? He has married out as much as you.'

'Helen is afraid of Peter,' said Lady Mary simply. 'And to be perfectly honest with you, so am I.'

'Well, I'm not,' said Harriet robustly.

'Of course not; but then, you're clever. Oxford, and all that. I got sent to finishing school, where I was bad at everything.'

'Everyone at Oxford would have been bad at everything at a finishing school,' said Harriet. She amused herself with a picture of Miss Hillyard learning deportment, or Miss de Vine learning charm.

'Oh, God, what's that?' said Lady Mary.

They were approaching a news-stand. The headline was no longer: 'Society Beauty Murdered', nor even 'Missing Actress'. It was: 'Hitler's Troops Reoccupy Rhineland. Versailles Treaty Defied'.

Harriet bought a paper. The two women tried reading it at once, but the smart wind tugged and folded the paper as they stood, and so Harriet rolled it up to wait till they got indoors. The Parkers had a pleasant, chintzy living-room in which one or two obviously Wimsey things — a lovely Dutch seascape over the mantelpiece, an elegant Louis Quinze secretaire — looked like refugees from another world. The two women spread the newspaper out on the sofa table and read it, heads together.

'Goose-stepping German troops began arriving in the Rhineland at dawn yesterday, seven hours before Hitler announced in the Reichstag that he had ordered the reoccupation of the demilitarized zone, and repudiated the treaties of Versailles and Locarno . . .'

'There's going to be another war,' said Lady Mary. 'We'll have to stop him.'

'I don't know,' said Harriet. 'Half the country is pacifist. And there will be many people saying we were too hard on Germany at Versailles, and he is only taking back his own back yard. Won't we just leave it to the League of Nations?'

'Do nothing, you mean?'

'It will amount to that, won't it? The League hasn't stopped Mussolini, or helped Abyssinia.'

'At least,' said Lady Mary, surprisingly, 'it should teach people that it's the right they have to be afraid of, not the left.'

'It might be wisest to be afraid of both,' said Harriet.

'I worked for the Communists for a bit,' said Lady Mary. 'They aren't anything to be afraid of unless you really are one of the bloated rich. I can't tell you how disgusted I am when very upper-drawer people carry on about the Bolsheviks, when Hitler and Mussolini are so much worse. They're only afraid for their own wretched bank accounts. I hate inherited wealth, it makes people stupid.'

'But it hasn't rotted Peter's brain?' asked Harriet.

'I don't mean Peter, I mean Gerald. Peter didn't inherit most of his — didn't you know? He had a family portion and he's doubled and doubled it over and over by his own efforts.'

'Surely that makes him a wicked capitalist writ large?'

'Oh, I don't know, Harriet, it's all so difficult. You think what an outrage to have all those servants when there are people starving and barefoot in northern cities, and then you think, well, at least your servants have boot leather and a job. But as for people running around supporting Falangists and Cagoulards . . . There are even people ready to suck up to Hitler. And he's such a vulgar little runt!'

'Who do you mean, Mary?'

'I mean Oswald Mosley, and that stupid Unity Mitford,' said Lady Mary.

'You may be right. I don't know anything about them. But the truth is the world is going to divide in two and heaven help people on the middle ground,' said Harriet, sombrely. 'Are you still a Communist, Mary?'

'Oh, no. Not really. But it is such a beautiful idea. Just like the apostles in the Acts, when you come to think of it. I mean, it isn't the Russians I like, it's the principle.'

'I once heard Peter say the first thing a principle does is to kill people,' said Harriet.

A noisy quarrel had broken out between the children while they talked, and Lady Mary pounced on her youngest, and confiscated the disputed toy. 'It's certainly going to be share and share alike *here*,' she declared. 'If you won't share the gun you shan't either of you have it.'

'If only that were true, Mary,' said Harriet.

Just then the front door closed behind Charles.

'You're early, Charles!' cried Lady Mary. 'Splendid. And look who's here.'

'Harriet!' said Charles, advancing and taking her hand in both of his. 'I'm very glad to see you here. Are you staying for supper? I tried to raise Peter today and they told me he's away.'

'I won't stay for supper at no notice,' Harriet said. 'You might be having chops. But I'd love it properly arranged, some time, and including Peter.'

'When he gets beck,' said Charles, 'tell him I'd

like a word with him, will you? We've found Mr Warren's blackmailers.'

Basher and Streaker had been immediately recognisable from Warren's description. The prison authorities had obliged by putting real names to the pseudonyms, and 'wanted' notices had been issued. A sharp policeman in Croydon had spotted the two men when called to a public house to deal with an affray. They were old lags, well known to the police, and Charles expected a good deal of surly refusal to co-operate, and an aggressive mastery of their rights, such as usually characterizes those who have a long-standing professional relationship with the police.

But in the event his first impression had been that the villains were petrified. Charles had taken one look at Basher's beefy countenance and vacant stare, and decided to interview the two together. If not quite simple-minded, Basher was obviously not very bright. Streaker, on the other hand, was the sort of sharp little alley-rat who flourishes on petty crime. Stripped of their nicknames they were Brown and Pettifer, respectively.

'You have been cautioned, I understand?' Charles began.

'Yes, sir.'

'You understand this is a very serious matter. A woman has been found murdered and we have reason to believe you had been issuing threats to inflict GBH on her. You are in a lot of trouble, my lads.'

'We done the blackmail, but we never touched the lady,' Streaker said. He seemed to be physically shaking, holding on to the table to steady his hands.

'Now then, let's take this from the beginning. I understand that you met Mr Warren in prison?'

'Yes, sir. Poor blighter didn't ought to have been in there. Couldn't look after hisself no more than a babe in the wood, Inspector. Got hisself picked on. Cruelty to dumb animals, that's what it is sending a helpless toff to mix with the riff-raff what's 'is Majesty's guests.'

'Warren was bullied in prison, you mean?'

'Tormented something terrible,' said Streaker. ' 'Ad his ciggies pinched, and people laughing when he spoke on account of his snobby accent, and messing up his food; you know what goes on, Inspector. So we took pity on him, Basher and me. Well, I took pity on him, and Basher threw a couple of louts against the wall, just in passing like, and so he got left alone.'

'And so having become his protectors you thought nothing of a little friendly blackmail?' said Charles.

'Not at first we didn't. But he hung around us all the time after that — well, you couldn't blame him what with certain people trying to catch him when Basher wasn't looking — and we had to hear how bloody wonderful his daughter was till we was sick of it. He went binding on and on about it till a saint would of throwed up. You haven't heard him, have you, Inspector? You'd be sorry for us if you had. Gawd, it was a relief when he'd served his time, and we was done with him.'

'Go on,' said Charles.

'Yes, well. A bit after we was out ourselves we seen her in the paper — lovely picture, called Society Beauty, Mrs Laurence Harwell. And I says to Basher, here, ain't that the bird Mr Warren was on about what was 'is daughter? So we bought the paper, and read all about it.'

'And decided to blackmail Mr Warren by threatening to harm his daughter?'

'Don't hurry us like that, Inspector. We might say somethink as we'd regret. He was always telling us as how she was working as a model, and we wasn't interested in that. We wouldn't try to milk a working girl. But the paper said she'd married a rich geezer, so we thought, well, if he's got a rich son-in-law, he oughter be in a position to pay us what he owed us. For looking after him, see? Well, anyone might of thought so, don't you think, Inspector?'

'Did Warren think so?' asked Charles, grimly.

'Didn't seem to mind too much at first,' said Streaker. 'Did he, Basher? Coughed up easy. We thought we was on to a nice little earner. Then he got sticky, and there's where we made our mistake.'

'You got greedy, did you?'

'We told him as we'd get his precious daughter. But we wouldn't have done it. You got to believe me, Inspector, we didn't mean it, only to frighten the old fool. I've seen Basher on the rampage more than once, Inspector, and it isn't a pretty sight, but I never seen him touch a woman, and I don't know what he'd do if I asked him to.'

'And yet, very shortly after your most serious threat against Mrs Harwell, you take yourselves all the way from Croydon to Hampton, and the next day she was found dead.'

'How did you know we was at Hampton?' said Streaker, visibly turning white. 'We deny that. Never been there in our lives.'

'I shouldn't deny it if I were you,' said Charles. 'We have a very good description from the ticket-collector.'

'Now see here, Mr Parker, don't you try pinning murder on us! We didn't have nothing to do with it. It isn't us you're after, it's the maniac in the woodshed.'

Whatever you say for the death penalty, Charles reflected, it doesn't always make the gathering of evidence easier.

'What maniac?' he asked. 'Look here, Pettifer, you have nothing to fear from me if you didn't do it. I might be going to prefer a charge of obtaining money with menaces against the two of you. But as to a charge of murder, if you calmly explain to me what happened, and if your account matches the other evidence we have at hand, it could even be helpful to your defence.'

'Well, Warren began to say he hadn't any more dough,' said Streaker. 'So we began to turn the heat up a bit, just to see if it was honest truth. And we thought if we gave the daughter a bit of a fright, Daddy might suddenly find he had a sock of money under the bed to share with us. You get the picture.'

'Only too well.'

'We snooped round the flats where she lived, and it was no go. Too much security; only one way in, and porters there night and day. But Warren had let slip that he might visit her at Hampton some time, so we went up there and asked around a bit, and found it easy enough.'

'How did you know Mrs Harwell would be there?'

'We didn't. We was going to smash up a few things, and leave a note to say next time it will be you. Only when we got there there were lights, and so we knew there was somebody there. So we hung about a bit in the garden, thinking it might just be a cleaner or someone who kept an eye out when the owners weren't around. The best place to hang around was a shed, down the side of the garden, under the trees, and we was just going in there when we heard him.'

'Heard whom?'

'Dunno who. Someone making a mad sort of gobbling noise.'

'He was very sad,' said Basher, suddenly, surprisingly. 'He was crying, Streaker. That's what it sounds like when you're crying your words out. *He* wouldn't know,' he added to Charles. 'Streaker never cries about nothing.'

'Someone was already in the shed, crying?' said Charles.

'Not just crying, mate, howling. And banging about. And talking gobbledygook.'

'You didn't hear anything of what he was saying?'

'He said, "Blast!" ' offered Basher. 'He said, "Blast! Crack your cheeks." '

'Piffle like that,' agreed Streaker. 'And banging 'is head against the sides of the shed.'

'So what did you do?'

'We was a bit took-aback. We just stood there, and then he burst out of there and run away.'

'What did he look like?'

'Have a heart, Inspector. It was pitch dark. He went past us like a cork from a bottle. 'Aven't got a clue what he looked like. Why don't you ask the ruddy ticket-collector what was so good at describing us?'

'All right. So the maniac ran off. Towards the house?'

'Round it. Towards the road perhaps. We didn't see. We was a bit shaken. We thought maybe another night would be better for our scheme, seeing as how we couldn't make out what was going on.'

'So?'

'So we left. We walked back towards the station, but at the bottom of the road there was a lorry waiting at the traffic lights, and we got a lift.'

'What kind of a lorry?'

'Farm truck. Full of cabbages, going to the

Garden. Took us all the way to town.'

'We should be able to find that,' said Charles. 'Not that that would let you out.'

'You want to find that maniac,' said Streaker. 'That's who.'

'We do; if he exists. A good description would help.'

'What's the good of saying that? I didn't see him; I can't help you. Telling you a fairy story wouldn't help. Look, you got to get us out of this, we never done it.'

'I shan't lay a murder charge this morning,' said Charles. 'A charge of blackmail will be enough to let us hold you in custody.'

'Will the beak give us bail?' asked Streaker, mournfully.

'I certainly hope not,' said Charles. 'The police will oppose it.'

Returning home, Harriet found Bunter in the hall. Or at least a pale simulacrum of Bunter, swaying slightly on his feet, and looking washed up. Since he was holding Peter's coat, she deduced that the master had returned along with the man.

'Your ladyship,' said Bunter, 'they tell me that you were disturbed . . . that is to say that a visitor to me . . . Forgive me, my lady, but she is not such a person as to understand the proper formalities of a gentleman's house . . .'

'It is my house, too, Bunter, and it was perfectly all right. I found Miss Fanshaw a most interesting person.'

'I will make sure that it never happens again.'

'Bunter, you look seriously exhausted. Go to bed. If Lord Peter requires anything tonight, I will see to it.'

'Thank you, my lady,' said Bunter.

Peter was found fast asleep, laid out on the bed still fully dressed. Harriet sat down on the foot of the bed and surveyed her property thus returned to her. Item: a sleek blond head, lightened now by a touch of silver at the temples. Item: a faint web of laughter lines radiating from the corners of the eyes. Item: a hawk's beak nose. Item: a mouth slightly longer than proportional to the face. Her lord and master, she reflected, seemed curiously absent from himself when asleep. He must be one of those people described by Miss Fanshaw, whose features when animated were very different from how they were when at rest. She remembered that he had been sleeping when she first looked at him possessively; they had been lounging together in a moored punt. He would have to wake up to get undressed, but it seemed unkind to hurry him. What was it he had said on the telephone, about a lying winter?

She picked up the book from the bedside. A stray quotation from Peter should always be sought first in John Donne. She found it there, quite quickly.

Methinks I lied all winter when I swore
My love was infinite, if spring makes it more.

262

12

Upon the king! Let us our lives, our souls,
Our debts, our careful wives,
Our children and our sins lay on the king!
                    WILLIAM SHAKESPEARE

All kings is mostly rapscallions.
                    MARK TWAIN

At breakfast Harriet was feeling some kind of
unease. She brushed away the offer of eggs and
bacon and kippers and black pudding, all presented in silver entrée dishes, and stuck to thinly
buttered toast. Her lord and master, who had
woken in the small hours, and celebrated his return in the fashion of the Duke of Marlborough
getting back from the wars, tucked in heartily.
Harriet eyed him warily. She rather hoped the
glow about him represented the aftermath of last
night, and not any aspect of his absence from her.
And about that absence — would he tell her what
it had been about? Before their marriage he had
abruptly disappeared from time to time, on secret
missions for the Foreign Office she had under-

stood; and this must have been another such. She would not have dreamed of asking him about it back then. It would have put him in an intolerable position to have to refuse to tell, and an awkward position if he told. A person who tells a secret, swearing the recipient to secrecy in turn, is asking of the other person a discretion which he is abrogating himself.

This at least, Harriet decided, had not changed. It would be as improper as ever to ask him to tell. She opened her newspaper, to read about the Rhineland. Hitler was offering conditions for peace. She looked at the pages bleakly. Perhaps a diffuse and uncertain fright makes one feel sick? Miss Gloria Tallant, she saw, was still missing. The police were widening their search.

'Will you be working this morning?' Peter enquired.

'I hope so. I mean to try. Unless you need me, that is . . .'

'I will hope to see you at lunch-time,' he said. 'We have a lot to talk over.'

'So, Charles, what's the scoop?'

'Amery has turned up, as you said he would. I have cautioned him and told him he is under suspicion of murder.'

'What has he done to deserve it?' said Wimsey lightly.

'Told us lies about his movements on the evening of the murder; demonstrated beyond doubt a motive for a crime of passion against the woman.'

'What lies has the silly fellow told you?' asked Wimsey.

'Well, at first he said he had never been anywhere near the bungalow in Hampton. He had found Mrs Harwell was not in town, and he had gone home disappointed, and the first thing he knew about anything was when he read it in his paper. But when confronted with the fact that the station-master at Hampton had seen someone of his description arriving at about six thirty on the evening in question, and was of the opinion that the person had not left Hampton by train that night . . .'

'He just might have overlooked him,' said Wimsey.

'Well, in the event, on being told about the sighting, Amery changed his story. He had been down to Hampton, that evening. He had walked up the lane towards the address he had been given, but then suddenly changed his mind about calling unexpectedly on Mrs Harwell, and after walking a little by the river he had gone home on a Green Line bus. Nobody, he thought, would have seen him arrive home that evening. I pressed him a little about the alleged strange conduct, going nearly there, and then not even knocking on the door, and he told us that she tormented him, played cat and mouse with him, and that he had suddenly decided that he couldn't face another episode of her cruelty.

'So then, of course, we asked for his fingerprints. We told him that if he had told us the

truth his prints could not be found in the bungalow, and we would be able to eliminate him from
the enquiry.'

'Whereupon, I suppose, he raised objections?'
said Wimsey.

'No, he didn't. Gave us the prints as meek as
a lamb. And they match the prints on one of the
sherry glasses.'

'So you conclude?'

'Well, Wimsey, he's lying. He might even be
the maniac reported by our two jolly blackmailers
— if there ever was a maniac, that is. The maniac
was howling in the woodshed, and then he ran
off in the general direction of the house, and I
suppose might have broken in. So if it was Amery
wailing in the shed, and if he did go in to the
bungalow, he is probably the last person to have
seen Mrs Harwell alive. And, logically, the last
person to have seen the victim alive . . .'

'. . . is the murderer,' said Wimsey. 'I take it
that you put it to Amery that he had killed her?'

'Oh, yes. We always try for a confession. But
he denies it emphatically. Would have died rather
than harm a hair of her head; adored her, cannot
bear to think of life without her . . . And a lot
more in the same line.'

'So why tell you fibs in the first place?'

'He was frightened and upset. Or so he says.'

'The thing now is to see what he says when
confronted with the prints on the sherry glass,' said
Wimsey. 'It's a pity that poets have such a poor
regard for truth, but he'll have to say something.'

'He has acquired a rather stroppy lawyer who will make sure that he says as little as possible henceforth.'

'I thought he was broke?' said Wimsey.

'Sir Jude Shearman has come forward to pay the lawyer.'

'Has he now?'

'He is apparently interested in Amery's plays,' said Charles, dryly.

'Which are certainly more commercial if he is to be in the news accused of murder,' said Wimsey. 'It's a strange world we live in, Charles.'

'I'll let you know what he says when we interview him again.'

Transcript of interview between Mr Claude Amery and Chief Inspector Parker, 9 March 1936, eleven in the forenoon. Present: the aforementioned and Sergeant Veal, stenographer; Mr Manteau, solicitor.

Amery cautioned.

Chief Inspector Parker: 'Mr Amery, I have to tell you that we know for certain you have been lying to us. Would you like to correct any part of what you have already told us?'

Mr Manteau: 'My client maintains the truth of his statement.'

Amery: 'Yes.'

Chief Inspector Parker: 'I think you should reconsider this statement, Mr Amery. Your fingerprints have been found.'

Amery: 'I might have fingered the door knocker while I was hesitating about going on with the visit or turning back.'

Chief Inspector Parker: 'Your prints are on the doorknocker, as you say. They have also been found inside the bungalow, on the stem of a sherry glass.'

Amery: 'They can't be! I saw her wash them up.'

Manteau: 'I protest. My client is being tricked into making admissions.'

Chief Inspector Parker: 'Would you like to vary your statement, Mr Amery?'

Amery: 'Yes, all right. I shall make myself look a hell of a fool, but here goes.'

Amery then made a statement. When he had signed it Chief Inspector Parker allowed him to leave, having warned him not to leave home without telling the police of his whereabouts, and instructed him to deposit his passport with the police.

Statement made by Mr Claude Amery, Scotland Yard, 9 March 1936, eleven in the forenoon:

I was very anxious to see Mrs Harwell. I had a personal matter of great urgency to discuss with her. On calling at Hyde House for the third time in a day I was told by the porter that Mrs Harwell was away, and I managed to persuade the man to divulge the address, which he had been given to redirect the post. On finding the address I took a train to Hampton, intending to surprise Mrs Harwell. I walked from the station to the bungalow, not wishing to take a taxi, in case it compromised her, since I knew that Mr Harwell was still in town. I arrived at about six in the evening.

Mrs Harwell was not very pleased to see me, and I formed the impression from the laid table, and her general manner, that she was expecting somebody else. However, she offered me a drink, and I accepted a glass of sherry. We sat and talked for some time, during which time she looked several times at her watch. Eventually she told me I would have to go, and showed me out. What with the disappointment at the reception I had received, and the unfamiliarity of Hampton, which I was visiting for the first time, I got lost, and missed the station. I wandered about for some time in the dark, and then had supper in a pub, of which I cannot remember the name.

Here there was a marginal note in Charles's hand. *Description fits the Hare and Hounds according to the local police, although that is some five miles from Rose Cottage. A darts match was in progress at the Hare and Hounds which was very crowded. Nobody remembers a person of Amery's description.*

After having a bite to eat, I was still angry at Mrs Harwell. I wandered about for some time although it had become extremely cold, and when I finally arrived at the station I found I had missed the last train. The thought came to me that while I was cold and stranded, a person unknown was dining alone with Mrs Harwell, and I returned to the bungalow, intending to hang about long enough to discover, if I could, who my rival was. At about eleven o'clock, as near as I could judge, my watch having stopped, I returned to Rose Cottage, and took up a position in the garden, where I could see anyone coming or going. There was a car parked in the driveway, the other side of the garden. I cannot tell what make or model of car it was; I am not interested in cars. Several times I advanced on the cottage, and looked in through the downstairs windows. The room was lit, and the curtains were not drawn, except those of the bedroom. I could see nobody in any of the living-rooms, a fact which led me to draw painful conclusions. It began to rain quite heavily, and I took shelter in the garden shed, from which I could see the lighted window of the bungalow. Unfortunately during my vigil I nodded off, sitting on a deck-chair, and I was woken by the sound of the car leaving.

At that point I went to the door of the house and knocked loudly, and for some time, hoping that Mrs Harwell would admit me for a second interview. I got no answer. I then wandered about for some time, very distressed, returning to the bungalow at about one o'clock in the morning, to try one last time. This time, getting no answer at the front door I walked around the *house to the back, and looked through the windows from the veranda. I saw Mrs Harwell sitting beside the fire. She could not have been unaware of my presence, because I was banging on the window pane, but she did not let me in.*

Finally realising that she did not wish to talk to me, being now very cold, and having spent all my money on the train ticket, and on supper, I began to walk to my mother's house in Barnes, which was considerably nearer than my lodgings in town. This took me most of the rest of the night. Eventually I got on the first bus of the morning going over Kingston Bridge, and arrived in Barnes at around half past seven. My ordeal having given me a severe chill, I took to my bed, and was unaware what had happened to Mrs Harwell until I returned to my London lodgings three days later, and found that the police had been looking for me.

Peter read this carefully several times through, and then took it to show it to Harriet.

'Give me the fiction writer's view of this, would you, Harriet?'

Harriet read it. 'I have some difficulty imagining Claude Amery as a murderer,' she said at last. 'Although he did say . . . I suppose the police will verify all this?'

'It might have been designed to be difficult to verify,' said Peter. 'We could buy Bunter a set of darts, and send him forth to loose them at a target in the Hare and Hounds; but even if he finds somebody who recognises Amery, that will only cover — what — an hour and a half? — of the fatal night.'

'It might be worth doing, just the same,' said Harriet. 'Can Bunter play darts?'

'If he can't it will be the first deficiency in the man I have ever detected,' said Peter. 'Bunter could be sent. But you realise there's a sort of catch to it, Harriet. If the man is lying, he will have made very sure that anything that could possibly be verified in his story will be verified. If he is telling the truth, then it's in the lap of the gods whether anybody will actually remember him or not.'

'As for the rest of the story . . .'

'It could hardly have been made to sound more completely incredible to a policeman if he had been trying.'

'I'm not sure it is incredible to me.'

'Can you say why?'

'I have no other but a woman's reason.'

'You think him so because you think him so?'

'You know, Peter, Claude is rather wet, but he's not stupid. Furthermore, he is a playwright.'

'So if he were to invent an entire scene . . .'

'It would hang together properly. It would be more believable than life. And it would have some dialogue in it; he likes dialogue.'

'You must allow for the literary form of the document. A statement made in a police station is paraphrased as it is taken down by a wooden-faced sergeant with a notebook and slow hand-writing.'

'You mean it may be only approximately what Amery actually said?'

'It should be correct in substance, though it may not be in prose style. The salient point is that it lets out Harwell completely. Can you think of a reason why Amery would do that falsely, and deliberately? Would he incriminate himself to protect the promoter of his play?'

'Surely not,' said Harriet. 'But how does he exonerate Laurence Harwell?'

'Timing,' said Peter. 'If Harwell was banging on the doors of Hyde House a little after twelve, and Amery saw Rosamund alive at about one o'clock.'

'Of course.'

'And in exonerating Harwell he looks likely to put the noose round his own neck. By his own account he was the last to see her alive. And by his own account he was desperate, and thought himself slighted by her. Incidentally, you were going to tell me something he said, just now.'

'She was playing cat and mouse with him, Peter. And he said if it went on he didn't know what he mightn't do.'

'And did you take him to mean he might injure her?'

'No, not at all. I took him to mean he might injure himself.'

'This is an unusual way of committing suicide,' said Peter.

'He can't realise. He must just think you will believe him.'

'Well, Harriet, people who are telling the truth may well expect to be believed, however preposterous the story sounds. And this one doesn't sound preposterous so much as exceptionally difficult to check up on. After all, he wouldn't be the first or last young man to be driven distracted by unrequited love. I'd like to ask him some questions; I wonder if Charles will let me talk to him.'

'What will you ask, Sherlock?'

'Whether he heard the dog barking. There is famously something highly suggestive about a dog that doesn't bark.'

Amery's lawyer had clearly told Amery not to talk to anyone unless he was present. Peter had some difficulty in arranging the interview he desired, and then was obliged to meet Amery in Manteau's offices, where he was confronted by a hostile witness, scowling at him, and poised ready to interject, 'Don't answer that!'

Amery stared at Wimsey with reddened, vacant eyes.

'I am sorry to trouble you, Amery,' Wimsey began. 'I have seen your statement to the police, and there are one or two points I would like you to enlarge upon.'

'My client does not have to answer any questions from you, Lord Peter,' said Mr Manteau. 'You have no standing in the matter.'

'None. I quite agree. But I may just possibly be able to help.'

'What do you want to know?' said Amery.

'I would like to know whether, during your repeated visits to the bungalow during the evening of the 27th, you heard the dog barking?'

'It barked when I first arrived,' said Amery. 'Damn thing was all over me. Rosamund put it in the bedroom.'

'Did it go on barking from there?' Wimsey enquired.

'No. It whimpered a bit, and scratched the door. Then it was quiet until I left.'

'But when Rosamund showed you out it began to bark again?'

'Yes. We passed the bedroom door to get to the front door, and that set it off.'

'Very well. Now later in the evening you returned to the bungalow, and spent some time standing around in the garden and in the garden shed?'

'Yes. I said so.'

'Did you hear the dog barking then?'

'Yes, just briefly. I was afraid it would give me away.'

'You thought that it had detected your presence outside the house, and was raising the alarm?'

'I was afraid so, yes.'

'Was it a good guard dog, then?'

'Heavens, no. Silly brute would bark at anyone, friend or foe alike. It just got excited, that's all.'

'But its barking like that might have made

somebody wonder why. Did it occur to you that it might be barking at somebody or something indoors?'

'No,' said Amery, slowly. 'It didn't. I assumed it was fussing about me.'

'And when you returned to the house for the third time, what then?'

'Well, I didn't hear it then. That's odd, isn't it?'

'That's what I thought. I mean, you seem to have been prowling about, knocking on windows . . .'

'My client —' began Mr Manteau.

'It's all right, Manteau,' said Amery crossly. 'I've already told the police that. What's the good of denying what I've already said?'

'In your own interests —' Manteau began.

'Don't you think I want all this cleared up?' said Amery. 'Lord Peter is trying to help. He must want Rosamund's murderer caught and punished; he knew her.'

'I did have the privilege of meeting her,' said Wimsey.

'And so you must have loved her too! She was the most beautiful person, Lord Peter, wasn't she? How could anyone have borne to hurt her? I'm the last person in the world who would have laid a finger on her; you do believe that, Lord Peter, don't you?'

'It's what can be proved rather than what I or anyone believes that will help us,' said Wimsey. 'So you were close to the house, and walking round it; you knocked at the front door, you entered the veranda, and you peered into the window of the living-room from there.'

'And she was sitting in the chair, taking no notice of me at all. She broke my heart, Lord Peter.'

'But the dog wasn't barking at you then?'

'No,' said Amery, frowning. 'I didn't think of it at the time. Perhaps she had let it out for a run.'

'It would surely have come straight to you, if she had done that.'

'I suppose it would.'

'You said it was all over you earlier in the evening.'

'My client cannot be supposed to be an expert in the behaviour patterns of dogs,' said Manteau.

'No. Well, one other thing,' said Wimsey. 'The sherry glasses. Earlier on Rosamund offered you sherry, and the two of you drank some together?'

'Yes. She had the table laid for dinner, but she just said, "You can't stay long. But since you're here, I suppose you'd better have a drink." '

'So you used two glasses? When you left the house, Mr Amery, exactly where were the glasses?'

'Back in the cocktail cabinet in the sitting-room,' said Amery without hesitation. 'She washed them up while I was there.'

'Did you see her wash them up?'

'Yes. She gave me to understand I was to make myself scarce, and she took up the glasses — there was still a sip left in mine — and she went with them into the kitchen. I was still talking to her, so I followed her, and I stood in the door and she went to the sink and washed the glasses.'

'Did she have any difficulty doing that?' Wimsey's tone was light and neutral.

'Difficulty? Whatever do you mean? She wasn't incapable or anything, just because she was beautiful. She'd had a hard life; she knew how to work. She —'

'Your prints were still on the stem of one of the glasses,' said Wimsey. 'Can you try to remember, very closely, exactly how the glasses were handled?'

'We just drank out of them in the usual way,' said Amery, frowning. 'Then she came across, with hers in her hand, and picked up mine from the little side table by the chair. Of course, Lord Peter, I have been wondering how fingerprints could have remained on the glasses after they were washed up. I thought that policeman had just made up my fingerprints on it, to trap me. But you see, she was holding them both together, by the rims, not the stems.'

'That accounts for your prints being unsmudged on the stem of the glass,' said Wimsey. 'And then?'

'She took them into the kitchen, and rinsed them under the tap.'

'Under the tap?'

'She put them down on the draining board. Then she took them one by one, holding them

278

by the bowl, the way one does to slosh a liquid round in a glass, and swirled the water round in them. Then she put them upside down on the draining board.'

'The tap was running all this time?'

'Yes. Then she wiped the bowls quickly with the glass cloth — very quickly — and walked back into the living-room and put them away.'

'Mr Amery, you are quite sure of the truth of this account?'

'Absolutely. You mean, no doubt, that it's funny any fingerprints survived all that?'

'Fingerprints can be very durable,' said Wimsey, standing up to take his leave.

'You will do all you can to clear this up?' said Amery. 'I am an entirely innocent man, and it's going to ruin me.'

'Oh, I wouldn't say that,' said Wimsey. 'A bit of notoriety is excellent publicity, don't you know.'

'Are you going to ask me where I went?' said Peter.

'I rather thought I had better not,' said Harriet.

'My dear Calpurnia! But though I am not Caesar, you are my wife; and I need to tell someone. Keep it under seven seals, but let me relieve my feelings.'

'Dearest, it is sometimes exceptionally hard to tell if you are fooling about or being deadly serious.'

'This time it's serious, and may even be deadly,'

he said. 'They asked me to recover some state papers. Now you ask me who from.'

'Certainly not. I will consent to ask you from whom.'

'A Babylonish dialect,
Which learned pedants much affect,'

murmured Peter.

'From whom had you to recover them?' said Harriet obligingly.

'From the King.'

'But I thought you said whatever it is had gone astray?'

'The thing is, he's been leading people the hell of a dance,' said Peter. 'The official papers get brought to him every day, and he sometimes looks at them and sometimes not. When he's at the Palace it's all right, because his staff keep a beady eye on secret papers, and they cover his tracks, and they pluck up courage and point out to him that his signature on this or that is urgent. But he goes down to Fort Belvedere every weekend, and he doesn't take his staff with him. And there's a panic out that when the dispatch boxes are at the Fort just about anybody could have a sight of them, and that, not to put too fine a point on it, he has funny friends.'

'Well, but . . .' said Harriet.

'But, Harriet?'

'Well, isn't that a bit exaggerated? I mean, he isn't stuffy, and all those official people round him are stuffy. But it doesn't mean he's showing state papers to a bunch of spies. He's just breaking the chaps-like-us rule, isn't he?'

'Is that how it strikes you?' said Peter. 'Would it strike most people like that? I wonder. Anyway, something desperately important went missing last week. The Palace staff concluded it had gone to the Fort with the King. So someone went down there to fetch it, and he was not let in.'

'Whyever not?'

'The Fort is the King's refuge from officialdom. Nobody on his staff dares show their face there. So a friend of mine — a Foreign Office man who was in my regiment — recruited me to talk my way in and see if I could get the document back; signed if possible, but back anyway.'

'Golly, Peter. But why should you be able to get it if someone on the staff couldn't?'

'Well, there are people I know . . .' said Peter vaguely.

'Go on.'

'When I got there I was shown into the drawing-room. Some of his guests were sitting around playing cards. Nobody asked me to sit down, so I stood in the corner like a dumb waiter. They didn't take any notice of me at all, certainly not so far as to guard their tongues. There were some appalling things being said. After a while I withdrew and asked one of the flunkeys if the King was at church. He smirked and told me the King was worshipping in his own fashion. I told him I had come to collect some papers, and he said,

"Why didn't you say so at once, sir?" and let me into the King's study, and left me there. Harriet, I could have been anybody; he didn't ask for identification.'

'I begin to see what you are worrying about,' said Harriet.

'I couldn't find what I wanted,' said Peter. 'There were dispatch boxes lying about, open, and papers spread everywhere, mostly lying face up. Then the lackey reappeared and said he thought I ought to leave. He said that if what I was looking for was not there, then it must be in the red box that His Majesty had taken with him when he left.

'Left for where? I asked. He did not know, but he thought it was for France. Anyway, to cut a long story short, His Majesty had hopped into his private plane and taken off from the lawns behind the house, and he was carrying a box with him when he went.'

'So what did you do?'

'I didn't know what to do. It was bad enough at Fort Belvedere; the damn thing was dynamite in France. I drove like hell for Oxford, and got Jerry out of bed in the House. Little beast was sleeping off Saturday night.'

'Peter, I don't follow you: what has Jerry got to do with it?'

'Nothing except an entrée to the Oxford University Flying Club. He came up trumps, got me an aircraft and a pilot. Do you remember Reggie Pomfret who fell for you so heavily? Well, your undergraduate admirer, would you believe it, has a pilot's licence, and we flew to Boulogne. Air control there had monitored a plane going over to Paris. Of course it might not have been the King's plane, but it was a Dragonfly. So I thought for a bit. I told myself he could not possibly be going to Paris; how could he go in mufti to Paris, where he is very well known, and would be recognised in two minutes? He couldn't so much as nip from a taxi to a hotel in Paris without being all over the papers, and then the fat would be in the fire. King or not, he isn't supposed to leave the country without telling anyone. So I just thought I'd go and look for him in Breteuil.'

'Where's that?'

'Near Paris; a little way out. I recalled that when he was Prince of Wales, ages ago, he had been sent to Breteuil to learn some French. One of the Breteuil boys was at school with me; I rather got the impression the Prince had got pally with the family. And the Count is a mixer, a political facilitator.'

'And what did you find?'

'Trouble. Fog. Pomfret couldn't find it at first. Then the fog began to lift, and stream away like steam from a kettle, and we spotted the château, and landed on a field in its home farm. Lovely place; absolutely simple and symmetrical, with two lodges in the shape of towers framing the approach. Makes Denver look like a mad architect's dumping ground. So I trudged up the drive;

there's a dry moat round the house and there was a white stag and his doe grazing in it. Unnerving, like some kind of dream. And as I reached the house, there's His Majesty emerging through the door, and a car drawing up for him. And Breteuil standing in the door to see him off. So I had to step up and intercept him and ask him for the thing. And he patted his pockets, and frowned, and then he smiled — he has a most disarming smile, Harriet — and said, "Damn! I've left it somewhere in the house. You'll see to it, Wimsey, I suppose?" '

'And had he left it in the house?'

'Yes, he had. Breteuil made me welcome enough, and we went to look for it. It was still in the dispatch box; I don't suppose he'd even opened it. But it was a relief not to find it lying face up where anyone could take a look at it. Anyway, I pocketed it, and then we found that the fog had thickened up, and we couldn't take off again. We had to hang around all day, and find a hotel for the night. To cut a long story short, we were grounded for three days.'

'So all's well that ends well?' asked Harriet. But something was weighing Peter down.

'There were others staying in the hotel where we found a roof over our heads,' he said. 'Others that I recognised. One of Ribbentrop's aides, for example, and Saxe-Coburg-Gotha. He's been running to and fro between London and Berlin, trading on his English royal connections, and supposed closeness to the Führer.'

'Mightn't that be coincidence, Peter? In a hotel near Paris?'

'Perhaps. Breteuil's other guests included a certain Mrs Simpson. She's the current inamorata.'

He pushed across the table to Harriet a French newspaper, showing a slim, elegant, rather square-faced woman getting out of a car. *'Elle qui sera la Reine d'Angleterre?'* ran the headline.

Harriet looked at it. 'Peter, it's not like you to be censorious,' she said. 'Have you never yourself dashed across to Paris to visit a mistress?'

'Oh, well, perhaps you're right,' he said. 'I must be getting old. But talking of mistresses, Harriet, I have some friends in Vienna who might need a bit of help.'

Harriet thought for a few minutes about the implications of that. She had heard of a certain opera singer . . . 'What kind of help, Peter?'

'Help getting out,' he said. 'The way things are looking, a Jewish family might like rather more than a theoretical border drawn on a map between themselves and Herr Hitler.'

'Of course you must help if you can,' said Harriet.

'I don't suppose she'd want to settle in London,' he said, thoughtfully. 'So you wouldn't have to deal with very much of her. New York would be more her scene. She used to complain bitterly that the theatre she sang in here was full of bad smells and damp Stygian effusions that affected her throat. Singers are awfully hypochondriac.'

'Was she fun, Peter?'

'Tremendous fun. Still is, I have no doubt. And you should hear her sing! Well, you will, unless . . .'

'Unless what?'

'Unless her appearance here should make you jealous.'

Harriet laughed. A deep, spontaneous laugh like a subterranean stream suddenly surfacing.

Peter looked suddenly shaken. 'My dear, I believe I must be making you happy,' he said, huskily.

13

Oh where, oh where has my little dog gone?
Oh, where, oh where can he be?

POPULAR SONG

Every crime has something of the dream about it. Crimes determined to take place engender all they need: victims, circumstances, pretexts, opportunities.

PAUL VALÉRY

'Have you found the dog, Charles?'

'That was sharp of you, Peter. Not exactly. But the blood on the carpet was dog's blood, not human blood.'

The two men were lunching together, in Peter's little office in the Audley Square house, on piles of sandwiches supplied by Mrs Trapp, and washed down by draught bitter brought up from the servants' hall.

'I thought so. Something nasty must have happened to the dog, or it would have barked every time Amery approached, not just on the earlier occasions.'

'That assumes Amery was telling the truth,' said Charles.

'So it does. And he certainly told me at least one whopper. So possibly he told more. Makes one uneasy when a fellow departs from the straight and narrow.'

'I'm afraid he is an obvious suspect.'

'Mmm,' said his lordship, with his mouth full of roast beef and mustard sandwich.

'I expect we shall find the dog, if we ever do, in the river,' said Charles.

'With its throat cut,' said Peter. 'No sign of a bloodstained knife with fingerprints, I suppose?'

'Not a trace, I'm afraid. That's probably in the river, too. We could look for it, I suppose.'

'What about bloodstained clothing? It would have made a dreadful mess.'

'Nothing of the kind found so far,' said Charles. 'There was blood on Harwell's shoes; but then one would expect that, given that he walked around the place before calling the police.'

'It's awfully amorphous, this case,' said Wimsey. 'Nothing to get one's teeth into. Let's survey the possibilities, one by one, shall we, and see if that gets us anywhere?'

'Right-oh,' said Charles. 'Where do you want to start?'

'Start with Harwell,' said Peter.

'He's right out of it,' said Charles. 'Rock-solid alibi. No motive.'

'Well, as you know, old friend, I don't like

motives,' said Peter. 'Toys for the jury. Who can tell a motive? Springing from the deepest secrets of the human heart and all that. Give me a method and an opportunity any time.'

'Even so. Harwell dined at his club, and was seen leaving at nine P.M. He could have walked home to the garages at Hyde House, picked up his car — fifteen minutes would you say? Not more. He could have driven himself down to Hampton, and arrived some time after ten; he could then have driven back to London and raised hell getting into his flat. But he couldn't have killed his wife before midnight, because Amery saw her alive at one o'clock. And he couldn't have left the flat and returned to Hampton in the early hours of the morning, because the porters lock all the doors at midnight and keep them locked until half past six, and you have to get them to let you out, and they didn't let him out. So he didn't leave again until after six thirty the following day. Face it, Wimsey, Harwell is in the clear. And you just can't sweep away motive like that; the man loved his wife, and had nothing to gain from her death.'

'It's been known for someone you love to madden you beyond endurance,' said Wimsey.

'Now who's plumbing the secrets of the human heart?' asked Charles. 'Compare Harwell's alibi with the ramshackle farragos offered by the other suspects.'

'Very well, let's. Our blackmailers.'

'Well, they admit to having been in Hampton,

lurking in the garden, and harbouring ill-intent.'

'But?'

'Well, none of the fingerprints inside the house belong to either of them. And they have a rather nebulous motive. They can't have intended to kill, because Rosamund dead was no use to them at all. They could have attacked her intending to scare her, and held on too hard. Brown is known as Basher, and is what one would call a heavy.'

'Could they have worn gloves about their evil deeds?'

'I suppose so. They're the sort of petty crooks who would know about fingerprints, and whose fingerprints are on record. I expect we could pin it on them, but . . . The thing is, Wimsey, they say they got a lift back to town around midnight on a lorry going to the Garden, and if we found the driver, and if he confirmed their story, then they would have left the scene too early; Amery says he saw Mrs Harwell alive later than twelve.'

'And you rather expect, I take it, that the driver will turn up?'

'Yes, I do.'

'You are probably right, Charles, but we can't eliminate them till he does. And so to Amery.'

'Well, to tell you the truth, I think he's our man. His story doesn't make sense.'

'Let's go through it all the same. He wanted to see Rosamund. He extracted the address from the porter at the flats, and took himself down there. Rosamund let him in and gave him a glass of sherry; then she saw him off. Instead of going he lurked around half the night in the freezing cold. Went off for some supper at ninish; returned to the garden. Saw a car parked there. Doesn't know what car. Still hung around; saw, or heard rather, car leaving. Was overheard gabbling in the wood-shed, but seems not to have realised anybody was outside it. Peered through windows and saw Rosamund sitting by the fire. She ignored him, whereupon he returned to London, going most of the journey on foot.'

'That's about it. Strange and unusual behaviour on the night of the crime, and a motive as wide as a cart-gate. She rejected him, and he got into a rage and killed her. And remember his story has been changed; until we found his prints on the glass he denied ever having set foot in the bungalow.'

'Yes, so he did. Something about all this is teasing the old grey matter, though, Charles. If Amery is telling the truth, his story totally exonerates the other suspects. So perhaps he did it. But if he did it, why would he tell a story that turns suspicion on himself? And if he's lying, it's an even odder thing to do.'

'But, Wimsey, he just doesn't realise what the implications of his story are. He's not a detective. And anyway it isn't really only his story we are going on. There's the pathologist's estimate of time of death.'

'Yes. But that's a bit wide and loose for the purpose, Charles. Suppose that the earliest possible time he gives us — eleven P.M., wasn't it?

— is the right one. Then, but for Amery seeing the victim alive later on, Harwell could have done it, and so could the jolly blackmailers. If the latest limit for time of death — two in the morning — is right, then really only Amery could have done it, unless it really is just another job of the Sunbury attacker.'

'We're still looking for him.'

'Well, meanwhile, look at this. These are shots that Bunter took for me. They are of the bed after you removed the body.'

Charles took the photos that Wimsey passed across the desk to him.

'What do you see?'

'Two depressions in the pillows.'

'Well, the right-hand one was the position of the head of the corpse, as found. The left-hand one stands to be explained.'

'A second person in bed with her?'

'A second person perhaps. But not exactly in bed with her; she was lying on top of the sheet and blanket, not between the sheets, wasn't she? And she wasn't undressed, Charles. That white slinky thing she was wearing is a cocktail dress, not a nightdress.'

'It had ridden right up, hadn't it? Could she have rushed to the bed in haste?'

'Possibility A: Rosamund takes lover to her bed in great haste. Once there, however, they lie side by side, with space between them, their heads thus making two saucer-shaped depressions a little distance apart. Possibility B: she struggles in

292

the hands of her assailant, and he pushes her down into the pillows in two different places in the course of the struggle. Possibility C: murderer pushes her head down into the pillows hard while killing her, then for some reason moves the body a bit. Lifts it, and puts it back slightly to one side of original position.'

'It's possibility C, isn't it, except that it wasn't the murderer. Harwell told us that he lifted her into his arms and sat for a bit when he found her, and then laid her back again. That has made the second depression.'

'Hmm. Don't you think if you lifted a body that should have been just beginning to get rigor, when you laid it back it would go down into the same position? There are possibilities D to Z.'

'I'll take your word for it,' said Charles, sighing. 'The thing is, Wimsey, I don't quite know how best to pursue this. What do you reckon we should be looking for next? We might find the dead dog, of course, but how far would that get us? We already know the poor brute was butchered.'

'I'm just as flummoxed as you are, Charles. I think Amery is the prime suspect so far, although there might be something we are completely overlooking. Otherwise why would he spin such a yarn? Only he must be a Jekyll and Hyde sort of a fellow: capable when playing Hyde of slaughtering pets, and murdering mistresses, and being a mild-mannered, self-pitying greenery-yallery sort of chap when playing Dr Jekyll.'

'Well, murderers can be devilishly cunning,' said Charles. 'Only, like you, I find Amery a puzzling suspect.'

'No puzzle about what needs doing, though,' said Wimsey. 'I'd rather like to see what Harwell thinks about the blackmailers' story; and we do very urgently need to know who Rosamund was expecting to eat that supper with her.'

'There might have been a demon lover?'

'There might indeed. And so far nobody has admitted to being the intended consumer of all that caviar and venison pie. Such a waste of a good dinner,' added Wimsey petulantly. 'Look, Charles, would you mind if I poked around a bit and talked to people myself?'

'You're welcome,' said Charles. 'Give it your full attention. You are at more liberty than a poor policeman, with two Bolsheviks and a bundle of dynamite in a left-luggage locker to investigate, four thefts of jewels, a missing actress, and an embezzler. I can do with all the help I can get.'

'Well, if you can somehow spare a copper to apply to the question,' said Wimsey, 'can we find out from Fortnum's exactly when that hamper for Hampton was ordered?'

'We've thought of that already,' said Charles. 'And as it happens there's an easy answer. The order department at Fortnum's doesn't note the exact time of calls, just the order in which they were received. But the telephone clerk there remembers that the call was cut off just before the conversation finished. Mrs Harwell had not yet given the delivery address. Luckily they had delivered to her in Hampton before, and they had the address in their records.'

'The call was cut off?'

'Which allows us to time it exactly,' said Charles, 'because the entire telephone exchange at Hampton was taken down by an electricity failure at five to twelve on the 27th, and the service was not restored until six o'clock.'

'So having ordered the hamper, Mrs Harwell might have been left with no way to invite the guest.'

'For whom, nevertheless, she set the dinner table. Do all the poking around you can, Wimsey. I'm at a loss.'

'Have you any news for me?' said Harwell, opening the door to Lord Peter Wimsey.

'Nothing definite, I'm afraid,' said Wimsey. 'There are some lines of enquiry opening up.'

'Come in,' said Harwell.

Wimsey followed him into the flat. It was bleakly elegant, and very untidy. The living-room had pale blue walls, and modernist furniture, all chrome and blue leather. A huge, deep-pile geometric carpet covered the floor; an electric fire stood in the tiled, curved fireplace, with a grille like a car radiator. Glass shelves displayed a few books and some expensive-looking ornaments. It struck Wimsey that the place looked as if it belonged to someone who carried no mementoes of the past at all; someone who had thrown away every piece of property, and bought everything new.

Harwell followed Wimsey's roaming glance.

'She liked modern things very much,' he said with a slight shake in his voice. 'My things are in here.' He opened the door to a large, book-lined study with a comfortable desk and old leather chairs. A picture of his father and mother in a silver frame stood on a side table. They shared the space with signed photographs of several famous actresses.

'Do you want to sit down?' asked Harwell. 'I'll get coffee sent up.'

'Thank you,' said Wimsey, taking a chair. 'Will you smoke?' Opening his case he offered Harwell a Villar y Villar.

Harwell declined, with a brusque gesture. 'So what have you to tell me?' he asked. He looked years older; haggard and dishevelled.

'It seems there has been some blackmail going on,' said Wimsey. He watched in astonishment as all the colour drained from Harwell's face, and the hand that the man had laid on the arm of the chair twitched convulsively.

'What blackmail?' asked Harwell hoarsely.

'I'm afraid your father-in-law picked up some undesirable acquaintances in prison,' said Wimsey. 'They took it into their heads that he might be induced to pay protection money if they threatened to harm your wife.'

'Harm Rosamund?' said Harwell. 'Is that what happened?'

'Well, possibly,' said Wimsey. He had a curious sensation of an ebbing away of tension in the man opposite him. 'I take it that you would confirm that you have been making payments to Mr Warren sufficient to enable him to pay blackmail demands, at least for a while?'

'Oh, my God,' said Harwell. 'I did wonder. You know, Wimsey, he seemed to need a lot of subsidies, but I thought, well, I thought it must be very hard to get by when you're not used to a limited budget. The truth is, I have absolutely no idea how much it would be reasonable for someone to need, to live simply, you know, but with dignity. I just thought he wasn't very good at managing, or I was being a bit miserly or something . . . Are you telling me he was being bled for money? How long had it been going on?'

'For quite a while, I'm afraid.'

'And — God forgive me — I told him it would have to stop; I told him I wouldn't be able to give him anything extra for a bit. Oh, Wimsey, it wasn't that that made them murder her, was it? I'd never forgive myself . . . Oh, I couldn't bear it. Why didn't he tell me what was going on? I'd soon have put a stop to it!'

'Let's take this calmly, one step at a time,' said Wimsey. 'Mr Warren was afraid to tell you, in case you involved the police. He had been told that if the police were brought into it, there would be a revenge attack on Mrs Harwell. You know him well enough, Harwell, to see what an easy victim he was for this kind of thing.'

'Yes, I do. Poor old chap must have been worried out of his mind.'

'And you must not think that your putting a stop to payments to Mr Warren is in any way responsible for the tragedy. The police think it very unlikely that the blackmailers were the assailants.'

'But why? Why rule them out?' said Harwell excitedly. 'If they were threatening her? Aren't that class of people likely to do anything?'

'As a rule that class of person is not likely to do something which removes their hold on their victim,' said Peter. 'But for the moment, they cannot be ruled out of the enquiry.'

'I should think not,' said Harwell, subsiding. 'I take it the police have them under lock and key?'

'Certainly. Blackmail is a serious offence. They can get fourteen years for it.'

'I think they ought to hang for murder.'

'Only if they did it, Harwell. If they did not, that would leave your wife's murderer walking around unpunished and free to do such a thing again.'

'Of course you are right. Forgive me; my feelings are rather out of control these last few days. I don't know what I'm saying. Incidentally, you don't know where my father-in-law is, do you? I haven't been able to get hold of him since the terrible occasion when I had to tell him of Rosamund's death.'

'He is very frightened,' said Wimsey, 'and I took the liberty of arranging a lodging for him where he is not likely to be found, and where he has a little company to keep him from brooding. His reaction is like yours: that if the blackmail has anything to do with it, he is partly to blame for his daughter's death.'

'But you don't think that is the case?' asked Harwell.

'No, I don't,' said Wimsey. 'Not that what I think has any particular importance. But, you told us, I think, that you did not see the table in the bungalow?'

'No; the room is L-shaped; I went through it without going round to the area where the table is. Does this matter?'

'Very much. The table was set for two. The question is, who was your wife expecting to dinner with her?'

'I have no idea,' said Harwell. 'Well, I could hazard a guess. It could only have been Amery.'

'Amery denies having been invited.'

'Well, perhaps he just dropped in. She was very hospitable, Wimsey.'

'She had ordered food from Fortnum's. It really looked as though she was expecting the guest, whoever it was.'

'Well, I don't know who. She had admirers. She drew everyone's eyes, wherever she went.'

'Could it have been a woman friend?' asked Wimsey.

'I suppose it *could*,' said Harwell. 'But I don't really think so. She felt very uneasy with people who had known her very long, and could remember her father's disgrace. Mostly we knew couples whom we had met together, since we were married.'

'I hate to suggest something you are bound to find hurtful,' said Wimsey, 'but could she have made a friend you didn't know about?'

'Of course she could,' said Harwell. 'I didn't set spies on her, or quiz her about everything she did.'

'Could I ask if you have looked at her correspondence? Might there be something to help us there?'

'By all means let's look,' said Harwell. 'We'll do it now if you like. Right away.'

He got up from the chair, and led Wimsey through to the bedroom. Limed oak bedstead and dressing tables stood around, with pea green handles, and an eau-de-Nil satin coverlet on the bed. Wimsey could not help feeling like an intruder in such sensuous surroundings. Beyond the bedroom was Rosamund's boudoir, fitted out with a stage mirror surrounded by light bulbs, and containing a little drop-flap desk. It was not locked. The two men pulled out of it its entire contents: a gold fountain pen; some headed writing paper and scented envelopes; a Liberty address book, a dozen or so calling cards, and some letters. They carried the letters back to Harwell's study, spread them on the desk and looked at them together.

Most of them were nugatory. Notes for dressmakers' appointments; a note from a woman friend thanking Rosamund for the gift of some used clothes. Another such thanking Rosamund for taking her out to lunch. A scrawled account in Rosamund's handwriting, keeping track of her dress allowance, in amounts that made even Wimsey blink and bite his tongue. And letters from Amery. A number of them, tucked into a Morocco writing case. Rosamund seemed to have kept every scrap she had ever received from him, for some of them were no more than one-line confirmations of an intention to meet. Then, from a little hidden drawer at the back of the desk, a bundle of letters tied in a blue ribbon, and marked 'His letters'. Wimsey thought for a moment it was treasure trove; then Harwell, spreading out the contents of the bundle said, 'These are all from me. She kept them . . .' and began to weep.

Wimsey retired quietly into the sitting-room, and sat down to wait for Harwell to recover himself. He had plenty to muse about.

In about half an hour Harwell reappeared, seeming calm again. 'I'm sorry,' he said. 'I didn't know she had kept them.'

'You have nothing to apologise for,' said Wimsey. 'I'm only sorry to have to upset you.'

'Will I have to show all that to the police?' asked Harwell, visibly shuddering.

'I shouldn't think so,' said Wimsey. 'After all, there is nothing there to get us a single step further. We still haven't an idea who she had invited to dinner.'

'And whoever ate that dinner with her was the

last person to see her alive, and therefore the one who killed her,' said Harwell, bleakly.

'Well, not exactly,' Wimsey told him. 'The table was undisturbed, the supper untouched. It looks very much as though the invited guest never arrived. But naturally we would like to know who he was, and why he didn't show up.'

'The only person I can think of,' said Harwell, 'is Claude Amery. And didn't you say he says he wasn't invited?'

'He seems to have been in the vicinity,' Wimsey said. 'But not invited. Whoever supper was for, if he is to be believed, it seems it wasn't for him.'

'What about Gaston Chapparelle?' said Harwell, suddenly. 'I'd forgotten all about him! But you know his reputation, Wimsey, and you should have seen the way in which he looked at my wife!'

'Hmm,' said Wimsey, thoughtfully. 'I'll get Chief Inspector Parker to ask him where he was that night.'

'Harriet, have you an urgent appointment with your Robert Templeton this morning, or would you be free to take a spin down to Hampton with me?'

'I'd be glad to come,' said Harriet. 'Robert Templeton can stew for a day; I'm sick of his company. But . . .'

'But me no buts, Harriet. I don't propose to show you anything gruesome. I just want a female accompaniment while I interview a young woman who might be unduly alarmed by confronting a titled nincompoop with an eye-glass.'

'But shouldn't you rather ask Bunter? I mean, he was always used to being your faithful side-kick; mightn't he feel . . . ?'

'What a saintly woman have I married!' said Peter. 'Who, far from indulging in the archetypal wish to reform her spouse, strives to keep everything unchanged. How very considerate of you, my dear.'

'Far from wishing you to change,' said Harriet, 'I would have you preserved as a historic monument if I could. Bunter, I feel sure, would wish for as little change as possible in the even tenor of his days.'

'But as it happens, Bunter himself has requested a day off. Something to do with a jamboree of photographers. Of course I agreed. The man has hardly had a day off since 1920.'

'Very well, then, I shan't give Bunter another thought. Who are we going to talk to?'

'You mean "to whom". To Mrs Chanter's daughter, Rose. I have arranged with Mrs Chanter that she and Rose will be at Mon Repos and expecting us at noon. Arise and go now, and I will describe the nine bean rows in the car. Put you in the picture, I mean. I'm sorry we haven't a better day for our jaunt, but at least it isn't raining. Oh, and Harriet, we should time the journey; remind me to take a note of the exact time we get on the move.'

'Fifty-one minuses,' said Harriet, as the Daimler pulled to the side of the lane outside Mon Repos. 'But there was a lot of traffic.'

'Thank you,' said Peter. They presented themselves at the front door of Mon Repos, and Mrs Chanter, in a sprig print dress, appeared at once, and showed them into the drawing-room of the house.

'You mustn't think I've got above myself, Lord Peter, my lady,' she said, taking Harriet's coat, and showing her to a chair beside the fire, 'I wouldn't make so free as to use my employer's house without asking permission. But Mr Sugden telephoned last night to say they would be coming home tomorrow, and I told him I would need time off because you would be wanting to talk to Rose, and he said to make you welcome here.'

'That's very kind of him,' said Peter.

'He is a kind gentleman, sir. Very kind. He and Mrs Sugden have been in Italy for her health this winter, but now they have to come home, unexpected, on account of the family trouble. He sounded worried sick, poor gentleman. Not that it's my place to talk about family matters outside the family, if you'll forgive me, sir.'

'Of course,' said Peter. 'Very proper of you, Mrs Chanter. Believe me, we shall ask Rose only what we absolutely need to know.'

'Here she is now,' said Mrs Chanter. 'Should I make you some tea?'

'Later, perhaps,' said Peter. 'But for the moment maybe you would like to stay in case there is anything you can add to what Rose has to tell us.'

Mrs Chanter sat down, as Rose came into the room.

Harriet had been amusing herself watching Peter's smooth manner as a detective. Now she turned her attention to Rose. The girl was pretty in that baby-faced way that often fades with youth, and well turned out. She was looking very apprehensive, and Harriet waited to see how Peter would deal with that.

'Rose, we think you may be able to help us find Mrs Harwell's murderer,' he began. 'We understand from what your mother told Mr Bunter that you were acting as Mrs Harwell's maid and housekeeper in the short time before she died.'

'She came down on the Wednesday,' said Rose, 'and she phoned and asked if I would open up the place for her before she got here.'

'What did you have to do, exactly?' said Harriet, wanting to claim a place in the conversation in case she had something more important to ask later.

'I drew the curtains, and brought in coal, and lit all the fires,' the girl said. 'And give the place a lick over with a duster, and took the dust covers off the sitting-room suite, and brought up some milk and bread from the village shop, and put a bunch of flowers in a vase, and filled some hot-water bottles to air the bed. Well, and of course I had to make up the bed first. Couple of hours' work.'

'And when did Mrs Harwell arrive?'

'About four o'clock, sir. She come up from the station in a taxi. She sent me down to the village to do some shopping right away. When I got back I had the supper to cook, and then I unpacked her suitcase, and hung up her clothes — she had the most lovely clothes, sir, you wouldn't believe — and then she said I could go, and come back the next morning.'

'And you did that?'

'Yes, I did.'

'So what did she ask you to do for her on the second day?'

'Just the usual things, sir. Just what I always did when I did for her: clean the grates, set the fires, make her breakfast, neaten the bed —'

'Woman's work, as is never done,' interjected Mrs Chanter.

'Was there anything else?' asked Peter, quietly. 'Did she give you a letter to post? Anything like that?'

'No, sir.'

'Are you sure, Rose? We think there must have been a letter.'

'She wouldn't have needed to give it to me, sir, because she took the dog for a walk before lunch, and she could easily have posted a letter herself.'

'I see,' said Peter. 'I see that you are a sharp sort of girl, Rose. You would have noticed anything unusual.'

'Well, there wasn't anything unusual to notice, sir.'

'And was Mrs Harwell quite her usual self? She didn't seem worried about anything?'

'She was a nervy sort of a person, sir. Very offhand with servants. She never chatted, like, or told you what was happening. Not a bit like Mrs Sugden in this house. Mum always knows just who is expected, and all the family news and that.'

'But Mrs Harwell was stand-offish?'

'Very. Yes, she was.'

'And so she didn't tell you that she expected guests for supper that night?'

'Well, yes, she did. She sent me off home as soon as I cleared her lunch things, which wasn't much because she only had a boiled egg and a rack of toast. And she asked me to come back at five to help with dinner. She said she was going to invite someone "when she could get through". I was a bit concerned, sir, in case she wanted me to cook. I thought it might be a bit much for me, and I said to her if only we had known, Mum would have been glad to cook something nice for her —'

'As I would have been ready to help out, naturally, given a bit of warning,' said Mrs Chanter.

'She said she had only just thought of it, sir, and it was a nice surprise for someone, and not to worry because she had ordered a hamper.'

'When had she done that?' asked Peter.

'It must have been on her walk before lunch, I suppose,' said Rose.

'And you have no idea at all who was expected?'

Peter's voice was very neutral, almost gentle, Harriet noticed. Calculated to give no unnecessary signals. What was it that welcomed little fishes in with gently smiling jaws?

'And when you came back at five, what were you asked to do?'

'Just set the table, sir.'

'Just the table? What about food?'

'The hamper had come. It only needed unpacking.'

'And for how many was the table to be set?'

'I can't exactly remember, sir. I think it was for two.'

'You can't be sure?' asked Peter. Rose shot a glance at her mother.

Then: 'It was for two,' she said.

'What did you think of the food you had to unpack?' asked Peter.

The girl looked very uneasy. 'It wasn't my place to think about it,' she said.

'You didn't think it was rather extravagant? Rather luxurious?'

'It wasn't what I would spend my money on, if I had her sort of money, if that's what you mean,' she said.

'There wasn't anything in it that you would have liked to eat yourself?'

'Not that I can remember,' said Rose. She wasn't looking directly at Peter. She was fiddling with her watch strap as she spoke.

'Well,' said Peter, briskly, taking a pencil and a notebook from his pocket. 'Let's have a list of what you can remember, shall we?'

Rose was silent. 'Come on, girl,' said Mrs Chanter.

'I just got it out of the basket and put it on the table,' Rose said, angrily. 'It was all wrapped up. I didn't take no notice of it.'

'Don't worry, then, Rose,' said Peter, putting his notebook away. 'Just tell us what happened next.'

'She said to wait till her guest arrived,' said Rose, 'so I sat and waited in the kitchen. And he never came. So there wasn't anything to do, and when it got late she sent me home.'

'She didn't name anyone? She just said "my guest"?'

'Yes.'

'And did she seem worried or upset when he or she didn't come?'

'Not particularly. She just said as I was to go now, and come back in the morning. So I went.'

'Did you notice what time it was when you left?'

'Somewhere about ten o'clock,' said Rose promptly.

'You didn't get in till after eleven, Rose,' said Mrs Chanter.

'I went for a bit of a walk down the lane,' said Rose, desperately. 'I didn't come straight back in. Any objections?'

'Yes, there is objections!' exclaimed Mrs Chanter. 'I've told you over and over again I won't have you walking around by yourself after dark! Don't you realise, my girl, as how there was a murderer lurking about somewhere?'

'I wasn't to know that,' said Rose, hanging her head.

'When you walked down the lane,' said Peter, 'did you happen to see anyone? Or did you see a car come or go?'

'There was a car passed,' said Rose, suddenly perking up.

'Was it coming, or going?'

'Coming up the lane, towards us here,' said Rose. 'I'm afraid I didn't notice its number plate or anything. Just that I had to step on to the verge to get out of the way.'

'All right,' said Peter. 'Look, Rose, is there anything else you can think of which might help us? I suppose you realise that you were the last person to see Mrs Harwell alive?'

'That's a horrible thought,' wailed Rose. 'You don't know that, sir. Anybody might of come in.'

'But you were sitting in the kitchen all evening. Wouldn't you have heard if someone came?'

'Yes. No, I might have nodded off,' the girl said. She was staring at Peter, and then at Harriet with wide blank eyes.

She's very frightened, thought Harriet. Now why should she be?

'It's mortifying to a sleuth,' Peter told Harriet, 'when people keep telling one fibs. Just about everybody in this case has slipped in a fib or two, about some trivial matter having nothing in particular to do with the case.'

'Are you thinking of Rose?'

'And Amery. And Harwell. But Rose is a case in point. Can you imagine unpacking a hamper and not noticing anything that was in it?'

'Perhaps one wouldn't take much notice if one knew that not a bite of it was for oneself,' said Harriet.

'I don't believe she unpacked the thing at all,' said Peter. 'But I don't think we can get any more out of her, do you? And I very much doubt if Charles and his merry men would do better. I've been racking my brain over it. Bunter is already known to be part of our baggage train; Mrs Chanter would confide in him while plying him with steak and kidney and spotted dick, but Rose would be in awe of him, don't you think?'

'Yes, I do. Bunter is a considerably more awful phenomenon than his master.'

'Thank you.'

'What about Miss Climpson's people?'

'None in their earliest youth, I'm afraid. And imperceptibly of a station in life slightly higher on the ladder than Rose.'

'Surrounded,' said Harriet, 'by that faint and fussy glamour that comes from being able to type? Peter, I know who you want. You want Mango.'

'Harriet, that's a stroke of genius! Can you spare her for a few days?'

'I think I might be able to remember how to dress myself,' said Harriet dryly.

'And do you think the girl would be willing?'

'I think she'd adore it, Peter. She worships you like a film star; and I'm sure she would find it thrilling to be involved in investigating murder.'

Peter hesitated, with his hand hovering over the bell. 'You know, this might not be a case of murder, Harriet,' he said. 'Contrary to popular belief, a dead body doesn't always mean capital murder. But even if what was done wasn't murder, we still have to find who wasn't a murderer.'

14

Through all the drama, whether damned or not
Love gilds the scene, and women guide the plot.
RICHARD BRINSLEY SHERIDAN

Report from Miss Juliet Mango to Lord Peter Wimsey:

Monday 16th March
Immediately on receiving your instructions proceeded to Hampton, and took rooms at the White Hart Inn. Gave myself out as a theatrical costumier, working on a film that had been projected to be shot this month. Succeeded in telling everyone in the hotel bar that the costumes for the film had all been destroyed in the studio fire at Elstree last month. Claimed that I was working in Hampton to be near the wardrobe mistress for the film, and that I needed a young woman the same measurements as Miss Kay Francis to model the dresses I was making. Aroused a good deal of interest with this story and several local girls are to come to see me tomorrow, Rose Chanter one of them. Have

ordered three bolts of satin and some trimmings from Lady Peter's account at Harrods, trusting that your lordship's words about no expense spared would cover.

Please tell Lady Peter that her amethyst serge dress would be very appropriate for her engagement to speak at the Hampstead literary luncheon party, since full mourning not appropriate in circles such as that, and it would be best to wear pearls with it rather than one of those collars. The dress is all ready pressed and hanging in the wardrobe for her.

I will report again tomorrow.
Yours faithfully,
J.L. Mango

Having read this missive, Peter passed it to Harriet. Harriet, deeply absorbed in reading the newspaper, took several seconds before she picked up the letter.

'What has attracted your attention?' asked Peter. 'Not the results of the Gas Light and Coal Company, I'll hazard.'

'No, not that. It's this case.' Harriet pointed at a headline which said: *Wife Killed by Husband. Three years penal servitude.*

'What is worrying you about it, Harriet? I have no need of the death penalty to deter me from murdering my wife. Nothing would induce me to harm a hair of her head. Never was wife safer . . .'

'It just seems to sort rather oddly with the judgement in the Buxton case,' said Harriet.

'Ah. Now that gentleman does seem to have been guilty of murdering his wife.'

'And in the summing-up reported yesterday the judge said it was not for the Crown to prove motive,' said Harriet.

'My dear, is it just the corrupting proximity of a criminologist spouse, or have you always read the law reports?'

'Always. Essential reading for the practice of my trade,' said Harriet.

'What is confusing here is the difference between motive and intent,' said Peter. 'You could probably base a novel upon it. Novelists like motive of course, as, Charles keeps telling me, do juries. Intent is much narrower, and easier to get a grasp on.'

'It seems a very slippery distinction to me,' said Harriet.

'I think it's clearer in practice than it is in theory,' said Peter. 'You might have a strong motive for wishing for the death of your aunt — if she is going to leave you a fortune, shall we say? But an intent to kill her is not the same thing. Most people with motives for murder never form the slightest shadow of an intent to kill. But now, supposing you have in fact killed your aunt, and it turns out you are her heiress. You might have more difficulty in rebutting the allegation that you had malign intent.'

'In this case the husband seems to have seized his wife by the throat in a paroxysm of rage,' said Harriet.

'Humm,' said Peter. 'Well, he's lucky to escape a conviction for murder then, isn't he? Because an intent does not have to go so far as being an intent to kill, to support a murder charge. An intent to inflict bodily harm is enough.'

'Otherwise, you mean, someone could stab someone else with a kitchen knife, and then say he had intended to wound, but not to kill the victim?'

'Precisely. It would become impossible to convict for murder. The assailant would always say that something short of death had been his intention. There's a further wrinkle to this. One is not allowed not to intend the obvious consequences of one's actions. Supposing, for example, that you belonged to a society for the destruction of ugly buildings. You drew up a hit list, and you went around blowing the abominations up.'

'Peter! What a wonderful idea; we should start such a society immediately, before London gets out of hand.'

'And then supposing that you were to argue that you had not foreseen that anyone would be injured in the process. The jury would probably think that you jolly well should have foreseen it. Another example: if the man on the Clapham omnibus would expect death to result from a stab wound through the heart, then it is not open to the assailant to argue that he did not in fact intend such a result. Unless he pleads insanity, of course.'

'I see. Well, in this case the man appears to

have fallen over on top of the woman while holding her by the throat.'

'Then I imagine the jury thought the fall was accidental, and that without it he would simply have let go, and she would have been left with nothing worse than a bruised neck. Can I see the report?'

Harriet handed the newspaper to Peter.

'Yes; you see they had had brawls before, which had not seriously injured either of them. To get a conviction for murder you would have to show that he had, or ought reasonably to have had, a belief that this time the assault would result in death, or at least in grievous bodily harm.'

'Three years isn't much, though, in the presence of a dead body, is it?' asked Harriet.

'He must have been most convincingly penitent,' said Peter. 'Is this maze of distinctions of any special importance to you, Harriet?'

'Yes, it is. I'm afraid my body in the reservoir may be the result of manslaughter, or unlawful killing or something, not of murder.'

'Does it matter? It's still a body.'

'Oh, it matters terribly. Murder is the only crime for a detective story. It has true glamour. Anything less is liable to strike the reader as perry to champagne.'

'What a ghoulish crowd the reading public must be,' said Peter. 'Couldn't you scrape home with a spot of conspiring to cause explosions? Embezzlement? Kidnapping? Counterfeiting coin of the realm? No, Harriet? Nothing but murder will meet the need? Then you must give your villain both motive and intent. As well as opportunity, of course.'

'I realise, if there has been murder, then someone pays for it with a life,' said Harriet, musing. 'Perhaps if the death penalty is ever abolished, a wider tariff of crimes will be available to detective story writers. Meanwhile, has Mango found anything?'

'See for yourself. So far, so good, I would say.'

Report from Miss Juliet Mango to Lord Peter Wimsey:

Wednesday, 18th March

Interviewed several local young women in my room at the White Hart today and selected Rose Chanter to model dresses for me, purporting to find her measurements the closest to what was required. She was delighted, and the conversation easily turned to Mrs Harwell, when she told me that the money for the modelling sessions would be particularly welcome as she had no more expectation of occasional earnings from the Harwells. I began to make a calico maquette for a dress for her, but have not yet cut the satin itself, as am hopeful that she will confide in me before I have touched the bolt, which would enable me to return the fabric for a refund.

Found Miss Chanter very talkative. She believes that she knows a good deal about film stars, and is eager to learn about stage costumes. Elic-

ited a good deal of detail about Mrs Harwell's wardrobe, and whole history of relations between Harwells and the neighbourhood. Have also been told about Rose's young man, Ronald Datchett, who is employed in the local boat yard, where skiffs and launches are made for sale and hire. Rose regards this as a good secure job as hire is not as seasonal as one might think. She would like to become engaged to Ronald, but her family are not keen on the idea. Mrs Chanter, I gather, is very strict with Rose, who has considerable difficulty finding a way of being alone with Ronald. They are restricted to one evening out each week, and must always say where they are going, and be back by eleven o'clock. I understand that Ronald walks Rose home after each excursion, but that cuddling in the bushes alongside the lane is cold and uncomfortable in winter weather. The girl made several envious remarks about the room in the White Hart with a nice fire burning, but I do not see why I should put her in the way of getting herself into trouble at Your Lordship's expense. Have formed the impression that Mrs Chanter's attitude is perfectly justified. Rose told me that the empty bungalow when the Harwells were absent was a sore temptation to her and Ron, but that he had been unable to find a way to break in without leaving signs of forced entry. Mrs Chanter keeps a key to the place, but it is on her ring of keys for Mon Repos and is never out of her pocket.

My attempts to lead the conversation into any

319

detail about the actual day of the murder have so far been unsuccessful, and I have been careful not to press enquiries too far, in case she becomes suspicious of me.

I hope you will not think it excessive of me to have had a dinner of roast beef today, as it was table d'hôte at a special price.

I will tender a further report as soon as possible.
Yours faithfully,
J.L. Mango

Report from Miss Juliet Mango to Lord Peter Wimsey:

Thursday 19th March

I hasten to make a report to Your Lordship as I have discovered something of GREAT SIGNIFICANCE. Rose came for a fitting session this morning, and in the course of much conversation she revealed to me that IT WAS NOT SHE who provided a servant for Mrs Harwell on the evening of her death!

It seems that what happened is this. Thursday evening is Rose's regular day for walking out with Ron, and that particular Thursday they had most eagerly anticipated, because Ron's parents were going to a regimental reunion party at the British Legion, and so Ron's house would be empty. When Mrs Harwell arrived unexpected and asked for Rose's services, Rose was in a difficulty. She could not tell Mrs Chanter that she was unwilling to spend the evening at Rose

Cottage, because she did not want to confesses to the reason. So she recruited a young friend to do the evening job for her.

She told me that she had been in mortal terror when questioned by Lord Peter that she would have the truth winkled out of her with her mother listening, and would be in terrible trouble. She thinks that Lord Peter knew she was lying, because she could not 'remember' what in fact she had never seen, the contents of the food hamper.

However, when Mrs Harwell expected Rose to return in the evening, a young girl called Mary Moles in fact turned up. Mary has just left school, and is only fourteen. I got the impression that Mary has rather a 'pash' on Rose, and would do anything for her. Rose persuaded her to take her place at Rose Cottage, so that the assignation with Ron could take place as planned. Rose understands from Mary that Mrs Harwell asked her to set the table, and then sent her on an errand which the girl could not accomplish. I cannot think of a way to interview Mary without 'blowing my cover' as a theatrical costumier. Will telephone this evening for further instructions.

Yours faithfully,
J. L. Mango

15

For in what stupid age or nation
Was marriage ever out of fashion?
SAMUEL BUTLER

'Harriet, something has happened.' Peter had entered the library in which Harriet was reading with scholarly application an account of the procedures of post-mortem examination of cadavers.

She heard in Peter's voice a note that made her at once close the notebook in which she was writing, get up from the table, and come towards him.

'Bunter has handed in his resignation.'

'Oh, Peter, no! Whyever? It hasn't anything to do with me, has it?'

'Why do you think that?' he asked her.

'Well, it was rather obvious he might find things very difficult when the master took a wife. Helen even suggested I should get him sacked — did I tell you? But I thought he and I had come to an understanding. I hate the thought that —'

'Well, it is your doing, but not in the way you

think. It is our happiness that has been the cause. Bunter wants to get married himself.'

'Oh, but that's *good* news! Wonderful!' said Harriet.

'Yes, of course,' said Peter. 'Of course it is. Beastly selfish of me not to dance for joy; but God, Harriet, it will be a wrench! Worse than that; he was my insurance cover, if you like, against making your life a misery if my nerves went to pieces again. I knew Bunter would always be ready to take the brunt of it, and you could just turn your back till it blew over. Now I don't know . . .'

'I would be ready to take the brunt of it,' said Harriet. 'For better or worse, Peter, in sickness or in health; don't you remember?'

'I remember perfectly; but I would rather you didn't have too much of the worse and the sickness to cope with.'

'But, Peter, does Bunter have to leave you if he marries? Is being a gentleman's gentleman a kind of celibate priesthood? Surely there are married servants — or does he want to go?'

'No, he doesn't. He does me the honour of being as shattered at the thought as I am. But I don't see what to do, all the same. Bunter's job does entail being under the same roof as me.'

'What usually happens when a servant marries?' asked Harriet.

'Well, they usually marry another servant. One either dispenses with their services, and off they go to a house which is looking for a married couple — cook, gardener or similar; or else one finds a job for the intended oneself, and keeps the twosome on.'

'Can't we do that?'

'Bunter is not proposing to marry a servant. The young woman is a photographer, I gather. It would be unimaginable to have her living here as a sort of permanent house guest.'

'Oho,' said Harriet. 'I think I have met her. What does she say herself?'

'Bunter hasn't actually asked her yet. Asked her to marry him, I mean. He broke the news to me first.'

'Peter, that's outrageous!'

'Is it? Perhaps it is. The truth is, Harriet, I am so taken aback I don't know what to think.'

'You are being rather Victorian about it, my lord,' said Harriet. 'Let's wait and see what answer Bunter gets, and meanwhile I'll see if we can think of a solution.'

'Yes,' he said. 'Would you mind if I played for a bit?' He had moved across to the piano, and lifted the lid.

'Music hath charms?'

'And I am excessively conscious of having a savage breast tonight.'

'What passion cannot music raise and quell? Play on.'

'Bunter paid us a dashed queer compliment tonight,' said Peter, with a catch in his voice. 'He said he had not previously supposed it possible to match physical passion with friendship.' And before Harriet could answer he sat at the keyboard and plunged into an intricate and convoluted fugue.

Report from Juliet Mango to Lord Peter Wimsey:

19th March
A very interesting development has taken place. Before I had made the telephone call I intended to make to Your Lordship for further instructions, Rose Chanter came to see me, bringing Mary Moles with her. The two girls had decided to consult me as to what they should do, as a person who knew more about the world than they did, and one who would not be likely to tell Mrs Chanter, or cause her to be told, of Rose's secret assignation. They are both, as you can imagine, my lord, deeply agitated by the scrape they have got themselves into, and Mary would best be described as petrified. She has realised, of course, that she was the last person to have seen Mrs Harwell alive, and she is afraid of being found out, and incriminated by her deception and silence. On the other hand, she is clearly very influenced by Rose, to whom she had sworn secrecy, and Rose is holding her to her promise.
This is Mary's account of what happened on the fatal evening. She went to Rose Cottage, and introduced herself to Mrs Harwell; she was very nervous, and half expecting to be sent away. She told Mrs Harwell that she had come to do what Rose would have been asked to do, as Rose was unwell. Mrs Harwell seemed very agitated. She wanted the

table set in a great hurry, although it was only five o'clock. She told Mary to set the table, while she herself unpacked a hamper.

Then Mrs Harwell was cross with Mary because she did not set the table properly. Mrs Harwell called her a nincompoop. I understand that Mary had never seen a table laid so elaborately, did not know how to fold napkins, or in which arrangement to put out knives and forks, and such like. When Mrs Harwell saw that she genuinely did not know what was required, and that she was upset, she told the girl not to mind, and showed her exactly how the job should be done, and they did it together. It looked lovely, Mary said.

But then the need for hurry was made clear. Mrs Harwell gave Mary a note, and her train fare, and asked her to take it at once to an address in London. She said she had not been able to get in touch because of the phones. She said she had been trying all afternoon, but if Mary went at once and caught the five thirty train she would be in time. Mary was very alarmed. She could not go to London without being later in returning to her home than her mother would have expected; her mother supposed she was having tea with a friend. And the whole task was beyond her; she had never been to London in her life, except once when an uncle took her to the zoo for her sixth birthday, and she had not the least idea how to find a London address.

On the other hand she was afraid of making Mrs Harwell angry with her again, so she took the note, and left the bungalow, and went off to find Rose, to give her the note and the fare, and ask her to take it to London.

It now appears that Rose had not confided fully even in Mary, because Mary did not know that Rose would be at Ronald's house, but trailed round the village looking everywhere she could think of. When at last she intercepted Rose and Ron coming home from an evening of love, it was nearly eight o'clock; much too late to deliver a supper invitation. Rose told Mary to go home. What about the note? Mary asked. Just chuck it, get rid of it, Rose said.

'What do I say when Mrs Harwell wants to know what happened to it?' Mary asked. Rose said that she wouldn't find out for several days, and she would never be sure if the person who said they hadn't got it really hadn't got it, or was just saying that. 'She wouldn't be the first person to be stood up for a supper date,' Rose had said. 'You could always say you lost it, so lose it now; just throw it away.'

BUT MARY KEPT IT AND HID IT IN-STEAD. The train fare she had been given was on her conscience too, until she put it into a Salvation Army collection box.

She was very alarmed by her evening's experiences, my lord. I would say she was an exceptionally silly woman, if I didn't have to bear in mind that she is a very young girl. As I have reason to know, my lord, it is very easy for a young girl to get herself into trouble with the authorities.

Well, the problem that they have now, my lord,

that they were putting to me for my advice was this. What should they do with the note? Rose was for destroying it; but Mary is very frightened of doing anything which, should it ever come to light, would get her into worse trouble. The murder has turned what was a mild scrape for both of them into a very serious matter. When you questioned Rose closely about the hamper and the table she realised only too well what a deep pit she had dug for herself, and that she might have got Mary into deep water too; but she is still very unwilling to make a clean breast of it all round. I have the impression, my lord, that she is more afraid of her parents than of the police.

However, it occurred to me to suggest that if they entrusted the note to you, you might find a way of making sure that the evidence was in the hands of the police, without anybody in Hampton ever needing to know a thing about it. I admitted to some slight acquaintance with you, my lord, and suggested that if the note were given to me, I could undertake to deliver it safely to you. The two girls have gone away to think about it.

I shall stay here another day to see what transpires.

> *Yours faithfully,*
> *J.L. Mango*

'It is a blessing beyond price,' said Lord Peter Wimsey, 'to have intelligent servants.'

Lady Peter Wimsey presents her compliments to

Miss Fanshaw, and would be grateful if she could call at Audley Square at her earliest convenience.

'I ought to tell you at once,' said Miss Fanshaw, turning to meet Harriet as she entered the drawing-room, 'that I have refused Mervyn's proposal.'

'It is in no way any business of mine,' said Harriet, slowly. 'And you are perfectly at liberty to tell me to mind my own business.'

'Oh, I don't mind telling you why,' said Miss Fanshaw. 'I wouldn't have come if I was going to be shy about it. I really hadn't realised what a wrench it was going to be for him — how genuinely hurtful — to give up Lord Peter. I mean, I know it's a blessing to be counted to have a decent master and a good secure job; I hadn't expected it to be an affair of the heart, if you see what I mean.'

'I do see, exactly. Peter is taking it badly too; they are both walking round the house bleeding invisibly like wounded ghosts.'

'Well, they can stop doing that,' said Miss Fanshaw. 'I have changed my mind. Mervyn can stay just where he is.'

'I don't know that that quite gets things back the way they were,' said Harriet. 'Apart from sounding as though it would be very painful for both of you.'

'I've been around a bit,' said Miss Fanshaw. 'I don't think it is a good idea for someone to come to a marriage having made enormous sacrifices. It ups the ante too much. Instead of merely needing to make someone happy, one would have to make them so happy as to make up for the loss. And somehow a loss and a gain tend to stand in separate columns, and one doesn't cancel the other.'

'How very sensible of you,' said Harriet.

'Do you really think so? My mother says it is hard-hearted of me. But I can't bear to have Mervyn do something for me for which I would have to be eternally grateful. I don't think I'm a grateful sort of person really.'

'Neither am I!' said Harriet. 'Look, I don't know about hard-heartedness; I was proposing we might try a little female hard-headedness about this. Would you slip your coat on again, and come with me?'

Harriet led her guest down to the basement floor of the house. A corridor from the foot of the stairs led between a door into the area at the front of the house, and a garden door at the back. Left and right, green baize doors separated the servants' quarters, and the kitchens and store-rooms. The glazed garden door opened to a brick path down the garden, past the dolphin and cupid statuary in the empty basin of the ornamental fountain. In the absence of water it was the dolphin that looked least at home; when the fountain had been in working order the cupid must have been uncomfortably wet. As in most London gardens there was a small rectangle of grass, surrounded by flower borders. A large old apple tree shaded the far end, and beyond was the mews. Down the damp path, and under the dripping apple branches the two women made for a door in this building. Harriet produced a key, and they went in. They were in a large dusty-floored room, with the Daimler parked at one end, and garage double doors behind it. Shelves and a workbench held the household's trove of tools and gardening equipment; cans of oil and a spare tyre stood against the wall. But the car and its clobber occupied barely a third of the space. The remaining area was still divided into stalls with mangers on the walls, and a tack-room at the other end. Beside the tack-room, an open-tread wooden staircase led to an upper floor. The two women climbed upstairs.

After the gloom of the nearly windowless space below, the upper room was bright. Again it was the full length and width of the building, but it had windows down both sides. On one side these windows gave onto the branches of the apple tree, which in its current leafless state permitted the back of the main house to be seen. On the other side the windows looked into the little mews street, cobbled and picturesquely neat, that ran behind the grand houses all along the street. When these houses were built the row of mews buildings behind them was necessary; people kept horses and carriages. Horses needed stables and grooms. Now the little street was lined with garages at street level, and flats above, or little bijou cottages with large windows where the stable and carriage doors had been. Opposite, a proud owner had planted window-boxes with trailing ivy.

Miss Fanshaw, with her hands thrust in the pockets of her coat, walked round the room, and looked out of each window in turn. At one end of the room a pretty little Victorian fireplace was still in position, with its grate filled up with sticks by a team of hopeful jackdaws, and then abandoned to time and the falls of soot. The wide old floorboards were thick with dust, in which the two women's footprints were discernible. Another, still steeper wooden stair led up again, and Harriet led the way.

Right at the top was a low run of attics, each with a little dormer window facing the street. An iron bedstead rusting in one of them indicated that here the grooms had slept. Without fires, it seemed, and by candlelight. But the windows were those pretty Georgian sashes with squared panes and narrow dividers. The corridor that linked the attic rooms was lit by dirty skylights. No outlook here into the garden. Harriet and the still silent Miss Fanshaw descended to the first floor again.

Miss Fanshaw looked quizzically at Harriet. 'One could divide off the garage space, and make a proper front door into the mews, with its own address,' said Harriet.

'Yes; I suppose such a thing could be done,' said Miss Fanshaw, non-committally.

Harriet plunged in. 'Lord Peter could afford to

do all this up very nicely,' she said. 'I think one might get a good three-bedroomed cottage out of it, with a pleasant living-room here, and a kitchen and dining-room downstairs. One could run a bell out here from the house, and Bunter would be only a step away. Don't you think?'

'Are you offering it to us, Lady Peter?'

'I suppose Peter ought to do that. I haven't put it to him yet. I wanted to know if it would seem possible to you, before starting a hare. I am asking you whether you think it would work out well; whether you could imagine living here.'

'Does Mervyn know about this?'

'No; it is a female conspiracy. A shot at a practical answer.'

'I hadn't thought there could be one. Could this really be spared?'

'Well, it isn't doing any good at the moment, except to spiders. Peter employs an architect; you could, you and Bunter could, work out what you want . . .'

'I don't think I'm very good at decorating and things.' Miss Fanshaw sounded dubious.

'My mother-in-law would be in the seventh heaven if we asked her to do colour schemes and arrangements,' said Harriet, smiling deeply at the thought of letting the Dowager Duchess have her head.

Miss Fanshaw walked to the end of the room, and stood looking thoughtfully through the apple branches at the garden.

'I can see this is a sort of solution,' she said.

'It would square the circle for Mervyn. And it's very good of you to suggest it. But I don't think it could work unless you and I were able to deal with any difficulties which might arise; unless we were to become firm friends.'

'I look forward to that very much,' said Harriet, holding out her hand.

'You were rather slow to follow my lead into matrimony, old man,' said the Honourable Freddy Arbuthnot. 'Couldn't think what you were waiting for all that time, until I met her.'

'I'm glad you appreciate her,' said Wimsey, lightly, leaning over the table to refill Freddy's champagne glass. 'My family are deeply divided on the subject. Denver keeps eyeing her as a possible brood mare, and St George as a possible let-out from all his responsibilities. The Duchess gives us both the benefit of her iciest disapproval, and my mother sings her praises without cease. Bunter is unsettled by the whole thing and is thinking of leaving me . . . I need all the agreement I can get.'

'Sorry to hear about Bunter,' said Freddy. 'That's a blow. He's been with you for ever, hasn't he? What's the rub?'

'Like master, like man. He wants to get married himself.'

'Oh, I see. Rotten for you. You can't decently try to stop him, can you? But look here, Wimsey, I wasn't actually making remarks about Harriet, but about Harwell. She passed it on to me that you wanted a bush telegraph message about him.'

'Yes, I did. Have you got something for me?'

'You were right. He has been raising money. Quite a bit of money. You know he has an interest in the Cranbourne Theatre?'

'Can't say that I did. Go on.'

'He is part of a consortium that bought the freehold seven years ago. A freehold is serious collateral; not like interests in plays. Anyway, Harwell raised a loan recently; short term, and used his share in the Cranbourne as security. Seems he needed money to launch this new play by Amery, and his funds were tied up in existing productions. Or anyway, that's the tale he told to my City friends. They found him his loan; he's regarded as very sound. Can one ask why you wanted to know?'

'Oh, you know what it's like. Fellow's wife found murdered, and one grows a gargantuan curiosity for everything about him.'

'A very nasty business, that. Can't help feeling sorry for the man. Lovely lady. Surely that one would be about love rather than money, Wimsey.'

'Oh, they get rather tangled together sometimes,' said Wimsey.

'Mm. Expect you're right. Both very important things, of course. Get entangled when you're married.'

'Things all right with you and Rachel?' asked Wimsey, looking sharply at his friend.

'Top hole, thank you. I was only thinking ruefully about school fees, and dowries and such like. You'll learn, given a bit of time. I always thought you were God's own bachelor, and would keep bed and board apart for ever — would have laid bets on it — and now look what happens.'

'Well, you may take Harriet out to lunch any time, subject to her acceptance, of course. I gather she enjoyed talking to you.'

'Jolly glad to hear it. Awkward sort of thing, really, talking to a brainy woman. Don't quite know what to say.'

'You talk to her exactly as if she were a man,' said Wimsey. 'Forgive me if I rush off; I have to call at Scotland Yard.'

'I'm glad to see you, Peter,' said Charles Parker. 'You remember that apparently vague suggestion from Harwell that Gaston Chapparelle might have been the mystery dinner guest?'

'Based on nothing but the way the man had looked at her? Yes, I do remember. It occurred to me that, after all, Harwell was paying the man to look at her.'

'Well, you know what slaves to routine policemen are. I sent someone round to ask him where he was that evening . . .'

'He says he was somewhere else, I take it?'

'Yes, he does. But he won't say where.'

'Has he had it explained to him how important it might be?'

'Naturally. He says it is a question of honour. I have brought him in to the Yard to try to overawe him, and it's like trying to overawe a brick wall. You wouldn't care to have a go at him, would you?'

'I'll try, Charles; but why should I succeed where you cannot?'

'Oh, you know, honour, Peter; more up your street than mine.'

Chapparelle was run to earth, with help from his cook, in the Garrick. He offered Wimsey a drink, and they settled in a corner of the smoking-room. Behind Chapparelle's chair an enormous portrait of David Garrick in fancy dress outshone the mildly overdone dress of the Frenchman: his too elaborate tie, his gaudy studs, his spats and snakeskin shoes.

'It is no good to ask me, Lord Peter,' he said. 'No good for the policeman to ask me, and no good for you — how you say it? Man for man.'

'This is a rather serious matter, you know,' said Wimsey. 'I haven't the least reason to think you involved in Mrs Harwell's death, but if you won't say where you were the police will have to decide whether to charge you with murder, or merely with obstructing them in the course of their duties. By comparison with the difficulties this will place you in, the admission that you were somewhere you ought not to have been . . .'

'The difficulties for me if I tell you are *une bagatelle*,' said Chapparelle. 'It is even good for trade. Women like the *frisson* of being painted by a well-known seducer. But for the lady with whom I spend the night these difficulties would not be slight.'

'A married woman, I take it?'

Chapparelle inclined his head.

'Look, old man, we must find a way round this,' said Wimsey. 'Otherwise you will find yourself subpoenaed, refusing to testify, and possibly in prison for contempt of court.'

'I am ignorant of the law of the English,' said Chapparelle. 'But the laws of honour forbid me to drag a woman's name in the mud. If I must go to prison, *tant pis,* I go to prison!'

'But if someone were able in secrecy to ask the woman in question to say whether you were with her, and if she said yes, there would then be no need for any breach in discretion. The whole matter would be laid to rest.'

'Can you imagine, milord, if you follow up a visit to a lady somewhat compromised by sending in the police?'

'I was about to suggest,' said Peter, 'that you might like to trust me with your account of the evening of the 27th, and with the name of the lady. That I would then find a way, with the utmost delicacy, of asking her to confirm what you say, and that Inspector Parker would then rely on my word for it that your alibi is corroborated.'

Chapparelle considered for some time. Then he said, 'It is all for show, this reputation I have with women. If I painted women in Paris, I would not cause a stir. A Frenchwoman expects to be seriously regarded; it is her due. But your poor cold English beauties, for them it is a thrill to stir the blood that someone looks at them for two seconds together; so I look hard, and I make a few remarks, and soon they are telling me that nobody has ever understood them before as I. It is pitiful, Lord Peter. If they are cold, these English women, it is because they are frozen with neglect.'

'It is perfectly true,' said Wimsey, reflectively, 'that the English inclination for decorum and privacy can as easily conceal coldness and indifference as it can passion.'

'It is this which makes your compatriots so interesting to paint,' said Chapparelle. 'Without concealment, where is the triumph of perception? But what I mean to say, milord, is that those that I paint I very seldom touch. My reputation in that department is greatly exaggerated. Only sometimes when the picture is finished there is a little crisis. Madame is very sad; she cannot believe that all that staring at her, all that agreeable attention to her person is merely *professional.* So it can happen that I pay her a little farewell visit, discreetly, you understand. I take a little gift with me. A souvenir of the sitting.'

'And on the evening of the 27th of last month you were paying a little visit?'

Chapparelle passed across to Wimsey a page from his diary, on which was written a name. 'Please to be *gentil,* please to be careful,' he said.

'Thank you,' said Wimsey. 'Your trust will not

be misplaced. Ought I in self-defence to ask you when your portrait of my wife will be finished?' A note of mockery had entered his voice.

'Ah, but with Lady Peter it is altogether another case,' said the painter. 'It was La Bruyère, a countryman of mine, who said it: that when a plain-looking woman is loved it can only be very passionately. I keep out of the path of the real thing, Lord Peter, as I would keep out of the way of an avalanche, or out of the mouth of a volcano.'

Mrs Hartley-Skeffington received Lord Peter in her pallid and austerely fashionable drawing-room. His request deeply dismayed her. 'How could I admit to such a thing, Lord Peter? My husband would divorce me,' she said. 'I should be ruined. Nobody receives or consorts with a divorced woman.'

'If Chapparelle's alibi is confirmed,' Lord Peter told her, 'then he will be of no further interest to the police. It is only if it cannot be confirmed that he might have to be questioned under oath, and in public. The penalties to him in that situation might be severe.'

She turned away from him. He waited quietly while she struggled with herself. Then she turned to him again.

'He was with me that evening,' she said, in a whisper.

'I am very sorry to occasion pain or embarrassment,' said Lord Peter, 'but I must ask you exactly where and exactly when you were with him.'

'He joined me at five o'clock, or a few minutes later. He left me again before daybreak; a little after five in the morning.'

'And where was this?'

She blushed deeply. 'We were at the boat club. My husband and I have a boat at Weybridge. A cabin cruiser with berths . . . Before Easter there are very few people around . . .'

'Thank you,' said Lord Peter. 'That would seem to deal with the matter.' He rose to leave.

'Lord Peter, wait. From something he said — that is, he let drop — I have reason to believe Mr Chapparelle had seen poor Mrs Harwell very shortly before he came to me. I am so very frightened, Lord Peter.'

'But you are quite sure Chapparelle was with you by five?'

'Oh, yes, I am. I was watching the clock; I was — God forgive me! — waiting for him eagerly.'

'Then be assured he can have had nothing to do with what befell Mrs Harwell; she was certainly alive after five o'clock. Chapparelle is out of it; and therefore, Mrs Hartley-Skeffington, so are you. Try not to worry.'

'That's it, then. We shall arrest Claude Amery,' said Chief Inspector Parker, when Peter reported to him, naming no names, but declaring himself satisfied.

'I hate to see you make embarrassing mistakes, Charles,' said Lord Peter, lugubriously. 'Have you found some sound evidence against Amery?'

'What would you call sound evidence?' asked Parker.

'His fingerprints in the bedroom? No? I thought not. There is nothing against Amery except his own story.'

'Which he has changed under pressure, and will change again, I imagine, should we find another scrap of evidence. Oh, we found the dog, by the way. Throat severed, carcass buried in the compost heap.'

'Ugh,' said Peter. 'Look, Charles, try to imagine Amery doing that.'

'It isn't any harder to imagine than what he said he was doing, prowling around all night for no particular reason. We eliminate all that can be eliminated, and what remains is the answer, Wimsey. Amery remains.'

'Well, we might be about to get our hands on another bit of evidence, Charles. Put your hat on and come home with me, and I will show you some missives from Harriet's personal maid, who has been misrepresenting herself in Hampton.'

Bunter met Wimsey and Charles in the hall.

'I attended the auction at Knight Frank and Rutley, as instructed, my lord,' said Bunter. 'We secured the *Alice in Wonderland* first edition. I took the liberty of paying a little above the amount you mentioned to me, however.'

'Excellent. I didn't think it would go to a thousand.'

'Nine hundred and forty-five, my lord.'

'You did quite right, Bunter. Be so good as not to mention it to her ladyship; I intend to hide it away against her birthday.'

'Very good, my lord. And Mango has returned, in a state of some excitement, if I may be allowed an observation.'

'Excellent,' said Lord Peter. 'We shall hear her out at once. Tell her to come to the library in ten minutes, will you?'

'Very good, my lord.'

'Oh, and be there yourself, Bunter. This is a council of war.'

Peter shed his coat and hat, and bounded up the stairs in search of Harriet. He found her already in the library, serenely reading Markham's *Handbook of Forensic Medicine.*

'You are about to be interrupted by an incursion of news,' he said. 'Prepare to meet thy doom. Well, not shine, of course, but quite probably somebody's. And here's Charles.'

'How good to see you, Charles.'

Peter handed Charles Mango's two reports.

'You expect Mango to have discovered something deeply revealing?' Harriet asked. She was exhilarated by Peter's sudden eagerness.

'I expect her to have discovered the identity of the person whom Rosamund Harwell intended to dine with her,' said Peter. 'The joker in the pack. The person, whoever he may be, who can displace Claude Amery as the obvious suspect. We shall see. Ah; see the conquering heroine come. Come in, Mango, and sit down. This is Chief Inspector Parker. He is in charge of the investigation. I have shown him your letters.'

'I'd rather not sit down, my lord, if you wouldn't mind,' said Mango, primly.

'Just as you like,' said Peter. 'Now, tell us all you can.'

'Well, my lord, my lady, Chief Inspector, Mr Bunter, it wasn't any too easy. I was determined to get hold of the note directly from Mary, and not have an arrangement in which Rose delivered it to me. I might have been doing Rose an injustice, but I thought the note was an embarrassment to her. It was only the note that had made Mary so frightened about keeping her agreement with Rose not to split on her. Without the note, it was only a little plot between two girls to let one of them have a quiet evening. With the note — and Rose had asked Mary to destroy it . . . Anyway, I managed to cut Rose out of it. I winkled out of them what they were doing the following morning, this morning, that is. Rose had to sit with her father, while her mother went shopping, and Mary had promised to do some ironing.

'So this morning I just walked round to call on Mary, and the moment she was alone with me, and Rose's beady eye not on her, she ran upstairs and fetched the note for me. "You've no idea what a relief it is to be rid of it," she said. "It's been giving me nightmares, Miss Mango, ever since I first clapped eyes on it." '

'The suspense is killing us, Mango,' said Lord

Peter. 'To whom is it addressed?'

'See for yourself, my lord,' said Mango. She reached into her bag and produced a small envelope, which she handed to Lord Peter.

He held it out so that everyone could see it. It was a lilac-tinted paper, and had been addressed in a sprawling, distinctive hand: 'Laurence Harwell, Esq.'

There was a silence. Then Peter reached for a paper-knife, and eased the envelope open. It had been lightly gummed, and he lifted the flap without tearing it.

'Gloves, Bunter,' he said.

Bunter brought him a pair of lightweight, suede gloves, and he put them on. Then he eased the sheet of paper out of the envelope, and spread it out on the table. All four of them leaned over to read it.

Dearest Laurence,

Missing you awfully. Do come down to supper here tonight, and we can go home together tomorrow morning.

Your rose of all the world,
Rosamund

'You know,' said Peter, 'if it wasn't for that blasted alibi, I could say exactly what happened. Exactly. Probably not murder, wouldn't you say, Charles? Manslaughter, like that case Harriet dug out of *The Times* the other day. After all, the poor blighter didn't actually *get* this note. He just went down unexpectedly, shall we surmise, and saw his wife in her pretty white dress, and the table laid for two . . .'

Harriet met Mango's eyes, and the two women frowned slightly.

'Peter, was she wearing . . . ?' Harriet began.

But, 'No, he didn't,' Charles was saying doggedly. 'Victim seen alive a good hour after Harwell was into his flat, locked in for the night. We have been over and over it with those hall porters, and we can't shake them. You are barking up the wrong tree, Wimsey.'

'I can't be,' said Wimsey, sadly. 'There is something we have overlooked, Charles.'

'The fact is that Harwell has an alibi, and Amery doesn't,' said Charles. 'You can come with me tomorrow and have a go at those porters one last time, if you like. I'm not a stubborn man. But it won't get us anywhere.'

'I'll take you up on that, if I may,' said Peter. 'Will you stay for a drink?'

'The usual, Chief Inspector?' asked Bunter, imperceptibly translating himself from colleague to servant again. Mango began to beat a hasty retreat.

'Oh, Mango,' Lord Peter called her back. 'That was very well done. Excellent work. We are all very grateful to you.'

Whereupon Mango blushed deeply, and fled.

Much later, when Peter was musing over his new purchase beside the library fire, there was a timid knock on the door.

'Come in,' said Lord Peter, in a terrible tone, annoyed at whatever it might be. 'Oh, it's you, Mango. Lady Peter has gone to bed. Leave it till morning.'

The girl stood her ground, looking terrified.

'What is it?' he asked, in a more gentle tone.

'It's just, my lord. I can't help wondering . . . that is . . . of course it's no business of mine to say things, but . . .'

'Don't be silly, Mango,' said Lord Peter, adjusting his monocle, and staring at her through it. 'Say what you have to say. I don't eat the servants.'

'My lord, could it possibly be just a coincidence, do you think, about Phoebe Sugden? I mean I know she doesn't seem to have been anywhere near Hampton, but somehow, when there's something horrible in the very next house, I couldn't help but wonder . . .'

'What are you referring to, Mango? What about Phoebe Sugden? Where does she come in?'

'I don't know if she does, my lord, but . . .'

'Sugden — the name of the people in Mon Repos? Mrs Chanter's employers?'

'Their daughter, my lord.'

'One Phoebe. What about her?'

'She's disappeared, my lord. The police have put out posters and everything.'

'Well, yes indeed, Mango, it does seem an odd coincidence. I'll have to ask Charles about it. I didn't know.'

'Oh, sir, didn't you see all those newspaper headlines?'

'Headlines? About Phoebe Sugden? No, I didn't.'

'Yes, you did, sir. You must have done. Phoebe Sugden is only her real name, sir. Her stage name is Gloria Tallant.'

Peter said, 'My God, how stupid of me! I must get hold of Charles at once. No, wait, it's late and he's a family man. At crack of dawn. Mango, thank you very much.'

'It's nothing, sir. I could have said earlier, only I thought you would have known. It's caused much more of a stir at Hampton, sir, than Mrs Harwell, what with Phoebe being a local girl, and her poor mother and father being local too, and her being a real star, a West End actress.'

'What do they think has happened to her, Mango?'

'Kidnap, or murder, or worse, sir,' said Mango with just a touch of relish.

'Any or all, to choice,' said Peter. 'I suppose Chief Inspector Parker will know about the police enquiry. You don't happen to be able to tell me when the young woman disappeared?'

'A week to the day after the murder, sir, I believe.'

'But not from Hampton? What am I doing keeping you up asking questions, Mango? Things do rather run away with me when I get the bit between my teeth. Patience till morning is my only course. Goodnight.'

When Mango left, Lord Peter picked up *The Times*, and looked for any further developments in the missing actress story. He could find no mention of it, but his eye did light, well down the page, on a story that a man had been charged with the Sunbury attacks. According to the report the man had been in hospital, unconscious following a road accident during the intervening period, and had recovered enough to be interviewed only on Tuesday. Widespread speculation attributing other crimes to the same person were accordingly discounted, and further enquiries would be pursued concerning these other incidents. The police were now anxious to interview anyone who had seen a Siddeley Sapphire erratically driven in Sunbury on the night of 27 February.

'Humm,' said Lord Peter, replacing the paper in the rack, and betaking himself to bed.

The bedroom was awash with moonlight, the curtains standing wide.

'Harriet?' he said softly.

'Yes, indeed. Who else should it be?' she said, laughing.

'I only wondered if you were asleep. Shall I close the curtains?'

'Not on my account. I love to see the moon and stars from the bed.'

'Then so you shall, Domina. O, moon of my desire, that knows no wane, the moon of heaven is rising once again —'

'Stop burbling, Peter, and get under the covers

349

before you take cold.'

'Here I come. I haven't palled on you yet?'

'Not at all. I appear to be insatiable.'

'Splendid. In a wife I would desire, what in whores is often found . . . I suppose whores must have been rather different in his day.'

'Absurd, Peter, you are absurd . . .'

'The lineaments of gratified desire — I know it, Domina, I know it.'

16

Don't put your daughter on the stage, Missus
    Worthington,
Don't put your daughter on the stage . . .
NOËL COWARD

These our actors,
As I foretold you, were all spirits, and
Are melted into air, into thin air
WILLIAM SHAKESPEARE

'Had you realised, Harriet,' asked Peter over breakfast, 'that Gloria Tallant and Phoebe Sugden are, or were, as I am afraid is more likely, one and the same?'

'No, I hadn't,' said Harriet. 'But — that explains it. I kept thinking that the pictures of Gloria Tallant looked familiar, and I couldn't think why. I'd never seen her. But, Peter, I had seen Phoebe Sugden.'

'Had you? Was I there?'

'No; it was while you were abroad. I saw her at the Ritz. Eiluned pointed her out to me. She was lunching with Laurence Harwell.'

'I've got to see Charles,' said Peter, abandoning breakfast, and leaving without more ado.

Harriet went from the breakfast table to her writing desk, and began to work, steadily. Miss Bracy soon had to lay down her knitting and rattle her staccato keys. The scene Harriet had reached was a nocturne — the reservoir by night. For various technical reasons it had not proved possible to remove the scene to Highgate Ponds, and the story was now taking shape without reference to London's rivers. A love-lorn youth was rowing himself gently across the surface of the silvery water, and would, when Harriet had set the scene, witness the slow surfacing of a dead body, whose horrid pallor would give him the fright of his life. For some reason the moon shone brightly in Harriet's prose, and she was enjoying word-painting the watery stillness and the glinting reflected banners of moonlight. She was just pulling herself together, and sternly admonishing herself with the rule that the reader's interest in description is quickly exhausted, when Meredith tapped on the door and asked if she was at home to Mr Gaston Chapparelle.

'Here?' she said, surprised. 'Oh, very well, Meredith, show him up.'

But she finished her sentence before going up to the drawing-room herself.

Chapparelle was contemplating the portrait miniatures of ancient Wimseys which hung beside the mantelpiece. He took her hand and bowed over it.

'Forgive the intrusion, Lady Peter.'

'Do you need yet another sitting, Mr Chapparelle?'

'No, it is not that. I need your intercession.'

'With whom? I am ready to help you in any way I can.'

'With Mr Laurence Harwell. I believe he is a friend of yourself and Lord Peter.'

'He is an acquaintance of ours, certainly. I don't know that I would expect to have any influence over him, though, Mr Chapparelle. Won't you sit down?'

'I am at my wit's end, Lady Peter.'

And indeed the Frenchman did look deeply agitated. Harriet experienced a sudden desire to be at Talboys, where people would have such a journey to reach one that one would not be at the mercy of other people's troubles all the time.

'What has Mr Harwell done?' she asked, trying to keep the sigh out of her voice.

'Rather it is what he has not done — or *ce qu'il refuse à faire*. You see, Lady Peter, I am to have an exhibition at the Reynolds Academy; it is a signal honour for a living painter. Naturally I am very pleased. My clients are very pleased. First their beautiful faces are to be seen in excellent surroundings for the world to admire, and then also the investment they have made in my fee is becoming highly profitable. Everyone is pleased except Mr Harwell. When I apply to him yesterday to borrow his painting for a month he refuses. He will not even consider.'

'How very odd,' said Harriet.

'I tell him the exhibition will be *un coup de foudre,* that all London will be talking about it, and he refuses even more *catégoriquement.* I tell him that the painting is indispensable; that it is the great masterpiece of my London period, that without it the show is *Hamlet* without the prince. He replies that I am a mountebank, that I have sold the picture to him and that it is no more concern of mine at all. I have been treated like a grocer, Lady Peter, or a shoemaker.'

'I am so sorry, Mr Chapparelle. I expect Mr Harwell is within his legal rights, but . . .'

'Art is not property,' said Chapparelle with dignity. 'Never have I been so insulted. Could you not explain to him?'

'I don't know that I could. I don't know Mr Harwell beyond the slightest acquaintanceship. Would the absence of the Harwell portrait really ruin the exhibition? You have painted so many interesting portraits.'

'In this one there was a unique metaphysic,' the painter said with dignity. 'Your portrait is a work of genius, madame, but you do not give the occasion for such nuance, such *double entendre.*'

'I hope you do not think me jealous of poor Mrs Harwell on that account. And surely we must make allowances for Mr Harwell. I will try to find a chance to talk to him. But I do not expect to have any influence on him.'

'Thank you, Lady Peter,' said the painter, taking his leave. 'Your portrait will be very soon ready. You could collect it until the opening of the exhibition. If, that is, Lord Peter will be ready to lend it when the time comes. I find that with Englishmen, one does not know where one stands.'

'And with Englishwomen, Mr Chapparelle?'

'Alas, madame, one knows very well. One is all too often out in the cold. The fires must be lit over and over again.'

'Charles, never mind the porters for the moment. Who is in charge of the disappearing actress case?' asked Wimsey, standing in Chief Inspector Parker's office.

'It's in my department. Bollin is the detective working on it. Why the sudden interest?'

Wimsey told him. Charles whistled softly. 'We've been missing something,' he said. 'I'll get Bollin to put us in the picture. But you're right; it can't be coincidence.'

'Interesting, that,' said Wimsey. 'As a matter of fact, Charles, surely it could. There *are* such things as coincidence; it's not like saying, "It can't be a unicorn," now, is it?'

'It's all very well for you to theorise. What I know is that if a copper says something is just coincidence it means they have given up trying to make sense of it.'

'And *sub specie aeternitatis* everything makes sense?'

'Even you, Wimsey, even you.'

Inspector Bollin proved to be a rotund young man, with ink on his fingers, and an impressive pile of papers in his hands. Charles introduced Lord Peter. On being asked about the connection, coincident or not, between Phoebe Sugden and the Harwell case Bollin became embarrassed at once. It was apparent that although Phoebe's home address was in his notes, he had not put two and two together and realised exactly how close together the two houses in Hampton were.

'I'm not on the Harwell case, sir,' he said miserably to Charles. 'It didn't occur to me to check . . .'

'We understand it is the talk of the town in Hampton,' said Charles mildly.

'Miss Sugden disappeared from an address in London, sir, at which she had been resident for approximately two years. I did not pursue enquiries in her childhood home, sir.'

'You were not to realise that the address was next door to one involved in quite a different enquiry,' said Wimsey helpfully.

'No, my lord, I was not,' said Bollin, heatedly. 'Not but what I would have happened upon it sooner or later.'

'Of course you would,' said Wimsey.

'Possibly,' said Charles. 'Meanwhile, what have we got in the case of Miss Sugden?'

Bollin launched into an account of the case.

Gloria Tallant, alias Phoebe Sugden, now aged twenty, had been sent at her parents' expense to a private dance and drama school, where she had done fairly well. Inspector Bollin had interviewed the principal of the college and received a distinct impression that the young woman's looks rather than her talent were her best hope of a big part. However, on leaving the college she had put her name on the books of several agencies, and by and by had achieved some very minor parts. Then she had had a stroke of extraordinary good luck. Sir Jude Shearman's new play required a leading lady with red hair, who could dance a few steps in the second act.

'She had red hair?' asked Wimsey.

'Very striking red hair, I understand, sir,' said Bollin. 'This is her picture and description.'

Wimsey looked at the photo and the details. 'I'm turning into an old married man, Charles,' he said, sorrowfully. 'A picture of a pretty woman leaves me cold. So, Inspector Bollin, our heroine lands a plum part.'

'It was for six weeks, sir. She had a bit of difficulty pleasing the director in rehearsal, but it was all set for the opening night. That's the background, sir. Then she didn't show up for the dress-rehearsal, or the opening performance, and her understudy had to go on in her place. Two days later the police were informed.'

'Two days? Why the delay?'

'It was very unfortunate. But the young woman's parents had gone abroad for the winter; the mother's health is uncertain, I believe.'

'Friends? Family?'

'She was living alone, sir, in a bedsitting-room in Southwark, quite handy for the West End. Apart from the people at the theatre there was just a boyfriend. I'll come to him in a minute.'

'And at the theatre they just assumed she had let them down?'

'That's about it, sir.'

'Do ambitious young women often skive off, leaving lead parts to the understudies?' enquired Wimsey.

'I don't know about that, sir, but the management didn't know this one well enough to know if she was reliable or not. No track record so to speak. They sent somebody to her flat, but he couldn't get in, and the neighbours didn't know anything. And when I asked a lot of questions, sir, it appeared that the director had told her off at the last rehearsal, the pre-dress-rehearsal, and upset her.'

'Do we know what about?'

'It was more or less about a certain line in the last act, I understand. He couldn't make her say it how he wanted, and she cried, and he told her she wasn't good enough to try that on, and she flounced out.'

'So when she didn't appear when she was supposed to, they thought she was sulking?'

'Paying him out. Making him sweat a bit. They thought it was . . .' Inspector Bollin turned to his notes, ' "A touch of the Sarah Bernhardts", they said.'

'But surely they realised it was serious when

she missed curtain-up on the first night?'

'Yes, they did, sir. But by then they had other things on their minds. Like whether Miss Mitzi Darling with dyed hair could save the day. They put a junior member of the management — well, someone from the ticket office — on to the job of trying to find her, and when she drew a blank they called the police.'

'I see. And you said there was a boyfriend?'

'Yes, sir. One Larry Porsena.'

'Another stage name, I take it? And by the nine gods he swore — what did he swear, Inspector Bollin?'

'A long deposition, sir. And no; it seems Porsena is his real name. Eye-tie parents, I gather.'

Charles flipped over the pages Inspector Bollin handed to him, and said, 'Give us the gist of this, will you, Inspector?'

'Gladly, sir. The gentleman was very fluent, sir. But what he says, roughly, is this. Gloria had an audition, at eleven in the forenoon, to which he escorted her. They were going to have lunch together afterwards, and before the dress-rehearsal for *Dance until Dawn*. Porsena left her at the stage door of the Cranbourne Theatre, and waited for her outside. She never came out. Of course he didn't know how long it should have been, but by two o'clock he was hungry, and browned off, and he went in and asked what had happened to her. He was told that there was no auditioning going on; that there was nobody in the building except the scene-painters, and he could make himself scarce.'

'And he jumped to the conclusion, I suppose, that she had stood him up?'

'Exactly, sir. He was very fed up. She had a part, and he hadn't; did I say he was a fellow-actor, sir? And he thought she was giving him the brush-off. So he just went off and drowned his sorrows. A couple of days later he went round to her place in the morning, to try to make it up with her, and of course he couldn't find her. Next thing he knew he read about in the newspapers.'

'And what did you make of him, Inspector?' asked Wimsey.

'Excitable sort of young man, sir. Genuinely fond of the young lady. Very worried about her.'

'I see. Would you think I was poking my nose in unnecessarily if I went and talked to him myself?'

'It's a free country, sir,' said Bollin, stiffly.

'Anything I find out will be reported back to you,' said Peter. 'It is your enquiry. It's just that people aren't always at their most confiding when talking to policemen. Chief Inspector Parker will, I am sure, make sure you get the credit for it.'

'Certainly,' said Charles.

'Thank you, sir. And as for taking credit, Chief Inspector, Lord Peter, we haven't got it cleared up yet. We have to find the young woman first. And at the moment she has gone without trace. A flighty young woman could have gone anywhere, with anyone, got into any kind of trouble.

Time enough to talk about taking credit when we've got to the bottom of it.'

'You are absolutely right, Inspector. I stand rebuked,' said Peter, meekly.

Larry Porsena opened his door to Lord Peter in his pyjamas, said, 'Oh, hell! Excuse me a moment,' and retreated, closing the door again. Lord Peter stood patiently on the landing and waited. The landing was in a lodging house: 'A Residential Hotel for Theatre People', as it called itself on the board outside. A card picked up from the table in the hallway proclaimed that hot meals would be available in the residents' rooms until two in the morning; that a friendly family atmosphere would prevail, but that drunkenness would not be tolerated; that young ladies and young gentlemen would be accommodated on separate floors; that laundry would be charged extra; that Mrs Malloney would ensure that the place was a home from home. One week's notice to be given on vacating a room.

Peter had read this far when the door was opened again, revealing a wiry, dark-haired young man with large features, dressed like Hamlet in a flowing white shirt and a black leotard.

'Stage clothes,' he said, gesturing vaguely at his attire. 'Malloney has impounded my trousers. I rather hoped you were my brother come to advance me the rent.'

'I am afraid not,' said Wimsey, offering his card.

361

'Golly!' said Porsena. 'Thank heaven! You're a famous sleuth, aren't you? Perhaps you can find her. I take it this is about Pheeb?'

Wimsey blinked, and Porsena said, 'Phoebe. Gloria.'

'Yes. I think you should hope that I shall not be able to find her.'

Porsena frowned for a second, and then sat down abruptly, and dropped his head in his hands. 'Oh, God,' he said.

'Let's hope I'm wrong,' said Wimsey. He waited for the young man to recover himself. The room was spectacularly untidy, and decorated with theatre bills and autographed photographs of the great and famous. Ashcroft and Olivier smiled glamorously across the bed. Gloria herself smirked at him over a naked shoulder rising from a deeply décolleté gown. Porsena's own publicity photographs looked back at her across his bed.

'I did tell the police everything I could think of,' said Porsena.

'I'd like to ask you rather different things,' said Wimsey. 'About her frame of mind in the previous few days. And on the day itself. Was she acting oddly in any way?'

'Several ways, actually. How did you know? I thought she'd gone round the bend.'

'She must have been very excited about the part in *Dance until Dawn*.'

'You bet she was. It was the big break. Everyone is longing for a big break. But it was only a short run, you know. If the critics slated her she would be back at the agency door, well down the queue. Only it went to her head. She didn't see it like that at all. She kept saying she was set up for life, and when I tried to make her see reason she just said, "Wait and see." '

'Mr Porsena —'

'Oh, do call me Larry. Everyone does.'

'Larry, did she say anything to give you an impression, even a ghost of an impression, that she was about to — well, abandon her old friends on a new cloud of glory?'

'Dump me for somebody more famous, you mean? Or at least somebody in work? Naturally, that's what I was afraid of. I was very fond of her, Lord . . . I don't know what to call a lord. Will Peter do?'

'Peter will do, within these four walls.'

'Well, Peter, we weren't exactly love's young dream. Just very good pals. Ever since I first bought her a coffee in the lunch break at college. We had a lot of fun together, and we had a sort of pact. You're a man of the world, I can tell you things I wouldn't tell the police. Anyone would realise that a girl living on her own in London might need an escort. But a young man in my position can find it useful to have a girlfriend too. It looks better. It allays certain fears. Of course I was afraid she would dump me — for her sake as much as for my own.'

'What do you mean by that, Larry?'

'Well, she was scatty. She hadn't quite got a grip on the hard world. You know the kind of thing: everyone was going to be kind to her, and nobody would be jealous, and it was going to be wonderful fun and never any hard work. Her parents' fault, if you ask me.'

'Bringing her up badly?'

'Bringing her up well. Letting her think the universe revolved around her.'

'And the result was she needed a protector, and you were it?'

'Got it. You're jolly quick on the uptake, Peter, aren't you?'

'I do my humble best. Anyway, you were saying you were afraid she might . . .'

'Only it took her just the opposite way. She was saying she would get me good parts; she would fix us both up, and we didn't have to worry again. I thought she'd gone bananas. I kept telling her it was only a part that she'd got. I don't know what you reckon, Peter, but I reckon that even very famous actresses, even the Gertrude Lawrences and Dorothy Lamours of the world, don't really have that much pull. I mean no doubt they get taken out to lunch, and into bed, if they want, I dare say, and no doubt they get seen around with powerful people, but I don't think they make casting decisions.'

'And she was talking like this on the basis of her first ever good part?'

'Exactly. Riding for a fall, I thought.'

'Nevertheless, she did have an audition for a part to take over when *Dance until Dawn* finishes?'

'So she said. I don't know what to think. When

she didn't come out after a couple of hours, I went in there and they said there hadn't been any audition all morning.'

'Yes, I have read your statement to the police. What do you think had happened to her?'

'Well, it's damned odd. I got a bit stroppy when the janitor gave me the brush-off like that, and he said, "See for yourself." So I went in and looked for her. In the auditorium, of course, and the foyer. The street doors were all locked up, by the way, so she couldn't have walked out that way. So then I ran along the corridors and opened all the dressing-room doors in turn, and the manager's office, and the wardrobe mistress's den — every door I could find. I was yelling for her, too. I ran around backstage. No luck. I don't know how she got out without my seeing her, but she wasn't there.'

'It wouldn't be easy to search a theatre completely, though,' said Lord Peter, musingly.

'You mean she could have been hiding?'

'Or hidden.'

'That's a terrible thought,' the young man said. 'I don't like that at all.'

'Sorry, and all that. Don't like to bring black thoughts. One more thing, though: did she do anything unusual in the week or so before she disappeared? Go anywhere she hadn't been before? That sort of thing?'

'Not as far as I know. She went home to fetch some clothes one evening — home to Hampton, I mean. I wouldn't go with her, I don't like suburbs much. I wanted to go drinking with some chums in town.'

'Thank you, Larry, you've been a great help,' said Wimsey, taking his leave. As he went, he tapped on the landlady's door, strategically situated beside the door to the street, and negotiated the release of Mr Porsena's trousers. There are some indignities from which he felt obliged to protect his fellow-men.

Alittle way down the street he slipped into a telephone box, and dialled the number for Scotland Yard. He spoke, not to Chief Inspector Parker, but to Inspector Bollin, and asked him to obtain a complete list of keyholders to the Cranbourne Theatre.

'Harwell's been having a bonfire,' said Charles, angrily.

'Where?' asked Wimsey. 'Surely those flats don't have open fireplaces, and there are no gardens.'

'He has a garden in Hampton,' said Charles grimly.

'Have you put a tail on him, Charles, in spite of telling me emphatically that I was barking up quite the wrong tree? Very wise of you.'

'Yesterday he drove himself down to Hampton and lit a fire in the garden. I told my man not to let himself be seen, so he had trouble seeing exactly what was going on. A lot of garden rubbish was burned, and a bundle of something from the boot of Harwell's car. Harwell didn't stay long, and he didn't enter the bungalow. The moment he left, we raked out the ashes, of course.'

'Bloodstained clothing,' said Peter. 'Canine blood.'

'Yes, probably. Clothing certainly, but the bloodstains might be gone beyond the scope of proof. It was a good fierce blaze. And perhaps there was something else in it as well.' Charles produced an envelope, and carefully slid the contents on to his blotting pad. A little scrap of darkly scorched fabric, no bigger than a postage stamp lay there. 'This doesn't look like part of a rich man's clothing to me.'

'Hmm,' said Wimsey. 'It's some kind of buckram, isn't it? I won't touch it, but I suppose it is stiff. Perhaps the kind of thing a tailor would use to interface lapels?'

'Ho. I hadn't thought of that. We'll get a Savile Row fellow to look at it.'

'What does Harwell say he was doing?'

'Getting himself into the open air for a bit. Clearing up fallen leaves. No law against it; there is a law against harassment. Why don't we concentrate our minds on getting Amery behind bars? You can imagine the sort of thing.'

'Only too well,' said Wimsey. 'But Charles, there must be something wrong with that alibi. If the porters won't budge, perhaps we should have another go at Amery.'

'To confirm what, exactly?' asked Charles. 'Oh, by the by, Wimsey, talking of confirmation, a lorry driver has turned up to confirm giving the jolly blackmailers a lift away from the scene of the crime well before eleven. So that eliminates them from the enquiry.'

'Well, we didn't really include them anyway, did we?'

'I suppose not. And I can't even nail them for blackmail, because Mr Warren won't press charges.'

'Won't he?' said Wimsey, astonished. 'Whyever not?'

'He seems to have got religion, and be in a mood to forgive his enemies,' said Charles. 'And for that, Wimsey, I blame you.'

'Dear my lord,
Make me acquainted with your cause of grief,' said Harriet.

'Am I musing and sighing with my arms across?'

'Well, I can see something is wrong.'

'Can you? And I thought I was making such a good job of keeping it to myself.'

'But why should you? Why not confide in your wife?'

'Because I am ashamed of myself. I'm behaving like a dog, Harriet. Selfish to the point of ugliness.'

'Because you ought to be pleased for Bunter, instead of grieving over him?'

'How did you know? Harriet, if you are going to see through my poor pretences like this, how ever shall I keep your good opinion?'

Harriet laughed. 'Peter, I don't think any less of you for discovering that Bunter's extraordinary devotion is repaid by attachment on your part. In fact, do you remember that moment in *Pride and Prejudice* when Elizabeth finally realises that she has been just plain wrong about Darcy?'

'No; remind me.'

'She is listening to an encomium from his housekeeper.'

'Bunter's devotion is my character reference? Of course I wish him every happiness,' said Peter. 'But it's almost impossible to imagine anyone else in his place.'

'Peter, look, all these traditions, all these rules that say a servant can live in, and a non-servant can't, and they must use pseudonyms, and so and so on — do we have to be bound by them? Can't we change anything?'

'The servants like rules,' he said. 'They know where they are then, and exactly what they must do to give satisfaction. It makes for a peaceful household, and I wanted a peaceful household; I wanted you to be free to work.'

'Your mother told me that it was up to you to make a home for me and bring me to it; not up to me to make a home for you. And I was relieved, because I didn't feel up to making the sort of home you would be used to; I was overwhelmed by it. But now I'm here . . .'

'Now you're here it is your establishment,' said Peter. 'You are the mistress of the house, and you do what you like in it.'

'Without regard to you?'

'Traditionally, if I don't like it, I retreat to my club. That's what men's clubs are for, and why they are populous.'

'Well, would you retreat to your club if I suggested that Bunter and the future Mrs Bunter could be installed in the mews?'

'I — well, I hadn't thought of that.'

'It would combine Bunter's continuing proximity with a separate roof over their heads.'

'Harriet, it would be a wonderful idea. I'm sure Bunter . . . but would the young woman accept it? Wouldn't it be a bit demeaning? I mean, I don't know what she's like, but . . .'

'I think you will like her, Peter. And I have reason to think she would accept a mews cottage with its own front door.'

'Have you now?' he said.

'I rather rashly mentioned the possibility of doing it up very smartly.'

'That's no problem; it would be fun, and come to that a good investment in the property. But there would be problems in day-to-day living, I suppose,' he said.

'But surely four intelligent people can find a *modus vivendi.*'

'What does Bunter think?'

'I don't know. You must ask him.'

Moments later she saw from the drawing-room window man following master down the rain-slicked garden path, through the darkening garden. Then a flickering light, like torchlight, showed successively in the three floors of the mews.

'All shall be well, and all shall be well, and all manner of things shall be well,' said Peter, returning to her an hour later. 'I have married a practical genius.'

'You would have thought of it yourself any minute,' said Harriet.

'But that's just the thing; I don't suppose I would. My sort's very hide-bound, you know. Running in ancient ruts. It's very liberating to be married to someone who is unimpressed by tradition.'

'Well, the news that I can alter things is going to my head rather. Could we change the tradition that puts us at opposite ends of the table when we lunch or dine alone? It's ridiculous that I have to get myself asked out to lunch by my husband to sit near enough to him for easy conversation.'

'Meredith shall be instructed to place us face to face across the middle of the board,' said Peter gravely. 'The king's palace shall be a queen's garden. I shall abdicate in your favour.'

'Couldn't we reign co-equal? There doesn't seem to be enough disagreement between us to justify revolutions and abdications.'

'A lesson, love, in love's philosophy? I am consumed with curiosity. What is the prospective consort of Bunter actually like?'

'Rather like me, I think. Perhaps from circumstances somewhat tighter than mine. Needed to earn a living, found a satisfactory way to do it;

interesting to talk to. Holds Bunter in high regard. In different circumstances she could have been a woman don . . . But, Peter, tell me what Bunter said.'

'I have never seen him evince so much feeling in twenty-odd years. He is overjoyed. I told him it was your idea.'

'You needn't have done that.'

'It is true my self-esteem is at a low ebb at the moment, but I am not so craven as to need to steal credit from my wife.'

'What has dented your self-esteem, my lord?'

'Harwell's alibi. But enough of that. Has the capable Robert Templeton plumbed the depths of Highgate Ponds?'

'I couldn't make that work in the end. I'm having to transfer the weirs to the outfall of a rural reservoir.'

'Too bad. I'll put the map away then.' Peter moved across to the side table where his old map of London was spread out.

'It's fascinating for its own sake,' she said. 'Did you know the London Hippodrome used to have water shows, and they could flood the tank from a river running below the building?'

'No, I didn't. I had heard of unwholesome smells from below the stage of the . . .' Peter glanced at the map as he began to roll it up. Then he stopped, and switched on the table lamp. Harriet heard him whistle faintly. She got up and joined him looking.

'What is it, Peter?'

'Here,' he said, pointing.

Flowing across the Seven Dials area on the map, which was marked as a marsh, was a dotted blue line, and the words 'Course of the Cranbourne?' It was one of a web of speculative water courses shown as tributaries of the Fleet.

Peter said, bleakly, 'Harriet, I think there might after all be a way out of the Cranbourne Theatre other than through the doors, and in that case, I think I know where Charles ought to be looking for Gloria Tallant.'

17

In stygian cave forlorn,
'Mongst horrid shapes, and shrieks, and
   sights unholy

JOHN MILTON

The Fleet flows out into the Thames at Black-friars Bridge. There is nothing to be seen of it but a cavernous black void giving out on to the slimy, grey, low-tide bank of shingle below the bridge. The water at low tide, and in dry weather, is shallow, seeping rather than flowing towards daylight and liberation in the Thames. Almost unrecognizable in thigh boots, and Water Board oilskins and tin helmets, Chief Inspector Parker and Inspector Bollin and Lord Peter Wimsey followed Mr Snell, the linesman, wading abreast in a wide tunnel in which the damp brick archway rose ten feet or so above their heads. Gradually the tunnel narrowed and darkened, and they needed their torches. The weight of water round their ankles taught them a sliding gait, shuffling rather than raising their feet. Caught in the torch beams, rats scuttled along a jutting course of bricks, staring undaunted at the light, giving back loathing for loathing. When the little party stopped, a chorus of echoing drips and trickling outfalls resounded in the cavernous space.

Harriet had been right, thought Lord Peter. She had looked at him somewhat greenly about the gills at the very thought of this expedition, in spite of its possible literary utility to her, and he had jumped at the chance. Since he had gaily promised her a full report he was honour bound, now, to keep up with the party and stay the course.

They reached the first weir after a few minutes. A bare iron ladder allowed them to climb over it in single file, and stand in the first of Bazalgette's great intercepting sewers. Unlike the sluggish water of the sleeping Fleet, this was rapidly flowing. Their torches showed an opaque brown fluid swirling past the ledge on which they stood. There was a very pervasive unhealthy smell.

'They used to be able to light the streets of London with the methane coming off this,' Mr Snell told them. 'In the days of gas light, of course. Now if any of you gentlemen has a box of matches, or a cigarette lighter in your pockets, I must ask you not to touch them. The slightest spark can cause an explosion here.'

'Does all this flow west to east by simple gravity?' asked Wimsey.

'In a way, sir, it does. But we have to pump it up over inclines two or three times on its way to allow it to continue by gravity. There is enough methane collected to drive the necessary turbines.'

Nearly opposite the point where they stood a dark tunnel entered the sewer through an arch.

'That is the old Fleet, gentlemen,' Snell told them. 'Follow me.'

They waded knee-deep through the sewer, and entered the tunnel carrying the Fleet. It was nearly dry under their feet. They began to walk along it.

'I would have expected an old watercourse like this to carry more flow,' said Chief Inspector Parker. His voice was muffled by the scarf he had pulled over his nose and mouth to filter the smell. Even so it boomed in the echoing passageway.

'When you confine a river in a culvert, sir,' he was told, 'you cut it off from all the little trickles that used to run into it. These days it's only storm water that the old rivers carry down; all the actual sewage is in these cross-routes. In dry weather the old river courses down here soon run dry.'

His little party fell silent. They walked for some considerable time, strung out one behind the other, walking in the sludgy deposit on the floor of the culvert. Here and there side tunnels came in, some of them seeping. It seemed like an age before they reached the middle-level intercepting sewer. Once again there was an iron stepladder by which the party climbed over the weir out of the Fleet and into the Victorian tunnel of the sewer. Completely disorientated now, they entered the upper reaches of the Fleet, and soon came to an outfall of some size, entering on their left. Their torches showed it some way back, to where a bend took it out of sight.

'This is what you might be looking for, gentlemen,' said Mr Snell. 'This is the first branch that might be draining out of Seven Dials.'

'Is this the Cranbourne?' asked Wimsey.

'Not that I know of, sir,' said Mr Snell. 'I don't know as there ever was a Cranbourne — not as such. To my way of thinking, I don't know as how the marsh under Seven Dials ever did flow out into the Fleet. And I never saw any Cranbourne marked on any of our maps.'

'Then what in Hades are we doing here?' asked the Chief Inspector.

'Whether it's the Cranbourne or not isn't the point, sir. If the marsh drains into the Fleet, then it comes in here. I would guess it comes down lots of little courses that have lost their names long ago along with their daylight. Maybe there was a Cranbourne once. Maybe it's somewhere through here or flowing into here. Maybe the whole district drained into the Cock and Pie Ditch; but we can't find that to walk up it.'

'Do these channels get inspected regularly?' asked Parker.

'Regular, but not often, sir,' said Mr Snell. 'There's hundreds and hundreds of miles of it under London. We have teams of flushers working, but it takes them a while to get round. Unless we gets a problem it might be more than a year before we come past somewhere.'

'Enlighten us, Mr Snell. What is a flusher?'

'A man what shovels the grit out, that accumulates in the sewers, sir. It would all silt up otherwise.'

'If you think this passageway drains Seven Dials, it's the one we want,' said Charles. 'Can we get up it?'

'You can, sir, but not standing upright. It might come to crawling in the muck, sir, as you go further up.'

'I'm afraid we must try, all the same,' said Charles. 'If this is the nearest outlet to Seven Dials.'

Wimsey shuddered at the thought, but the group began to stoop and shuffle onwards. And then there was a noise, a rhythmic low booming sound like the slow firing of cannonshot.

Mr Snell's demeanour changed at once. 'Back up!' he cried. 'Quick about it, if you don't mind!'

There was an undignified scramble backwards towards the Fleet tunnel. 'This way! Look lively, sirs.' As Mr Snell spoke the tunnel sighed in their faces a gust of its foul breath. This was followed immediately by a blast of turbulent, roaring wind.

'What's happening?' cried Inspector Bollin in alarm.

'That was the topman banging the manhole cover in its hole to let us know it's raining up there,' said Snell. 'Don't be frightened, gentlemen, we have a minute or two. Up these steps here — hurry along, please!' A note of genuine alarm had entered his voice. One after another

378

the group climbed on to the footholds of the ladder, going straight up through a shaft in the roof. Mr Snell was last in line. As he got his hands on the rung below Wimsey's feet a deafening crash of sound, like the surf on a huge foreshore, rose past him. Looking down, Wimsey saw a roaring deluge rising below the man. He locked his left arm through the nearest iron rung, and, leaning down, offered Mr Snell a hand. Mr Snell got a foothold on a rung above the bubbling and rapidly rising surface, and the two men climbed clear. A disc of white daylight topped the shaft they were climbing in, with the swaying black outlines of the policemen moving above them.

They crawled out of the ground in the Clerkenwell Road, in the middle of the street, with cars going past them on both sides. The topman stood over the manhole, holding a flag to warn the traffic. The gutters were sluicing with rain, and pouring water down the throats of the drains.

'We are a good way east of Seven Dials,' observed Wimsey.

Mr Snell seemed untroubled by the rain, but then, a drenching with clean water must have been a welcome change for him. 'Ah, sir, who knows where they all are?' he asked.

'All who?' asked Wimsey, startled for the moment with spectres of many corpses, when one was bad enough.

'London's rivers,' said Mr Snell. 'You can bury them deep under, sir; you can bind them in tunnels, you can divert them and stop them up and forget about them, you can lose the map, and wipe the name out of mind, but in the end where a river has been, a river will always be.'

'You're a poet of the sewers, I see,' said Lord Peter, appreciatively.

'We will have to try again in drier weather, I take it?' Chief Inspector Parker asked, turning his collar up against the battering rain.

Meanwhile, beneath their feet the sluggish Cranbourne in its nameless course had roused itself, and spewed out its secret contents into the torrential Fleet, and the Fleet had tossed and carried it down over the succession of weirs, and out into the turning tide of the rain-dimpled Thames, which in turn took it onward, down-stream, to surface below Tower Bridge on the tidal mudflats. The captain of a tug would see it, and summon the Port of London Authority launch. The body of a woman would be recovered. But nobody would be able to tell at what point it had entered the water.

18

See how love and murder will out.
> WILLIAM CONGREVE

Here, take my picture; though I bid farewell
Thine, in my heart, where my soul dwells
　　shall dwell
> JOHN DONNE

'Harriet, do I smell?'

Harriet considered the matter. 'Yes, my lord. Quite distinctly. Of carbolic soap.'

'Oh, as long as it's nothing worse. Bunter has been scrubbing me all over for twenty minutes, but it still lingers in my nostrils. Or perhaps it's a psychological smell, a kind of olfactory battle-fatigue.'

'I take it you have been searching for missing actresses?'

'Down the drains. Or up them, rather, since we entered them at the outfall. We didn't find anything, but then before we reached our destination rain stopped play.'

'A pity. Robert Templeton has found his corpse

while you were out, and I was hoping for a hideous detail or two to flesh out the description.'

'Fleshing out is an unfortunately happy expression. I have married a ghoul. Are ghouls like the crones of fables, do you think? Do they turn into princesses if one embraces them? Upon your assurance that I do not reek I shall experiment . . .'

Peter put his arms round Harriet, and kissed her. The moment she flinched, he released her, and said, 'Harriet, what is it? What is wrong?'

'There, love, don't look so stricken; nothing is wrong.'

'You quite frightened me. Did I hurt you? I don't know my own strength, sometimes, what with Mr Matsu's training.'

'Peter, it's nothing. Just this stupid collar is so stiff it scratched me.'

'Let me see.' He moved behind her, and undid the collar, one tiny hook by one, and uncurled it from her neck. 'Yes; the blasted thing has grazed you,' he said. 'It's drawn blood!'

Harriet went to the mirror over the mantelpiece to look. Minuscule droplets of blood stood on a tiny abrasion on her neck.

'It's nothing,' she said. 'Kiss me again.'

But Peter was standing in the middle of the room behind her, the collar in his right hand, and frowning. 'I — excuse me a minute,' he said, and went to the telephone. She heard him through the open door asking for Sir James Lubbock.

'James, something has come up . . .'

Meredith came in. 'Is it all right to draw the curtains, my lady?'

'Yes, thank you, Meredith.'

'No,' Peter was saying, 'very tiny surface marks. Quite localised. They couldn't have been obliterated in some way by bruising? Yes, of course you looked carefully, but — yes, I see. I see. Thank you.'

Peter put down the telephone, and looked at Harriet abstractedly. 'There were no such marks on Rosamund Harwell's neck as there are now on yours,' he said. 'Harriet, can you think of any reason under the sun or the moon why someone might put a collar on to a woman already dead?'

'To cover the marks of strangulation?'

'The face was as much disfigured as the neck itself,' he said, 'and the face was naked.'

'I don't know; let me think. Could someone have been dressing her — could she have been naked when she was killed, and the murderer have dressed her afterwards?'

'That would be harder than it sounds. Getting clothes on to a completely inert body would be a struggle. And why? Why was the murderer doing it?'

'I don't know why. But it would explain a mistake like the collar.'

'A mistake? Why do you call it a mistake?'

'Well, I was a bit baffled when I heard she was wearing that. So was Mango, I think. Rosamund had such exquisite taste. And nobody with the least idea at all of dress would wear the white

383

collar with a white dress. The whole idea of the thing is to soften the effect of wearing black.'

'So she was dressed after she was dead,' said Peter miserably. 'Oh, Harriet, I loathe this case!'

'I don't know what to say, my dear. I hate to see you miserable, but . . .'

'But you don't like to suggest that I disengage myself and go fishing because of the way I reacted to that suggestion last time?'

'No; because I want to see the stupid woman avenged!'

'A woman, however stupid, being on your side?'

'In what conflict, Peter? Are men and women at war?'

'We are not,' he said. 'At least *we* are not.'

'No, indeed,' she said. 'I think what I meant was that I wanted to see the weak protected against the strong, and stupidity is a form of weakness.'

'A potentially lethal form,' he said. 'Nothing is weaker than a murdered corpse; and this one was not wearing when it was murdered the collar it was wearing when it was found.'

'So she was murdered when undressed?'

'It would seem so. And that suggests a sexual crime.'

'But are you surprised? In view of who she was and what we know about her it was always likely to be so, wasn't it?'

'It was likely to be a crime of passion. But logically a man could be provoked by rage and jealousy and desire as easily by a fully dressed woman as by one lying naked in bed. More easily perhaps.'

'I see what you mean; a sexual crime suggests one perpetrated by a stranger.'

'A stranger who leaves no trace, no finger-prints.'

'A husband or a lover, then. And acting at a level at which people are impossible to know. At which it is hard enough to understand even one's own partner, let alone anyone else's.'

'A level at which one is doing well to under-stand even oneself,' he said.

'As when I took all those years to discover that I needed you?'

'That was my fault. All that peacocking and manoeuvring. I was overbearing; trying to win you by overpowering your resistance. Every at-tempt I made made it harder for you to accept me, because acceptance would have been surren-der. In my own defence all I can say is that I eventually realised that I could not win a free spirit like yours in such a way. And that never, in my most benighted and insufferable moments, could I have played such games sexually. It was all heart and mind stuff.'

'Dearest,' she said, holding out a hand to him, 'let's not divide the lusts of the flesh from heart and mind. And lusts are only joys — did you know? It's just the Anglo-Saxon word for joy.'

'Is it indeed?' he said, taking her hand. 'An insight lost with the Norman Conquest, with which my ancestors were intimately connected.'

'You seem exceptionally eager to take blame for things tonight, my lord. Is it that which is making you so unhappy about all this?'

'I suppose so, Harriet. Touch pitch and be defiled. There's a game that men and women play. It isn't our game and so our knowledge of it is anecdotal, if extensive. The woman puts up a show of reluctance. Respectability is chaste; or she doesn't like it; the man is fired up by resistance, he storms the citadel. Perhaps she seems to like being overcome; perhaps she concedes from pity or love or mercy for his need and must be paid in gratitude. It's a dangerous game; it contaminates love with power.'

'And it could easily go too far?'

'Very easily.'

'Do you remember when you bought me that dog-collar in case I got strangled in Oxford, you showed me two pressure points in the neck . . .'

'Yes. A human being is very fragile in certain places.'

'And might be strangled almost by accident?'

'Might die in hands that intended only to overpower. Or in the hands of someone who got a frisson out of a show of strength. The kind of strength disgustingly called manly.'

'But that would not be murder. It fails your definition of intent.'

'Yes. And if Gloria Tallant turns up unharmed a manslaughter verdict on Rosamund Harwell is the best the prosecution could hope for. If she turns up dead, that's a very different matter.'

'There could be no connection.'

'Back to the realm of unhappy coincidence. I'm afraid there is a connection. But for the moment, will you tell me with your woman's intuition whether the husband or the lover was more likely to use excessive force?'

Harriet thought about it. She walked to the window and considered it, looking out unseeingly into the street. 'I would have to say I think it would be more likely to be Harwell,' she said. 'He has a dominant personality. Claude — whatever I might say about his powers as a poet — strikes one as rather defective in what you just called manliness.'

'That's the devil of it,' said Peter. 'Here we go round the mulberry bush. Again. As far as corroboration is concerned, Harwell appears to be telling the truth and Amery to be lying. One is almost tempted to suppose a conspiracy between the two of them.'

'No,' said Harriet. 'While she was alive their rivalry would absolutely prevent that; and once she was dead whoever killed her would be so hated by the other.'

'I think you are right. I must beat about the bushes some more.'

'Well, before you do, how about a little unforced Anglo-Saxon joy? Here I stand, uncollared . . .'

'That's the thing about me. I could never storm a citadel, however ill-defended. The only thing that tempts me is a wide-open gate, and the trumpets sounding welcome.'

'Alone of all your sex?'

'Well, not quite alone. In a minority. I have always been like that, as wicked Uncle Paul could tell you. He regards it as a weakness.'

'No doubt he would love to tell me. But I think I would rather explore without a guide.'

'No maps of the interior?'

'Just surveys of my own making. What kind of trumpets do you want to sound your welcome? Bach trumpets?'

'Could you manage a natural trumpet?'

'Yes,' she said, 'I think I could.'

Monsieur Gaston Chapparelle was announced unexpectedly shortly after breakfast.

'I give myself the pleasure, madame, milord, of observing in person the effect of my work.' He was followed into the room by Meredith, bearing a large flat rectangular parcel.

'My dear fellow,' said Peter, laying aside the newspaper, and rising to greet the Frenchman. 'There was no need. We would have come to collect it.'

'The observation I have promised myself, Lord Peter, is on both of you together. Had I merely sent a message that the portrait was ready to be collected, one or other of you would have come; I could not command you both to present yourselves. I am not Louis Quinze.'

'A pity,' observed his lordship. 'You would

have done rather well at it, I think.'

Monsieur Chapparelle inclined his head.

'Now, where should we set this up?' asked Peter. 'Where will the light be good?'

'Perhaps you would put the parcel down on the table, Meredith, and bring us a high-back chair to prop it on,' suggested Harriet.

'Be so good as to turn your backs for the moment,' said Chapparelle.

Peter turned to Harriet, smiling. She observed that he was in a state of excitement, like a little boy expecting a treat.

'Please to look now,' said Chapparelle. With hands on her shoulders Peter turned her gently round.

Deeply startled, Harriet saw looking back at her from the canvas a person she had never seen in the mirror. A guarded and somewhat defiant expression possessed her familiar features, the beetle brows, the candid steady gaze, and thick bushy dark hair. This much she could recognise. It was the face of someone who had suffered hurts; all that she knew. What came new to her was a different nuance: a gaze of someone with a secret confidence, with a look of eagerness and expectation, someone serious for the moment but about to laugh . . . someone vindicated and triumphant.

She was far too striking to be beautiful; for the first time she saw the connection between her plainness and her strength of mind. Looking at Peter she saw him mesmerized; for a moment she saw on his face a ghost of the baffled desire and admiration which had afflicted him in the past.

'Hmph, hmph,' said Chapparelle, looking very pleased with himself. 'I tell you I am a genius.'

'Indeed you are,' said Peter, recovering himself. 'I am deeply in your debt.'

'You are in my debt for five hundred guineas, milord,' said Chapparelle.

'Come, sir, you know I was not referring to money,' said Peter. 'I am indebted to you for what you can see, and for being able to paint it. I did not know that anyone but myself . . .'

'I am delighted that I have pleased you, Milord Peter. You are not too pleased to be generous, *j'espère*. You allow that I take the portrait back for a month during the exhibition? If all my clients should be pleased in the fashion of Mr Harwell, I shall be ruined.'

'You must excuse poor Harwell,' said Peter. 'He has not the original to keep him company. I shall find it very hard to part with this, even with Harriet herself to look at every day. But of course we will lend it — if you think that an analysis such as that will win you clients.'

'Clients, perhaps not. People are afraid of me. *Ils ont raison.* But it will bring me glory. It is nearly the best thing I have ever painted. It will be the centrepiece of the show.'

'It will dazzle the discerning, certainly. If you will step down to my office, we will make arrangements for your guineas.'

'It has been a pleasure, Lady Peter,' said Chapparelle, taking his leave.

'Well, where shall we hang it?' said Peter, bouncing back into the room. Harriet blushed slightly at being found still staring at herself. 'Why don't we move that rather silly Fragonard from the wall in the library? Then I could see you while I play the piano. I'd like that. Is it picture-hook ready?'

He lifted the picture from the chair, and turned it round, finding the brass eyelets in the frame and the picture wire neatly in place. Then he stopped, and stood gazing. His attention was so intense that Harriet walked across the room and joined him. The picture was painted on a light brown finely woven canvas, stretched on a wooden frame and tightened with wedges driven in at all four corners. The surplus canvas was folded over, slightly puckered. Peter put his monocle in his eye, and stooped and stared closely at the upper right corner of the thing. Then he turned to Harriet and said, 'Harriet, I think I know why Harwell won't lend his picture. I'm afraid Chapparelle will never see it again. I'm afraid it has been burned.'

'Oh, Peter, no! Surely not! That would be criminal — and why ever?'

'Exactly. Why? I suppose you didn't see it, Harriet?'

'Yes, I did. It was in the studio while mine was being painted. I admired it greatly. It was better than anything else of his.'

'You amaze me.'

'Yes, really. It had an extra dimension compared to his other work. It was very clever; it showed her two ways.'

'Harriet, sit down and tell me about it. Tell me everything you can remember.'

'It wasn't flattering; it was strange, rather. It showed her tight-faced, frightened, almost. She looked very hard and selfish.'

'Cruel; but not untruthful . . .'

'Too cruel to be truthful, Peter. But the thing is, he painted her the other way as well. She was holding a mask; a mask of her own face, shown very beautiful; ethereal, almost.'

'A mask? What sort of a mask?'

'You know the sort of thing — as in the Venetian Comedy, a full painted mask, held up in front of the face on a stick. It was wonderfully real; it showed her as the world sees her — idealised, but very true to life.'

Peter had gone suddenly rather pale, and was looking at her oddly. 'Of course, a painter can show anything,' he said, 'a unicorn, a chimera, a cloud of putti; it doesn't mean there ever was such a thing.'

'Oh, but there was,' said Harriet. 'He had it made for him by a clever young colleague. It was done in papier-mâché. I saw it myself. A beautiful and ingenious thing.'

'My God, Harriet, that alibi!' said Peter. 'Don't you see? Or wasn't it real enough — did it really look exactly like her?'

'Well, it was inhumanly beautiful,' said Harriet

slowly. 'I think perhaps it wouldn't have deceived anyone for long who wasn't in love with Rosamund.'

'But Claude Amery was in love with her,' said Peter. 'He saw Rosamund's dead body with the mask in front of the face, held in place by the collar. Harwell must have known he was lurking around in the garden, and set it up.'

'Could that possibly have worked?'

'On a distraught and freezing lover by moonlight? I think it could. Harriet, I've got some checking to do. I'll be back in an hour or so; but I must chase Chapparelle back to his studio for the moment,' said Peter, ringing for Bunter. When Bunter appeared he said, 'Bunter, would you ring Chief Inspector Parker, and ask him to call here later in the morning if he can manage it? And ask him if he would be so kind as to bring the samples from the Hampton bonfire.'

Chapparelle's studio was in the same state of confusion as before. The canvas on the easel showed a handsome, rather flamboyant young man in an open-necked shirt. He was posing as Byron; he was being painted as a cad. The artist's penetrating eye was working as usual. Peter asked what had happened to the mask.

'You didn't give it to Harwell along with the painting?'

'*Non,* milord, I did not,' said Chapparelle. 'He paid for a painting, and a painting is what he got. The mask I have given to Mrs Harwell herself. It is a souvenir of the time we have spent together.'

'You paid Mrs Harwell one of your little fare-well visits?' asked Peter.

'Certainly.'

'So the last time you saw the mask it was in Hyde House?'

'No, milord. It was in a bungalow in Hampton. Mrs Harwell was very pleased with it. She put it in a vase to make it stand upright on the stick, so that she could feast her eyes on it.'

'When were you at the bungalow in Hampton?' asked Peter, astonished.

'On the afternoon of the 27th of February,' said Chapparelle.

'And nobody saw you, coming or going!' exclaimed Wimsey.

'I was rowing myself in a little skiff down the river. These boats can be hired at Hampton Bridge, Lord Peter. Nobody thinks that the man in the boat goes somewhere, only that he is rowing for the pleasure of rowing. They are very *chouette,* the boats; one can visit a friend with a landing stage, one can visit a friend in a river boat . . . I spent ten minutes with Mrs Harwell. Just to give her the mask.'

'You did not tell me this when we last spoke.'

'You did not ask me about the afternoon, monsieur, only about the evening. About all what you asked me, I have told you.'

The two little scraps of canvas, one of them scorched, lay on the desk in Peter's office.

'Not a tailor's interlining, but an artist's sized canvas,' said Peter.

'Forensic will tell for certain; but it looks like it to me,' said Charles.

'We are getting somewhere at last,' said Peter.

'Yes; but I'm not clear quite where. Harwell burned his wife's portrait; and then, you are saying, used the mask —'

'No, Charles; first he used the mask. He arrived unexpectedly to find his wife in suspicious circumstances: table set, all ready for someone. He hasn't seen the note; he doesn't know it is all prepared for *him*. And he *has* seen Amery hanging about. There is a scene; he kills his wife. The mask is at her side; Chapparelle has given it to her that afternoon. I think perhaps she has set it beside the bed where she can enjoy looking at it. Harwell puts the mask over her face and props her up where with any luck Amery will see her, and bolts for town. It works; Amery confirms his alibi. But now the portrait is potentially lethal; he can't afford to have anyone reminded of the existence of the mask.'

'Hold on, hold on,' said Charles, 'you go too fast for me. Has he burned the mask too, do you think?'

'No,' said Peter, 'I'm fairly sure he got rid of that earlier. He would have realised at once what a danger that presented to him; I think perhaps he didn't realise till Chapparelle wanted to borrow it that the portrait itself was dangerous too; that he couldn't keep it to mourn privately over it, that at any minute someone might try to get a look at it.'

'All right, so he got rid of the mask immediately. Before he called the police the next morning, I suppose. How? Did he burn that too? The fires were out and cold when the scene-of-the-crime team got there.'

'I don't know,' said Peter. 'How does one get rid of papier-mâché?'

'One boils it,' said Harriet. 'I've seen Sylvia use and re-use the mush for her arty little maquettes. You cut or tear it up and put it in a pan of boiling water. It disintegrates into a mess like porridge.'

Peter was staring at her like one who had just received a vision of light. 'The blocked sink,' he said. 'How stupid I am! The blocked sink, great heavens! The blocked sink. The blocked sink that makes all things clear. All this time, Charles, I have been convinced that there was something fishy about Amery's story because in his graphic description of Rosamund washing glasses he seemed all unaware that the sink would have filled up. But he's in the clear: the sink was clear; Harwell blocked it the next morning getting rid of the mask. The fellow was telling the truth. He must be asked one simple question — did he see Rosamund move when he looked through the window? — and released without a stain on his character.'

'We have to prove a story as well as propose it,' said Charles, doubtfully.

'Bunter mine!' said Peter. 'When you found

your photography frustrated by a blocked sink, did you make efforts to clear it?'

'I did, my lord, but without avail.'

'So when you left it, it was still blocked?'

'It was.'

'And what will have happened to the sink since? Has anyone been using the bungalow?'

'No,' said Charles. 'Not unless Harwell has lent or rented it. When he drove down and lit the tell-tale bonfire he didn't go into the house. I'll send someone at once to get a sample from that sink-trap. And we will indeed ask Amery your question.'

'Can I do that?' asked Peter hopefully. 'After all, I did think of it.'

'You can accompany me in an unofficial capacity,' said Charles.

'No,' said Amery. 'She was quite still. She was just sitting there, ignoring me.'

'Are you perfectly certain, sir, that she made no movement at all the whole time you were tapping on the window and looking through, and calling to her?' Parker's voice was quiet, almost gentle.

Amery frowned with the effort to remember. 'She let her hand fall,' he said at last. 'Her hand was lying along the arm of the chair, and she let it fall to hang down towards the floor.'

Wimsey shuddered slightly. He could imagine the arm slowly sliding off the smooth surface of the chintzy chair. Dead weight — newly dead;

later there would have been stiffness.

'But her face, sir; did you see any expression cross her face? Could you see clearly enough for that?'

'Oh, I could see her clearly, all right,' said Amery, suddenly fluent. 'She had that frozen expression — she was good at that. She didn't move a muscle. She used to do that to me; just when I thought she was encouraging me she would put on the ice-maiden act, going suddenly cold and remote. She could chill you to the bone with that expression. Like an angel, like a statue; it would strike me to the heart, but I couldn't resist it.'

'*La belle dame sans merci* hath thee in thrall?' murmured Wimsey.

'Yes,' said Amery. 'That's about it, really. Nothing like poetry for hitting the nail on the head. She was even very slightly smiling as though my anguish amused her. She was freezing me out, and I had never seen her more beautiful.'

'She may have blown hot and cold as you say, sir,' said Charles. 'But on this occasion — would it help you to know that she was not ignoring you; or at least we believe not. We believe she was already dead.'

Amery went a very pale greenish colour. He stared at Charles for a moment, and then staggered to his feet, saying, 'Excuse me a moment, I think I'm going to be sick,' and hastened from the room.

'Poor chap,' said Charles, looking after him. 'Born with one skin too few, I suppose.'

'I don't think it's inborn,' said Wimsey heart-lessly. 'A cultivated condition. But this is all a bit rough on him. Are you going to tell him he leaves without a stain on his character?'

'I'm going to tell him he is clear of suspicion, but will be needed as a witness,' said Charles. 'Before I collect a constable or two in case of trouble and go to arrest Harwell.'

'I wish you wouldn't do that quite yet,' said Wimsey.

'Whyever not?'

'Come and talk it over quietly in the George and Dragon across the street? Meet you there when you've said your piece to Amery.'

'I feel sorry for the poor blighter, really,' said Charles, sipping his pint. 'That must have been an exceptionally exasperating woman.'

'Condoning murder, Charles? Can I believe my ears?'

'Well, throttling her was going rather far,' said Charles, in the tone of one making a concession. 'And I don't know that we're out of the woods, Wimsey, even if, as I suppose we will, we find paper detritus and flakes of paint in that drain. He's going to deny it, and it's going to sound so preposterous to the jury.'

'How long do you think it took?' asked Wimsey, musing. 'He had to haul the body through to the bedroom, and lay it on the bed. He had to remove and destroy the mask.'

'You mean we should check the times for the

morning as well as the night before?'

'I expect you'll find there's at least an hour unaccounted for before he telephoned the police. I take it they will have logged that call?'

'Certainly,' said Charles. 'But the jury will easily believe he spent the time weeping and wringing his hands.'

'No, they won't,' said Peter. 'They won't believe he shed a single tear for his wife, although I'm sure he did, because they will be hanging him for murdering Phoebe Sugden. I shall be the only man in England, or woman for that matter, who believes his grief for Rosamund is genuine.'

'You know something I don't, then, Wimsey. As far as I know there is no connection between the two cases except the odd coincidence of the girl's home having been in Hampton. Don't tell me again you don't like coincidence; neither do I, but . . .'

'I did tell you, as a matter of fact, Charles. You can't have been attending.'

'To what?'

'Mr Porsena's story. He says Phoebe cum Gloria had been home to Hampton to fetch some clothes.'

'So?'

'So perhaps she saw Harwell there, some time in the evening. When he says he was wandering round London streets, and we think he was murdering his wife. The simplest possible thing, Charles, to lose one's life over. She saw him — they passed in the lane — or, yes, that's it, when he drove up to turn his car outside his neighbour's gate, it would have been nearly eleven at night, but the girl was just leaving with her clothes, or was coming back from the pub, or whatever.'

'But did she know Harwell by sight? He wasn't often in Hampton, and she wasn't living at home.'

'As a matter of fact I'm sure she knew Harwell. Harriet saw her once lunching with him at the Ritz.'

'So she could smash his alibi; or rather his story.'

'And pretty quickly she realised it. She was reading the *Daily Yell* and such stuff.'

'She could have come to the police and told us.'

'But there were no flies on that little madam. It was much more useful to go to Harwell and apply a little blackmail.'

'If she was blackmailing him we should be able to find the money. Money leaves traces as clear as footprints, and longer lasting.'

'Not money. Something far more desirable, something to dream of, burn with longing for, lose one's name over, consume oneself with envy over.'

'And not money?'

'Glory, Charles. Parts. She was an indifferent actress and she longed for lead parts. Not only for herself, for her boyfriend too. She saw herself and her cronies taking over every part in Harwell's productions from here to eternity. He sent her to eternity by a shorter route.'

'She drowned. The autopsy found no signs of injury. She could have fallen off a bridge. It could have been any bridge in London.'

'It could. But I think, don't you, that it is time we had a look at the Cranbourne Theatre?'

'I can get a warrant, if you like, and ransack the place.'

'I thought I might go in for a spot of entrapment. I know you can't dabble in the black arts, but I could. Harwell is a creature of impulse, I think.'

'Impulse? You say that in the face of that elaborate farrago with the mask?'

'Like a chess player who makes bad mistakes, but then is very good at recovering the position. A man who can't bear to lose, who thinks he has a right to win, who thinks the rules of God and man do not apply to him. I do see, Charles, that the chances of connecting him beyond reasonable doubt with a body floating loose in the Thames are not too good. We need his help; we just might be able to shake him into saying something foolish. Look, this is what I have in mind . . .'

19

Down, down to Hell, and say I sent thee thither
WILLIAM SHAKESPEARE

The Cranbourne Theatre had been built in 1780, and retained some of the grace and glory of the baroque age. Its boxes and galleries curved gracefully round the stalls, its proscenium arch was crowded with riotous putti in ormolu bas-relief, and the ceiling was painted lavishly with blushing clouds and the undercarriages of flying angels. It had been built as an opera house, and in the days of Handel and Mozart had served as one; now far too cramped for that purpose, with too small an orchestra pit and nowhere to store elaborate scenery, it had become simply one among many London playhouses, although still the most elegant.

Wimsey presented himself at the stage door, and declared himself to be an architectural historian. He would be obliged if he could be shown round the building. He was especially interested in the fabric.

The doorman was very sorry, but there was a

rehearsal in progress; there could be no admittance to the stage or auditorium.

'It affects their nerves to have people listening to rehearsals,' he said. 'These artistic people have terrible nerves, sir; you wouldn't believe.'

Wimsey quite understood; but as it happens the point of interest to him was the foundations of the building.

'Funny you should say that, sir; you'd be amazed if I told you what we has down there. I'd like to take you, but I can't leave the door.'

Wimsey expressed himself willing to find his own way, given simple directions.

'At your own risk, sir. You will be sure to mind your footing, won't you?'

Wimsey promised faithfully that he would. As a seeming afterthought he left his card on the counter.

'If any of the managers is in the building . . .' he said. He slipped round the back of the stalls, unseen, he supposed, by the actors on the stage. The director was sitting in the front row, shouting at his cast. Wimsey slipped through the doors marked Emergency Exit, and instead of pushing on the bar-locks and going out into the street, turned through an unmarked green door into the backstage area. At once the building turned its seedy private face to him. Not here the glorious gilded make-up of the foyers and auditorium; here everything was painted a dim and faded shade of green, the paint battered and flaking with age. Ancient worn lino covered the passage floor.

Wimsey passed the wing-flats of the stage set, glimpsing sideways the actress in paroxysms of emotion, throwing her arms wide and her head back, and crying: 'Duty! What is duty compared to love?'

'Oh, for God's sake, Suzie, get some feeling into it!' yelled the director.

Behind the stage was a cavernous gloomy space full of props, ropes, coils of electric wire, flood-lights, unused equipment of every kind. Two young actresses were sitting quietly on a bench, smoking. Seeing Wimsey they made guiltily to put out their cigarettes — it was obviously for-bidden to smoke among all these inflammables — but he raised a hand to them and slipped quickly through the door at the far back corner. It was totally dark beyond the door. Wimsey took a torch from his pocket, and by its pencil of light found a light switch. In front of him was a brick wall, but a flight of steps led downwards to his right. A chain across the steps held a swinging notice: 'Authorised persons only'. Wimsey un-hooked the chain and descended. A dank, un-healthy smell rose to meet him, the smell of cold stones and damp timbers, of country churches in winter.

At the foot of the flight of stairs he found him-self not in a basement, but at the top of a bot-tomless pit. He was on a kind of catwalk. At the far end another iron staircase led down to a lower walkway, and below that yet another. Dim light bulbs strung out on wires shed a scanty light. The walkways had a single strut by way of handrail on the right, and on the left were unguarded over the sheer drop. Wimsey whistled softly to himself, and began the zigzag descent.

The lovely building above him was resting on massive timber piles which rose vertically out of the pit. Not single trees; the balks were made of bundles of tree-trunks, bound together with iron bands. Cross-bracing timbers wove a web between them. The iron walkways descended crazily like a path for Gulliver in the land of the giants. The light bulbs were defeated by the depth and extent of the darkness.

Wimsey switched off his torch, and looked away from the lit platform on which he was standing. His eyes adjusted slowly to the gloom. There was a forest of the standing timbers. He tried to understand. Had these supports been driven into marshy ground, as Venetian builders had done, to raise their fantastical structures? And since here there was no lagoon to be brimmed twice every day by the tide, had the marsh dried up, shrivelled down, been washed away, leaving the underpinning standing proud? Washed away — that was it — for he could hear the sound of water. A gentle running sound, filling the space, softly echoing all around him.

Very gingerly Wimsey leaned over the inadequate railing, and shone his torch downwards. Way below him, as far down again as he had descended already, was a black stream. It ran in an open culvert across the floor of the pit. On one side it emerged from a brick arch, and on the other disappeared into a tunnel. There had once been an iron grating across this point of exit, but only rusty fragments of it remained.

'The Cranbourne, I presume,' said Wimsey. 'I am pleased to meet you, though I find you in reduced circumstances.'

He shuddered at his own thoughts as he looked down. And then he heard a door slam above and behind him, and rapid footfalls ringing on the iron grid of the catwalk.

Harwell's voice said, 'What in hell are you doing here, Wimsey? You're not an architect.'

'I am looking for ways out of this building other than through the doors,' said Wimsey.

Harwell was silhouetted against one of the random light bulbs; it was too dark to see his face. His bulk, however, his broad shoulders and burly build, were clearly apparent. 'And why would you be doing that?' he asked. His voice told everything that his shadowy face did not: he was fighting for self-possession and there was in it the unmistakable undertone of fear.

'I am trying to account for someone's movements.'

'Whose?' asked Harwell. There it was again; the slightly raised pitch of the voice.

'Miss Gloria Tallant,' said Wimsey. 'Unaccounted for between a mysterious audition in this theatre, and the mudflats of the tidal Thames. However, this' — he pointed at the running river in the depths — 'is clearly a possible route.'

'One might certainly lose one's footing here,' said Harwell grimly, descending towards Wimsey.

'What did you do?' asked Wimsey. 'Lure her as far as that last door and just bundle her over the rail?'

'What did *I* do?' asked Harwell. 'How foolish you are, Wimsey, a true effete aristocrat. You suspect me of two murders; what makes you think I will stop at a third?' He came down another flight of the crazy staircase. 'You are rather vulnerable, standing there,' he said, reaching Wimsey's level.

'I am well able to defend myself,' said Wimsey coolly. 'But in this narrow space I could not do so without tipping you over the edge. Be warned.' But the truth was Wimsey could well see that any struggle would almost certainly lead to both of them going over. In the light of uncanny clarity cast by danger he saw suddenly that he was in peril that he should not so blithely have risked; he was a married man now, and his life was not unequivocally his own to hazard. Perhaps Harwell had come to the same conclusion as to the danger they were in; anyway he was standing on the other end of the length of walkway, poised but still. Wimsey said, 'As a matter of fact, you are wrong. I do not suspect you of two murders. Only of one.'

Harwell blinked. 'What do you mean?' he said.

'You didn't murder your wife, Harwell; you didn't mean to kill her, did you?'

Harwell shuddered. His face looked gaunt and

hollow-eyed in the shadows.

'It was an accident, wasn't it?' said Wimsey softly. When he got no answer he went on, 'No jury would find it murder; no jury would want to hang you; if it were not for all that fooling around with the mask you would probably have walked free. Of course you will lose the sympathy of the jury when they see that your efforts to avoid confessing what had happened involved deliberately attempting to incriminate another man. But however severe they feel about that, they won't find it murder. The prosecution would probably only try for a verdict of manslaughter. It's the other one which is going to hang you. Why did you do it? She was blackmailing you, I suppose?'

'Oh, yes. You don't imagine I would have anything to do with a little slut like that from choice? As a favour to her family I saw her once to advise her in a general way about a theatrical career; and then she saw me that night in the lane, as I was driving away. She could break me at any minute. I would have paid her, you know, Wimsey, paid her for the rest of her silly life, but she wanted something I couldn't give her. I do have influence over productions that I finance; of course I do, but even I can't make managements give good parts to bad actresses. She didn't leave me any choice. And nor do you, of course. I'm sorry about you; I rather like you, though Rosamund didn't. I like brains, even in meddling aristocrats. Besides,' he said, pausing as though the thought had just struck him, 'I'm sorry to upset your wife.'

He lunged suddenly forward.

'I shouldn't do that, if I were you,' said Chief Inspector Parker from the darkness over their heads. 'It won't help you; every word of your conversation has been overheard, by myself and my constables here. Just stand quite still while we come down to you.'

'That's a filthy trick, Wimsey,' cried Harwell. 'Aren't you ashamed to corner a man like a rat?'

'You are not quite cornered,' said Wimsey quietly. 'There is one move you could make. One short cut. You have only seconds to make it.'

Harwell looked down at the forty feet or so of sheer drop from where he stood to the dark gurgling water below. Then he shook his head, baffled, and stood waiting for one of Parker's men to handcuff him and lead him away.

'I was so angry with her,' said Harwell. 'I just had a sort of brainstorm. She owed me everything — didn't she, Wimsey?'

There were four men in the little shabby cell in the police station: a stenographer, the Chief Inspector, Harwell and Wimsey.

'You understand,' Harwell said, appealing to Wimsey. 'You know the story. I had done everything for her, I indulged her every whim, we were tremendously happy . . .' He stopped and shook his head. 'We should have been tremendously happy, but things kept going wrong somehow. I had to keep trying again; I had risked a ruinous deal to raise money for Amery's play just to please her. I knew she flirted with Amery but I didn't think she would . . . When I got down there unexpectedly and saw she was expecting someone I just saw red. That fool Amery was blundering about outside, so I knew it must have been him she was expecting, and she was lying down on the bed. I took her by the neck, and I shook her . . .'

He looked up at his interrogators with an expression of baffled understanding, as though something had just come to him. 'If I hadn't loved her so much, I wouldn't have been so angry,' he said, 'and I was shouting at her; she tried to hold me off, she was saying something; she was saying, "No, Laurence, no." That's what she usually said when I wanted her. Only this time I didn't beg and coax. I overpowered her. I took what I wanted; my due. What she owed to me and nobody else. And then I realised — I realised that she . . .' Harwell sank his head in his hands. 'She lay so still. The damn dog kept barking and barking, and I was overwrought, so I — it's quite hard to kill a dog, do you know that? It was harder than killing Rosamund.'

'It's all too easy to understand what happened so far,' said Parker quietly. 'What I don't understand, sir, is why you didn't face the music. All that moving the body and playing about with the mask, locking doors and breaking windows: why did you do it? It has only made things much worse for you.'

Harwell looked up at them hollow-eyed. 'I

411

couldn't face what people would say,' he said. 'We were the most-talked-of lovers in London. I couldn't bear people to know it had come to that. I had a reputation as her husband; it gave me cachet to be the one she relied on — and I did love her, really I did!'

'So you took steps to escape the blame for it,' said Parker.

'I couldn't bear her poor bruised and flushed face, lying there on the pillow, so I covered her with the mask. I was sitting beside her when I heard someone on the veranda, and I saw Amery looking into the window. And then I thought of something I could do.'

'That was very wrong of you,' said Parker.

'It serves him right!' said Harwell. 'Rosamund was mine; mine alone. If he had left my wife alone I couldn't have touched him. I thought I had managed it at first,' said Harwell. 'I thought I had covered my tracks. I locked the bedroom door, and then broke through it. I locked the front door behind me, and went round and broke a window so that it would look like a break-in. I didn't think to try to open the door through the broken glass, so that wasn't as clever as I thought it was. But I thought I was getting away with it, and Amery would have to take the blame. Then I got into one difficulty after another. That stupid poncing Frenchman wanting to put the portrait on display, for instance. I couldn't have that. I didn't want anybody to remember there had been a mask. So I burned the picture. And it was all I had left to remember her by . . .' His voice shook.

'Can we move on to the disappearance of Miss Phoebe Sugden?' asked Charles.

'Oh, her,' said Harwell. 'I thought you overheard about all that. Wimsey worked it out, curse him.'

'I shall need a formal statement from you, overheard or not,' said Parker.

'She was a stupid little bitch,' said Harwell. 'She doesn't matter.'

'I think you will find, sir, that she does,' said Parker.

20

For who hath but one mind ḥath but one face.
JOHN DONNE

'Pitiful, really,' said Peter to Harriet, telling her about it. 'A man without self-control, and without self-respect. One must make allowances, I suppose, for the power of a cold-hearted sexual tease to drive a man to distraction.'

'Being a sexual tease is not a crime for which one deserves to die,' said Harriet sadly. 'But what do you mean about Harwell having no self-respect? I thought he had rather a good opinion of himself.'

'They go together, oddly. Son of a famous father; he puts his money into a showy business, with a lot of glory washing round any success; he doesn't do terribly well — not as well as Sir Jude Shearman, for example. And then he does something that makes everyone know his name and admire him. He can wear his beautiful wife as a woman wears diamonds in public. How she loves him! How he loves her! What a romantic story!'

'So if people think she has been murdered by

an intruder, or by a lover, he keeps the aura of a tragic hero.'

'But if he is discovered to have murdered her himself the whole thing turns into Grand Guignol. He loses the name of virtue. Precisely.'

'Do you feel any sympathy for him at all, Peter?'

'Very little. Should I?'

'People have been comparing Harwell rescuing Rosamund with you marrying me.'

'Stupid of them,' he said.

'We are different?'

'Yes. Look, Harriet, Chapparelle could not have made any kind of point about you by painting you twice in the same picture; you are unmasked all the time. You face the world as what you are, come what will. It is that which made me love you on first sight, and all these years since. It is that which I admire in you, and which I cannot manage for myself. I fool about all the time, covering myself in my title, my reputation, a capacity for foolish wit.'

'But, now you come to mention it, Peter, you have been fooling rather less of late.'

'I am grateful to you, Domina,' he said.

'Whatever for?' she asked.

'You do me the inexpressible honour of taking me seriously,' he said.

'But not gratitude, Peter. Not that. It's such a hateful thing. A horrible great blunderbuss with a vicious recoil.'

'It's safe when it's subsumed in love,' he said.

'Who is so safe as we?' she murmured.

'. . . When none can do
   Us injury, except one of we two . . .'
Treason to us   John Donne

he said, and she heard the undertone of triumph
in his voice. 'You have unmasked me,' he said,
'and loved me all the same.'

'So you feel no particular urge to throttle me?'

'Not at the moment. But do not presume on
that too far.'

'I shall be careful. I do have something to tell
you, Peter.'

The telephone rang.

'My dear, I'm sorry about this, but I must go.
Will your news wait?'

'Yes, if you must go. What has happened?'

'Another little diplomatic hitch. I hope it won't
take as long as last time, but . . .' He had already
got that frozen, abstracted expression.

'Peter, before you go, what happened about
Rosamund Harwell's note?'

'Nothing. I put it away in the drawer marked
"pending". Why do you ask?'

'Did anyone tell Laurence Harwell about it?'

'I certainly didn't,' said Peter. 'And I doubt if
Charles did. It isn't necessary for evidence in the
face of his confession, and on the whole I think
it would be merciful to spare the Hampton girls
the witness-box.'

'But he should know. He should know she
wasn't deceiving him with someone else.'

'Should he? Won't that make his remorse more

416

pungent, if he is remorseful? Dr Johnson said somewhere that the remembrance of a crime committed in vain was the most painful of all reflections. But, Harriet, I haven't the time to spare thought for Harwell now.'

'Of course,' she said. 'Off with you, and back as quickly as you can.'

'I'll put a girdle round about the earth.'

The library door closed behind him.

There were voices in the hall. And then silence in the house; for the moment no servants moving audibly, and a great sense of absence — as consciousness of Peter's presence ebbed away.

Harriet paced up and down in the library. She lit a Balkan Sobranie, and extinguished it half smoked. A simple and terrible thought had occurred to her. It was not Laurence Harwell she was thinking of; she was thinking of Rosamund. Of what would be fair to her. Was this the great sisterhood of women coming into play?

'She was not the sort of woman of whom I could have made a living friend,' Harriet reminded herself. 'And yet I do feel like befriending her ghost.'

The note should be shown to Harwell, she was sure of that. And as soon as may be; he had none too much time left. How? She telephoned to her brother-in-law.

'Charles, supposing I wanted to visit Laurence Harwell, how could I do it?'

'Remand prisoners have visitors,' he said,

cheerfully. 'You would just find out the visiting hours, and present yourself. He's in the Scrubs. But —' He broke off as it occurred to him that Harriet must know perfectly well that remand prisoners can have visitors, and would surely risk deep discomfiture in doing what he had just suggested. 'What does Peter say?' he asked.

'He's called away again.'

'Hard luck,' said Charles. 'I don't like it when this happens too often; I can't help thinking it means deep trouble breaking out somewhere. It's only too easy to imagine these days. Couldn't it wait till he's back?'

'It's like having toothache and dreading the dentist,' she told him. 'Better to get it over with.'

'Well, you know best. But, Harriet, I do hope if you ever felt lonely or down — well, Mary would be delighted to see you, you know, any time.'

'Thank you, Charles, I'll remember that.'

She still hesitated. And then it dawned on her that if she did not summon up the courage to face the shades of the prison house she would, instead, have to live for ever with the knowledge that she had funked it. That even Peter's love, her liberty, the ring on her finger, had not succeeded in freeing her from the ordeal of being tried for the murder of Philip Boyes, had left her disabled, left her unable to do something which she thought she ought to do. She found the telephone number she needed; she enquired for the visiting hours; she put on her coat. Going to

Peter's desk — it was unlocked — she found Rosamund's note and put it in her pocket, and went out.

It was, of course, a different prison; she managed quite well approaching the gate, announcing herself, sitting in the waiting-room. Only when the guard appeared to conduct her to the interview-room, and she had to walk, escorted, down the passageways, accompanied by the rattling of keys as the security gates were opened, and the dreadful sound of the gates clanging shut behind her, did she begin to quail. The place smelled of human misery; somewhere someone was shouting, and the sound echoed and boomed in the stone and iron spaces. But when she sat down at one end of a table, facing Harwell sitting at the other; when the little window to the side showed her the familiar blur of a face watching through glass; when the door was clanged shut behind her, and she heard the sound of the lock, bitter recollections of the past swung up to hit her somewhere; she reeled under the impact of memory. But memory came to her rescue, for she found she could remember and command also the numbing detachment from her surroundings, the narrowing focus that held the attention blinkered rigidly on what would happen in the next few minutes, and reared away like a frightened horse from any prospect more remote than the present hour.

She turned her attention on the sullen, silent

man sitting opposite her. His leonine form and tawny hair reminded her of an animal in the zoo. His eyes were dull, his gaze baffled.

'You?' he said at last. 'Why should you come?'

'I have something to tell you,' she said.

'Does your bloody husband know you are here?' he asked.

She blinked at the insult offered to her by his swearing in her presence. 'As a matter of fact, no,' she said.

'And what would he say if he did? I wouldn't have let my wife go calling on murderers. But then, I wouldn't have spent my time pursuing them. Is it a family taste?'

'Mr Harwell, I might have more idea how you are feeling than you realise,' she said.

'Oh, might you?' he said. 'But you didn't actually do it, did you? What do you think it feels like really to have murdered someone?'

'I'm sorry; that was impertinent of me. I can't imagine what that would — does — feel like.'

'So what are you here for? Have you come to flaunt your innocence under the nose of the guilty?'

'I wanted to tell you something about Rosamund,' said Harriet.

'I would have forgiven her in a minute or so,' he said, his voice suddenly unsteady. 'But do you wonder I was angry? I gave her everything, everything she wanted, for herself or for anyone; I had half ruined myself to get her pet poet's play put on; but she should have been grateful; she owed it to me not to fool around with another man. Do you take lovers, Lady Peter? Do you have secret assignations? Or does owing your life to Wimsey make you toe the line?'

'I have come to tell you that she didn't, that she wasn't making secret assignations.'

'And what can you know about it? Why the devil should I believe you?'

'I would like to tell you that I think it was my suggestion, innocently made, that persuaded your wife to spend a few days at the bungalow. We were talking, and I said it might be fun, and might please you, if she set about some decorating there. As you can imagine, I have since greatly regretted making the suggestion.'

'Did you also suggest setting up a candlelit dinner for two?' he said after a moment.

'This is the invitation Rosamund sent,' said Harriet. 'With great ingenuity it has been found.' She put the note down on the table between them, and withdrew her hands into her lap. Both of them glanced at the watchful presence at the surveillance window before Harwell picked it up. He read it.

'Rosamund gave that to an unreliable messenger, late in the afternoon of the day that she died. It should have been brought to you at your club. It went astray,' said Harriet, gently. He was looking at her with an ashen face. 'I thought you ought to know,' she said. 'I hope that it does not make your suffering any worse than it necessarily must be.'

He said bleakly, 'She might have told me, if I

had not had my hands around her throat.'

Harriet stood up, ready to go. 'If there is any-thing that I or Lord Peter can do for you . . .'

'Nothing can be done for me,' he said. 'I can pay for a good lawyer. Wait; let me talk to you a moment. Nobody else will listen to me ever again. I thought, you see, that I had been so wholly, so horribly deceived; that I had made such a com-plete fool of myself, giving abject adoration to a loose woman . . . poor Rosamund! How terrible for her: she must have thought I had come in answer to her summons, and I — and I . . .'

'I am afraid I ought to take that note back with me,' said Harriet.

'Oh, yes!' he said eagerly, pushing it across the table to her. 'But, yes, there is something you could do. Ask Lord Peter to make sure that this note comes out in court; that the blame all lies where it ought to lie, and her name is cleared of any stain. I shall get what I deserve, but let her reputation be unblemished.'

'I expect the note can be used as you wish.'

'To show it was a terrible misunderstanding; that it was neither her fault nor mine.'

'Goodbye, Mr Harwell. I am sorry for you.'

'I shall be able to think of her without bitterness in the time that remains to me,' he said. 'And thinking about her is all that is left.'

Harriet picked up the note, and signalled to the warder that she wished to leave. She walked away down the interminable corridors behind the warder with a kind of disorientated astonishment at being able to go; at being let free. When the outer gates closed behind her she broke, childlike, into a run, gulping in great lungfuls of the grey, cool open air of the London street as though she had surfaced from drowning.

'But you didn't have to do that,' said Peter Wimsey. 'I would have done it, I would have taken your word for it that it was the right thing to do.'

'You would have protected me?' said Harriet.

'I would have spared you the affront to your feelings. It must have been gruesome for you.'

'And that's just why I had to do it. I had to know that I wasn't still walking wounded; that I could do what was needful just as anyone else would.'

'Almost anyone else would have felt ready to leave Harwell to his fate.'

'The truth about himself, about what he has done must be bad enough; to leave him suffering the torment of the damned over an untruth, over the false idea that Rosamund had betrayed him . . .'

'I hope he was grateful to you, Harriet. I doubt if he could have had the slightest idea of what pain it must have given you, what memories it reawakened.'

'He was very glad to be able to think her innocent, and to engross the blame to himself. And, my dear, I am no longer in flight from memory. To be in a prison again cost me a pang or two,

I won't deny it. The ordeals of the past were terrible at the time, but they brought me to you. See, here I am, perfectly calm. In fact, Peter, you look the more harried of the two of us; was your errand difficult?'

'They use me as an emergency message-boy these days. The message was duly delivered, with certainty and in secrecy. So I suppose it was not difficult, and that I have succeeded in it.'

'But it has left you very depressed, I see.'

'Ah, love, let us be true to one another,' he said, taking her in his arms, 'For we are here, as on a darkling plain . . .'

'Is it as bad as that?'

'I'm afraid so. I think we have been living in the eye of the storm, and mistaking it for calm. We shall find ourselves at war again before all this is sorted out.'

'And all these people around us who are saying that after all the Rhineland is part of Germany; that the Versailles Treaty was unfair, that Hitler will negotiate a peace when Germany's just demands are met . . .'

'They believe what they hope, Harriet. But they are wrong.'

'War is so terrible a thing.'

'Don't I know it! And the next one will be worse than the last. The machinery for inflicting death and destruction is better than it was. Mussolini's tactics show the way; we must expect to have poison gas used against civilians, and multiple other horrors. I'm not surprised that people have no stomach for it. And this time we shall go into the fray with the Americans sworn to neutrality, and the country led by an irresponsible and pro-German King.'

'You are very hard on him.'

'I suppose one should remember half his family are Germans. The talk is, he wants to marry that woman.'

'Which woman?'

'Mrs Simpson.'

'But she's married to somebody else.'

'She can get a divorce. The fact that he's the head of the Church of England and if he did such a thing it would split the country top to bottom has apparently escaped his attention.'

'It's very hard on someone not to have the person that they love,' said Harriet.

'He can have her. He just can't marry her.'

'I offered to live with you, once, without being married to you. You took it badly.'

'So I did. Perhaps I am being curmudgeonly. How do you put up with it?'

'I just point it out to you and wait for a change in the weather.'

'The thing is, Harriet, I can understand perfectly a bit of fooling around. Carrying on like Jerry; he knows he has burdens to carry when he inherits the title, he can see how it weighs on his father, and he wants to play the boy out of school while he still can. But when you do inherit; when the responsibility is yours, you have to do your duty.'

'I do see that, Peter; even though I think nobody has had as little freedom of choice as the King has since the abolition of slavery.'

'He could abjure his title, I suppose; renounce the crown. What is contemptible is trying to keep the thrones and titles and wriggle out of the responsibilities. Enough of this; you had some news for me.'

'Yes, I have, my lord, although I might have chosen the wrong moment. This isn't the best time, I take it, to be giving hostages to fortune?'

'My dearest, are we really?'

'So it seems; some time in October. You'll think me incredibly foolish, but I wasn't keeping an exact check. I didn't even notice at first; I kept feeling sick, and I kept thinking there were reasons for that. Chapparelle purported to see some mysterious change in me, and I thought he was just flannelling. Eventually Mango put two and two together, and sternly admonished me to go to the doctor.' She was talking rapidly, watching him to see what he felt.

He said, 'Domina, it will be all right; you will be all right, won't you? What did the doctor say?'

'He gave me an approximate date, and told me to drink plenty of milk. He measured my hips and told me that if my interior dimensions were in the usual proportion to my exterior ones there would be no cause for concern. Peter, it's nice of you to react by worrying about me — but are you pleased?'

'Pleased?' he said. '*Pleased?* That's no sort of

word for it — my blood rejoices in my veins! I can feel the eternal stage-hands shift the scenery around us as we stand.'

'What scene gives way to what, my lord?'

'In all the vanished legions of the past,' he said, 'the Vanes and Wimseys glory in our light, wearing ancestral titles down another swathe of years.'

'Oh, Peter,' she said, smiling, 'I told Jerry once I was tempted to marry you just to hear you spouting nonsense.'

'And the future,' he said, suddenly sombre, 'opens up before us real and urgent.'

'That's not nonsense,' she said. 'Do we do right to bring a child into the present time?'

'There's what we can do for any child of ours,' he said, 'and there's what no one can do for any child at all.'

'They make their own way, you mean?'

'They claim or renounce their inheritance in their own time, and make or break the time accordingly. We shall lavish every gift we can on ours, but we cannot give it safety.'

'You know, until this happened I would have said that I no longer cared a fig for the fate of the world as long as you and I were together.'

'Let Rome in Tiber melt, and the wide arc of the ranged empire fall? No, Domina, that's not our style. If there's another war we shall have to face it, and we shall have to win it,' said Peter.

21

Hanging and marriage, you know, go by
  Destiny

  GEORGE FARQUHAR

You know, my friends, with what a brave
  carouse
I made a second marriage in my house . . .
  OMAR KHAYYAM

*Extracts from the diary of Honoria Lucasta, Dowager
Duchess of Denver:*

29th March
  *Peter came in just after breakfast, exultant,
to bring news that Harriet is pregnant! Much
rejoicing together. He says she has been not
very sick, but nevertheless told him that he
must see to it that she has a cup of tea in bed
every morning, as tea before getting up was the
only thing any good against morning sickness
in my case, and it might run in families. The
remedy, I mean. Peter pointed out that Harriet
not in the family in that sense. Quite right, of*

428

course, *but she seems like a daughter to me. Told him so. Did not add more so than Mary, as it seemed disloyal. Besides, I am very fond of her. Mary, that is.*

Well, now there will be family confabulations! Wonder if Helen will be glad at prospect of reserve heir, or annoyed at loss of prospect of Peter's money for Jerry. Went to Garrard's to buy spoons for christening present, and then bought gold and garnet brooch for Harriet instead. Baby can, indeed must, wait. Coming out, bumped into Peter on same errand. Longed to wait to see what he chose, but thought better of it.

Arrived home to find Gerald and Helen waiting. Gerald cock-a-hoop about it, saying he always thought Harriet a sensible woman who would know what was expected of her — would have told her himself if Peter hadn't forbidden him. Helen worried that Harriet not aware how to bring up children of upper classes, but said at least she would now have to give up writing 'those dreadful books'. Told her I hoped not, as I would lose favourite reading. Don't know why Gerald makes me so cross. He said it would be a relief not to have to lean so hard on St George; thought privately it would make Jerry even harder to call to order, but didn't say so. Told Gerald it would probably be a girl. Decided not to give brooch to Harriet till tomorrow, to let Peter get in his gift first.

30th March

Called round at Audley Square after lunch, excuse to see decorations in mews, but really to give brooch. Enormous perambulator with ridiculous coachwork and huge embroidered sunshade being delivered from Swan and Edgar's. Present from Jerry. Very absurd, but amused Harriet, can't think quite why. She very touched at my little gift, and looks very happy. Said she hoped I could remember all about babies, and anything she ought to know, as her own mother, of course, not available. Told her I could remember in grim detail, but not really true. Will have to find the volumes of my diary for child-rearing years. At Denver somewhere, I suppose. Suggested Mary as source of more recent reports.

Had to drop several hints to be shown Peter's present, but managed it in the end. Got shown into Harriet's little study to admire nice ebony inkstand with cut-glass inkwells and silver mounts, rather spoiled, I thought, by somewhat moth-eaten goose-quill pen, with all the feathering removed from one side. Foolishly wondered aloud why Peter had not bought a nice silver fountain pen in Garrard's while he was about it, but it seems the inkstand was bought just to set off the ancient quill pen, point of which is that it had belonged to Sheridan Le Fanu. Felt somewhat out of depth.

Told Harriet I should need to be well prepared for clever grandchild, and asked her to recommend really good novel. She said I might like

War and Peace, *as it was a story about families,
but* Peter Rabbit *would be needed sooner. Met
Bunter's intended at bottom of garden, looking
at progress on converting mews. Sensible young
woman with large hazel eyes, reminding me of
peppermint humbugs. Said could she have lots
of yellow in colour scheme as it reminds her of
sunshine and sand. Said yes, of course, but will
have to do scheme for drawing-room over again,
to get rid of pink. Pink and yellow impossible
together. Just a glimpse of Peter, as I left, looking
smugger than ever. Wanted to hug him, but
Meredith standing at the door with my coat. By
dinner time felt quite worn out with feeling
happy. Tried thinking about those poor Abyssini-
ans to compensate, and took it rather too far.
Must ask Franklin to remind me how to knit.*

31st March
  *Bunter's wedding day fixed for 3 August so
must chivvy architect; decorators will need at
least a fortnight. Found some very pretty dining-
chairs with needlepoint seats in Waring and Gil-
lows; wonder if Bunter would like them? Chairs
not decoration, precisely. Must not go too far and
interfere. Got up a delicious colour scheme in
yellow and blue and sage green. Decided to play
safe and show it to everyone — Peter, Harriet,
Bunter and Miss Fanshaw — before ordering
papers. Helen called and said she should think
Bunter should be grateful and not expect to be
consulted. Asked her how she would like it if she*

was made to live in horrid colour scheme. She replied she had lived in Denver 'as she found it'. Admit she has a point. Shudder to think what she would have done if allowed to alter the old place.

28th April

Called on Lady Severn and Thames as it is the fourth Tuesday of the month, and my day for visiting. She tells me the new baby will be called Matthew if it is a boy. Said I couldn't think where she got that idea, as the only Matthew in the family is a poor cousin whom Gerald keeps on at Denver, fussing about in the library. She said she had it from Peter himself, and that I should pray for a boy as if they have a girl they will call her Keren-happuh. Wonder if she is losing her grip, at last? Will ask Peter about it as soon as possible.

14th June

Quiet supper in Audley Square, just the three of us. Discussing Mrs Simpson; Uncle Paul has sent French newspapers all saying the King will marry her. Peter saying he would have to abdicate in favour of his brother the Duke of York, as no such thing as morganatic marriage in England. Can't believe he would do such a thing; the King, I mean. Talk turned to thorny question of Bunter's wedding present. Harriet suggested the Paul de Lamerie candlesticks. I said, 'Oh, no, not those, Peter is so fond of them.' Harriet said that was the trouble with being immensely rich; when you wanted to give a costly present it had to be something that cost you to part with. Got the distinct impression that Peter agreed with her.

3rd August

Bunter's wedding day. St James's, Piccadilly. Bunter turns out to be terrifically High Church and they had **Panis Angelicus** *sung by Aurelia Silberstraum, newly arrived from Vienna whom I think Peter once . . . well, that's all in the past, though I rather think he pulled some strings to get her papers sorted out. Service packed, and full of music critics and press-hounds, rather better behaved than the criminal reporters, all lurking by the steps to the organ loft, wanting a word with the soprano. Bride slipped in almost unnoticed. Wearing shell-pink satin, very becoming. Bunter and Meredith (the best man) looking strained. Would swear Bunter's eyes were moist as bride approached the altar. Must be mistaken — too unlike Bunter. Harriet in loose dark red dress, has begun to have that slightly leaning backwards gait. Said to Peter that pregnancy suited her, and he said she looked like a treasure ship making into harbour. Old self clearly not entirely snuffed by middle age. Rather too much incense for my liking, but when Aurelia S opened her mouth was* **thunderstruck!** *Thought entire church would lift off the ground and float into the Empirean — if there are empires in the sky*

— may have got the word wrong. Quite under-stand what the fuss over her is about.

Reception at the Bellona Club, in private rooms. Bunter's mother, very large and enfee-bled, brought up in service lift, and installed in armchair. Wedding presents all on display — spotted Peter's candlesticks at once. All Peter's servants above level of housemaid among the guests, all very well turned out. Mrs Trapp re-splendent in powder-blue two-piece and wide-brimmed pale blue straw hat trimmed with pansies. Bride's father made rambling speech, obviously very proud of his daughter. Quite right too; I do so admire these modern women who can do things. Saw couple off from side door — front halls forbidden to women. Amazed to see the happy couple depart in Peter's Daimler. Said he must be even fonder of Bunter than I had thought; Harriet said large car needed to carry equipment for photographic tour of Highlands. Went home rather depressed; often feel depressed after having a good time, wonder why?

Helen called round before dinner, outraged. Says it makes family look ridiculous to have had master married hugger-mugger in Oxford with strange dowdy company (she means women dons) and man married with ludicrous pomp in proper way in London. As for operatic stars sing-ing church music, indecent level of showing off. Surprised at Bunter, would have expected him to know his place. Lots more similar remarks. Told her that it was natural to feel miffed when she herself not invited. Felt considerably cheered up. Anger must be good for the blood.

25th August

Sent Franklin to Hatchards for copy of War and Peace, *thinking today good time to start long book, gap to fill now job on Bunter's house finished. Silly woman came back with* Anna Karenina, *saying it was the nearest thing she could find. Got as far as first sentence, then stopped to think. 'All happy families resemble one another, but each unhappy family is unhappy in its own way.' Great author has got that the wrong way round. I think unhappiness is much the same whatever the reasons for it, and happiness is a quirky odd sort of thing. Surely nobody before has been happy in precisely the way that my Peter and Harriet are? Must be reading the wrong book — will ask Harriet to lend me* War and Peace.

AUTHORS' NOTE

Laurence Harwell was found guilty of the manslaughter of his wife, and the murder of Phoebe Sugden, and was hanged for the latter offence on 14 July 1936. He left an annuity to his father-in-law and the bulk of his fortune to charities for out-of-work actors and actresses. Mr Warren lived with Mr and Mrs Rumm for the rest of his years, and learned to play the harmonium for their prayer meetings.

Claude Amery's play *The Suspect* was put on in August 1937, financed by Sir Jude Shearman. It was a huge success, and laid the foundation of his long career as a playwright.

Gaston Chapparelle was parachuted into eastern France in 1941 where he organised a cell of the Resistance, and acted as a secret agent for British Intelligence. His cover was never broken and he was given the Légion d'Honneur in 1948.

Bredon Delagardie Peter Wimsey was born on 15 October 1936, and his brothers Roger and Paul in 1938 and 1941. During the war Peter Wimsey served in military intelligence. Harriet took the children to Talboys, and lived quietly there until 1945. Bunter tried to rejoin his old regiment, but was refused on grounds of age.

Early in the war Mrs Bunter's studio prospered, taking pictures of young people in uniform, but in the Blitz a direct hit demolished it, and the Bunters, with their son Peter Meredith (born December 1937) joined Harriet in Pagglesham, where they rented a cottage near Talboys, and Bunter organised a super-efficient contingent of the Home Guard. Meanwhile Lord St George became a fighter pilot, and Helen, Duchess of Denver, went into the Ministry of Instruction and Morale. (See the *Spectator*, 17 November 1939.)

Harriet Wimsey continued to write detective novels, branching out somewhat from the conventions of the form. The work which she completed just before the birth of her first son, though darker and more psychologically realistic than most detective fiction of that time, was hugely popular, and well reviewed in the literary press, thus confirming her in the new direction she had taken. Her monograph on Sheridan Le Fanu took her a further ten years to complete.

Dorothy L. Sayers abandoned the writing of *Thrones, Dominations*, some time between 1936 and 1938 having become deeply involved in the staging of *Busman's Honeymoon*, and then with the writing of religious plays, followed by her life's crowning endeavour — a translation of Dante's *Divine Comedy*. She died suddenly in 1957 leaving the last thirteen cantos of the *Paradiso* to be completed for her by her friend Barbara Reynolds. Peter Wimsey had not left her when she ceased to write about him; in 1937 she described him as a permanent resident in the house of her mind, and said she found herself bringing all her actions and opinions to the bar of his silent criticism.

Dorothy L. Sayers was unusually willing to collaborate with others; she shared the writing of *The Documents in the Case* with Robert Eustace and the playwriting of *Busman's Honeymoon*, which preceded the novel, with Muriel St Clare Byrne. On the great translation of Dante she recruited and received the assistance of scholars, notably Barbara Reynolds.

Jill Paton Walsh read *Gaudy Night* in her early teens, and was inspired by it with an ambition to study at Oxford, the achievement of which has· put her life-long in debt to Dorothy L. Sayers.